For

Jamaica

by
Craig Gallant

PLAYGROUND of the PIRATES

For Jamaica by Craig Gallant
Cover image by Howard Pyle
This edition published in 2023

Winged Hussar Publishing is an imprint of

Winged Hussar Publishing, LLC
1525 Hulse Rd, Unit 1
Point Pleasant, NJ 08742

Copyright © Winged Hussar Publishing
ISBN PB 978-1-945430-88-6
ISBN EB 978-1-958872-28-4

Bibliographical References and Index
1. Historical Fiction. 2. Pirates. 3. 17th Century

Winged Hussar Publishing, LLC All rights reserved
For more information
visit us at www.whpsupplyroom.com

Twitter: WingHusPubLLC
Facebook: Winged Hussar Publishing LLC

A Dutch fluyt

For Jamaica
The Men and Women of the West Indies

The Squadron
Aboard the galleon *Ultimo Arbiter*

Commodore Solomon Hart, her captain
Myles Booth, her first mate
Zachariah Rees, her quartermaster
Mao Kun, her sailing master
Lincoln Watts, her surgeon
Atieno Haji, her ship's cook
Dante Poza, her carpenter
Theodore DeVillepin, Julien Durand, Ettiene Lalande, and others, her gunners
Efrain Gallo and Lorenzo Marti, her boatswains
Vincent Ancel, Jacques Soyer, Brian Ball, Sidney Day, and many others, her crew

Aboard the light frigate *Jaguar*

Jonathan Fowler, her captain
Benedict Haviland, her first mate
Dennis Flynn, her quartermaster
Sarah Jolie, her sailing mistress
Michael Chin, her surgeon
Old Eryk, her ship's cook
Enrique D'Or, Juan Ramirez, Sheila Lee, and others, her gunners
Francois Caron and Louise Deveaux, her boatswains
Christophe Billet, Jordan Belanger, Pierre Cochet, Archer Harris, and many other, her crew

Aboard the brigantine *Bonnie Kate*

Eamon Maguire, her captain
Shanae Bure, her first mate
Mathias Sylvestre, her quartermaster
Martin Ruiz, her sailing master
Hector Fraga, her carpenter

Jorge Carballar, her ship's cook
Isabella Sanz and Aidan Allen, her gunners
Axel Perry, her boatswain
Alonso Costa, Filip Carita, Martin Tenorio, Anna Green, Aston Hunt, Hamish Sloane, Matheo Serre, Armand Carpentier, Tian Rodier, and many others, her crew

Aboard the brigantine *Syren*

Sasha Semprun, her captain
Renata Villa, her quartermaster
Dominique Bienvenida, her sailing mistress
Sun Hai, her surgeon
Corine Beauvais and Kyra Barret, her gunners
Gabriella Bevier, her boatswain
Morganne Giraud, her cook
Dominique Blanc, Aimee Bougie, Pilar Castex, Rebecca Chapelle, Lillie Wood, Raya Barker, Ada Pallazo, and others, her crew

Aboard the sloop *Chainbreaker*

Thomas Hamidi, her captain
Sefu Barasa, her quartermaster
Billy Deever, her sailing master
Aurora Imarisha, her surgeon
Cassius Black, her gunner
Matthias Claire, her cook
Charles Lafitte, Georges Browne, Felix Azizi, Mosi Shae, Usian Welles, Orlando Rubio, Raul Ikeno, Simon Moya, and others, her crew

Aboard the sloop *Laughing Jacques*

Bastian Houdin, her captain
Cesar Japon, her quartermaster
Jean Martin, her sailing master
Luc Masse, her carpenter
Xavier Noboa, her gunner
Albin Leblanc, her boatswain
Killian Pasteur, Roche Touchard, Lewis Cook, Deacon Stewart, Rowan Elliot, Angel into, Marcos Saenz, Ramon Ocampo, and others, her crew

For Jamaica

Other Ships
Aboard the brigantine *Chasseur*

Sidney Greene, her captain
Euan Kaur, her first mate
Niko Barnes, her quartermaster
Rupert Poole, her sailing master
Leonard Butler, her surgeon
Harrison Reid and Ralph Davis, her gunners
Kayden Berne, her boatswain
Zain May, her cook
Jeremiah Campbell, Hudson Gray, Jenson Ward, Rory Thomson, Haider Andrews, Travis Saw, and others, her crew

Aboard the sloop *Chaucer's Pride*

William Kay, her captain
Alvin Simms, her quartermaster
Derrick Vallance, her sailing master
Joseph Wryght, her gunner
Ben Suther, her boatswain
Dillan Kane, her cook
Fred Salley, Taylor Whinn, Janson Moore, Roger Haley, Hal Arnold, Tavis Schnare, Vernon Waldrip, Abe Lewis, and others, her crew

On Tortuga

Bertrand d'Ogeron del La Bouere, the governor

Severin Serre, owner and proprietor of the *Lazy Dog Tavern*
Andre Marchette, barkeep at the *Lazy Dog*
Nadine Berthelot and Renee Boudot, serving women at the tavern

Cedric Daucourt, publican of *Daucourt's Public House*
Emmeline Daucourt, his wife
Claudine, Lea, and Jules, their children

Filip Chartier, proprietor of *Chartier's Counting House and Victualers*

Mabey, a young Taino outcast

Port Royal

Thomas Modyford, the governor

Captain Lachlan Porter, a prominent citizen

Jamie Hall, owner of *One-Eyed Jack's*
Lucy Knight and Liz McDonald, barkeeps at Jack's
Hallie Sharpe and Alyssa Ryan, serving women

Denis Flynn, patriarch of a prominent merchant family

For Jamaica

Prologue

1652 ~ Hispaniola, One Mile East of Santo Domingo

It was a memory.

And so, like all memories, there was no telling if it was a true recollection of events as they had happened or a patchwork quilt of impressions, images, half-remembered stories, and wishes that had accumulated over the years.

The world was bounded by rickety walls of rough wooden slats, bright sunshine stabbing through, penetrating the hot, steaming darkness.

What furniture the world contained was overturned, much of it broken into unrecognizable tangles of wood and rope. The dirt floor was scattered with shattered bits of pottery and glass, a pathetic collection of rice and corn ground into the dust.

By the wreckage of a cot was a suspicious shape, the hint of a rounded shoulder, the suggestion of splayed legs beneath a dun wrap. One twisted shape might have been an arm, flung high over what might have been a face.

Garish red was splashed across that corner of the world.

In the opposite corner, alone and hunched against the sudden changes that had wracked her world, was a girl of five or six years old. Her skin was a smooth nut-brown, her wild black hair a halo of innocence around a face dominated by wide, staring blue eyes. Under other circumstances those eyes would be striking, but in the here and now of the broken world, they merely reflected the horror of life's fragility made manifest to a mind too young to comprehend.

The girl's head pivoted, staring at a stretch of rough wall moments before a doorway appeared, the irregular door kicked roughly open, spilling familiar sunshine and strange, harrowing smells into the world.

An olive-skinned man in a faded red shirt entered the world through that glaring rectangle of light, casting about him with an intent, narrowed gaze. He took in the shape in one corner and sniffed, turning to leave before those dark eyes fell upon the girl. Their eyes met without fear or shame. Then he scanned her body up and down once as if evaluating her upon some criteria she could never have understood.

With another sniff, the man shrugged and turned back to the door.

"Anything, Martin?"

They were the first coherent words to be spoken in this shattered world in some time. And although the girl could not understand the language, there was a strength and confidence in them that sparked something buried deep in her mind, below the dull echoes of the shattering of the world.

The man in the red shirt stopped in the doorway and looked back into the world. "Just a girl, captain. Same's been done for the mother, looks like, as the others."

A curse from outside this world was enough to make the girl flinch. The words had been in Spanish, a language she *did* understand. And the emotion behind them was neither gentle nor kind.

"Eamon, what's the point?" A woman's voice this time, from a little farther away.

The man stood aside, and another figure entered the world. He towered over the girl, the sunlight streaming through the doorway gleaming off his bald head. A tangled beard wreathed a mouth set in a hard, angry line as eyes that flashed a golden-brown glared into the shadow of the girl's world.

The man glanced at the shape in the corner with its crimson splashes and horrible stillness wincing. Then he looked at the girl, and all of his anger seemed to drain away.

"Eamon, we've got to get going before the dons arrive. You know they have a sloop ready at Santo Domingo. Isabella isn't going to be able to get us much warning on foot."

But the man did not seem to be listening to the woman outside. He only had eyes for the girl cowering in the corner, now pushing with her bare feet against the dirt floor, trying to press herself through the wood of the wall.

"It's okay, girl." The words meant nothing, but the man's voice was soft, with a singsong accent she had never heard before. He approached slowly, lowering himself down gracefully onto his knees. "It's all over now."

"Lies aren't going to help her, Eamon." The woman who had been berating the man from outside stood in the doorway.

She was tall, dressed much as the man was, in tight brown trousers with a black coat over a white shirt. She, too, bore a long, curved blade at her hip. Wild dark hair wreathed an olive-skinned face, a red cloth tied over the loose curls. Her eyes were dark as she took in the remnants of the room, resting at last upon the girl's weak struggles.

"There's no one left, Eamon. If she's lucky, the dons will take her back to Santo Domingo. She might end up as someone's servant, or maybe even with the church. Either way, nothing for her is over yet."

The man shook his head, his eyes not moving from the girls. "She's coming with us, Sasha."

The woman snorted. The man in red, standing behind her, sniffed again.

"Eamon, I don't think that's wise. You promised you'd listen to my advice."

But the man's attention was entirely wrapped up in the girl's half-hearted attempts to escape. He looked around and found a tattered blanket far enough from the cot to have escaped most of the red flood from the shape on the floor.

"It's going to be alright." Again, the words were meaningless, but their lilting cadence, and the soft, gentle tones, reached her where perhaps a monologue in perfect Spanish might not have.

"Captain, we have to go." The woman's voice was hard. "You haven't been here long enough to understand what you're doing. The girl needs to stay here. There's no place for her on the ship. And Cayona's no place for a child."

The kindly man's smile never wavered. "No place on Tortuga is any place for any creature of god, Sasha. Still, we seem to have been doing well enough."

He moved closer again, draping the blanket around the girl and putting one strong arm across her slight shoulders, muttering comforting, meaningless noises the entire time.

"Captain Hart will not be pleased you've taken an escaped slave aboard, Captain. If you lose his sponsorship, we won't have a home. Governor Le Vasseur doesn't much like Englishmen." The woman's tone was harder, now, her eyes boring into the back of the man's head as if trying to push the sincerity of her words into his mind through sheer force of will.

"Call me an Englishman again and I'll toss you overboard." But the warm tone seemed to undermine the words. "And bugger Hart." The man in the red shirt snarled, and the man called Eamon felt the girl stiffen in his arms at the tone. "If that great carrack of his could even raise anchor I'd be more concerned with that."

The woman cast a sour glance over her shoulder. "Belay that, Ruiz. Our newfound Brethren have elected the good Captain Hart to lead us. His good graces are worth more than the governor's right now, if we want to operate out of Cayona Harbor."

He had picked the girl up, wrapping her in strong, gentle hands. "She's no more an escaped slave than I am." The man's voice shook with the effort to control a growing anger as he carried her toward the doorway that led out of the close confines of the hot, copper-tainted world. "She's a child, with no part in the crimes that brought her to this place." His voice seemed to catch. "Back home, we wouldn't have called any of that a crime. We'd have called it heroism."

"The color of her skin will argue against that in these waters, Captain. You'll be guarding her for the rest of your life."

"Nonsense. Sefu has nearly the same color skin, and his neck's never known a collar."

The woman shook her head, sending her hair snaking down her back with the vehemence of her argument. "Barasa's from the Barbary Coast, and his eyes and his skin are not at odds with that fact. This girl? Where is her father, eh? I'll tell you." Her tone slid easily from the hard sense of argument to the bitter heat of anger. "He'll be about a mile or two to the west, Captain. He'll be some landowner, or some overseer, living in Santo Domingo, with no more care of her existence than of a mosquito on the arse of his next conquest as she works his field."

The man hitched the girl up onto one hip and held a hand, palm out, toward the woman. "Peace, Sasha. I agree with nearly everything you're saying. But is that any reason not to save her from what must come next? We have no idea what happened here. Someone went through some pains to make it look like a Taino raid, what with the arrows and all. But have you ever known the natives to strike at such a pathetic little village, minding its manners in the jungle, scratching out a harmless existence from dirt and sea? Jesus, Mary, and Joseph, girl. You know who did this."

The woman stifled a reply, shaking her head again, but this time the gesture lacked the force of her early denial.

"You know the dons better than any of my other crew. These little settlements of escaped or forgotten slaves form all the time, they're allowed to eek there way along for a little while, maybe a year or two, and then they're wiped away. If we hadn't been sailing off the coast these last few days, trading with them for fish and news, I have no doubt they wouldn't have even gone through the effort of hiding their involvement."

The girl's world expanded then as the man carried her outside. She saw the ramshackle huts all around, most of them collapsed, with more of those odd, still shapes scattered around. The usual colors, dun and tan and brown was augmented here and there with more of the garish red.

Her mind refused to take in details, sliding from one shape to the next, never settling on any one for long. Strangers walked among familiar paths, gathering up what little food or metal the village had boasted.

"Hart might not like it, but he doesn't have any right to dictate how I run the *Bonnie Kate*. As long as the crew is with me, he'll have no choice but to keep his trap shut. That's how things work over here, right? I might as well take advantage of the total lack of discipline."

The man in the red shirt snorted again. "He could keep us from his leads, Cap'n. He could send the others out, keep us at anchor till the ship rots out from underneath us."

The man they called captain shook his head. "Won't happen." They were walking through the jungle, moving down the slope toward the beach, still hidden behind the thick verdant veil. "Look, I know I'm not in Waterford anymore. The *Bonnie Kate* no longer holds a Letter of Marque from the Confederacy, and all of the old enmities and alliances mean nothing. But privateer or buccaneer, I won't be letting any old Sasanach like Hart dictate to me or mine what we might or mightn't do. If he feels like flexing those Flemish muscles of his, we sent more than our fair share of his brothers to the bottom of the Irish Sea in our time."

These words were heard by several of the men and women heading down toward the beach, and most of them laughed heartily. There was an edge, though, that made the girl tense in his arms again.

"Very brave words, Captain." The tall woman with the curly hair muttered, waiting until most of the others had gone on ahead. "Still, Hart can do much to hurt us here. He has Le Vasseur's ear, and the other captains will follow his lead. If he decides to take the girl's presence as an insult or, worse, a provocation of the authorities here on Hispaniola, it will not go well for us."

The captain held the girl more tightly to his broad chest and shook his head. "No, Sasha. I don't think you understand. We don't have a choice here, now." He shifted the girl so he could look into her eyes. His own began to fill, and he shifted her again, to hold her close.

"The old world is falling apart. We can't even follow one year to the next who is at war and who is at peace. Are we supposed to aid the Spanish this month, or should we be burning their ships to the waterline? What about the French? The Dutch? And who are we, anyway? When I arrived here two years ago the *Bonnie Kate's* crew was entirely Irishmen I had known for years. Now at least half are from countless other places as far removed as your own Santiago, Barasa from Africa. Hell, I've even got Englishmen hauling canvass and swabbing the decks, for the love of God!"

They walked without further words for several moments, the sparkling waters of the little cove beckoning them through the green shadows of the jungle.

When the woman spoke again, her voice was soft, a hint of pain searing through all of the other emotions. "She's not your little girl, Eamon. They're gone, and you can't bring them back."

The man's step faltered for a moment, but then he continued on as steadily as he had before.

His own voice was steady when he finally replied, as they stepped out of the trees and onto the sand, the sleek lines of the brigantine *Bonnie Kate* resting peacefully just offshore. "This isn't about Katie or her Ma, Sasha." He hitched the little girl around again to look once more down into the calm, clear blue eyes. "If there's to be any peace for us here in this New World, it's going to be because of wee bairns like her."

Chapter 1
1674 – Cayona Harbor, Tortuga

The confines of the captain's cabin of the *Bonnie Kate* made it a less-than-comfortable place to hold such a meeting, but with the Commodore having already denied the enterprise his blessing, the remaining captains of the squadron had decided that Captain Maguire's ship was the next best option.

Besides, it was well known that he kept a better selection of wine than even Hart himself.

Maguire smiled as he settled back into the comfort of his chair. The others were sharing chests and benches, with Thomas Hamidi of the *Chainbreaker* having folded his enormous form into a sitting position on the floor to better afford room for his big, dark-maned head.

He hoped none of the noticed the threadbare rugs, the tarnished silver, or the fact that he had not replaced a single stick of furniture in years. A captain of the Brethren had a certain standard to maintain, after all. It wouldn't due for them to notice he wasn't spending the money he was supposed to dedicate to such fripperies.

He didn't want them to start wondering *where* all of that money might have gone.

"Are we sure they'll be there when we arrive?" Captain Fowler, the grizzled old captain of the light frigate *Jaguar*, was, curiously enough, the timidest captain in their little squadron. "We don't need the Commodore or Governor D'Ogeron wroth with us, and our holds none-the-richer for it, neither."

A bark of laughter nearly sent Bastien Houdin, captain of the sloop *Laughing Jacques*, falling off the little keg he was using as a seat. Bastien was also the squadron's only French captain, and under the circumstances, his good opinion carried more than its usual weight. "Jonathan, you old nanny-goat. Next, you'll be arguing we join the others cutting down trees and smoking stolen cow hides up on the mountain. Why don't you give *Jaguar* to me? I'll show you how to use her."

Fowler lurched off his bench, nearly sending his quartermaster, Dennis Flynn, tumbling onto the deck. "You miserable, frog-eating worm—"

"I would happily offer you satisfaction, *monsieur*, if you would care to name the place?" Captain Houdin remained seated, but his smile had taken on a predatory edge.

Maguire left them to it, gesturing with one hand when it looked like Sasha was going to enter the fray. There was no danger of Fowler ever letting something like this go too far. And even now, with Cromwell cold in his grave these fifteen years or more, and Charles II on his father's throne, it still warmed Maguire's Gaelic heart to see an Englishman discomfited.

He was honest enough with himself to admit that this was probably more than a small consideration in choosing to continue with the current caper despite Commodore Hart's uneasiness with the plan.

Sure enough, when Bastien continued to stare gaily into Fowler's red-rimmed eyes, the old Englishman cursed under his breath and rammed his steel home. "You are not worth the trouble, Houdin. I often ask myself why the Commodore even allows your little boat to sail with us."

That seemed to stick a little more than any attack on his nationality might have, and Maguire wondered if the fool had finally pushed even the genial Frenchman too far. Bastien loved his little sloop, and there was no denying that the *Laughing Jacques* and Hamidi's *Chainbreaker* were far better suited to many of the tasks the nimble little squadron took up than the larger ships. But one would have to be blind not to see that Bastien, at least, aspired to helm something larger one day. And if he saw any way to help fate along, that day would come sooner rather than later.

"Can we get back to the business at hand?" Sasha Semprun had been serving with him almost since his arrival in these waters. She was still tall, still powerful, her mane of dark hair still free of any hint of a lighter hue. She was a captain in her own right, now, the sovereign ruler of the brigantine *Syren* and her all-female crew. There was not a captain in the squadron, including Maguire, who would cross her when she scented prey.

"I concur." From his place on the floor, Captain Hamidi should not have been able to command their attention so easily, but that deep, gravelly voice could cut across the chaos of a boarding action with ease. In the confines of the *Kate's* small captain's cabin, it was nearly painful.

"Right." Maguire sighed. Maybe Fowler would get himself killed in a duel some other day. "To Jonathan's point," he nodded toward the captain of the *Jaguar*. "The *Marie Lajoie* and the *Courageux* are still where they dropped anchor this morning, in that little bay just off La Ringot."

The two merchant fluyts had been hiding in Cayona Harbor for days under the impression the governor would protect them from the buccaneers who still called the island home. Maguire had thought the man was allowing his French sensibilities to overwhelm his other senses where the tricolor was concerned, but when Commodore Hart had agreed, he had revised his opinion.

If Henry Morgan had still called the island home, things might have turned out differently. Governor D'Ogeron had a great deal more respect for that old buccaneer than he'd ever had for Commodore Hart. The Commodore was cut from much more politic cloth.

If the squadron as a whole could not go after the French vessels, however, perhaps Maguire could persuade a couple of his fellow captains to go against the old man's wishes.

It wasn't as if they were sailing with a navy, after all. The Brethren of the Coast knew a certain amount of loyalty to each other, but it was more a rambunctious family than the iron-shod discipline of the Royal Navy.

And due to a little silver splashed prodigiously around the harbor before they eventually decided to risk the homeward passage, the *Courageux* had suffered a mishap only an hour out of Cayona. The cables from the wheels to the rudders, terribly frayed and poorly maintained, and helped along by the effort of a couple of dock rats with negotiable ethics, had snapped.

"Tian has eyes on them, and the relay remains unbroken from the headlands to the gable room of the Lazy Dog. There's been no change in their disposition since they put in around noon."

"No change, unless your man in the tavern's decided to have a few instead of keeping a steady watch." Benedict Haviland, *Jaguar's* first mate, was made of firmer stuff than his captain.

Maguire smiled. "That's why I've got Aston in the gable room. No worries about him being lured out of there by the questionable charms of the Dog's girls or grog."

Another bitter voice barked a laugh. Cesar Japon, quartermaster on the *Laughing Jacques*, was a stark contrast to his jolly captain. "The *priest*." The man's Castilian accent managed to convey more contempt in the word than it should have been able to muster. "Unless he hears Neptune's call from the harbor and leaps head-first from the window."

Maguire waved the concern away with a casual hand. Although, he had to admit, Japon had a fair point. Aston Hunt was a former Anglican deacon whose torture at the hands of the devout Spanish navy upon his capture years earlier had fair broken his mind. The man now earnestly believed himself to be the first of a resurgent priesthood in service to Neptune, lord of the waves. Ninety-nine times out of a hundred he was a consummate sailor and one of the best crewmen aboard the *Bonnie Kate*. But that one time when his newfound zeal got the better of him could be spectacular.

"He's got a cup of saltwater with him, and I made sure he'd have plenty of seaweed in the room while he waits. He won't let us down."

"And I'd rather have Hunt drunk on seawater watching my back than any of you with half a cup of rum in sight, any night of the week." Sasha snorted, and the others chuckled and nodded amiably.

Maguire gave the woman a quick smile of thanks, then continued. "So, our prey is caught, my friends. They are at our mercy, ripe plums waiting to be picked, and all we need do is sail around the headland and take what is ours."

"Governor D'Ogeron—" Fowler's muttered objection was half-hearted, sensing the tone of the group swinging against him.

"The governor need never know what's transpired so far from his manse." Maguire shook his head. "Look, my friends. Tortuga is not what it once was. I tell no secrets in saying the words. Most of the English captains have taken the Crown's offer and returned to the bosom of the throne, bearing Charles's paper and drinking his grog in the snug confines of Port Royal."

He sighed. Had he had his way, the *Bonnie Kate* would have been among them in one shake of a lamb's tale, regardless of his own personal feelings about the Britishers. "Many more who have stayed are out in the jungles of *La Montagne*, cutting wood so better men can sail the waves."

He knew that was unfair, but his anger at the ever-changing life of the Caribbean buccaneers was never far from his thoughts. He had fled Ireland as she fell to the forces of the Protector, all of Europe engulfed in endless petty wars that left princes like Rupert of the Rhine and even Charles II himself shrugging wryly while the commoners paid for the game in blood.

But he had arrived in this new world only to find the old animosities and enmities remained. In fact, he was starting to believe that the constant shifting of alliances and combatants back home was having an amplifying effect on the frayed nerves of the European populations of these new seas rather than the dampening he had once hoped for.

He would never understand those who abandoned the freedom of the waves for the security of the land. Day to day he smiled at them and waved away their concerns; but in the silence of his heart he could see them as nothing more than cowards.

"Under the constant surveillance of the governor, weighed down by countless edicts and declarations from Paris and beyond, we would never have two sous to rub together, were we to follow his every whim."

"And Hart is nothing more than his creature, at this point." Hamidi's growl made the bulkheads of the cabin shake. "Has the *Ultimo Arbiter* ever even left Cayona? Have any of you ever seen her sail?"

Maguire knew full well the answer to that question. *Jaguar* had been the first ship to join the self-styled Commodore, years before the *Bonnie Kate* had traded the gray waters of the Irish Sea for the brilliant blue of the Caribbean. And although Fowler had not been her captain then, he had been a mate. And in his cups he was more than willing to admit he had never seen the flagship, *Ultimo Arbiter*, a captured huge Spanish galleon, leave the safety of Cayona's harbor.

"The governor—" Now Fowler was sounding petulant, and he knew it. But the man seemed constitutionally incapable of keeping his mouth shut at times like this.

"Which governor?" Even Captain Houdin was losing his patience. "How many governors have ruled over Tortuga since Hart's been sitting aboard his ill-gotten floating fortress? The English have owned the island, the French, even the Spanish returned for a time back in '54. And during all of that, Hart has squatted on the well-painted decks of his immobile ship like some princeling guarding his precious scrap of land."

"The sheer weight of metal the *Arbiter* brings to bear—" Haviland was pale beneath his close-cropped blonde beard, but this was a battle he and his captain had fought many times before, and Maguire had to assume the man found it tiring. He was no idiot, like his captain.

"That argument might have borne up before the forts were completed." Japon still considered himself a Spaniard at heart and was more surly than usual when the *Arbiter* entered the discussions. "There are now more guns between those forts than both of that antique's broadsides combined. Eventually you are going to have to face the fact that there is some other reason she remains at anchor after all these years. Has she ever even been careened? Christ, man, her hull could well be fused to the bottom of the harbor at this point."

"Enough." Maguire knew the flavor of the room now and knew that there would be plenty of crew available for his plan. He had no need of *Jaguar* if either Boutin or Hamidi were willing to bring their sloops into the fray. He knew he could always count on his old first mate if a plan was sound. *Syren* would never be far from his wake if his course was true.

"I move we vote." Bastien's smile could be misleading. Maguire had seen him stab an unarmed man in the chest with that same expression brightening his eyes. But his ire had been raised by Fowler's weak arguments, and there was an eagerness for loot that could not be denied. "*Laughing Jacques* supports Captain Maguire's motion. I vote we relieve these French of their finer baubles and send them on their way."

"*Chainbreaker* will sail with you." Hamidi knew an easy score when he saw one. And his crew of free Africans and escaped slaves had done handsomely whenever they followed *Bonnie Kate* out of the harbor.

"You can count on *Syren*, Captain." Sasha seldom referred to him by that title since taking it up herself. When she did, it usually meant she was trying to make a point. Her quartermaster, Renata Villa, nodded fiercely behind her. The woman was well over six feet tall with jet black skin marked all over with shining tribal markings and dripping with gold rings around fingers, wrists, and neck.

"Excellent. Captain Fowler? The disposition of the *Jaguar*?" Maguire had won. He could afford to be civil.

"Perhaps a Spanish target? Or the Dutch? Everyone seems to be against the Dutch this year."

Japon made to stand, hampered by the low ceiling as well as his captain's hand on his corded wrist.

"Do you know of any ripe Spanish targets, captain?" The reality was that there were none, and they all knew it. And although the Dutch might be at the bottom of the proverbial heap across the Ocean right now, and a perennial favorite target of the governor, they kept their holdings in the New World well-protected. It took some luck, these days, to fill a hold with anything more than smoked meat or rough lumber without a paper from the governor of Port Royal or Santo Domingo.

The new rules, again.

"The French are protected—"

"Captain, you need not feel you must join us." Maguire stood, minding his head. The low ceiling made grand gestures harder, but probably kept things a little more civil, as well. "The Commodore knows of my overall intentions. He does not approve but has given us leave to pursue them independently if the fluyts and their crews are not harmed. If the *Marie Lajoie* and *Courageux* do not return safely to France it will be none of our doing, and our crews will be well-satisfied with what we take away from the venture."

"How do you intend—"

"The means are none of your concern if you do not wish to bestir *Jaguar* from her moorings, Captain." Maguire gestured toward the door with a tilt of his head. "All members of the squadron will get their proper shares, I assure you. Now, if you do not mind, we would hear your vote, and then those of us committed to the affair should like to finalize the plans, I think?"

The other captains and their mates and masters nodded gravely.

Seeing how things had gone, Fowler nodded as well, but his face was grim. He stood, and Haviland stood with him. The small blonde first mate was one of the few officers in the squadron who could stand in the cabin without fear of striking his head against the deck above.

"I will notify the Commodore of your intentions. I trust we will not all rue this decision. The squadron needs the governor's good-graces, captain, or we lose the only home we have."

That was not entirely true, Maguire reflected as Fowler and Haviland negotiated the small door and closed it behind them. The *Jaguar* would be welcomed at Port Royal if it wished to take up the king's commission. *Bonnie Kate* could also accept Governor Lynch's offer. Hell, even the *Syren* would most probably be able to take advantage, if Sasha wished. But Bastien Houdin would never be able to trust the English peace, and Jamaica's plantations made the island no fit place for a free African to call home.

That was no chance he would have ever asked of Hamidi and his crew.

If the squadron were to stay intact, there were few places where they might operate with impunity outside of the protected harbor of Cayona. Still, the governor was a weak, venal man, and his usual cut, beneath the fig-leaf of an early yule gift, would be more than sufficient to keep him from looking *too* closely at the fate of these two ships as long as their crews were not abused.

"Well, now that we've lost them, where are you keeping the good rum, Maguire?" Bastien made as if he were going through the sea chests along the rear bulkhead. "I know you've a bottle or two stowed away for special occasions."

"I'd say getting out to stretch our legs without Fowler glaring disapprovingly down at us from his quarterdeck is special enough." Hamidi laughed. "I think in this company, we can be free with our contempt for the English?"

Maguire smiled with a nod and produced a smoked glass bottle from a box beneath the low table. "You know me too well." He poured out several fingers for each of the men and women present.

"He's not wrong, you know." Renata Villa mumbled as she bowed over her tumbler. "Tortuga's time is almost done. The Brethren are scattered. There may come a time when Port Royal may be the only choice."

Maguire shook his head. "No. Things might look bleak now, but the squadron stays together. Something will come up."

"You wanted to go to Port Royal years ago." Bastien pointed out. "When the offer was first made."

Maguire held a hand up. "Only if we could all take it together and remain free of the twisted forced trade. I believed we could. I still do, to be honest, but I understand Thomas's objections," he nodded toward Hamidi's bowed head. "And yours, Bastien. We won't be going to Port Royal unless we are all going to Port Royal. And for the time being, that's not an option."

Reality shifted so quickly in the Caribbean it often felt like a dream, or a nightmare. Usually that was to his dismay. But he secretly found comfort in that transience on this one issue. If things would shift just enough for his fellow captains to find a home, there as well...

"So, how are we going to relieve these Frenchmen of their livelihood without relieving them of anything else?" Sasha smiled into her own drink. "I've been eager to hear this since you mentioned their sad misfortune."

Maguire smiled, happy to let the matter of Port Royal settle for now. "Well, it's funny you should mention that." He saw an answering gleam in her eyes before he continued. "I was thinking this might be a task for my first mate."

Chapter 2
1674 ~ Cayona Harbor, Tortuga

"If you don't get another signal before the next bell, we should send someone." The man's voice was soft and amused. "He might have lost himself staring into that jar of water you gave him."

Shanae lowered the spyglass with a slight twist to her mouth. Aidan Allen was often as amusing as he thought himself, but when he wasn't, he was usually just annoying.

She had chosen Aston Hunt, the man they called the Priest, to take the high watch in the Dog. If the man had succumbed to one of his quixotic moods, it would go poorly for her.

She was almost certain he had understood the gravity of his assignment, however.

Almost certain.

They stood together at the *Kate's* port bulwark, the stain of Cayona smeared against the verdant jungle beyond, the ship still all around them as the crew tried to pretend there was no imminent action in the offing.

"He'll be fine." She cursed the waver she heard in her own voice. Captain Maguire would never have shown such doubt.

"Oh, he will be," Aidan responded. "My concern is more for the rest of us. You know, those of us who *aren't* under Poseidon's personal protection?"

She gave the *Kate's* younger master gunner a look and then raised the spyglass once again. Aidan was careful not to mock the sad man to his face, or even before the rest of the crew. But when they were alone, and the subject came up, he was seldom able to deny himself these little digs.

She shook her head, but before she could reply she saw a light flash in the dark recess of the window above the Tired Dog. She held up one hand after the first gleam. Two more followed, and she breathed a sigh of relief.

Not only were the two French fluyts still in place; so was the Priest.

"All's well." She lowered the glass and turned to rest against the rail. "Now we wait for the others to come to their senses, and we can heave anchor." His handsome smile nearly gleamed in the harsh sunlight as it sparkled off his blonde hair. She wrinkled her nose to show how little it affected her.

She walked toward the aft rail, taking the small flight of stairs two at a time as she ascended to the quarterdeck. She nodded to Martin Ruiz, the

Kate's sailing master, where he stood at the wheel.

Across the harbor, like a gaudy red and white wall gleaming in the sun, sat the *Ultimo Arbiter*. The old galleon presided over the harbor like a matron over wayward charges. Although, the glaring holes of her gun ports, open to the slight tropical breezes, gave a dark shade to the comparison.

She had once been a Spanish ship, of course. And there were stories bandied about the squadron and the harbor of how Commodore Hart might have gained her. Shanae tended to disregard the more wildly heroic tales of stern chases and battles on the open sea; she found herself more inclined to believe the whispered stories of Hart purchasing the becalmed hulk from some crooked don captain one of the many times Tortuga had exchanged hands among the old powers.

The man just didn't seem the type for feats of valor.

"I know he doesn't bestir himself often anymore, but he didn't even send Boothe to the captain's little meeting." Aidan spoke softly, looking up into the hills beyond Cayona. The captains and most of their seconds were convened beneath their feet, and the aft windows of the captain's cabin were only feet away.

"I'm the first mate of the ship, Allen. If I didn't know who was visiting, I wouldn't be long for the post."

He gave her a quick, wicked smile, but didn't push further on the subject.

Shanae sighed, settling her gaze back on the distant shape of the *Arbiter* as she sat at anchor. She had grown up within the squadron. She didn't remember anything of her life before, despite all the stories the older hands were always eager to tell her. They spoke of a village destroyed, wiped off the surface of Hispaniola with nary a survivor other than her young self.

She kept her face calm, her eyes serene, but doubt boiled beneath. Captain Maguire had all but raised her, with the help of the squadron. Surely no one thought she had earned her position as his second on her own merit? She struggled every day to dispel any doubts they might have, but still she felt they persisted.

It was one of the reasons she rarely accompanied him when the captains met in council. There was no need to embarrass him before the others, no matter what he might say.

Footsteps interrupted her dark thoughts, and she turned to see the gray head of Captain Fowler emerge from below, Benedict Haviland rushing to keep up.

Shanae nodded to her opposite number and muttered to Aidan. "Have Axel bring the *Jaguar's* boat around."

The gunner gave a jaunty half-salute and moved toward the forecastle, where the *Kate's* boatswain stood with several of the younger crew.

"Captain, your boat will be along in a moment. I trust things below remained civil?" She smiled, her glance shifting from the captain of the *Jaguar* to the first mate.

Fowler's only reply was a dismissive grunt, but Haviland was a little more forthcoming. "I think you knew what was going to happen before we ever pulled alongside, Bure."

She smiled with a shrug. "There's no telling in our trade, Ben. There's always room for adaptation."

He gave a short laugh, and they both ignored Fowler's dark gaze. "I wish you all well, if for no other reason than the *Jaguar's* shares."

She nodded, casting a casual glance aft to where the big frigate rested at anchor at the mouth of the harbor. She glanced aside to see Fowler moving forward to hurry the boat crew as much as he might, and she turned back to the *Jaguar's* first mate with a pitying glance. "Active shares would have given you more."

The little blonde man nodded, a hot spark in his green eyes. "I've a feeling they'll be talking about this action as far off as Port Royal and Maracaibo." He looked up at her. "The two of you must have something fine planned, to gain enough booty to justify hoisting anchor and yet avoid the governor's ire. The Sun King won't be pleased that you plucked two of his plums. I've heard whispers this will make even Morgan or L'Ollonais jealous they weren't here."

She laughed at that. "It won't make Morgan love Captain Maguire any deeper, that's for certain. And you know neither of those grandstanders would sail with our sad little squadron even if they back amongst us."

"Well, it'd be nice, for once, if they were here to see what the squadron can do, is all. Even if we can't be there with you."

She shrugged. Fowler and Haviland had left the council early, obviously deciding not to participate in the action. That meant they were outside the seal of silence, and thus privy to no further information. "Louise won't even feel the pinch." She jerked her chin to the waist of the ship, where Fowler was already scrambling over the bulwark and down the ladder to his boat. "I do believe it's time for you to take your leave, First Mate Haviland."

He smiled ruefully and raised two fingers to his forelock. "Good evening to you, First Mate Bure."

She acknowledged his words and then turned back to the water.

"Good luck, Shanae." He whispered as he walked past, and she nodded again, begrudging him a brief smile.

Aidan returned, nodding to Haviland as they passed. He hopped up onto the quarterdeck and resumed his position beside her.

"They're making for the *Arbiter*. Not even pretending they're headed home." He whispered to her, still conscious of the captains below.

Shanae shrugged. "There's no reason for them to. Captain Maguire's already told Hart what we intend, in general terms. He didn't like it, but they're not going to try to stop us."

He snorted. "I'd like to see them try."

She gave him a pitying look. As if this would come to the squadron battling fighting amongst itself. "Attend to your business, sir. Your gun crew could do with some additional drill, I think."

He gave her a bright smile. "My crews are already excellent. Besides, whatever you and the captain have planned, it doesn't much involve the carronades, or he'd have had me down in the magazine readying more charges. There's not much he can be intending with six shots." He leaned toward her, his smile turning devilish. "No, my dear. I do not believe old Captain Maguire intends to blast away indiscriminately at those pretty little fluyts." He raised an eyebrow with melodramatic zeal. "I've no idea what you've planned, but I've no doubt it'll be exciting."

She allowed a slight smile of her own and shrugged. "Only time will tell, gunner."

His own smile grew even wider. "That's master gunner, first mate."

She snorted. "Since when?"

He gripped the edges of his vest and rose onto his toes in his best imitation of a High Street dandy. "Are we not buccaneers, first mate? Do we not forge our own paths? Since I decided my own damned self!"

She laughed despite herself. "I'm not certain how Isabella is going to feel about this."

He puffed his chest out. "She's a big girl, she can share the glory." But then he looked furtively around. "She's not nearby, is she?"

She smiled. "I think she was forward, working on number one." The foremost nine pounder cannon on the starboard side was always causing her and Aidan trouble. "You can call yourself a master gunner if you want, just so long as you don't expect a master gunner's shares"

He looked hurt, but the humor never left his eyes.

The hatch in the bulkhead forward of the quarterdeck opened again and the rest of the squadron's officers erupted from the stifling heat of the captain's cabin and onto the main deck of the ship.

"Shanae, where are ya, lass." Maguire's smooth brogue rolled across the deck and she hopped to the railing, meeting his gaze as he turned to scan for her. He nodded. "We're agreed, as you and I discussed. The game's afoot, as the Bard might say."

The others laughed at this even as they moved to the bulwark, waiting their turn for the small boats to come around.

"Who to command?" She asked, her back straight.

"One boat from *Chainbreaker* under Black, one boat from *Syren* under Gabrielle, and one boat from *Laughing Jacques* under Leblanc."

That made sense. With shore parties like these, the captains usually assigned either their boatswains or a gunner to the boat. Of course, that left the *Bonnie Kate's* boat as yet unclaimed.

She looked at him, not wanting to give him the satisfaction of asking, and he looked up at her, clearly not intending to give her an inch.

The decks of the ship grew still as the crew and the officers of the other ships sensed something happening. A tableau had formed, with Maguire and his first mate staring calmly at each other over the railing, a small, almost identical smile twisting their lips.

Maguire looked away and she knew a moment of victory, but he didn't look back, instead turning to the captains with a jaunty wave. He saw them off, ignoring her completely, and she turned on a heel to look back out over the water, watching as the small boats took their crews home.

"Any further word from on high?" Maguire came up beside her, gripping the railing lightly in hands scarred from a life at sea.

It took her a moment to realize the captain was referring to Hunt in his high perch. She handed him the spyglass and nodded toward the distant roof. "Signaled just a few minutes ago, captain. The prey has not moved."

He grunted, raising the eyepiece to his face. "Hadn't moved as of an hour ago or more, you mean. It takes time to pass that signal over half the island. I don't want to wait any longer than we have to."

"It's going to take them hours to run new cables, sir. We've got time."

He smiled with a nod. "I've no doubt, Shanae. I'm not too concerned." He turned toward her, his smile only widening. "Now, about our boat."

"I was thinking Isabella or Aidan, sir. Percy's only a child, not even a year as our new boatswain."

The boy squawked indignantly from the forecastle deck, but several hands laughed and pushed him back while he smiled good-naturedly.

"You make an excellent point, Shanae." The captain seemed to consider her words, and she felt her heart sink. "If we send Isabella, who would have over-all command, do you think? Gabrielle? *Syren* has precedence over the other two ships, and we don't want to seem greedy. Or Black? *Chainbreaker's* just a sloop, but he's been with the squadron the longest of the other three."

She considered the names, struggling to remain detached from what was happening. "I would say Black, sir. He's obviously the most formidable, and the most level-headed in action."

Maguire nodded, giving her a clear-eyed look filled with pride. "I think that would be the perfect answer to that little exercise. Luckily, we don't have to worry about it."

A little twist in her gut accompanied a quick flush of anger.

"Sir?"

He laughed, and she had to suppress a very real urge to knock him into the harbor.

"You'll have command, obviously. It was your plan, after all. *Kate* and *Syren* are near equals in class, and you've got more seniority in the squadron than almost anybody I could name. Besides, Sasha told me she wouldn't send her boat if I didn't allow you the command, so that was a closed deal before the council was even ended."

She felt a rush of gratitude for the tall captain of the *Syren*.

"You'll have to pick your own shore party. I want the four boats ready to put out before we leave the harbor, and I want to leave the harbor ten minutes ago." He turned toward the crew, gathered now in the waist and the ratlines, eagerly awaiting his orders. "Alright, boys and girls, make for open sea." He turned toward the ship's sailing master. "Martin, we'll follow *Syren* out, leaving *Chainbreaker* and *Laughing Jacques* to catch up as best they can."

"Aye sir." The little Spaniard tossed half a salute. "Leave room for *Jaguar*?" The amused grin twisting the man's impeccable goatee showed he was in on the joke.

"No, Captain Fowler has opted for a passive share for himself and his crew, Mr. Ruiz."

"More for the rest of us, then, Captain." Mathias Sylvestre, the *Kate's* quartermaster, walked up to them. "It's been a while since we've strained the hold, captain. She'll be good for the exercise."

"Indeed, Mr. Sylvestre." He turned back to her; an eyebrow raised in curiosity. "Who will you be bringing, Miss Bure?"

She looked out over the crew, their eyes shining eagerly. How could so many of them want to follow her into battle? Admittedly, there should be little actual fighting if her plan worked, but they couldn't know that.

She saw Aidan trying to get her attention with a surreptitious gesture, his eyes skittering between her and the captain. *Kate's* boat would probably be the only one with two officers aboard, but that didn't matter much. She wouldn't have wanted to face danger without Aidan Allen by her side. She nodded.

"Allen, sir, if you don't mind?"

He smiled, and she didn't like the expression much, but he nodded. "Who else?"

The boat would carry about six more, and she quickly pointed out five of the best scrappers the *Kate* could boast.

Each clearly met with the captain's approval, but she could see his curiosity building as to who might be called out for the last seat.

But she had a promise to keep.

"We won't be leaving for a bit, right sir?" She pointed out the scramble of activity aboard the other ships. "None of the others knew we'd be leaving so soon. We have a little time?"

He nodded, but the line between his eyes deepened. "Probably. Time for what, though? I don't want to be scrambling when we don't have to be."

"I promised Aston a place in my boat for his service in the Dog, sir. You know none of the others would have managed it half so well."

Maguire seemed surprised for a moment but nodded at once. "True enough, Miss Bure. We wouldn't want such leal service to go unrewarded."

She hated it when he pushed that bilge, but she was glad enough that he would wait for Aston, she let it go.

"Signal to the Dog, Aidan? A lantern from the main topmast, if you'd be so kind?"

He nodded and shouted at a crewman near the main topsail yard.

"You've made arrangements?"

"Costa and Greene are keeping a boat at the western quay. The three of them promise they can make the entire journey in less than one bell."

He nodded, casting his gaze back toward shore where the little stone jetty that serviced the western portions of the town was hidden by several other ships resting at anchor. "Costa and Greene. Good choices. We might have missed them, if we'd had to leave sooner."

She had been waiting for this, and she was ready. "It was a calculated gamble, sir, but if you had declined to wait, they both assured me they could pull hard enough to be back aboard before we made it out of the harbor."

He smiled. "I approve, Shanae. You choose wisely. Hunt is a good man, despite his ... difficulties. I have no doubt he will serve you well."

She was glad to hear it, despite her own convictions. She watched the other ships of the squadron readying for action and leaned against the taffrail. "So, there will be just about thirty of us, all told? We had hoped for a few more."

"Fowler was never going to join us." Maguire shrugged. "We could tow a jollyboat with us, put a mixed crew into it from all the ships. It wouldn't be—"

"No." She spoke without thinking, and knew at once her tone had been sharp, but she knew what she was about, and she needed him to know that. She had no intention of adding a mixed crew, and the dangers of miscommunication that could bring with it, on this adventure. "I'll make it work."

He smiled. "I know you will. It's past time you had a command of your own."

That sent a cold shiver down her back despite the tropical heat of the day.

This wasn't a command. It was an action, nothing more.

"If it works, sir."

"It'll work, Shanae. It'll work."

The captain turned back to shore, smiling at the sight of a lone, gangly figure lurching toward the quay.

"You're better than you know."

She was thankful for the familiar words, as false as they might feel to her.

Chapter 3
1674 ~ La Ringot, Tortuga

Aidan slapped at his shoulder with a curse, glaring at the smear of red and black the devilish insect left behind. Armand Carpentier, a topman from the *Kate* and one of the best dirty fighters in the crew, hushed him from behind. Grudgingly, he nodded.

It seemed like an eternity since they had put out from the ships, following Mabey, their small, enigmatic little guide. They had begun the laborious portage across the little headland toward the bay holding their intended prey, the little Taino flitting in the shadows ahead of them, his easy movements seeming to mock their clumsy progress. Each boat crew had been left to their own devices to carry their charges overland through the jungle, and he gave a silent prayer of thanks, once again, that he was with Shanae and not with the *Chainbreakers* or the *Laughing Jacques*.

He was certain Shanae had spoken with Gabrielle, the little red-headed boatswain from the *Syren*, long before the mission was finalized. Both women had had their boats loaded with cut-down lengths of spar, a little wider than the hunting trail Mabey was guiding them along. The lengths of spar were being used to roll the vessels along, pulled and pushed by grunting, sweating crew. A pair of sailors would take the rearmost spar up when the boat passed it, carrying it forward and placing it before the rounded prows to continue the journey.

Because they weren't lifting the full weight of the boats, they had been able to load the craft down with most of their supplies, and several men and women could rest at a time, except when their path went up or down the steeper slopes.

Aidan thought he'd caught Mabey, glancing back at them from the darkness ahead, grinning evilly more than once.

He smiled himself, wiping sweat from his forehead with one dank sleeve, and cast a look back at the other two boats. The *Chainbreakers* under the command of the big former-slave, Cassius Black, labored in intense silence, their dark skin gleaming with sweat. Black himself bore the full weight of the boat's prow upon his broad back, his bright eyes fixed intently in the middle distance, navigating their course as if by the feel of the trail beneath his bare feet.

At the rear of their little formation came the men of the *Laughing Jacques*. They weren't laughing at the moment, having tried, in turns, dragging, carrying, and pushing their boat along the muddy ground. It had been quite impressive, seeing how long the men had kept their spirits high before the grim reality of their situation had settled in.

Aidan assumed Captain Houdin had given his men a bit more than the half-ration of rum Captain Maguire had suggested.

Sooner than he would have thought possible, it was his turn once again to take his place at the ropes. He tugged the stiff gloves over his sweaty hands and bent to with a will, determined that Shanae does not see him flag. It would be bad enough for the others from the ship to see him hard pressed, but the first mate had not stopped moving since their boats put out, and he would be damned if she would see him any less equal to the task at hand.

Soon enough they should meet up with the relay crew the captain had placed strung through the jungle, anyway. Their boat was going to be considerably more crowded on the final leg of their journey, but it would be worth the added effort when they arrived. Even more so, for the assistance they could offer in taking the boats down to the water.

He slowly realized the *Syren's* boat had halted, and so eased his hold on his own rope. Shanae was standing at the crest of a dark hill, looking down into the jungle, Mabey standing beside her. After a moment's pause, he decided that his rank afforded him a little leeway. He nodded to Hunt, behind him, and stripped the gloves off to join Shanae, their guide, and the *Syren's* boatswain as they contemplated the far slope.

"It's too steep to keep going the way we've been." Gabrielle rubbed the red stubble of her head with one broad hand, her brows low. "We're going to lose at least one boat if we try, and probably some hands along with it. There's no better path?"

Mabey shook his head, thin arms folded over his bony chest. "No. Only much worse."

Shanae wiped sweat from her forehead with a sigh. Her nut-brown skin glistened, and her blue eyes were steady as they took in the scene before them.

She nodded, glaring at the rutted track. "I didn't want to have to rig up any lines, but I'm afraid you're right."

Aidan dipped his head sagely, feeling the time was not entirely propitious for a quip. He felt a presence looming up behind him and turned to see Cassius Black pushing through the shining undergrowth by the side of the trail, skirting around the boats. The big bald man looked down at the slope and grunted.

"So, this would be what the block and tackle is for, then." His voice was low; the others made room for him.

Shanae's grin was bright in the green shadows of the jungle. "I didn't want to have to do it, but if we did, I didn't want to have to go without, either."

Black's answering smile was fierce. By the time the little blonde boatswain from the *Jacques* staggered up to join them, they were breaking up, moving back to their boats to gather up the rigging gear.

"Ropes?" LeBlanc's breath was coming in ragged gasps. He had not been shirking his own efforts at the rear of the column.

"Ropes." Aidan nodded, finding himself the last man still standing at the crest. "You all okay back there?"

The boy grimaced. "I'm not sure I would have agreed to this if I'd thought it through."

Aidan laughed and slapped him on the back, ruing the gesture at the wet clap of sound as he struck the sweat-drenched fabric.

*****

They worked efficiently, everyone happy to be free of the crushing weight of the boats for a while. Several topmen from each ship completed the bulk of the work, fixing blocks and lines from the top of the ridge down into the dimness of the gully below, under the dull, slightly-amused eyes of their guide.

After the actual trek, rigging the block and tackle seemed the work of mere moments, and all too soon they were lowering the *Syren's* boat down the slope, crew grunting above and below as they struggled with the weight. Shortly, the craft was at the bottom, pushed off to the side, and the next boat made the descent.

Soon enough, they were once more pushing their way through the jungle, Mabey disappeared into the gloom ahead. Occasionally, now, they could see the gleam of the sea through the dappled shadows ahead, and Aidan gave another silent prayer. He was at the back of the boat this time, pushing along, marking the coming and going of the crew switching out the spars as they moved. Each pass they made marked another step in their forward progress.

Two of the *Jacques* and one *Syren* had already succumbed to the heat, and were left behind with water skins to regain their strength while the rest of the party prepared themselves by the shore.

He shrugged some of the tension out of his shoulders when he was next relieved and moved up to walk beside Shanae and their guide as she picked her way through the wreckage left behind by the passage of the lead boat.

"Any idea how much farther we've to go?" He tried to direct his friendly question at the guide rather than his first mate. He didn't want to presume upon their friendship, knowing full well how much her current command weighed upon her. But the unceasing round of back-breaking labor, short rests in the fetid, steaming jungle heat, and then more work at the ropes was starting to take its toll on all of them.

He wanted to spit a curse as the little Taino man seemed to ignore him completely, and Shanae cast a dark glare in his direction. Then she then shrugged. "You know *La Ringot*. There aren't any decent maps of this entire region. My best guess? I'd say we had less than a mile to go. The relay party should be just up ahead."

Even though he had appeared oblivious to the exchange, Mabey nodded at this.

Aidan decided not to dignify the gesture with a response. "But even that far might take forever in this God-forsaken jungle." He looked out into the darkening jungle. "You know, they should have heard us by now. If they were anything more than lollygagging layabouts, they would have come out to help long before now."

He said it mainly in jest, the light-hearted complaint of a man more than willing to pull his fair share. So, when he saw the shadow cross her face at his words, he fumbled a step in concern.

"What is it?"

She jerked her chin forward. "You're right. They should have come out to meet us by now. If someone on the ships saw them, or worse yet, if they were found by a foraging party..."

He shook his head. "No need to worry. Alonso was in command? He wouldn't have been caught out like that."

Alonso Costa had been with the *Bonnie Kate* nearly as long as Aidan. The ferret-faced little Spaniard was a devil at cards, but he was also a sailor who knew his duty and wouldn't shirk.

"He's also not the kind to rest on his haunches while there's work to be done." Her normally confident tone was dark. "He's not here waiting for us, and there's got to be a reason."

Without consulting him further, she pushed forward, around the lead boat and its grunting, straining crewwomen, to find Gabrielle.

Mabey, with one quick glance over his shoulder at Aidan, moved to follow her. Was there a nervous edge to the man's expression?

Aidan tried not to be offended by Shanae's abrupt departure. She was in command, after all. And he wasn't here in his capacity as a master, but just another fighter to help pull off her daring caper.

It still stung, to have been dismissed so easily, however.

"Heavy weighs the crown." The words came in a harsh whisper, and Aidan almost shoved the gangly man into the bushes by the side of the trail before he pulled himself short.

"Hunt." It was half acknowledgment and half curse. He hated it when the Priest snuck up on him like that.

Aston Hunt only smiled vaguely through his tangled beard. "Heavy nonetheless." He gestured forward to where Shanae and the guide had disappeared. He was holding the small vial of dark green glass she had given him years ago. It always hung around his neck now by a hempen line, and Aidan knew from experience it contained nothing but a slug of seawater. For some reason, Hunt clung to it as if it was filled with the most precious liquid on Earth.

Aidan found the Priest's presence mildly disturbing. Not because of his madness. There were plenty of mad folk in the squadron. Hell, there were damned few men and women sailing with the Brethren of the Coast who *weren't* mad, when you looked close enough. It came with the territory.

No, it wasn't Hunt's madness that set him apart, but how often he seemed to see the deeper truth of things long before any but the captain, and maybe Shanae, knew what was happening. You might not always know what he was talking about, but more often than not, upon reflection or in the fullness of time, his words would come back with a haunting weight you hadn't noticed in the moment.

"She takes everything very seriously."

Aidan knew Shanae bore a soft spot in her heart for the creature, and so always tried to go out of his way to be patient.

"Seawater sings in her veins, gunner. There is none more serious in all our lord's realm than she."

Sometimes, he made it hard, though.

"She thinks something might have happened to the relay party." Often the best way to deal with Hunt was to ignore the wilder pronouncements and act like he was just another member of the crew. "She's worried."

The madman took that in, his wild eyebrows settling low over his fever-bright eyes. "She may have need of my council."

"I doubt that Hunt. You should—"

But the man was gone, crashing loudly through the undergrowth.

Aidan cursed. If the Priest interrupted Shanae in her work ahead, and she learned that he had been the last to have the lunatic in hand, she would not be gentle with him.

"Hunt, wait!" He raced after the man and came up short as he rounded the lead boat and took in the scene before him.

He nearly choked.

The light had been failing beneath the dense canopy overhead for a while; the distant glimpses of sky to the west showing the deepening red of a gorgeous Caribbean sunset.

But in the vague, shifting twilight of the jungle, Aidan could clearly see why the column's progress had halted so abruptly, and he wondered if their venture had failed before it had really even begun.

A party of Taino natives was standing before Shanae and the other officers, their dark skin gleaming with sweat, bows drawn in their hands, their faces flat and angry.

There was no sign of Mabey.

It was a miracle Shanae had not drawn on them, he thought. She seldom spoke about how she had first come to the squadron as a small child, but there were plenty of tales whispered among the various buccaneer ships, and many of them spoke of a native raid on a small colony of escaped slaves, leaving only the little Shanae alive.

He didn't know how she kept her calm. If *he* had been confronted by the people who had killed his family, no matter how long ago, he was certain no power on Earth would be able to stop him from reaping a terrible vengeance.

But instead, Shanae merely stood in the middle of the trail, speaking in a calm, reasonable voice.

"What halts our progress, gunner?"

Aidan closed his eyes, pinching the bridge of his nose in exasperation.

"She's got everything in hand, Hunt. We should probably keep our distance." He looked up to reason with the priest, only to catch a fleeting glimpse of the man taking off down the gentle slope at a dead run.

"Hunt, stop!" He shouted, then grunted. He recognized the look on the man's face. When he got these notions into his head, there was no stopping him short of physical restraint.

And if those Taino down there were feeling quarrelsome, that might be necessary.

He jogged after the crazed sailor again but remained silent otherwise. He had no interest in drawing the attention of any of those bows.

Shanae stood with Gabrielle and Black flanking her, all of them keeping hands conspicuously away from their weapons, although he was happy to see that Black's pistols appeared primed and ready if they were needed.

"We wish only to pass along the trail." Shanae's words were soft, but there was no give in them. "We mean no harm, and we do not hunt. The Europeans in the bay will be gone by tomorrow if you give us leave to pass. If we are forced to turn back, there is no telling how long they will stay. And each day, they will continue to fish and forage. How much damage will *they* do?"

Aidan didn't think turning back and dragging the damned boats all the way across the island again was in the cards, but his heart skipped a beat at the thought.

He wasn't going to be able to pretend indifference if the promised end of their journey, so near at hand, was denied them.

In his moment of despair, he scanned the natives again and realized there were not as many as he had first thought. In fact, a large number of the people further down the trail weren't Taino at all. They were crew from the *Bonnie Kate*, trussed up like pigs, sitting disconsolately on the floor of the jungle.

The relay crew had been keeping watch over the French merchant ships, passing the information they gathered across the island back to Cayona. They had obviously run afoul of the natives.

The light continued to fade, and he knew that time was not their friend.

"The Brethren and the Taino have no quarrel here." Shanae's tone had gotten harder. She was clearly sensing the passage of time.

One of the natives, a little old man whose face was so wrinkled, the folds nearly swallowed his eyes, barked a laugh.

"There are no more Brethren of the Coast. You? Your squadron? Those who were once Brethren have fled, disappeared over the waves, or invaded *La Montagne* and *La Ringot* for their wood, areas sworn to the Taino in the time before the Spaniards were driven out."

Aidan grabbed Hunt by the collar, thinking to pull him back before he broken into the tense ring, but the man surged ahead, breaking his grip, and stumbled between Shanae and Gabrielle, nearly falling to his knees before the little dark man.

"Friends! There is no need for strife amongst us!" He held his hands up to show that they were empty, and then turned to give a look the madman probably assumed was reassuring to the mates.

It only succeeded in sending a shiver down Aidan's own, sweat-drenched spine.

"I know you for fellow travelers, friends!" Hunt held up the container of sea water. "The Ruler of the Waves guides your lives as surely as he is the sovereign of our own course. He provides for us all, and in times of danger and want, he sees that his children are fed and safe."

"Hunt, that's enough." Shanae's voice was stern. She did not reach out to grab him, but her voice was cold. "This was—"

"No, m'lady." He shook his head, his greasy locks swaying maniacally. "The Master of the Trident speaks through me!"

He turned back to the Taino, eyes aglow with madness, or something else. "Those two ships that befoul your home waters are our gift from the Lord of Horses. They are meant for us. And in accepting this gift from our god, we will rid your land of their unwanted stench."

"Alright, Hunt." This time Shanae did reach out. "I need to handle this…"

Her words faded away as she watched the smile stretch across the ancient man's face. There was an amused respect there that had not been there before. With a few muttered words to his followers, the crewmen down the hill were freed, rubbing their wrists ruefully, giving the natives dark glances as the small warriors faded back into the jungle.

The old man turned back to the officers, but he addressed Hunt, not Shanae. "Your god, not ours. But we honor him all the same. You will see these ships and their men gone?"

Hunt bowed low, and Aidan almost laughed at the gross theatricality of it all. "Cacique, we will see them off without delay."

The term gave Aidan pause. He knew it meant leader, or captain, in the Taino language, but how had the crazed sailor learned it?

The man smiled and nodded, then looked to Shanae. "If they are not gone tomorrow, there will be a reckoning." And he disappeared after his kin.

Aidan shivered again, despite the heat. The Taino were usually a peaceful people, unless provoked. But when they decided to unleash their wrath, they were the equal of any fighters who walked the Earth, no matter their lack of sophistication or advanced weapons.

Hunt turned to Shanae; the look of puppy dog eagerness almost painful to witness. "M'lady, the way is clear."

She shook her head, her face an unreadable mask, and then smiled with a heavy sigh. "Hunt, if you do that again, I'm going to arrange for you to meet Neptune face to face sooner than you might like."

Mabey did not appear again, but this close to the water, they hardly needed him. No doubt the man would be halfway back to Cayona by now, ready to spend the silver Shanae had given him at the start of their journey at any pot house that might welcome such as he.

The boats were set to moving once more, and soon enough they were all gathered beneath the eaves of the jungle, looking out across the smooth, placid waters of a little bay at two dark shapes floating at anchor about a hundred yards out.

The two fluyts were ablaze with lights as the night's watch lit lanterns and hung them around the ships. The buccaneers crouched low in the green shadows and watched. There were no boats out, and there did not appear to be any boarding nets rigged.

From all they could see, the Frenchmen had no idea they were being stalked.

Now all they had to do was wait for full dark, ready the boats, and prepare for the arrival of the *Bonnie Kate* and the other ships of the squadron.

The hard work was done. Now the dangerous work could begin.

Chapter 4
1674 - Doux Bay, Tortuga

The old pressure began to build behind her eyes.

Shanae trusted Captain Maguire completely, and she knew that her own planning and preparation was sound. Nevertheless, before any action, a rising tide of self-doubt always turned her blood cold and drove a spike of ice up into her forehead.

The feeling was as familiar to her as the *Kate* itself. And with it came two companion thoughts, every time.

The first was the calming assurance that, no matter what doubt might assail her before such endeavors, she had always risen to the occasion. Her abilities and her training had always overcome the near-paralyzing fear before battle was joined.

The second was that one day, that might not be the case.

But she was damned if a couple of French merchantmen would be the hill upon which she died.

She trained the spyglass on the headland off to their right. Nothing but dark, rolling waters out beyond the protection of the little bay; beyond the glittering lanterns that were her natural quarry. There was no sign of the squadron, but it was early yet.

She glanced behind her crew, at the low mountain the islanders called *La Montagne*, in their gallic lack of imagination. The moon had not yet risen above the crest, and until it did, she would not worry.

But looking back at the mountain reminded her once again of the Taino, and how tense the situation had been before the priest had intervened.

She felt a slight smile twist her lips as she thought of Hunt. He was a madman, and no mistake. But that madness had its place in a world that made as little sense as this chaos beyond the line.

But the Taino, on the other hand, were a factor to be considered on nearly any island in the region. Especially here on Tortuga, where so many of the Brethren had given up the sea-going life for the relative peace and security of providing wood to the ravenous expansion of the colonies scattered across the islands.

Those buccaneers who had turned to the logsman's trade had pushed deeper and deeper into the Taino territories, expanding far out past the sugar fields and plantations. They had pushed the natives farther and farther into the mountains and the eastern-most coast of Tortuga, called *La Ringot* by the

French.

Of course, they would be angry. Of course, if they captured anyone they perceived as being of the same ilk, they would look askance at their presence and perhaps take out their frustration and anger concerning their diminished status on the island on those hapless travelers.

She should have taken that into consideration. She should have had her relay crew better protected, forewarned, and better armed.

She felt cold sweat trickle down her spine. They could have been killed.

Damnation, they could have been killed, and her entire command could have been ambushed and lost as well.

She tried to shake the heavy weight of fear away, but it settled ever deeper into her bones.

And now she was to lead a desperate assault on those ships with these same men and women she had almost gotten killed once today already?

"Stop."

The word was calm, quiet, and after her initial jump, she realized that none of the others could have heard it, never mind the sentries on the French ships.

She turned her head and found herself looking into Hunt's bright green eyes. The man's black hair hung down over his face in lanky strands, and yet the expression on that face was wholly composed.

"You've got to lead out there now. The natives are gone, satisfied with our offering to the god and to them. What has passed is past. Now is all that matters."

She opened her mouth, but had no idea what she was going to ask. Had he read her mind? How did he know what she had been thinking? How did he know when they were supposed to leave?

But as she looked again over *La Montagne*, her jaw snapped closed. The sliver of moon was just peaking over the mountain's edge, crisp and clear in the tropical night.

It was time.

She nodded her thanks to the man even she called the priest from time to time, and then looked aside to where Aidan rested, a black hat tilted down over his face. That man could sleep anywhere.

"It's time." She did not whisper, knowing instinctively how clearly the hissing of a whisper carried over water. But her voice was low and urgent.

She was happy to note the taste of eagerness in it.

Once again, her fear and doubt had receded at the moment of action.

One day they may not. One day they may swell up to overwhelm her and paralyze her.

But this was not that day.

The men and women around her eased into action, sliding the boats on the smooth, still-warm sand from underneath the jungle canopy and into the blood-warm waters.

If the moon had been any bigger there was no way this plan could have worked. As things were, they would be rowing hell-bent-for-leather across the silver-gilt waves for a hundred yards before they reached their prey.

If the captains did not complete their part of the plan even a bunch of French merchantmen would have little trouble seeing her small crew off with heavy casualties.

She hopped into the *Kate's* boat as Armand the topman and Tian Rodier, an escaped slave that had chosen the ship of his rescuers over the vessel that housed the majority of his people in the squadron, pushed them into the gentle waves. Off to the side she watched as the boats from *Syren*, *Chainbreaker*, and *Laughing Jacques* slid into the water as well.

The oarlocks had been muffled with sailcloth, every raider was draped in dark fabric, soot streaking their faces. Weapons were sheathed, as per her orders, but they were blacked with soot as well.

She felt her heartbeat heavily in her chest as her oarsmen bent to their tasks, muscles bunching and relaxing in easy unison. The bow of the boat sliced through the small waves, every ill-timed splash setting her teeth on edge.

One of the oarsmen, Filip, missed a wrist turn and his oar flapped, flat-bladed, into the water. The passengers aboard the boat tensed, and the man shot a sheepish glance back at where she crouched in the bow. She watched the ships ahead, saw no signs of sudden, concerned, movement, and waved his fear away.

For the first part of their journey the boats would have the cover of the jungle shadows behind them. Hopefully, they would be just four darker spots moving through the tropical night. But soon they would be too far from the shore, clearly visible beneath even the paltry light of the waning moon.

Without a distraction to draw their attention out to sea, the lookouts aboard the fluyts would have to be blind not to see them. Without warning, they could be looking down the muzzles of the big swivel guns mounted around the railings of the ships.

She extended the spyglass again and put it to her eye. She spotted the dark silhouette of the steeply sloping headland, the tops of the trees outlined in bright silver, and then swept the field of view to the left, out to sea.

At first, she saw nothing, and began to despair. Very soon now she would have to make the call. Did they forge ahead without the distraction of the squadron, most likely taking heavy fire from the topmen and light guns of the cargo ships before they could close the distance, or did she give the order to retreat back into the island shadows, giving up their one chance to take the Frenchmen unawares and thus minimize casualties on both sides and the chance that they would have to pay an even steeper price with the governor?

She didn't know what would be worse: the loss of face among the squadron from a failed mission, or the difficulties they would all have to deal with should the caper succeed in a messy, half-assed fashion.

And then a flash of light caught her attention down the dark tunnel of the spyglass. A wide smile washed the fear away.

No buccaneer in his right mind would rig that much light for an attack. *Bonnie Kate* came sweeping around the headland under full sail, another incongruous element to the scene. There was no caution in her movements, no stealth in her approach.

And as her green and gold hull broke completely from the island's shadows and into the moon-splashed waves, three more shapes, all equally as brazen in their lack of light discipline, all as equally flashy in their sail-plans, came crashing around the little jetty.

The roaring of stentorian orders echoed across the water as the four ships came crashing into the little bay. A brilliant flash of muzzle-fire erupted from one of *Kate's* forward guns, followed by a whistle and a towering splash out beyond the two fluyts.

Shanae grinned broadly as Aidan cursed behind her. That shot would have served no good purpose under normal circumstances, and obviously offended his sensibilities as one of the ship's chief gunners.

More roars echoed across the water. More towers of white foam reached up to the star-spangled sky.

Cries of panic and fear echoed across the bay. She swept the spyglass down upon the Frenchmen, and her grin turned savage as she noted the dark specks of their crews rushing to their starboard sides.

She had no doubt every eye aboard those ships was strained out to sea, watching the laughable display of the squadron's approach.

Seasoned Caribbean hands would have never been fooled by this ruse. The buccaneer ships had fired far too early. They carried far too much canvas to make a stealthy, careful approach. In fact, there was almost no way, short of blind-drunk lookouts or a full gale, that anyone could fail to notice the coming of the squadron.

And that was exactly what they had planned.

By now each of the four ships were firing their guns in ragged, undisciplined rhythms that left almost no time between each shot. Towering fountains of water rose up all across the bay. A naval officer with any experience at all, or a buccaneer with even a single season of raiding under her belt, would have seen this for either a blatant subterfuge or the worst gunnery in the history of warfare.

But the French merchantmen saw only a dire, immediate threat.

There was chaos on the decks of the fluyts. Men rushed here and there, pointed, firing small arms into the night, or scrambled around the pathetic little deck guns, hoping against hope that they could fend off this overwhelming, if clumsy attack.

Shanae growled her pleasure and barked a brief command to her oarsmen. They bent to with a renewed will, and the boat surged across the water, the distance between them and the towering merchant ships shrinking with every pull.

At this signal the other boats began to heave ahead as well. The men and women crouching in the boats readied their weapons; belaying pins, shortened gaff hooks, and clubs for the most part. She had ordered her people to keep their firearms stowed for the initial assault.

But that meant that as they boarded, they would be facing foes bearing far deadlier weaponry. That took discipline and trust on the part of her people, and that cold little voice in the back of her mind began its insidious whispers once again.

Did they trust her that much?

Should they trust her that much?

It would soon be time for them all to see her fight once more; a sight some of the newer hands had never witnessed. These moments were rare, and oft retold in the quiet watches of the night.

But then, so far, they had always gone her way.

If she was killed in the next few minutes, that tale would be told as well.

It would just be a different story.

Ahead, heedless of her inner turmoil, the starboard fluyt continued to grow, eclipsing the view of the sea beyond.

Brigs from the late 17th century

Interlude 1
1655- Aboard the Syren, *Cayona Harbor*

"So, you must be Maguire's girl."

The girl looked up as she clambered over the side and onto the *Syren's* main deck. The woman who had spoken towered above the newcomer, her sleek black skin shining in the sun. She had no hair, her scalp marked by strange, dark scars in a circular pattern.

"My name is Shanae." The girl stuck her lip out. The crew of the *Bonnie Kate* took her very seriously. They accepted her as one of them, and there were no comments about her being a girl or belonging to anyone. She was already one of the best lookouts, and easily the best powder handler on the ship.

It was only when she went into town that her age became an issue, and the people, men and women both, treated her as some oddity. The men, for the most part, laughed at her, while the women seemed to think she was in some kind of danger; their reactions ran from sadness and concern to a breed of fear she couldn't hope to understand.

She'd gotten into more than one fight while ashore, but the town wasn't the ship. There were too many people, too much territory to cover, to establish a reputation that might keep folks from bothering her.

She had been with Captain Maguire for five years. He was a kind captain, a fair captain, but he expected her to carry her own weight, and to make her way with the crew as best she could.

She stood as tall as she could, stretching out her spine and looking straight up into the dark face so high above her own. She barely came up to the woman's waist, but the flash of bright white smile brought an easing of the tension clear in her stance.

"Very well, then. No one's girl but your own." The woman bent down, dark eyes sparkling in the bright sunshine. "You should fit right in here."

Captain Maguire had taken the *Kate* to Port Royal and sent the girl to the *Syren* for the duration. He had not explained why.

The girl had not been away from the ship since she had made it her home when she was a child.

She rubbed one forearm savagely across her eyes and looked away.

The tall woman looked down at her, her face impassive, then tilted her head toward the aft of the brigantine. "You're familiar with the layout? Captain Semprun is expecting you in her cabin."

The *Syren* was very similar to the *Bonnie Kate*; finding the captain's cabin should prove no challenge at all.

She sniffed, then nodded. Without a backward glance she walked past the tall woman, her back ramrod straight, and moved toward the low hatch.

She missed the tall woman's gentle smile as she went.

At the end of the companionway beneath the quarterdeck, Shanae rapped on the small door and pushed it open at the call from within.

The cabin was much like Captain Maguire's, if a little better maintained. Maguire was a man who liked a tidy ship but kept his own space a little more cluttered than one might have expected. It was clear that Captain Semprun was a different kind of leader.

The small space was divided into two compartments with a dark curtain. The lack of bed, bunk, or hammock rigging meant the sleeping quarters must be behind the curtain. Two thirds of the space was visible. A small desk, several chairs, and a small table sat about the room, unsecured from the places along the bulkheads where they would be stored for action. There were two long guns, probably six pounders, tied down against the outer walls, pointed toward the stern. Two chase ports, currently open to allow the free circulation of air, showed where the *Syren* might surprise some naval cutter thinking to snap up a buccaneer on the open sea.

At the desk sat Captain Semprun, bending over a chart, several small books piled around her. She looked up and smiled, her curly black hair hanging loose down either side of her face.

"Welcome, Shanae. It's been a while."

The woman's voice was deep but feminine. It held a strength that seemed the equal of Captain Maguire, if of a different timbre.

"Thank you for letting me stay with you, ma'am." The girl bowed slightly. "I shan't be any trouble."

That made the captain smile. "I have no doubt, girl." The dark eyes became serious as she indicated one of the chairs, waiting for Shanae to take a seat.

"Now, Shanae, I would like to talk with you for a spell concerning your time aboard the *Bonnie Kate*. Are you happy there? Are you treated well?"

The girl looked puzzled at the words, then nodded. "Yes, ma'am. I'm treated quite well. Captain Maguire treats everyone aboard the ship fairly, so long as they do their work."

The woman's eyes narrowed. "I know. I was a member of that crew for a long time, remember."

The girl nodded in response but did not speak.

Captain Semprun leaned forward, her elbows resting on her knees. "You are not mistreated? You have not been ... abused, in any way?"

The girl's frown deepened. "I don't know what you mean, ma'am. No one is abused aboard the *Bonnie Kate*."

The woman looked away, a slight smile twisting her full lips. "You know there are no men aboard the *Syren*."

The girl gave another wordless nod.

"Because of this, there is a certain ... safety, aboard the *Syren*, for a girl, that cannot be guaranteed aboard any other ship, no matter how diligent and conscientious her captain might be."

That seemed to sting the girl, and her dark brows lowered menacingly toward the bridge of her nose. "No one is abused aboard the *Bonnie Kate*, ma'am."

That seemed to satisfy the tall captain, and she leaned back in her chair, taking a longer moment to stare at the girl in open appraisal.

"Captain Maguire says you're passably well versed in fighting. You don't look like much, a little slip of a girl like you. I've a mind to see you better prepared in that regard, while you're with us, if you'd allow me the indulgence."

The girl's eyes tightened, her lips a thin line. "I wouldn't want to be any trouble, Ma'am. I'm sure Captain Maguire just meant for me to berth with you while he visits Port Royal. He shouldn't be gone more than a few weeks. I mean to earn my keep, either way."

The dark woman smiled at that. "Oh, you'll earn your keep, have no fear. But I believe I would feel better about your future after a little more training in the application of disciplined violence."

The girl followed the words without expression, nodding only at the end. "Whatever you believe to be the best use of my time, ma'am. Might be I've more edge than you've noticed, though."

Semprun didn't smile, but there was a tension around her eyes that almost seemed to convey a similar expression.

The captain leaned forward; her arms crossed on the small table before her. "Why did he go to Port Royal? Do you know?"

The girl's face tightened. "Business. He didn't say, ma'am. He's not in the habit of telling me more than I need to know. I'm just another member of the crew."

That, more than anything, caused the sardonic ice in the big woman's eyes to melt a little. "Of course." Then she cocked her head slightly to one side. "And why didn't you go with him?"

The question was asked in a way that clearly let the girl know the captain had her own theory. "You know the way of it, ma'am. Anyone with African blood is dissuaded from joining a ship of the squadron making for Port Royal."

The captain nodded, one hand making a rolling gesture for the girl to continue. "The English policy toward Africans on Jamaica is a mess. Men and women both have been seized more than once. Merely being glimpsed from the docks is sometimes enough to offend, depending on the mood of the English that day."

Captain Semprun sighed, shaking her head sadly, and then rose. "You are correct, of course, Shanae. And yet he still ventures to Port Royal, eh? He hasn't brought the *Bonnie Kate* there in a while, I think."

"Not since I joined the crew, ma'am. No." The girl was quick, almost as if she was setting to cut the captain's thoughts off before they could wander further. Or to prove that she knew the history of the ship.

"But he's gone himself a time or two." The captain leaned casually against a support beam. "Leaving the ship and her crew behind for a few weeks here or there?"

The girl was completely still, fists at her sides. "That's common knowledge, ma'am."

The woman turned, then, to look out one of the hatches into the glaring sunlight. "Of course, it is. But why?"

Then she seemed to shake something off and turned her smile back toward the girl. "I've asked Corine Beauvais, one of my crew, to set up on the forecastle for your first lesson and assessment. Don't let her pretty smile fool you; she's tough as any man in the squadron. If there's anyone here can sharpen that edge you've started, it's her. There'll be no slacking aboard the *Syren*, Shanae. We'll have your best or Captain Maguire can find you sleeping with the dogs ashore when he returns."

The girl gave a sharp nod and turned toward the doorway. As she reached the threshold, she turned. "I'll follow orders, ma'am, but I think you'll find I am quite capable of taking care of myself."

She was gone before the captain had a chance to respond. She stood alone in the cabin for several moments, a strange twist to her lips, until the tall African woman returned.

Renata Villa was an escaped slave, much older when she had fought for her freedom than Shanae had been when the *Bonnie Kate* had plucked her from that scene of slaughter on Hispaniola three years ago.

Renata shared her captain's concern for the girl. But as they locked stares, both smiling grimly after a silent moment, it was clear they both approved of her current state.

*****

Outside in the bright sunshine, the girl glanced around the main deck of the ship, noted the bustle of regular shipboard work, and moved toward the small forecastle, where a squat blonde woman was standing beside the foremast step, waiting for her.

There was a small table set up by the woman's hip, a bit of sailcloth tossed over it, concealing several objects.

"You must be Shanae." The woman's French accent was thick, but not nearly as thick as half the townsfolk in Cayona.

The girl nodded, scanning the little table.

"I'm Corine Beauvais. The captain wants to know what you're capable of. I was told you're pretty good in a fight?" Muscles rippled in the woman's arms. When she smiled, it seemed that years melted from her tight, rigid face. She couldn't have had more than a few years over the girl's own decade.

The gnarled fist lashed out at her face, and the girl staggered back, bending with the blow so that, even as the knuckles grazed her cheek, there was little resistance to their passing.

Shanae spun to lose the momentum of her dodge and the strike, settling into a fighter's crouch, drawing the back of her right hand over her mouth and looking with dispassionate calm at the streak of blood there.

The woman's smile never wavered. "Captain wanted to know what you're capable of," she repeated.

The girl's answering smile couldn't have registered on the woman before a counterattack of frenzied blows flashed out, pushing her back across the forecastle.

One lucky punch slid beneath the woman's hasty guard and struck her on the chin. There was no noticeable effect, but whether it was because of the girl's slight frame, the experience of her opponent, or the woman's solid jaw, was unclear.

Except that the woman's smile widened even more. "*Touché*, girl. Well done."

The woman relaxed, rising out of her fighting stance, and moved back toward the table. "You've got potential, if we can teach you to harness that energy, and use it more wisely."

Then she grunted as the girl planted a sideways kick into the back of her knee.

The woman went to the deck with a yell of surprise, then rolled quickly to the side, narrowly avoiding the next kick, aimed at her head.

"Alright!" The smile had slipped, and the woman rose with a wary glance at the girl.

A crowd had formed in a semi-circle on the main deck below them, the crew of the *Syren* looking up, smiling appreciatively. Some were even calling advice to the other woman, none of it complimentary.

"That's enough. We're all impressed. You took me down. Let's get some water and—"

But the girl had spun to the table, pulled off the sheet, and revealed an array of weapons laid out there, as if for a lesson or inspection.

There were several pistols of varying sizes, as well as a dizzying collection of knives of almost every conceivable shape.

A little hand flashed out and the girl held a short, heavy oak rod, across her body in a passable guard position. Her grin had shifted into the eager, savage expression of a small animal.

"Girl, there's no need—"

Two vicious swings whistled through the air, causing the other woman to weave away, her blonde hair flying.

"I have a name." The girl growled the words, and the growing crowd of women on the main deck roared their approval. This seemed to annoy Beauvais, who nodded, one hand up in a pacifying gesture.

"Sure, you do. Now put the stick down. We don't—"

Two more lashes with the baton flashed in the sun, the second landing with a meaty thunk against the woman's raised forearm.

The two fighters glared at each other from beneath their raised arms, the girl's eyes widening slightly while the woman's narrowed with low cunning.

Before the girl could react, bringing the rod back for another blow, the woman's foot lashed out, sweeping the girl's feet out from beneath her. She hit the deck hard, air crashing from her lungs as the woman continued her sweeping move, dropping one knee down on the center of the girl's chest.

The rod was yanked from her hand, tossed away toward the forepeak, and she was hauled upright by one arm, left to twist painfully, her feet barely on the warm wood of the deck.

"Enough time to calm down, now, sweetling?" The woman growled in the girl's ear, and even after the waif nodded painfully, she let her swing for a moment before dropping her.

When the girl looked up, angry and sullen, she was surprised to see that the woman was smiling widely. The women on the main deck cheered.

"Not bad for a first day, girl. We've got some honing yet to do, but there's a lot here to work with." She nodded, looking the skinny girl up and down. "A lot to work with."

*****

Her duties aboard the *Syren* were many; the captain kept her running from morning till sunset. But there was a large part of every day, there on the forecastle, dancing around the shadows of the foremast, that Shanae and Corine Beauvais would share that little scrap of ship and batter at each other for hours on end.

Corine Beauvais was vicious, giving no quarter until the girl could hardly stand, sweat splashing the burning deck, creating a further hazard as they sparred.

For the first week Corine worked her with the batons, leaving the knives, cutlasses, and other weapons as an enticement to greater efforts. Before the first week was out, no one could touch the girl with a baton, while she would land far more blows than she missed in return.

Beauvais found herself wondering if taking on this challenge for her captain had not been a mistake.

As good as the girl was with the hardwood rods, she proved even more proficient with the various bladed weapons. She had an instinctual awareness of the orientation of any blade and could weave a protective cocoon around herself with the smallest dirk or the heaviest cutlass. She could land a series of blows in rapid, staccato succession before an onlooker could register the attack had begun.

But it was more than just proficiency with the various weapons that began to set the girl apart. She truly enjoyed the work, as well. There was nothing she looked forward to more than sparring with a worthy opponent. And when she began to regularly best Corine, others on the *Syren's* crew stepped up to match her.

By the end of the third week, the girl was holding her own against the towering Renata Villa herself, the enormous woman grinning through every sweat-drenched bout.

She proved herself with the firearms as well, both pistols and long guns, able to land a shot on the forecastle from the quarterdeck more often than most of the grown women on the crew. But she never came to love the powder like she did the blades.

At one point, one evening after the day's work had been finished and those members of the crew who had not gone into town were lounging about on the deck, she challenged Kyra Barret, another young crewwoman who more than enjoyed dueling, to a contest. Barret was given three loaded pistols, Shanae three balanced knives, and the two of them faced off, aiming at targets set right over the shoulders of their opponents.

Captain Semprun nearly forbid the contest, but a grinning Corine begged her to stay back, and with a silent glance at each of her young charges, the woman did so.

Corine dropped a kerchief between the two, and when it hit the deck, three loud eruptions echoed out over the harbor, bouncing back from the glittering lights of the town.

When the smoke had cleared, two of Barret's shots had landed, one in the center of the target, one clipping the edge closest to Shanae's ear.

All three of Shanae's blades were sunk into the center of the target behind the other girl, quivering with the force of their strikes.

The crew of the *Syren* had screamed their approval at the display, even Kyra Barret smiling widely as she flicked one of the knives with one painted fingernail.

The moment cemented the girl in the crew's affections.

*****

One afternoon, with sweat dripping off her forehead into the gentle swells of the harbor, the girl turned to find Captain Semprun standing nearby, looking out toward the mouth of the harbor and the distant dirt forts that guarded it.

The entire time the girl had been aboard the *Syren*, she had seen how well-trained the crew was. The women were worked mercilessly, spending a large portion of each day with pistols and blades.

She had asked the captain why, once, and Semprun had looked at her with strangely flat eyes. "Most women are at a disadvantage in strength and stamina when the action gets in close with men. We must overcome this with speed, agility, and accuracy, and those things only come with training."

The girl had tilted her head at this, giving the tall woman a puzzled glance, but thought no more of it. But that day, with the sun sinking slowly behind the hills to the west, and with the captain standing nearby, sharing the moment, she clearly had another question.

"Why don't you train, if it's so important?"

The captain looked down with a wry grin, as if the girl had puzzled something out.

"If you never let them see you train, if you never let them see you sweat, or land a poor blow, or get struck with a blunted weapon, something happens in the mind of your crew, Shanae."

She looked out again over the water. "The only time my crew, or anyone, sees me swing a blade or fire a pistol, it is in deadly earnest. Blood will flow. I flatter myself to think I am rather good at such things, as well, and so, a mystique arises around me."

The girl thought about that for a moment, then turned back to look out over the water. "So, it's a pantomime, then."

The woman's smile broadened. "Something like that. As a leader, you may someday find that much of the job is creating an image in the minds of those who follow you. If you can enhance that image, make it stronger in their minds, do something to separate you from the common walk of man, you may find they garner more from it than you might think."

"You fool them into fighting harder." The girl's voice was firm, but a little sad.

"Does that disappoint you? It is an illusion, something you would do well to learn about, regardless of the path life shows you. Creating an image like this can often be better than the most rousing speech. And there is no fault in getting more from your people, Shanae." She looked like a beautiful statue, staring out over the crimson-dappled waves.

"They will often fight better under the power of this mystery, and in doing so, they may survive where others might not."

The girl nodded again, then sighed.

With her own nod and a slight smile, the captain settled in beside her, to enjoy the sunset.

*****

The *Bonnie Kate* had been gone for just over three weeks. Shanae and Corine were resting with their backs against the foremast, eyes closed against the brutal heat of the tropical sun, when a call from the crow's nest above on the mainmast snapped them out of their musings.

The green of the *Kate's* hull was dark against the bright, glowing water of the harbor as she cleared the headland to the west and made for a mooring off the aft starboard quarter of the *Syren*.

Shanae bounced up as if on a string and was making her way toward the hold where her meager possessions had been stowed during her sojourn with the women of the *Syren*.

Captain Semprun watched her approach from the forward rail of the quarterdeck, a strange smile on her face that seemed equal parts affection and concern.

"Shanae, are you so quick to leave us?"

The girl looked up, a smile tugging at her lips, and flicked a thumb over her shoulder. "*Kate's* back, ma'am. I've got to get home."

The captain nodded, watching her descend, and was there still when the girl reemerged into the light.

"Shanae, you will always have a place here on the *Syren*, should you wish it." The woman's voice was intense, her eyes direct.

The girl stopped her skipping advance across the deck and turned, her own face somber.

"Thank you, captain. That means more than you could know." She turned her head to watch as the other brigantine slid across the rolling surf of the harbor. They were already preparing a boat to fetch her home. "I will always be grateful to you for everything you've done for me, but Captain Maguire is my captain. And the *Kate's* my ship."

Faster than seemed plausible, the *Kate's* boat was alongside, the girl was hoping over the rail, and she was gone.

Semprun smiled to herself as she turned back to her cabin.

For some reason, it wasn't quite as annoying as usual to realize that this time Maguire might just have been right.

Chapter 5
1674 ~ Doux Bay, Tortuga

Shanae forced herself to stand straight in the bow of the boat as the crewmen hauled on the oars for all they were worth. As the little craft surged forward, the view before them was quickly eclipsed by the *Marie Lajoie* towering above.

Fluyts were not overly big ships, as far as the full scope of their kind were concerned, but they were large enough. Only the *Arbiter* and the *Jaguar* could really compare, from the squadron. And from the pitching deck of boat, the flank of the *Marie Lajoie's* hull rose up like a solid wall of dark wood.

Off to her left she watched the glowing wakes of the other two boats approaching the *Courageux*. Judging from the commotion on the distant ship's deck, the entire crew was still lining the starboard rails, immobilized by the squadron's approach. Weak French curses rose to the heavens.

Of course, there were no nets rigged along the sides of her target, but that would pose little challenge to the buccaneers of the squadron as they moved in for the strike.

Beyond the bulk of the ship swelling before them she could still hear the booming echo of the squadron's guns as they rolled over the waves. Distant splashes reassured her the gunnery was as poor as intended, and she shot Aidan a quick grin. He gave her a sour look which melted into a mischievous smile.

There was nothing quite like the feeling of a plot coming together.

The bow of the little boat cracked against the side of the fluyt and lines sailed up into the darkness overhead. Two of the hooks bit into the rail and were pulled tight as a third slithered briefly before splashing down in the churning water between the boat's gunwales and the heavy planking of their prey.

She had no time to worry about the sound of the splash as she scrambled up the rope. Her people knew better than to try to race ahead of her.

When Shanae boarded a prize, she was always the first over the side.

She grasped the rail with one hand and hoisted herself up and over with a grunt, landing in a crouch, her bare feet slapping on the warm wood of the main deck.

A solid line of dark backs blotted out the view of the squadron's noisy approach. Some of the sailors gripped cutlasses or belaying pins, while others seemed more content to pull at their hair or harangue their neighbors in babbling French.

She felt her lip curl in disdain. This is what made such men fair game in this world. There was no place on the waters for a man who could not keep what he claimed as his own. The earth had been seeded with just such weaklings for the enrichment of those strong enough to seize what they wanted.

She rushed toward that line, pulling the two wooden rods from her belt. She would follow her own orders to the letter. She understood full well the reasons behind the captain's insistence that they do everything in their power to keep the French sailors alive.

That wouldn't be saving many of them from waking up with brutal headaches, however.

She aimed for a burly man, one of several who had managed to arm himself in the chaotic rush of the ship's panic. She ran as quickly as she could, conscious of the sound of her bare feet on the deck, gliding across the polished wood like a ghost.

The poor man never even knew the true threat had arrived before the baton cracked across the base of his neck and sent him sprawling into the other sailors before him, a dead weight, his weapon clattering to the deck at their feet.

The crowd of sailors surged away from the falling man, looking down at him with startled cries, and Shanae wanted to laugh at the looks on their faces.

In their defense, of course, they probably assumed the man had been cut down by a splinter or a long gun shot from the squadron's fire.

Never mind that not a single ounce of led or iron had come anywhere near either fluyt. The Frenchmen were too far gone to notice.

Before the sailors could marshal any kind of defense, she swung wide with the other baton and brought it up against the side of another man's head. That man's eyes crossed, a vaguely accusatory tilt to his eyebrow, and he sank gently to the deck.

Her wooden weapons struck three more times as a tidal pull of bodies drew the crew of the fluyt away from her and toward the raised quarterdeck.

By that time, the rest of her crew were on them, swinging clubs and pins with wild abandon, their howling cries drowning out the screams of their quarry.

Shanae took a moment to glance off to the right where the squadron was drawing in sail, all four ships slowing, their cannons silent. It would take a while for them to bleed off their momentum and come around, but nothing she had seen on the *Marie Lajoie* led her to expect she would have any trouble subduing them long before the others arrived.

"To the depths with you, cretins!"

The voice was unmistakable. Hunt's lean form came crashing out of the darkness, a cudgel of heavy driftwood huge in his hands. He swung the club with strange glee as the Frenchmen shrank away, pushing their fellows against the quarterdeck's bulkhead.

"Your lord wearies of your foolishness!" A sailor was dashed to the deck. "You are a blight upon His waves!" Another flew off into the wildly shifting shadows. "Poseidon requires nothing from you now but your breath!" He surged forward, one scrawny arm stabbing out, and caught a wild-eyed sailor's throat in his long, gaunt hand.

Shanae smiled. It was always comforting to watch Hunt at work. His rantings invariably terrified their opponents, while battle was the only real time his own colleagues seemed to appreciate the man's flair for the dramatic.

Then she realized what Hunt was doing. The poor Frenchman was being forced back, arms windmilling wildly, toward the starboard rail.

While she had no particular objection to some of these sailors taking an evening swim, she needed to preserve them as well as she could. If Hunt was allowed to run the man backward into the rail and then off, there was no telling what kind of injury he might sustain; and, stunned, he might drown before regaining his senses.

"Hunt! Stand down!" She lashed out with one long baton and sent it slicing into the priest's chest lengthwise, slowing his headlong rush to the rail without causing too much pain with the impact.

The man's fever-bright eyes blinked, then some modicum of clarity returned. He looked at her then, seeing her for the first time, and nodded.

Almost as an afterthought, he struck the relieved Frenchman on the side of the head with the gnarled branch and watched with clinical indifference as the man added his body to the growing pile of unconscious crewmen on the deck.

By the time she turned back to the action, the fighting was all but over. Most of the crewmen of the fluyt had managed to retreat up onto the quarterdeck, huddling in a tight press against the aft rail of the ship, their hands in the air, their eyes downcast, desperate not to give offense.

Aidan was striding back and forth before the cowed mob, his face a mask of boredom. Over his shoulder rested a short Taino paddle. There were several other *Kates* around him, as well as men and women from the other ships.

In the midst of the Frenchmen was a man whose ludicrous uniform could only mean he was the captain. His face was contorted with fear and anger in equal measure as he shouted something to Aidan's back.

For his part, the gunner didn't even seem to hear the Frenchman.

Shanae moved along the rail, taking stock of the last pockets of resistance shrinking around the bow of the fluyt.

She enjoyed the appreciative looks in her own peoples' eyes as she passed. They seldom saw her fight, and only ever when the battle was real. Clearly, she was still able to cut an impressive figure through a melee.

In her inspection she walked past a small boat secured to the deck keel-up just aft of a large cargo hatch.

Something about the canvas around the boat picked at the back of her mind, but before she could turn to give it a second look, a boom echoed over the water from the other fluyt and she smiled as a cry went up from her own people. She looked over to the *Courageaux* in time to see her colors fluttering down into the dark waters of the bay.

"Shanae!" The sudden warning cry came from the quarterdeck, and she whipped around, the batons coming up into a ready position as she spun.

An enormous sailor was charging from beneath the small boat, brushing the loosened canvas easily aside. The man was huge, easily the tallest person she had ever seen. He rushed at her with a vicious-looking gaff hook raised over his head. His eyes were dark, but his face was calm. There was no sense of mindless fury, but rather calculation and resolve.

This man knew who to remove, among all the buccaneers who had boarded the ship in the darkness and confusion.

Shanae thought the man was giving her far too much credit if he believed killing her would save his ship, but it showed more thought and planning than anyone else on the deck of the merchantman had displayed.

She brought the batons up, crossing them over her head, and blocked the downward swipe of the hook's pole with a sharp crack.

For a moment they were face to face, his green eyes reflecting sparks of lamplight before she shoved him away with a prodigious effort.

Those eyes widened slightly, and she smiled as she swept her weapons out and back in, right for the man's head.

The blond Frenchman ducked with more dexterity than she would have expected from a man of his size, knocking both of her batons aside with the shaft of his gaff before bringing its butt up and into her stomach.

The pain was immediate, the heavy pole striking with all the man's prodigious strength. She felt her feet leaving the deck for a moment and feared she might not be able to remain upright as she danced back, trying to find her balance, knowing he would be following up, chasing her as she fell.

And he did. The hook rose again, and again she noted the total lack of anger in his face. This was a man going through the motions of a task that needed to be done; there was nothing personal in it at all.

She realized she wasn't going to be able to regain her feet. She was too far off-balance; she could not get her feet back underneath her. The hook gleamed with a flat malice as it swept toward her.

She had been right all along. She wasn't equal to this task.

She was going to die on the deck of this pathetic little French merchantman.

She felt her left foot gain purchase on the deck and pushed without thought, launching herself sideways as the vicious hook swept past.

She struck the deck hard and rolled with her momentum, rising up into a crouch, batons already raised.

The man was on her before she had time to catch her breath, the shaft of his makeshift weapon crashing in from one side and then the other in a rapid flurry of blows. She felt the hook pluck at her sleeve, a scratch burned across one cheek, and a pull on her trousers made her fear he had drawn blood there as well. She scuttled back farther and farther until the bulwark pressed against the small of her back, the waters of the bay glittering far below.

The entire time, despite his obvious success, the man's face had not betrayed a moment's satisfaction.

She couldn't help but be impressed with his control.

Now, if only he was exerting that control on something other than trying to kill her.

She ducked under his next attack and threw herself to the side, lashing out with a quick blow that slid under his guard and struck him in the side with a dull sound. The impact nearly jarred the stick from her hand. It felt as if she had hit a tree.

Somewhere far away she could hear shouts and cries, but her mind was focused on the moment, on this imminent threat to her wellbeing and the faith the men and women of the squadron had in her.

The hook hissed past her face as she turned to avoid the cut, but it caught in her shirt with a stinging pain that told her she had been pinked.

She cursed under her breath, lungs burning with exertion, and brought both batons down on the man's wrists before he could recover. If she could knock the weapon out of his hands it might be enough; maybe earn herself enough time for a dialogue; something she was realizing, she wanted more with each passing moment.

It was as if she had brought her rods down on a stone wall. The man grunted at the impact, but there was no noticeable effect on his hands as he brought the gaff hook around for another series of blows.

Shanae's arms were numb, the muscles burning dully with the exertion of trying to stay alive.

And still there was not the slightest gleam of satisfaction in those hard, green eyes.

And then the eyes shifted. The merest shadow of doubt crossed the Frenchman's broad face, and Shanae glanced down to see that his foot had snagged in a coil of rope and canvas cast off from the boat that had concealed him.

With a slight kick, the tangle flew from him, and his head came back to regard her, but in that moment both batons, one after the other so fast the impacts came with a single sound, struck him on either side of the head.

It was a quick blow, sacrificing strength for the speed to get them in before the man's guard was raised once more. But they were enough to stagger him back.

He released one hand from the shaft of the gaff hook, holding it up as if to wave her away, the weapon still strong in the other hand, but a renewed surge of energy filled her.

The batons were a blur in her hands, fanning first one way and then the other, striking blow after blow; wrist, elbow, forehead, hand, chest. The rhythm of their fight had changed now, and it was the man's defenses that were coming a half-breath too late. He was guarding against a blow that had already struck by the time the next attack began.

Finally, she saw an emotion in his face.

Respect.

And then, with a prodigious grunt of effort, she brought both sticks down on the top of his head.

One of the batons snapped, the end spinning off into the darkness. The other bounced off his skull, her own hands stinging from the impact.

Those calm green eyes regarded her for a moment longer, and she was afraid her best had not been enough after all.

Then he crumpled where he stood, his legs giving out underneath him.

It was all Shanae could do not to collapse beside him. She forced herself to straighten despite a painful stitch in her side. She regarded the broken baton for a moment before tossing it onto the prone man's still back.

"Are you alright?" Aidan was beside her, a look of awe on his handsome face. "That was unbelievable."

She barely heard him. "Tie this one up." She nudged the blond giant with one toe.

Aidan nodded, gesturing for two sailors from the *Kate*. "He's a brute. Best not have to deal with him again before we take our leave."

She looked up, then, shaking her head. "No. I want to talk with him before we take our leave."

She turned and began to pick her way through the wreckage and the unconscious bodies toward the quarterdeck, where several of her most experienced people were securing the captain and forcing the rest of the crew down onto the main deck of the ship.

'Wait, what?" Aidan rushed after her, skipping to catch up. "He almost killed you!"

She smiled. "Exactly. That hasn't happened in a while. I think Captain Maguire will agree. He's got just the right kind of temperament for the life."

The gunner had more to say, but she left him behind as she took the short staircase to the quarterdeck two steps at a time.

"Shanae!" A gruff voice from the main deck called out. All talking faded at the sound, and she went to the forward rail, resting her hand on the smooth, polished wood, and looked out over the main deck of the fluyt she had just taken.

Hunt was standing amidst the other raiders, brandishing the driftwood cudgel over his head. "We'd follow you to Hades' gate, my lady!"

She frowned. She hated it when his idiosyncrasies were voiced before a crowd. The crew seldom reacted well.

Her concern for the fallen priest was such that she hadn't even really processed the meaning of his words.

Then the men and women around Hunt began to nod vigorously. Their own weapons rose into the air, and soon their raucous cheers were rising up to the glittering star overhead.

"Kissed by Poseidon himself, my lady!" The lunatic was grinning furiously. "Kissed by Poseidon himself!"

She found herself smiling back as the *Bonnie Kate* drew up alongside, the crew there cheering in response.

The smile faltered, then. The men and women aboard the *Kate* had no idea what had happened on the *Marie Lajoie*. They weren't cheering for her, but for the loot they would all be carting back to Cayona. They had no idea what had happened aboard the fluyts as they had torn past with their ludicrous load of canvas.

But then the mob below her redoubled their own cries, drowning out the other *Kate*s. These men and women *did* know what she had done. They knew what they had all done.

Her smile returned as she waved her unbroken baton over her head in response.

Chapter 6
1674 – Cayona Harbor, Tortuga

The raucous sounds of celebration echoing off the water only served to heighten Boothe's annoyance at his current situation.

Sitting on the wide porch that skirted Chartier's Counting House and Victualers, he had a fine view of the squadron resting at anchor in their usual spots. It was almost as if they hadn't been gone for two days.

Almost.

There was no way those bilge rats would be carousing this late into the dark watches without the fresh gold off those French merchantmen weighing down their pockets.

Boothe wanted to kick the fragile railing before him, but he knew old Filip Chartier wouldn't appreciate the damage, and it wouldn't do for the Commodore's first mate to be angering the chief money handler in Cayona.

He looked down at the papers in his lap for the hundredth time. Letters of credit, each avowing a healthy amount of coinage in Chartier's vaults in the name of Solomon Hart, independent man of business and definitely not Commodore of a squadron of buccaneers who had just flouted the governor's wishes and taken down two merchant ships flying French colors.

He shook his head, grinning bitterly despite himself. Maguire was a clever bastard.

Officially, the squadron had been out testing some new sail plans, and the new rigging on the *Syren*. Even the Commodore had known that to be a lie, but a large part of leading such a group, Boothe had learned over the years, was to know when not to give an order. Give an order you knew wouldn't be obeyed, and you were begging for someone to come along and remove you.

And so, knowing full well Maguire and the rest were flaunting his wishes, Hart had had no choice but to remain in Cayona Harbor with Fowler and the *Jaguar*, chewing on the bitter taste of betrayal, with a chaser of undeniable envy.

The men and women of the squadron hadn't chosen the life of buccaneers so they could float and rot in a harbor while fat merchantmen sailed blithely past each day. They were like barely trained dogs, straining at their leads, desperate to taste the blood of their natural prey.

Boothe understood the Commodore's plan, and his wishes to create a permanent home for the buccaneers on Tortuga like they had once thought it might be nearly a decade ago.

But it was a path fraught with danger and difficulty, and Maguire wasn't making it any easier. Boothe didn't know how much longer Hunt was going to be able to placate the governor and his French sensibilities before they were going to have to make their move.

Out in the street, a rowdy bunch of sailors wandered past, shouting and laughing with drunken abandon. Their harsh voices echoed off the dark buildings to either side of the winding road as they made their way up from the harbor.

Heading toward the Lazy Dog, if he had to guess.

His bitter smile slipped, and the grimace that replaced it, just as bitter, twisted his handsome face into a mask of frustration.

He was torn. A very large part of him was furious for Maguire and the others for their flagrant disregard of the Commodore's plans. With this foolish attack, however they had managed it and however they intended to get away with this plan, the relationship between the governor and the squadron, always tense, was only going to get worse.

But a small voice in the back of his mind, the voice that had first suggested he leave the King's service to join their sworn enemies, the Brethren of the Coast, snarled in frustration.

That part of him, the true reaver he felt himself to be, wished very much that he had been with the others last night.

To hell with it, and to hell with all of them.

He pushed himself upright and rose with a slight groan at his protesting legs.

Boothe stepped heavily down the wide steps of the counting house and onto Cayona's high street. It swept up in a gentle curve from the harbor, the buildings an alarming, eclectic mix of architectural styles and periods defying both form and function.

Cayona might be a flourishing town, but there was no confusing it with the more successful cities growing up throughout the area. It certainly couldn't compete with the likes of Santo Domingo, Havana, or even Port Royal's fevered energy.

Cayona has seen its best days, no matter what the others might like to think. The place had been on the decline for over a decade, and nothing was going to stop that deterioration now.

A pair of snarling dogs erupted from the shadows between two ramshackle buildings on his right, snapping at each other in an alarming knot of fur and violence that rolled across the street and into the shadows on the other side.

Even the dogs on Tortuga were savages.

The party of buccaneers that had passed Chartier's had stopped halfway up the rise toward the second tier of the town, just around the corner from the counting house. Boothe slowed as they came into view. He was well aware of the low opinion many of the crew from the squadron's smaller ships had for anyone who sailed aboard the *Arbiter*.

And he was honest enough with himself that his lip twisted in bitter amusement as he thought the word *sailed*, as well.

As deeply in their cups as this group obviously was, there was no guarantee his position as first mate on the Commodore's ship would see him safely through their midst.

In fact, depending on the prevailing opinions after their successful raid on the French fluyts, the first mate of the *Ultimo Arbiter* might seem like an ideal target for their high spirits.

He hooked a thumb behind the sheath of his long knife. He hadn't thought to bring anything more intimidating ashore with him. In retrospect, he could see that might have been foolish optimism on his part.

He took a breath to settle his nerves and leaned into the hill, resuming his climb. These fools might have forgotten the kind of damage Myles Boothe could do with a long knife, but Boothe hadn't.

Before he reached the group, however, they bumbled back into loud, cackling motion, rolling up the hill like a confused avalanche. One or two cast glances back down the hill toward him, but either they didn't recognize him, or they didn't find his presence galling enough for comment.

Ramped up as he was for violence, he wasn't sure how he felt about that.

The group arrived at the tall, tilted shape of the Lazy Dog as it loomed over them at the top of the street. Shoving, laughing, and crying out as they compressed themselves into the confines of the small front door, the group disappeared faster than he would have thought possible, and for a moment he was alone on the street.

It was warm, of course. It was always warm. But it would be far warmer inside, where the close confines, packed bodies, and the ever-present musty odor of men and women who lived on the water would combine to create a familiar, uncomfortable fug.

It always seemed strange to him, given the natural environment of a sailor, how they always seemed to crush themselves into close, smelly confines whenever given the chance.

With one last intake of the fresh, humid air, he pushed open the door and stepped into the fetid tavern.

He squinted into the blazing lights of lanterns hung about the walls, his eyes unaccustomed to the brightness after brooding for so long in the dark. The milling throng of bodies that pressed in from all sides threatened to crush him, but they offered an anonymity that he was thankful for after his dark thoughts out in the street.

He pushed his way through the crowd, keeping the pressure constant but not violent or sudden. There was no need to start anything now that he was so close to his goal. With the addition of rum and ale to the mix, he was certain any provocation, combined with recognition, would result in drawn steel.

The men and women who would be considered officers in a more formal squadron would be taking up the tables along the shadow-haunted back wall, raised up on a dais that provided them a good view of the Dog's main floor.

In fact, although he couldn't make out faces at this distance, given the lack of lanterns there, he had no doubt they had seen him enter, and would be well-aware of him by the time he broached the mob.

They would assume he was there to speak for the Commodore. They might even be marshalling a defense of their actions, although he knew where blame for that scheme should be laid.

He felt the bitterness twist his lips. He couldn't just be another buccaneer with these people; not anymore. As the first mate aboard the *Arbiter*, he was the Commodore's creature, not his own man.

At least as far as these others were concerned. He liked to think he had more independence than that.

Although he was coming to fear his peers might be more correct than he wanted to admit.

The dais was set apart from the rest of the tavern by a rail that mimicked the forward rail of a quarterdeck. Severin Serre, the old buccaneer that owned the Lazy Dog, had set the main floor of the inn out in as close an approximation of a sailing ship as could be achieve, going so far as to place his office above the raised dais, where the quarterdeck of a warship might have been. The man liked to boast that the rail, indeed, had been taken from a British naval ship he had bested off the coast of Cuba back in his marauding days.

Boothe had inspected the railing once in the light of day and would swear that no British ship had ever carried woodwork that shoddy into battle. But he allowed the innkeeper his little conceit.

The tables on the dais were all small, the better to allow those crews calling on any given night the ability to arrange them to their liking. As Boothe put one booted foot on the lowest step and surveyed the scene before him, he grimaced. This was going to be even less pleasant than he had anticipated.

Most of the tables had been pushed to make a long board across the back wall, leaving only three or four stragglers behind, hosting two or three lesser members of the squadron who had not been deemed worthy to join the august assemblage at the back.

He took a deep breath, trying his best to ignore the funk, and stepped up onto the dais.

In the middle of the long table, facing him with one arched eyebrow, was Shanae Bure, of course. There were several bruises clear even beneath her dark skin, and a cut over one eye glistened wetly in the lamp light. She didn't seem to be in any pain, however. Sitting amongst her court like a queen from the old world, Shanae looked imperiously up at him, not deigning to stand. The others around the table, nearly all mates and masters from the lesser ships of the squadrons, took her lead and remained seated as well.

This was less of an insult than it might have been during his navy days, when suitable deference to rank was far more rigidly applied than in the world of the buccaneers and flibustiers of the New World.

As they watched him approached their eyes were flat, faces expressionless. He reflected that even back in his service days, he might not have been greeted with too much additional deference. Shanae was first mate of the *Bonnie Kate*, after all, despite her age, and although that ship was vastly smaller than his own *Arbiter*, their nominal ranks, in that other world, would have been similar enough to allow her the leeway to be rude if she wished.

As it was, this wasn't insolence, per se, but rather an understandable testing of the situation between nominal peers ashore. The precedence of the ships in the harbor had very little to do with what was about to occur here in the Lazy Dog, except insofar as most of the sailors of the squadron had come to view the *Arbiter* with something less than utter respect.

"Boothe, what brings you out on such a night as this?" Her voice was flat but not rude. A continuation of the dance, then. Eventually, someone would flinch, and the true weather gauge would be revealed.

"I thought I'd come to congratulate you all on your recent action." He kept his voice cool, reasonable, and moved to pull back the only empty chair at the table, across from Shanae.

There was a solid thump from under the table as he reached, and the chair slid toward him a fraction of an inch. He paused, puzzled, thinking that someone might have pushed it toward him, to welcome him into their company.

Then he saw the bright, cruel smile on the dark face of the amazon sitting next to Shanae; Renata Villa, quartermaster aboard the *Syren*. The lamplight gleamed off the tribal scarring that crowned the woman's shaved head, and she leaned forward slightly.

The toe of her booted foot moved side to side on the chair he had intended to claim.

He stared at her for a moment, then smiled. There was no reason for this to get any uglier than it already was, and he wasn't about to allow a quartermaster from a mere brigantine to shake him. He would say his piece and move on. There was no reason for him to stay any longer than necessary.

It didn't often rankle him, the lack of respect the crews of the smaller ship seemed to confer upon the *Arbiter* and the *Jaguar*. The other four ships, brigantines and sloops, were more practical for the type of actions buccaneers favored. When hunting larger prey crew from the galleon and the frigate would often join the smaller ships. And when, on those rare occasions a mightier prize made herself known, the *Jaguar* would lead the squadron out on the chase. Everyone did their part, pulled their weight, or they didn't share in the spoils.

The *Arbiter's* place in this balance was a little odd, but the Commodore had schooled him sufficiently in the political realities of operating in these waters that he knew the huge ship had to remain behind to bolster the guns on the small forts in guarding the harbor and keep the governor happy.

The balance had been thus for longer than he had served with the squadron and having risen to the position of first mate of the behemoth galleon, it had brought him a happy, comfortable life.

When he wasn't required to search out the mates and masters, of course.

He sighed. There was better food and drink, and company, aboard the *Arbiter* anyway.

"We appreciate your words, Boothe." The forced Spanish accent of the little quartermaster from the sloop *Laughing Jacques* grated on his already tested patience.

"Would have appreciated your hands on an oar more." Someone down the table muttered, and there was general mirth from the others.

He glanced in that direction and saw a jumble of faces, most of them Africans from *Chainbreaker* and the paler expressions of the *Jacques'* mongrel crew.

He ignored them and looked back at Shanae. "The Commodore thanks you for your work, and for the gifts you graciously delivered to Chartier's." He searched for a moment for the right words to continue. "He trusts that similar gifts were delivered to the governor, as per the standard arrangement?"

The smile she gave him them was worse than all the dark looks and amused gibes he had received since he entered. "All of the formalities have been observed."

He forced himself to smile in response.

"I think, despite the irregularities, if the sums are similar for the governor, your captain may have been proven correct in this after all."

Aidan Allen, the blonde gun captain sitting to the woman's right, barked a laugh. "The sums were more than adequate, Boothe. I delivered the cheques from Chartier's myself, spoke to the governor's factor directly. He was most pleased."

"The necklace you gave him for his wife probably didn't hurt any." A heavy woman at the far end of the table was grinning evilly at the gunner, who nodded back with an answering grin.

"You seem to have come away with even more booty than you had expected." He turned back to Shanae. "Governor D'Ogeron, once he realizes the truth of the events, might not be so sanguine as his man."

"We gave that French peacock no reason to complain." Aidan's smile slipped. "He got his money, and more besides. It's more than he deserves, keeping us locked in the harbor for weeks on end.

"That's not the governor's doing." The short, dark-skinned fat man nearest to Boothe's position turned, hooking one arm over the back of his chair. "The Commodore gives him that power. The Governor's got no way to stop us if we wanted to leave."

That was true enough, but not a course he wanted these men and women sailing down at the moment. "We have a good thing here on Tortuga. The Commodore has arranged a situation that sees us protected, gives us a homeport, and at the same time provides us with rich pickings when—"

The fat man spat over his shoulder at Boothe's feet. "Rich pickings. *Rich pickings*? When was the last time—"

"Sefu, I think that's enough." Shanae smiled at the man as he turned back to her, then raised her head to regard Boothe once again. "Are there any other messages the Commodore wishes for you to deliver?"

He felt a pressure building in his throat. Was it possible these fools didn't realize what they were doing?

He pulled the empty chair violently from beneath the table, sending Villa staggering forward for a moment as her booted foot was dragged with it, almost pulling her under the table. She slid herself back up in her chair, rising frighteningly above everyone else against the wall, and glared at him as he settled himself in the chair.

"I don't think you fully understand the possible impact of your action against those ships, Shanae."

She leaned forward, elbows on the table, and grinned at him. "Why don't you explain it, First Mate."

The woman was going to get them all killed for her pride. "When word gets back that you hit those two ships, ships that were under the protection of the governor of Tortuga, the French authorities are not going to be pleased. Further, we won't be seeing more of their kind putting in here. Where are you planning on taking up the trail, if not Cayona Harbor? You'll see the pickings run slim here quite soon, mark my words."

The statement seemed to have no impact on the woman at all. "I disagree, Boothe. We killed no one, we left them with enough cargo to justify their return. They were directed to make straight for Calais, and I believe, having looked into each of those captain's faces, that they fully intended to comply with those demands. It will be months before word of what happens comes back this way. There won't be any impact, for now, on shipping through Tortuga. No one will be any the wiser."

"And who knows, by next week there will be a whole new list of allies and enemies from the Old World." Allen twisted his mouth as if he had just tasted something sour. "Maybe it'll be the Dutch out of favor? Maybe England will be siding with the Spanish against the French? How they keep track of who should be killing whom at any moment I don't know. How are we're supposed to know, half a world away?"

"I'm not even sure why we should care." That last comment was from a tall woman at the other end of the table.

"Not that we've been depending on shipping through Tortuga for a while now." Villa leaned over as well, her not inconsiderable height emphasized in the gloom. "Who, other than friends of the governor, has come through Tortuga in months? The scent we've been catching has had more to do with our own work, sailing the old routes, putting in at places like Port Royal and Santa Domingo, and developing friendships there. The Commodore and the governor have been nearly useless in that regard, and they might do well to remember that the next time they decide to make demands."

It was true. They had lost all sense of the Commodore's intentions in Tortuga. Santa Domingo? Port Royal? This lot would never pursue the life of the forced trade, serving as the lapdogs of the venal merchants of Port Royal. And the Spanish would never have them. Where else did they think they could go?

"We have a home, here. Would we be welcome in Santa Domingo?" He glared around at the Africans sitting at the table, Villa, and the men and women off *Chainbreaker*. "Would you be welcome in Santa Domingo?" Then he looked at the Frenchmen and the Spaniards. "Would they receive you with open arms in Port Royal?" Then he lost his temper and slammed the table with one open fist. "Hell, none of you would be welcomed at Port Royal!"

Shanae shook her head. "Things are changing there. The others—"

He sneered at the light of hope in her eyes. "Every buccaneer that would have been able to shift their moorage to Port Royal did so years ago. You think Morgan is going to change his tune toward your captain now? And you lot? You'd end up on a gibbet or an auction block in a whore's minute."

He expected them to explode at that. He anticipated rage to match his own sudden outburst to answer his words.

Instead, they just looked at him, their eyes flat once more.

They didn't believe him.

Was it possible they knew something he didn't know? Was it possible Maguire's foolish hopes concerning Port Royal were more than just fairy stories?

He took a deep breath, forcing down the frustration that swirled up to mix with his anger at their indifference.

"Well, whatever we poor mortals decide here, it'll have no impact on the real world. The captains meet even now aboard the *Arbiter* to decide our next course of action."

Many of the heads around the long table nodded. It seemed their captains had felt little need to keep the meeting a secret.

He didn't know what to make of the fact that none of them seemed concerned at all.

"There will be ramifications from last night's action." Even as he said the words, they felt weak and pathetic in his own ears.

Judging from the faces staring back at him, it might have been the first thought he had had since entering the tavern that they would have agreed with.

He rose, forcing himself to push the chair gently back under the table, even quirking an eyebrow at Villa as he did so.

"Well, I'll leave you to your well-deserved revels, then."

He turned to leave and was halfway down the low stairs when Shanae's voice called out to him. He turned to see her standing at her place, the injuries on her face somehow granting her even more dignity.

"Next time, you will be welcome to sail with us."

He almost missed the final step, which would have been a fine punctuation to his ridiculous visit. He paused to regain his equilibrium and then nodded over one shoulder as he turned back toward the door.

What could she have meant by that?

Chapter 7
1674 ~ Cayona Harbor, Tortuga

Maguire settled back into the plush cushion of his chair and forced himself to stare into the dark depths of the brandy in the crystal glass cradled in his worn hands. He did his best not to think of the relative cost of each item, or of the drink in his hands. He knew the Commodore hoped to impress his captains with the venue of the meeting; why else would they not be ensconced in the warmth of Daucourt's public house, where they usually met for such events?

Cedric Daucourt was a fast friend of the squadron, a merchant who had long ago decided it made more sense to ally with the buccaneers of Tortuga than to try to slip cargo past them. His family always made the captains feel welcome in their home, providing all manner of drink and the fine conversation of his well-educated wife and children.

Their relationship with the dapper little Frenchmen was one of partnership and friendship, not the servitude of the forced trade of Port Royal. It was a key source of his hope for the squadron's future in Jamaica: that they might work with merchants, and not for them. Because of that, he always enjoyed sharing their home for meetings like this.

The man's willingness to abet his attempts to seem to spend more money than he did was just one more aspect of his friendship that Maguire cherished all the more.

But instead, they had been summoned to the *Ultimo Arbiter*, to sit in state with their Commodore as if somehow they had all awakened into a nightmare world where the navy had accreted itself around their lives and transformed their freedom and independence into the stiff confines of military discipline.

Summoned was the right word, too. The messages he and Sasha had received, each hand delivered to their respective cabins by uniformed boys in the black and red of the *Arbiter*, had been very haughtily worded. He was sure, if he had had the time to consult with Thomas Hamidi and Bastian Houdin, he was certain they would have said the same.

What was Hart's game, with all this foolishness? He grimaced into the amber liquid; nothing would make him leave Tortuga faster than the Commodore trying to impose any further control over their lives.

"Gentlemen, and lady, I believe our repast having been concluded, we might move to more weighty matters?" Hart smiled around the table, and Maguire noted quickly that despite the misgivings of the junior captains, nothing had kept them from Hart's fine food.

Truth to tell, it had been a meal to rival anything he could remember having had in years. Even Daucourt would have been hard-pressed to match it.

"I was thinking we could repair to the stern gallery, perhaps? The sun should be setting over *La Montagne's* shoulder right about now, the view is stunning from this height, I assure you."

A subtle dig at them all for coming from smaller ships? It was impossible to tell with the man, and Maguire knew that he tended to attribute every word out of the Commodore's mouth with ill intent when he was in a foul mood.

And he was in a foul mood now; all the more so because by every right he should be in a *fine* mood indeed. He should be celebrating last night's haul or basking in the admiration of the other junior captains aboard his own ship.

Instead, he was here, little more than a set piece in Commodore Hart's pantomime, the worn nature of his best frockcoat more of a concern than the moral of his men.

Out on the stern gallery the heat and closeness of the cabin was little relieved by the early tropical evening. He kept to himself, in the forward, starboard corner, between the stern bulkhead and the ornate, red gallery railing. He took a sip of his drink and fought the urge to throw the priceless glass into the harbor.

"Now, if I might be indulged for a moment," Hart had settled into a heavy, throne-like chair his sailors had brought onto the gallery for him, his frockcoat and trousers pristine, as always. "You all have every right to feel proud of what you accomplished last night."

Maguire shot a hooded glance at Sasha, where she leaned against the railing toward the middle of the gallery, and Hadid, whose hulking dark-skinned form was half in and half out of the companionway door leading onto the gallery.

Both returned his gaze without comment.

Bastian was smiling, as always, nodding at the Commodore as if there was no cause for tension among them.

Ironically it was Jonathan Fowler, captain of the light frigate *Jaguar*, standing over the Commodore's shoulder and glaring at them all with unconcealed anger, who Maguire was sure showed the only genuine emotion on the stern gallery.

"The plan was excellent, bleeding the prey without killing it, leaving enough to salve the stakeholders' anger and ensure that the captains would continue on their way without causing a local problem was ingenious."

Hart turned slightly in his chair to look directly at Maguire, and the captain forced himself to stand straighter to hear the pronouncements of the man they had all agreed to follow for the time being.

"Captain Maguire, I understand the assault itself, carried off without casualty to attacker nor defender, was led by your most excellent first mate. Please present Shanae with all our compliments on a job well done."

The other captains nodded, and Bastian leaned forward to pat him on the shoulder. "*Très bien, mon ami.*"

"Thank you, Commodore." He struggled to keep his voice civil. He forced himself to remember, once again, that the man had no real power over any of them. Any ship of the squadron could leave anytime it liked.

It was a question of options, however. And he was none too sure how many of those any of them had, given the current climate.

"However," the Commodore's voice took on a sad undertone that threatened to wash away Maguire's resolve to remain civil. "We must not lose sight of the practical realities that dictate our lives. Striking French ships was, as I stated before the fact and I maintain now that the deed is done, reckless and ill-considered. What if something had gone wrong? What if either of those gentlemen had been killed, or one of their ships destroyed?"

"Irrelevant." The deep, rumbling voice of *Chainbreaker's* immense captain rolled over the gallery. "None of those things occurred. If you wish to speak, please keep the conversation to reality."

Sasha nodded, standing up a little straighter, and even Bastian's smile faded a little. Fowler's features only darkened further.

"Alright, then." Hart straightened himself in his chair with a nod. "We shall speak of things as they are, and not as they might have been or," he looked toward Maguire, eyes narrowing. "Or of how we would have them."

Before the captain of the *Bonnie Kate* could reply to that look, the man continued.

"The political realities back home are, as ever, tumultuous."

"Your home, not ours." It was Thomas, again, but the others nodded their agreement. Even Maguire felt himself agreeing, despite his lingering affection for his native Ireland.

Hart gave the big man a sour look but nodded grudgingly. "A good point, captain Hamidi, but hardly relevant, as you would say. Tensions between the old powers there dictate the alliances and rivalries here, and things are, as ever, entangled and confusing at their heart, without the added confusion of the cross-oceanic voyage to further stir the mix."

He gestured with one languid hand at the harbor, where two small sloops rigged for cargo, their tricolor French flags fluttering at their stern, sat at anchor. Other than the local fishing craft, small personal boats, and the ships of the squadron, the harbor was empty. "I need not remind you what flag flies over Governor d'Ogeron's manse. At the moment, the English and the Dutch are only now testing the waters of peace, while the French still hold the Dutch as foes. And at last report, relations between France and Spain have deteriorated as well. Currently, we may attack the Dutch at our leisure with careful enough planning, while striking English ships may put us in jeopardy and God alone knows the dispensation between the French throne and the Spanish."

The man looked tired, and for once, Maguire wondered if there wasn't some genuine feeling there after all.

"Governor d'Ogeron, the official stance of Paris notwithstanding, has made his own enemies among the Spanish, as you know, leaving us ever-vulnerable should the French remove their official protection from the island, and creating for us a precarious perch at best."

Maguire stifled a yawn. These tribulations were exactly the reason he was so eager to seek a new home in Jamaica, if only he could get the pieces aligned. The Commodore's own plans for the squadron had become more and more irrelevant to him, as the old man's attitudes toward Jamaica, the other buccaneers, and Tortuga had made themselves known.

"I think the time may be ripe for us to look to Jamaica." Hart's voice was heavy and brought Maguire's head up with a snap.

The other captains began to voice their confusion as well, in a rising babble that threatened to drown out all sense on the stern gallery.

Fowler whistled with the sharp, penetrating sound he was known for, and the other captains settled down at once, glaring at the scowling captain of the *Jaguar*.

"I know, this is not what I have envisioned for us. I have argued for patience and persistence here in Tortuga for many years. But perhaps our opportunities here have fled. Perhaps we have been caught out by time, and I have missed our best chance to make this our permanent home."

"But you've said all along that Port Royal was no fit home for the squadron." Sasha's voice was short and cold. "You've made your case time and time again. What changed?"

Hart crumpled a little more into his chair. "You all have reminded me, once again, what we can accomplish when we work together. As a joint enterprise, combining all our varied strengths and capabilities, we are nearly unstoppable. There are national navies at work in these waters who could not stand before us, were we to venture forth in strength. Hell, we could perhaps even rival the efforts of Henry Morgan himself, if we wished! Perhaps chaining ourselves to Tortuga no longer serves our needs." He signed, looking toward the sinking sun that now bathed the stern of the huge ship in crimson light. "Maybe it never did."

"Chains seem very much to the point, as far as my crew and I are concerned, at any rate." Thomas ventured out into the red sunlight, standing before the Commodore with his corded arms folded heavily across his barrel chest. "Many on this gallery here have made the case to me and mine, many times, that only chains await us should we try to put in at Port Royal."

"And you've made an excellent case, time and time again, of how my crew might be viewed by the remnants of Cromwell's brood." Sasha cast a glance over her shoulder at Maguire as she turned to the chair. "I don't think I'd be eager to bring the *Syren* into Port Royal after your tales of weal and woe."

Maguire's brows dropped. What was Hart doing? The transfer to Port Royal had been the major point of contention among the captains for years, and the Commodore had always argued for staying on with his friend d'Ogeron. Why this sudden shift in position?

And then Hart looked directly at him, and something strange and dark slithered behind the man's eyes. Before Maguire could even be sure it was there, it was gone. But the Commodore smiled thinly and gestured to him with one open hand.

"Aemon has been making an excellent case for the move for a long time. Aemon? Would you like to restate your arguments now?"

Maguire shook his head. Now was not the time. He knew that. He had been too quick to think they could shift to Jamaica years ago, when the other English buccaneering captains had followed that bastard, Morgan. Many others had moved on to Petit Goave, leaving Tortuga nearly empty of the Brethren.

He had been eager to follow, but he saw, now, that the time had not been ripe. It still wasn't ripe. His preparations were not nearly complete.

Before he could voice an objection, he heard his own words issuing from Fowler's mouth, and he felt his jaw drop.

"With one major score to fill our holds, we could arrive in Port Royal with repute sufficient to free us from our feared constraints."

The words were fair, but the man's flat eyes never left Maguire's. Despite the warmth of the evening, a chill slid down his spine.

It felt like a nightmare, where his own words were being used for some strange purpose he could not fathom.

"Sufficient to free us." Thomas Hamidi barked a laugh that boomed out over the harbor below. "Interesting choice of words, Fowler." He spat the name. "Considering you would be under no such danger yourself."

Sasha nodded, then looked again to Maguire. "Eamon, had you not reconsidered your own thoughts on this matter? There have been English captains, as recently as this past summer, who danced the hempen jig for slaving after taking Spanish prizes."

"They danced the jig, aye." Fowler grinned, but there was no mirth in the expression. "Because the crown prefers its servants be circumspect when dabbling in the flesh trade. That danger can be mitigated, if the purse we bring to Jamaica is sufficient."

Maguire wanted to stop this madness. There was no such prize on the horizon. The Spanish treasure fleets weren't even ripe for dreaming of, having both already returned to Spain.

"Port Royal—"

"Is not an option at this time." Thomas's voice brooked no rebuttal. "I will not sail my people into that lion's den until such time as Lynch and the Council has proven their interest in the flesh trade is at an end, one and all."

"*Syren* will not enter Port Royal either." Sasha's tone was firm as she moved to stand beside the black-skinned giant.

"We French have never felt comfortable in Jamaica. Not under the Spanish, nor since the English conquest." Bastian was smiling again, but he gave Fowler a pointed look before continuing, "Your Charles has been no more welcoming since his ascension."

Hart looked perplexed. But still, there was something about the expression that bothered Maguire.

"I hear your arguments. Hell, I've made them myself, many times. But what is there here on Tortuga for us? Relations with d'Ogeron are strained. Merely the presence of my *Arbiter* and the coin from your last brave caper may not be enough to secure our continued welcome here. The shipping in the area runs dry, most of our Brethren have fled or moved inland to harvest wood and meat for those of us still willing to ply the waves. I truly believe Port Royal may be our best chance."

Maguire snorted at this. The Governor's insistence that the *Arbiter* remain in port to augment the number of cannons mounted in the small forts at the mouth of the harbor was an old story, one that had been used time and time again to justify the enormous ship's being unable to join the rest of the squadron.

He had his own suspicions why the ship never left port, but what did it matter if the governor was a coward, or the Commodore? For all intents and purposes, it was all one. The *Arbiter* gave the Commodore the prestige to nominally command the squadron, and the squadron had done quite well, historically, without her help in action.

"The governor was happy enough to receive his share of the fluyt's return." Maguire had found his voice at last. He would be damned if his plans for the squadron and Port Royal, still in their infancy, would be commandeered or tainted by Hart and Fowler. "My people caught no hint of our imminent expulsion."

Hart gave him a smile whose pitying edge might have brought him to blows in his younger days. As it was, he maintained his temper, barely, and opened his mouth to continue.

Fowler spoke before he could. "I sense too much dissent for this new plan, Commodore."

Hart looked at the other captains and nodded slowly. "I agree, Captain." He waved wearily with one hand. "Very well, then. We shall remain in Cayona Harbor for now. I will speak with the governor on the morrow and assure us of his continued good will."

The older man slumped in his chair as if in defeat, and Maguire wanted to applaud.

It had all been a performance. He could see that now.

Even more than he had suspected, the entire evening had been set for the sole purpose of raising the possibility of shifting the squadron to Port Royal, a consummation he had ever been against, and then putting that plan to rest based on all the old arguments.

Maguire wanted to spit on the well-polished deck of the gallery. If there had been any doubt of his read of the situation, it was banished by the arrogant smile Fowler gave him as he spoke again.

"Come now, Captains; a few more prizes like last night, and we could turn this entire island around."

Hart nodded as if the thought hadn't occurred to him. "That is true, Captain. If we could strike out from here and continue to build our accounts with both Chartier's and the governor, we could soon own both. With that kind of power, what limit might there be to our ability to rediscover the island's former glory?"

Sasha shook her head, giving Maguire an alarmed look. She, too, must have realized what had been done. "The island's main strength has fled, Commodore. To the forests, to Petit Goave, to Port Royal. It is scattered. Our few ships are not going to recapture that faded glory, no matter how many governor's we frustrate."

Bastian stepped forward. Now the masters of *Laughing Jacques*, *Syren*, and *Chainbreaker* stood side by each, staring down the Commodore and the captain of the *Jaguar*.

"We took those two prizes in direct contravention of the governor's wishes, Commodore. And before them, when was the last major strike we managed? It had been far too long."

Hart nodded in agreement, then leaned forward, one elbow rested on the arm of his chair, the other raised, almost in benediction. "True, Captain Houdin. True. But Governor d'Ogeron will not be governor forever."

There was an ominous echo behind those words that Maguire, never a friend to the governor, did not like.

And then Hart tilted his head down in agreement. "Our friend Bertrand has been feeling rather nostalgic for his homeland the last few times we have spoken, truth to tell. I fear his string of defeats abroad weigh on his soul." Again, that look of sadness that was almost, but not quite, dripping with sincerity.

"With most of our Brethren fled, a strong naval presence could prove decisive in determining the next governor."

Fowler nodded. "And if d'Ogeron were so moved as to put in a good word back in Paris, who knows who might ascend to the chair on the hill."

Bastian snorted, and Maguire wanted to kiss the man. Fowler and the Commodore had just overshot their mark, and as the other captains smiled in response, it was clear that they had all seen behind the little farce's curtain as well.

"Tell me, Commodore," the little Frenchmen said through his accustomed grin. "Do you intend to have this chair carried all the way up to the manse, or will you be settling your arse into the well-worn ruts in d'Ogeron's throne?"

Maguire expected for the Commodore to show some anger at this. Fowler's eyes flashed, of a certainty. But instead, Hart smiled, shaking his head as if sharing the joke. "I wouldn't presume to dream so high, Captain Houdin. This chair, right here, is sufficient for my needs."

"For now." Thomas rumbled, and there was no humor in the giant's voice.

Hart's smile faded as well as he looked up at *Chainbreaker's* captain. "Indeed, Thomas. But would any of us have chosen the rover's road, if we were not looking to the next main chance?"

Their laughter slowed at that, although they were all still smiling.

Somehow, Hart had brought the tension and the danger of the situation back under his control while still having set the seeds he wanted to plant in the fertile ground of the captains' imaginations.

Maguire frowned. To what end?

He needed not wait long for the answer.

"There is another matter I would like to put before the council of captains, if you would all allow me to be so bold."

Now, the mirth faded quickly, and Maguire was heartened to see the edge returning to Sasha's gaze.

"I have been approached by a game young man who wishes to join our little circle of companions."

That was interesting, even to Maguire. The squadron had not added a new ship in years, when Bastian had brought *Laughing Jacques* into the harbor. He had been searching for his countryman, Francois L'Ollonais, who had been away. L'Ollonais had never returned to Tortuga, having died in Panama on that very outing, and given no other real choice, Bastian had joined the squadron not long after.

The addition of a captain and a ship to the squadron was not an event to be taken lightly, nor without the full consent of the captains in council. Yet Hart's tone seemed to carry with it the weight of a decision already made.

That sat poorly in Maguire's chest.

"This young man's name? Would we know of him? Has he any prizes we might recognize?" Maguire moved to stand to Thomas's left. Now the captains of the smaller ships presented a united line before Hart and Fowler.

He prayed it would make a difference.

It felt like it would not.

"He is young, alas." The Commodore waved one hand dismissively as he settled back in the chair. "He has not yet made a name for himself. But he brings with him a newly-fitted brigantine, the *Chasseur*. And a hold full of provisions and material to set the squadron up smartly for whatever our next great adventure might be."

Maguire's eyes tightened. There was, yet again, something behind the Commodore's words, lurking there like a Taino ambush, but he gave nothing away.

"This young paragon have a name?" He asked again, noticing how Hart had let this detail slide.

The Commodore nodded. "Greene. Sidney Greene. Second son of a merchant house of Port Royal, I'm told. A house of some repute, I believe."

Maguire's expression tightened further. He knew the name.

"I'm familiar with the Greenes of Port Royal." At his tone, he caught the other captains glancing sidelong at him. "Wealth built upon the forced trade, with little regard for their partners."

Forced trade, the act of entering into illegal shipping contracts with foreign powers only to pass along the manifests and itineraries of their contracted ships for buccaneers to snap up at their convenience, had lined many a wealthy Jamaican family's coffers. It was frowned upon by both the crown and many of the more righteously-minded Brethren, but there was no doubting its efficacy.

The other captains frowned at that, looking back to Hart for his reaction.

"I know nothing of his family's dealings, only that he wishes to join us here on Tortuga, and brings with him both material, connections, and a powerful ship that would be a boon in our future endeavors."

"I will not partake of forced trade." Thomas growled. "Many of my people taken in such dealings are returned to shackles long before the rest of the booty thus enlarged makes it to Port Royal."

"*Syren* will—"

This time it was Fowler that cut Sasha off. "Captain Semprun, Captain Hamidi, there is no danger of this. The squadron will not partake in the forced trade." He looked down at Hart. "Isn't that right, Commodore?"

The old man nodded, waiving away their concerns with a relaxed hand. "Of course not. The dealings of Greene's family is immaterial to us. We will continue as we have, merely stronger than we have ever been."

"We *will*." Maguire quirked an eyebrow at the pair. "It sounds as if the decision was made before we ever came aboard, gentlemen. Are we to assume you present us with a *fait accompli*?"

Again, Hart waved away the concerns of his captains. "I have merely extended an invitation for Captain Greene to join us on a probationary standing. If the man proves an ill fit, we will bid him be on his way, and none of us the worse for the moment."

"How long will this status last?" Bastian's humor was buried deep, now.

Hart shrugged. "One action? Allow the boy to stay with us for a single action, and if things do not go smoothly, we will part ways with the *Chasseur*, and that will be that."

"*Chasseur*." Bastian's voice was low. "A strange name, for a ship out of Port Royal."

"Visions of grandeur, is all, I'm sure, Captain Houdin." Fowler smiled his oily smile. "I'm certain there is nothing more to it than that."

"And that he wishes to make his name on Tortuga, a French possession." Hart agreed. "The name makes more sense in light of that intention. And in fact, that fact should go far to alleviate much of your concern, Aemon." That smile he had not fully trusted in over a decade returned. "It is an ill-fated ship that is named and renamed on a whim. I'm sure young Greene intends to stake his newfound reputation upon that ship. I think you will find him refreshingly earnest; all in all, an excellent addition to our company."

"On a provisional basis." Maguire folded his arms. He would not let the Commodore slip this by so easily.

Hart nodded, his expression somber, for what that was worth. "On a provisional basis, certainly."

It was the only assurance he was going to get, he realized. This departure from previous precedent sat poorly with him, but at the moment, he did not see that he had any other option than to accept the Commodore's current ploy as a given.

Still, he would watch this Greene, and he would see that Shanae kept her eyes open as well.

At the first sign of treachery, he would see their newest brother consigned to the bottom of the sea before he allowed the boy to interfere with his own plans for the squadron.

A Spanish Galleon of the 17th century

Interlude 2
1658 – Aboard the Ultimo Arbiter, *Cayona Harbor*

"So, you must be Maguire's girl." The man's voice was not unkind, but neither was it welcoming.

The man grinning down at the girl wasn't young, but he wasn't old, either. He had the English accent of most of the men and women serving aboard the *Ultimo Arbiter*, which set him apart from the more varied crews on the other ships of the squadron, aside from the frigate, *Jaguar*.

"My name is Shanae Bure. I'm to be taught navigation while I'm with you." She took a moment to catch her breath from the climb, looking around at the expansive main deck. The mainmast was as big around as the bole of an enormous tree, reaching right up into the sky. Fore and aft, the foremast and the mizzenmast seemed nearly as large and tall. The masts underscored the sheer size of the *Arbiter*.

From the water, the ship was a massive wall, double rows of gun ports glowering down on the world. On deck, it was like being on top of a mountain, isolated from everything all around.

Small bands of crew stood around, looking curiously at the newcomer. One particularly greasy-looking crewman in dirty white trousers gave her a strange smile, sun gleaming through thinning blonde hair.

She looked away.

"The Commodore would like to greet you aboard himself, Shanae, if you'll come with me?" She nodded, sniffing dismissively at the grandeur around her, and nodded aft, for him to proceed.

He laughed, then, and she stiffened. But he moved off, and she followed.

"I'm Boothe, the quartermaster." The man said over his shoulder, big hands folded at the small of his back as he strode across the polished deck toward the bulkhead leading to the aft cabins and storerooms; steep ship's ladders led up to the quarterdeck to either side.

Boothe led the girl through a hatchway that was more a large door on a building ashore than a ship's door, and into a long hallway with more, slightly smaller doors leading off to either side. There were lanterns hung occasionally on the walls, but none of them were lit this early in the morning.

At the end of the hallway stood a door that would have done a counting house proud. Heavy, studded, with cast iron fittings that looked like they could withstand a battering ram, the wood was old and stained with age and use and smoke.

The quartermaster, Boothe, rapped sharply on that door, and the sound fell flat and dull, a further testament to the strength of the wood.

"Come." The voice was pleasant enough, muffled by the thick door, and Boothe pushed on the dark surface. The slab opened smoothly at the pressure, and the girl was led into a chamber that might have been in a palace.

The captain's cabin was divided into several areas, including a heavy partition that must have hidden his sleeping quarters. There was a heavy desk along one bulkhead, with several chairs before it and one large, throne-like seat behind. Across the room was a long, elaborately carved table surrounded by matching dark wood chairs. Other pieces of furniture were scattered around the space, holding glittering bottles, dishes and glassware, fine weapons on display, and maps and charts that seemed to be arranged more for show than for practical use.

Everything in the cabin had been as it was for a long, long time, and there would be no way to secure the room for a voyage short of weeks of determined work.

It made the whole display more sad than impressive.

"Welcome!" The man behind the desk stood, a grin peeking through his pale blonde beard. His hand flicked out to drop something behind a heavy box on the surface between them; a pair of spectacles. Watery blue eyes squinted down at the girl, corners crinkled in an attempt at good humor.

"You must be Shanae." The Commodore moved around the large desk to stand before her, regarding her as he might a well-trained hound sitting at her master's command. "I asked Captain Maguire to second you to my ship so I might get to know you a little better, Shanae, while he's away."

The girl blinked as if in surprise, then nodded.

"I know Captain Maguire's ship is a different kind of place." The man paced back and forth before the large gallery windows at the stern of the ship. "The squadron is a carefully-balanced machine, and I often wonder if your captain fully appreciates the kind of determination required to maintain that balance."

The girl raised one eloquent eyebrow, but otherwise remained a silent, attentive statue.

The Commodore whirled on her. "What do you know about our governor, girl? Does Captain Maguire ever mention Governor d'Ogeron?"

The girl blinked at that, but whether it was at being addressed as 'girl', or at some memory of such a conversation was impossible to say.

"Not that I'm aware of, sir."

The Commodore nodded once and then looked back at the harbor spread out far below. Eventually, he seemed to shake himself out of some troubling thought and turned away from the view.

"Well, I think you should probably report to the quarterdeck. One of my mates will have been expecting you." He quirked a kindly grin, but his eyes were distant, as if he had already moved on to more important matters in his mind. "I do apologize if your tardiness causes undue strain on your first day aboard."

The dismissal was clear. The girl turned to see the tall man in the elaborate facial hair still standing by the door, a strange half-smile twisting his mustache out of its careful alignment.

"I'll bring her to Kun, sir." He reached out and drew the door open, gesturing for her to move through ahead of him.

The companionway was warm after the well-aired captain's cabin, the sun streaming through the outer hatchway baking the floor with its tropical heat.

Climbing the ship' ladder up to the quarterdeck was like scaling a high wall, and the girl was again out of breath as she turned around at the top to survey the prim order of the main deck far below.

"This her?" A voice with a harsh accent caused the girl to start, and she turned to see a short, round man regarding her through thick spectacles. He stood by the tall wheel, the sharp shadow of the mizzenmast rising up behind him. A strange, thin mustache looped down over his mouth to dangle like a cat's whiskers to either side.

"This is she." The tall man, Boothe, gently moved her toward the wheel, where the bespectacled man awaited her with foot-tapping impatience.

"Be gentle, Kun. She might not be used to your Oriental wit."

Before the man could elaborate, he had turned and was hurrying down the steps to the main deck.

The girl looked to the man standing by the wheel and seemed to relax as she saw he was smiling. "You'll have to forgive Boothe. He's new to the position of quartermaster and feels the need to comment on every member of the crew to prove he knows us." The man's almond-shaped eyes narrowed in amusement. "As if he's proving anything, noticing that I'm not from around here."

The girl smiled in response. "You must be Mao Kun. Captain Maguire told me to pass along his compliments, and he hopes you are doing well."

The short man's own grin faded somewhat. "Of course, he did. He would." Behind the thick glass, the man's eyes seemed sad. "How is the old fish-eater?"

She shrugged. "Well. I think he's gone to Port Royal again. You're to teach me navigation while he's away."

Kun nodded. "I am. Although if I know Captain Maguire, I'm fairly certain you know more than most of the lubbers you'll find on this ship already."

She stepped around the wheel to stand beside the sailor, reaching out to run one small hand along a spoke. "Probably."

There was no false modesty in her voice, and it brought something of the man's smile back to his round face.

She looked back at him. "You were from the *Bonnie Kate*."

A flash of something passed over his face and he nodded. "Used to be, lass. Used to be. Took the Commodore's offer to join the *Arbiter* soon after you joined the *Kate*. Been locked up here ever since."

The girl looked puzzled. "Why?"

"Why did I take the offer? Or why have I been locked up here ever since?"

She shrugged, looking through the wheel at the broad main deck so far below.

"It was quite a step up, to join the crew of a galleon. And the Commodore's crew gets a bigger cut of any booty." That shadow passed over his face again. "And Captain Maguire suggested it."

She tilted her head at that, looking back at him puzzled. "He did? Why would he do that?"

This time, the man's smile and the sad cast to his eyes were perfectly matched. "I think probably for this moment, miss."

Her face twisted in confusion, but then she looked away. "Please call me Shanae."

This time the smile burned away the shade. "And you will call me Kun. We have a lot to discuss, Shanae. The Commodore intended for old Horace, the sailing master, to instruct you. It took more shares of rum than I'd care to say to switch the duty with him, and the old man can certainly put the grog away. But for the rest of your stay with us, you and I should be left more or less to our own devices."

"To learn navigation." She said the words in a flat tone that gave nothing away.

He responded with the same tone. "Indeed."

She smiled.

*****

The girl rested against the forward rail of the quarterdeck and looked down to where a work party was laying out an enormous stretch of canvas for rigging. Above, another group of men and women were removing the sun-bleached fore topsail, so it was most likely going to replace that.

Off the port bow of the galleon the *Syren* rocked at anchor, with the town of Cayona behind. Closer, just to starboard, was the much larger *Jaguar*. There was no motion on either ship. Those buccaneers aboard were probably hiding from the heat or in town, spending the dregs of their last take.

Only aboard the *Ultimo Arbiter* did life follow this rigid, disciplined structure.

By the look on her face, she didn't like it.

"Here comes *Chainbreaker*." The girl started at Kun's voice, turning to glare at the little man, but he was at the railing, leaning over, not looking at her.

She moved to join him. "Where'd they go?"

Kun shrugged. "No one tells me anything. South, I think? Maracaibo? They tend to keep away from Santo Domingo and Hispaniola." He sighed. "There aren't very many ports safe for an entire crew of Africans, to be honest, lass."

He said this last with a sidelong glance at her, taking in her dark complexion with an almost apologetic smile.

The girl didn't seem to notice.

"Why do you think Captain Hamidi only employs Africans? They're not all former slaves, I know."

Kun shrugged and turned back to watch the little sloop glide into the harbor. "No, he has several freemen aboard, and several of the crew are directly from Africa; including that new quartermaster of his, Sefu. I'm not sure, to be honest. It might be cultural? It might be that they feel more comfortable with their own folk."

She shook her head, watching as the dark figures scrambled about the rigging and the deck, making ready to drop anchor as she glided in beside *Syren*. "There are Africans on every crew. I haven't noticed them treated any differently than anyone else in the squadron."

He sighed. "Maybe Hamidi trusts his fellows more than he trusts the people whose folk put him in chains."

"Perhaps Captain Semprun would have similar sentiments for the *Syren*." She looked thoughtful. "Perhaps there is some safety in seeking out similar folk."

The little man shrugged. "Perhaps. I've never known virtue or vice to discriminate along any such lines, however."

She smiled at that, then looked back up the hill behind the line of low buildings circling the harbor. "What does the governor feel about *Chainbreaker*? You said there were not many harbors open to such a ship."

Kun turned to settle his weight against the bulwark and looked up at the distant hills of Cayona, where the dirty white of the governor's manse could be seen through the high jungle trees. "He sends messages to the Commodore every now and then, whining. But the Commodore sets him right, and they have a dinner, and the whining stops for a while."

The girl cocked her head toward him. "So, the Commodore protects *Chainbreaker* and her crew?"

That seemed to take Kun aback. "Of course, he does! The Commodore is constantly keeping the peace with the governor, with the local businesses, and the other buccaneers who call in at Tortuga. This ship may not move far, my girl, but she sees a lot of action nonetheless."

He turned back to the table they had set up behind the mizzenmast, a bit of canvas rigged over their heads for shade. "Now, let's take a look at those charts again, you can plot me a course from here to Maracaibo and back, to show me what you've learned."

The girl's shoulders slumped, but she moved toward the table, her eyes already picking out the necessary charts and reaching for a pencil and a scrap of paper.

"Kun, still working?" The voice was harsh, oily, and both the short man and the girl looked to the ladder with hooded expressions.

"Ball." Kun muttered the name as if it tasted bad, turning away from the sailor in the dirty canvas shorts and tunic. "We are."

"Please," the man stumped up onto the quarterdeck and gave the girl a particularly greasy smile that never seemed to reach his dark eyes. "Call me Brian, Kun. We've been shipmates for how long?" His thinning pale-blonde hair danced fitfully in the slight breeze.

The navigator leaned over the charts and muttered something neither of the others could hear.

"You know Kun, lass. He's all seriousness when there's a task at hand." The man stood with his thumbs stuck in his belt, the table between them, and gave her another smile as if he truly believed third time was a charm.

She gave him a sickly half-smile and went back to the charts herself.

"I'm just tryin' to be friendly, yeah?" He put his broad hands on the charts and leaned down into their field of vision. "You keepin' the girl all to yourself up here, Kun? No way to be a good shipmate, now, is it?"

The little man's head shot up sharply, and he threw a quick glance at the girl before rounding on Brian Ball. "You know what the Commodore said. You'd best stand down and go find somewhere else to be, or I'll let Boothe know—"

"Boothe." Ball sneered, leaning one dirty shoulder against the mast. "Boothe's a pup. What's he gonna do? And besides, what've I done? Just bein' friendly, is all. And you both so standoffish." His eyes narrowed and he gave the girl another, closer look. "You been cold since you come aboard, girl. Ain't many women on the *Arbiter*, to be sure. And this ain't how we play things here, no it is not."

The girl straightened, her shoulders settling back. When she wasn't slouching, or leaning against anything that might be about, she was quite tall.

She looked directly into the man's eyes, and the brass in his gaze shifted a little under her scrutiny.

"I'm not of the *Arbiter*, Mr. Ball. I'm from the *Bonnie Kate*, and that's how *we* do things. I'll thank you for leaving us to our work, now, without further distraction."

The dismissal was harsh, far more than most seamen would accept from a slip of a girl, but it was delivered with such calculated indifference, Ball was halfway to the ship's ladder before he seemed to know it.

"I'll see you around, girl. I'll see you both around." He tossed this last sally as he disappeared over the edge of the quarterdeck. His attempted sneer was weakened by the speed of his departure, but there was a brittle solidity to his attitude that promised trouble ahead.

"I'm sorry about him." Kun muttered, before the man's nappy head was even below the deck. "I've spoken with Boothe, but nothing seems to keep him away." He looked up at her then, eyes tightening behind the spectacles. "He hasn't approached you when you were alone, has he?"

Her gaze shifted from chart to chart, pulling those she felt she needed closer. She answered, but her voice was distracted. "No. I'm honestly not concerned, Kun. He's harmless."

The worry in the older man's face was evident, but the girl wouldn't look up, and so he shook his head, leaning over to watch her work, obviously trying to dismiss his own apprehension.

By the time Shanae had put together the route from Maracaibo to Tortuga, they had both forgotten about Brian Ball.

*****

"You haven't done any training in arms since you came aboard. Perhaps you should join us." Boothe sat near where the girl was eating her lunch, both enjoying the shade of a rigged sail in the forecastle, a nice, gentle breeze off *La Montagna* taking the curse off the afternoon.

She looked a little startled and shook her head. "No, thank you, Quartermaster. I've other duties to attend to."

He looked a little annoyed at that. "Please call me Myles, Shanae. Or Boothe, at least. We aren't so formal as all that, even on the *Arbiter*."

She shrugged. "Alright, Boothe. Thank you, but I should really be about my studies. I've been sent here to learn more about navigation. I should focus on that."

He seemed vaguely put out by the reply but nodded. "Kun tells me you're a quick study. I've heard from some of the ladies of the *Syren*, over the years, about your times with them. You've spent some time training aboard her, too, I believe."

She finished the chunk of chicken she had been eating and rubbed her hands against her thighs as she stood. "I did. And I do. But here and now, I should be focusing elsewhere."

He stood to join her. "I just wanted you to know you were welcome. Many of the men have mentioned that you weren't joining in the training." He leaned closer. "Some have expressed a concern you would not be able to protect yourself, if the need arose."

That seemed to confuse the girl. Her voice was cold as she responded. "Would I need to protect myself aboard the *Arbiter*, Mr. Boothe?"

"No!" A look of anger flitted across his face. "Of course not!"

"No, I thought not." She nodded, and then turned to skip down the stairs onto the main deck. "Things are done differently here, I know. But I have never feared for my person aboard the *Kate* or the *Syren*. Things couldn't be *that* different on the *Arbiter*."

She moved at a steady clip across the deck, past several men she recognized. Each smiled tentatively toward her, their looks lingering on her longer than she was used to, but none had more than a quick, casual greeting.

Kun was waiting on the quarterdeck, as he always was, and then turned to the array of instruments he had laid out on his little table.

The girl looked down at the table with a smile, the men behind her forgotten.

*****

The girl pushed herself away from the stern bulkhead of the poop deck and stretched, throwing a last scrap of flatbread into the harbor behind her to be fought over by the screaming gulls overhead.

"I hope *Kate* gets back soon. I don't think I have much more to teach you." Kun rose as well, with a slight grunt. He brushed crumbs off his chest, picking a larger bit off and popping it into his mouth. "I suppose we could start taking out one of the ship's boats, and you could row me around the harbor each day."

The girl smiled and shook her head. "I don't think that was what the captain had in mind."

The man's round face turned serious. "Perhaps, as we have this moment, you could tell me what you *do* think he had in mind?"

She looked out over the harbor, the sky blazing red above, throwing ruddy shadows across the water and into the jungle to the east. "I think Captain Maguire wanted you to show me the squadron from the *Arbiter's* point of view." She shrugged. "And learn how to plot a course from Charleston to Port Royal without hitting Florida, perhaps."

Kun's eyes turned thoughtful. "That sounds like something he'd want. And what did you see?"

"It's a lot more complex than it appears from the decks of the *Kate*." She turned to lean an elbow on the high railing of the poop deck, gazing down to where *Syren* and *Chainbreaker* lay at anchor. The former's blue hull was dark with the coming night, its gold trim flushed with the red of the dying sun. The latter's black hull was already disappearing into the darkening waters, only the reddish glints of silver trim outlining her shape. "Keeping this many different ships together for as long as he has must be a terribly difficult task."

"The governor doesn't always help, either." Kun mumbled. "He's happy enough for the *Arbiter's* guns, of course, and for having his own little navy, when he gets to feeling his oats. But he doesn't like word getting back to Paris that there's a ship of Africans infamous for calling his island home. And that says nothing of the *Syren*, which, I believe, they view as entirely unnatural."

The girl smiled at that. "Well, they've always got the *Arbiter* and the *Jaguar* to give them the appearance of honesty."

"And the *Kate*." The man's voice was wistful.

"Well, the *Kate's* special no matter what." She replied, before pushing away from the railing. "Well, I think you, Mao Kun. You have been an excellent teacher and a friend. I think I'm going to go down and take stock of my things, just in case."

"You've taken up in a corner of the gun deck, yes?" His eyes had darkened just a bit. "Would you like me to join you?"

Most of the crew were on deck as the cool evening breeze swept in to take the sting out of the day. Below would only be the few men and women sleeping off their work shifts or their last bender ashore.

She shook her head. "No, I'll be fine."

He nodded, watching as she descended onto the quarterdeck and moved around the mizzenmast and the wheel. "Give a shout if you need anything. There will always be someone nearby."

She cast a dazzling smile over her shoulder as she slid down the steep way to the main deck.

The stairway below decks was just aft of the two big ship's boats lashed to the center of the main deck. She had walked this path well over a hundred times in the past week or more and didn't hesitate even when she realized it was darker than she had expected. The sky was now a deep crimson fading to black in the east, and shadows seemed to be growing all around her.

Night fell quickly in the islands, and there was often a period of near-total darkness before some master or mate thought to kick the crew into lighting lanterns for the night's watch.

The stairs were steep but solid. It seemed more as if one were going downstairs in a building rather than belowdecks on a ship. And as the main deck disappeared above and behind her, and the darkness swam up to muffle nearly any sight of the gun deck below, she paused.

The girl stood there for a long moment, slowly scanning the deep shadows all around, before she hopped onto the deck with a shrug and began to move toward the stern where she had strung up a hammock near one of the hatches into the officer's mess.

When an arm reached out of the darkness and snaked about her throat, she stopped, stock-still.

"Now, girl. Time, I think, I continue your education aboard the *Arbiter*."

It was Brian Ball, his face flushed, his breath shallow, as he moved around, shifting his grip on her neck so that he could maintain his hold but get a better view of her face.

The girl showed no emotion.

"You see, I think you've been livin' a sheltered existence, over there on the old *Bonnie Kate*. You've been shielded from some o' the harsher realities o' the rover's road, and I think a gentle hand like old Brian's might be just the way to ease you into the Brethren good and proper."

He looked her up and down, a strange gleam in his dark eyes. "I do indeed."

She cleared her throat but made no other move. "Realities?"

He smiled. "Well, that there are only certainly things a buccaneer is truly entitled to." He shifted his grip again, so he was holding her by the shoulders. "A buccaneer is entitled to that which they can keep, and that which they can take, and nary anything more."

Her eyes narrowed. "Are you proposing to take something from me?"

The smile turned greasy. "Why, it don't have to be like that, no. Lass, this could be more a question of giving than taking. I've got other things I could teach you as well, I warrant."

It was as if the light in his eyes had kindled an answering gleam in her own. "And what's that?"

"Well, now, those things that pass between a man and a woman, o' course." He moved his face closer to hers, the stubble on his cheeks scratching as he grazed her cheek with his own, roughly. "The passing of idle time in the quiet places of the ship."

She had moved away slightly at the scratching touch but stilled again. "Are you suggesting we find ourselves a quiet place?"

He was extremely close, now, his sour breath washing over her. "Commodore's just had one of the goats butchered. The stalls still empty down on the orlop deck. Hell, it's probably still warm."

Their lips touched as he pressed his face against hers.

She let the contact linger for a moment, although she did not match the grinding movement of his head.

A voice, lost somewhere up above, was calling out her name with some heat.

Ball's head jerked back, looking up as if he could see through the deck low over their heads. "What's that?"

Her lips quirked into a slight smile; the first expression she had shown since the encounter began. "My protectors, I would imagine. Poor timing, as always."

The man's dark eyes went flat. "Damned if they'll rob me of my sport, girl." He grabbed her more roughly and began to drag her toward the stairway.

"Wait!" She resisted for the first time. "I think we're done here."

"You weren't paying attention to your lessons, girl. In the life of a buccaneer, you keep what you can keep, and you take what you can take, and that's an end to it. And if you're not giving, I'm taking."

He grabbed her by one wrist and began to drag her again toward the stairs.

"I don't want this." She repeated the words, and there was something in her voice that brought him up short.

"Listen, girl. As bad as this might seem, it can get worse, right?" He jerked his arm, and a knife blade gleamed dully in the dim light from above. "You don't want this to get worse, do you?"

He looked as if he was going to say more, but then stopped as he saw something in her eyes.

"Oh, futter this." He pulled on her arm, bringing his other around to threaten her with the knife, closing on her throat.

She ducked, twisted, and slid around him, all in a single motion that left him holding nothing but air, the knife hovering over his own wrist.

"Go, now, and this will be an end to it." Her voice was low, serious.

"Damned if I will." He muttered, squaring on her once again.

Overhead, the voice repeated her name with more energy.

The sound seemed to spur him to sudden, violent action. He lunged for her, and she slid beneath the grab, rising up behind him to give a gentle prod in the backside with one foot.

The man lost his balance and came crashing down to the deck with a soft grunt of pain.

"You little bitch. You're going to regret that."

He charged her, head low, eyes wild, knife leading the way.

With casual-seeming speed, she stepped aside, slapped his knife hand out of line, and brought her knee up with crushing force into his groin.

"Bitch!" He muttered, and in answer other voices responded from the main deck. The pounding of feet echoed all around them.

"Bitch," he repeated, and brandished the blade again, standing awkwardly, pressing one elbow into his hip. "This ends now."

He moved without further comment, his knife flashing out with all the speed and strength he could muster. She slapped it aside again, but this time he pulled back in, changed his attack, and thrust again. The girl was hard-pressed, then, to keep the blade from her flesh as he attacked over and over. With each stab he gave forth an explosive, disgusting grunt.

The knife's blade slid across the girl's forearm, leaving a red slash that immediately welled with blood.

"It needn't have gone this way, girl." He was panting now, his greasy flesh slick with sweat, and a flat, empty hunger in his eyes.

He started toward her, and her palm shot out, meeting his charge with its own solid strength and impressive speed.

Her hand struck him in the nose and a sickening crunch snapped out across the gun deck even as a storm of feet rushed down the stairs.

Brian Ball was standing still, swaying slightly, the knife dangling loosely from his limp hand.

"What in the name of hell are you playing at, Ball?" It was Boothe, with Kun right behind him, clasping a belaying pin.

Ball did not respond.

The man's eyes were wide, staring straight ahead as if they could penetrate the gloom of the gun deck, and were looking into some amazing mystery.

A single bloody tear wormed down his cheek, and he fell over backwards.

His chest was still, his eyes open, staring sightlessly at the deck above.

"What—" Boothe moved forward, Kun following closely. Someone on the stair had a lantern, and the shadows began to dance wildly among the cannons, stores, and beams of the ship.

"You're hurt!" Kun moved around Boothe to grab Shanae's arm. Blood was flowing freely, dripping onto the deck.

"It is time I take my leave." The words were low, but clear and strong.

Boothe stared down at Ball, then back to the girl. "How did you know the *Kate* was back?"

"Captain Maguire will send a boat right over, I'm sure." Kun murmured, wrapping a bit of sailcloth around her wrist.

"I'm sure he will." She replied.

But her eyes were hard, focused on something in the middle distance only she could see.

Chapter 8
1674 ~ Cayona Harbor, Tortuga

"I don't know what the old man's thinking." Aidan's voice was petulant, but Shanae could forgive him for that. The entire squadron had been on edge with the word that Hunt had invited a new crew to join them without consulting the other captains.

Shanae might not be a captain; she might not be steeped in the nuances and subtleties of command, but she realized a problem when she saw it. The Commodore's break with the traditions of the squadron, as well as the Brethren themselves, meant trouble.

She shrugged. "No one is happy, Aidan. At this point, Captain Maguire suggests we keep a weather eye out and see how things develop."

Aidan grunted. "The captain knows more than he's telling us." They were resting casually on the small forecastle of the *Bonnie Kate*, their morning duties done, resting in the slight shade of a rigged scrap of canvas, backs against the foremast. He rolled against the mast to come shoulder to shoulder with her, looking at her with narrowed eyes. "He knows something about this Captain Greene and he's not letting on."

She ignored the look, watching the mouth of the harbor. "He's mentioned the name. I don't think he knows this man in particular."

"The captain spends more time at Port Royal than anyone. He knows every family on that coast. You're telling me some sprig from the merchantmen with aspirations of piratical grandeur somehow escaped *his* gaze?" The gunner snorted and settled back against the mast. "Not bloody likely."

She wished she could disagree. Captain Maguire *did* know more about Port Royal than anyone else. His knowledge of the families, the factions, and the infighting there always seemed to verge on the preternatural.

But now that such information might prove helpful, he had clammed up tight.

It had to have something to do with the Commodore.

Although Captain Maguire liked to play his cards close to his chest, she thought she knew something of his eventual intentions concerning Port Royal. She didn't know how he intended to neutralize the danger to a significant portion of the squadron's crews, but she knew he must have some sort of scheme in mind.

"Well, if they intend on further dividing shares for an entire new crew, they better have a plan for finding much bigger prizes." He tilted his head toward her without shifting his own gaze from the horizon. "There's rumblings among the crews. No one's happy, especially everyone who went in on the two fluyts only to see a goodly portion of the booty shifted over to *Arbiter* and *Jaguar* despite *their* crews sitting safe and pretty back here."

"That's the deal, you know that." She was always frustrated when this topic came up. There was an arrangement, and each captain had agreed to it. And each captain had been elected by the various crews. It wasn't a perfect form of governance, and often allowed for an unscrupulous dog to bribe his way onto the quarterdeck for a time.

But Shanae had faith in her people. Give buccaneers enough time, they always sniffed out a rat.

She pushed against the mast with her back and rose smoothly to her feet. "Come on. I want to work the gun crews through their paces today. We gain nothing sweating under the noonday sun, griping about things we have no way of changing."

He rose as well, looking up into the clear blue of the autumn sky from beneath one raised forearm. The sun pushed down on them with heavy, oppressive heat. "My people won't be happy, exercising the guns on a day like today."

"Good. An unhappy crew will focus on us, and the pains and complaints of the moment, and will think less about the future, which none of us can know, and none of us can change."

"That's a little too deep for my people." He smiled, though. "They may just go straight to throwing you into the harbor."

She laughed and hoped he couldn't tell it was forced. "Well, at least then I might be a little cooler."

*****

Several weeks had gone by before the anticipation of the squadron, winding up to a fever pitch, was finally rewarded.

Shanae was working with Ruiz the sailing master on the quarterdeck when a call from aloft drew every hand's attention to the starboard bow. She took out her spyglass and snapped it open, focusing with the ease of long practice on the speck that had just crested the horizon, headed straight for the harbor.

She could barely make out the white cloud-shapes of sails coming into view. The lookout up in the crow's nest would have had a better vantage from his height, and she was certain the man, Hamish Sloan if she wasn't mistaken, would not have called her attention to the ship if it wasn't the one they'd been waiting for.

And if it looked at all dangerous, there would have been a lot more urgency in the call. As it was, Captain Maguire had, over the past few weeks, maneuvered their ship closer and closer to the mouth of the harbor, position-ing her so that her lookouts would be the first to spot an approaching ship.

And so, the rest of the squadron, just as eager for news but not as well-situated, would find out from the *Kate* that their new sister had arrived.

If, in fact, those sails she was watching belonged to the brigantine *Chasseur* out of Port Royal.

There was an even chance the ship was some other brigantine, brig, or two-masted ship. It might be a merchantman, it might be a courier of some kind, come with news for the governor. It was at least reasonable to assume it wasn't an enemy, however.

You would have to be a fool to attack Tortuga with a single ship, what with the forts and the *Arbiter*, not to mention the buccaneer squadron that still made the island their home.

The ship remained hull down beneath the waves for longer than she would have liked, and she began to wonder if her sense of time was playing tricks on her, when Ruiz, standing beside her at the taffrail, muttered under his breath.

"*Maldito puta!*" He spat over the railing into the shimmering waters of the harbor.

Shanae smiled. "Language, Martin. Would you kiss your mother's hand with that mouth?"

Ruiz laughed, still staring out at the distant ship. "Who do you think taught me such colorful expressions, *senorita*?"

More of the crew, alerted by Sloan's call, were moving to the star-board bulwark. More spyglasses were snapping open, sweeping the horizon, looking for the ship.

"Enough!" It never failed to amaze Shanae, how the warmth of an Irish brogue could so quickly turn to a vicious, whip-cracking snap of com-mand.

Maguire stepped onto the main deck of the ship, slipping the wide brim of his good hat over his shaven scalp and pulling at the waist of his frock coat.

Shanae's brows dropped. Captain Maguire was never one to stand on ceremony, and usually dressed for comfort and utility rather than the frippery the Commodore and Captain Fowler favored.

She turned back to look at the ship, now visible to the naked eye, sliding up over the horizon.

Who were these people that the captain should care to dress in such heavy gear despite the heat?

"Do we want to be seen as nothing but gawking children? Go about your duties. Show these Port Royal layabouts what it means to be a bucca-neer of Tortuga."

The men and women of the *Kate's* crew turned toward their captain. Shanae spun around as well, no real idea what he meant.

"Break open a cask!" Maguire's smile was brighter than the sun. "First mate," he turned to Shanae. "The primo grog, from my cabin, if you please. A double ration for everyone." He turned back to the small crowd gathering in the waist of the ship. "Polish up those jacks, boys and girls! I want the gleam of their hoisting visible from *La Montagne* to the poop deck of that Johnny-come-lately brigantine approaching!"

There was a roar of approval from the crew as Shanae, her own smile wide, head shaking at the mysteries of command, stooped to go back into the captain's cabin and fetch up the keg.

She was quickly relieved of the heavy load as soon as she came back into the sunlight, and the cask was passed hand to hand until it came to rest before the captain, now standing idly by the mainmast.

"Now, my lads and lasses, I procured this lovely specimen from the captain of the *Marie Lajoie*. He was loath to part with it, but I knew, even as I unstoppered the cork and sniffed me a sample, that its rightfully place was aboard the *Kate*, awaiting a special occasion."

The men and women crowding around shouted again, many laughing and slapping the backs of their comrades.

"I can think of no more special occasion than to show these Port Royal dandies how we do things in Tortuga, no?"

This time the shout was almost deafening, and Shanae was glad she had eased out to the edge of the crowd.

But even as the cries from the *Kate* drifted away over the gentle waves of the harbor, she thought she heard echoes, and turned back to look toward the town of Cayona, wondering what they might be celebrating.

And then she realized the other shouts were not coming from the town, but the other ships.

And then she realized that it was not all the other ships. There seemed to be raucous crowds gathered around the main mast of the *Syren*, and in the bows of the *Chainbreaker* and *Laughing Jacques*.

Somehow, Captain Maguire had managed to coordinate with the other captains who had gone against the two French merchantmen, a seemingly impromptu revel at the approach of Commodore Hunt's newest addition to the squadron.

She could think of no better way to differentiate the buccaneers of the Brethren of the Coast, the last remnant of that rare breed, from any other seagoing force in the known world.

Instead of salutes with the guns, lines of uniformed side parties, and the tootling of horns, the crew of the *Chasseur* was being treated to a haphazard group of misfits all getting resoundingly inebriated as they passed.

She looked for Aidan, knowing how much the gunner would appreciate the captain's game, but realized he was nowhere to be seen.

She cast a glance back over the heads of the crew to where the captain stood. She was more than a little alarmed as she saw that his smile was gone. He was staring off the starboard bow with a level, steady gaze.

Something more was happening here than a little irreverent gesture at the Commodore's, and this new captain's, expense.

There were others missing as well. Costa and Carita, both members of Aidan's best gun crew, were nowhere in evidence. She would have sworn the gunner had been lounging on the forecastle deck with many of his gun crews while she was working on the tiller with Ruiz. Isabella Sanz, the *Kate's* senior gunner's mate, had been with them as well.

Now that she was looking, she couldn't find any of the men or women who had been with Aidan before the alarm was sounded.

She began to push her way back toward the mast, intending to demand Captain Maguire tell her what was happening, when she felt a grip on her shoulder. She spun to stare into Aidan's eyes and wanted to slap the smile off the man.

"What in the name of all that's holy—"

He handed her a silver tankard. "Drink?"

She had no interest in drink but took a sip out of habit.

"Water." She wanted to spit it out. It was lukewarm and tasted none-too-fresh.

He nodded. "Yeah. He's promised us double shares tonight, when the rest of you slobs are sobering up enough to watch the new arrivals."

She looked down at the cup, over to where Maguire gave her a quick smile, and then back to Aidan. "So, all of this..."

"Will tweak the noses of the Commodore, Fowler, and hopefully every Jack and Jill aboard this new ship."

"But just in case there's some fly in the soup..."

"*Syren*, *Chainbreaker*, *Jacques*, and the *Kate* will all have gun crews as sober as judges, with loaded charges and balls at the ready." He took the cup back and raised it in a silent, ironic toast to the captain. "There better be another one of those kegs in his cabin, or there'll be hell to pay when Isabella and the others hear of it."

Shanae smiled at last, relaxing. "There was another. Two more, in fact."

Aidan's own grin widened. "I wonder what he's got planned for that last one?"

*****

They were once again on the forecastle, backs resting against the foremast, watching as Axel Perry called out the rhythm for the *Kate's* boat crew, making for the distant, glowing bulk of the *Arbiter*, carrying Maguire to his first meeting with this new captain.

"So, why do you think the Commodore accepted this new pup's request to join our merry band?"

Aidan's voice was distant and mellow. His silver tankard, now drained of water and rum both, rested by his side.

Shanae shrugged, then realized that the gunner would never be able to see her from his vantage. "I don't know."

"I still say, if they're going to join us, we're going to need to start looking at bigger prizes. And the Commodore has been getting more timid of late, rather than less. If we hadn't taken on those fluyts, we'd be provisioning on credit at this point, and many of the boys would be heading for the hills, having stolen every axe and adz in storage."

"Maybe that's it. Maybe he thinks, with another brigantine in company, we can take on something more impressive?"

There was a moment of silence as Aidan chewed over her words. "You don't think he's contemplating a move against the dons, do you?"

Shanae shook her head, taking another sip of her own rum. "No. Even if the *Arbiter* could bestir herself from the harbor, we wouldn't have the strength for something like that."

"Hmmm." Aidan pushed his head against the mast and looked up at the stars overhead. "Could be he means to separate us, send us all out in different directions?"

She rocked forward, away from the mast, and shifted around so that she could look at Aidan and the shadowy silhouette of the *Chasseur* at anchor behind him. "I don't think so." She stood and went to the railing, resting her elbows on it and staring at the new ship.

The crews of the four smaller ships of the squadron had been rowdy, indeed, as the *Chasseur* had come to rest at her anchorage. And many a good-natured taunt and insult had been tossed back and forth by way of greeting.

But the deep green hull of the new ship had bothered her for some reason. It was too neat, too tidy. It reminded her too much of the Royal Navy ships she had seen.

Port Royal, she had always believed, had a little too much of England about it to be a comfortable fit for her. She knew Captain Maguire meant for them all to shift to Jamaica at some point, and she was willing to give it a go when so ordered, but she couldn't shake the feeling that something about that place went counter to the deepest realities of what it meant to be Brethren.

Many of her old friends had taken the governor's offer, shifted their flags and taken the king's papers. They were now little more than vain-glorious auxiliaries to the king's naval strength, or trained attack dogs for the merchant families of Jamaica.

The appearance of the *Chasseur*, trim and ship-shape and shaking her world with its presence, only further twisted that knife.

Why would the Commodore want another ship? In a pinch, if it was crew he needed, he could always recruit from the men and women who had turned to the logging trade on the mountain. There had to be some buccaneers up there who were having second or third thoughts about that life.

But instead, Hunt had brought in a whole new ship.

Why did he feel the need for a whole new ship?

Unless it had less to do with spreading their threat range out over a wider area, and everything to do with being able to bring to bear more threats on a small, isolated target?

"What if he's planning on attacking a fort, or port, or some other land-based mark?"

Aidan lurched to his feet unsteadily and joined her at the railing. "Oh, hell no." He shook his shaggy blonde head. "No. Taking on a fort? That sort of thing's for heroes and fools. Dead heroes and fools, more often than not. Charging into the guns of a prepared position? Sailing against big guns being fired from a steady platform as we thrash about on the waves? No thank you."

He shook his head again, even more vehemently, and glared through the night at the watch lights aboard the frigate across the harbor. "No, ma'am. Old lady Allen didn't raise her little boy to die on a beach somewhere."

She was a little surprised by his attitude. The man was no coward, and it wasn't entirely true that sea-borne assaults were all that rare. Hell, even Governor D'Ogeron had led his share of assaults; although none of those had turned out too well. But she couldn't fault Aidan's overall assessment. Attacking a fort, even with an extra brigantine and the guns she might bring to bear, would be a dangerous matter.

"What did she raise her little boy for, then?" She wanted to change the subject, since there wasn't anything they could do about things for now anyway.

He smiled at her with a roguish grin. "Oh, Mrs. Allen fully intended for her little boy to die comfortably in bed, ma'am." He looked up at the starry sky and sighed. "In a big, comfortable bed."

And then he grinned a wicked little smile at her. "From exertion."

Chapter 9
1674 - Cayona Harbor, Tortuga

"I will be damned!" Aidan was not even trying to hide the bitter anger that churned in his chest at the news. "I will be damned to hell and drink with the devil!"

"Probably, but I don't see how that affects us here and now." The woman smiled languidly and pulled him back down onto the pile of old sail-cloth and rags. "You know, your inability to focus on the task at hand could be taken as a personal slight."

He glanced down at Isabella and shook his head. "I'm sorry, Bella, I can't."

The woman looked annoyed, but sat up, adjusting her clothes. "You're not going to have a choice, Allen." She stood, shaking her long black hair out. "We're all going to be heading south, and before you know it, we'll be hoisting tankards of mead, or wine, or whatever the Dutch drink, and we'll be making use of whatever they sleep on to celebrate our continued existence and the glory of being alive." She gave him a sour look. "Some of us will, anyway. Feel free to stand on the beach and spit into the wind, if that's going to make you feel better. I'll always be willing to spend your shares."

She left the tight confines of the orlop and headed back up onto the deck. "You better reconcile yourself with this, Aidan. The ship's got no room for a gunner's mate without the spit to face some return fire." She turned at the hatch and grinned down at him. "I wonder, if there's only one, would I get a larger share? See you on Bonaire, Romeo."

He watched her feet disappear, the hot sun flashing behind her, and then settled back on to his haunches to sulk.

He knew he was sulking. He was familiar with the concept. Usually, when the mood took him, he'd go find a willing woman among the crew and disappear for a quick tumble to get his mind off his troubles.

But from the moment Shanae had mentioned a coastal assault, his nightmares had been frequent and violent. He hadn't had a decent night's sleep in days.

And now, as word spread through the squadron that this was exactly what the Commodore intended, he wanted to scream at the heavens.

Who was this Captain Greene, anyway, to plant such a notion in the old man's head? Some merchant's son from Port Royal, with no experience behind him and a ship his daddy bought for him? What did he know of at-tacking a land target from sea?

Aidan barked a short, bitter laugh. And the Commodore was suppos-edly going to be joining them for the first time in living memory! The crew of the *Arbiter* were scurrying about in preparation and had been since before the *Chasseur's* arrival.

Of course, no one believed the *Arbiter* was ever going to leave Cay-ona Harbor, but it was nice of the old man to pretend, to make them all feel better about things.

"Aidan?" Her voice sent a quick shiver down his back and he turned to see Shanae peering down into the darkness. "Everything alright?"

He flashed her a quick smile. "Of course. Just hiding from the worst of the sun."

As far as excuses went, it was terrible. Deep in the orlop, you might be safe from the glaring sun, but the heat of the bastard, baking every inch of the ship above and around you, was enough to crush the will to live.

Still, during the daylight watches, it was one of the few places you might hope to steal a few moments of privacy.

Even as he thought this, he saw Shanae's eyes shift to the pile of cloth in the corner, and the side of her mouth pulled up in an amused gri-mace.

"I see. Well, I'll leave you to it." And she turned away.

"Wait." He hopped up and joined her. "I'm done moping, promise."

The look she shot him over her shoulder did not say much for her faith, but she waited all the same.

"Could you answer me one question, though? If I promise to smile for the rest of the day?"

She gave him a darker look. "You sorely overestimate the value of your smile."

He waved that away. "Why would Captain Maguire agree to an attack like this? Why, after all this time, would we turn from the sea to the land?"

They were on the main deck, now, with crew moving around them, nodding to her deferentially, making rude faces at him behind her back. But her eyes, those sparkling blue eyes, were only for him.

They were not happy.

"What do you think you know?"

That stopped him cold. "Just the scuttlebutt everyone knows."

Her looked turned even colder. "I had given you more credit for quickness than that, Aidan." She looked out at the *Chasseur*, her expression inscrutable. "And I'd have thought you'd have given the captain more credit, as well."

That rankled, but he was too far gone to care. "Captain Maguire has kept us on the blue for as long as he's sailed these waters. We've avoided venturing onto the land in all that time. Look what it did to L'Ollonais! Look what it's done to the Governor! Why now? What does he think we have to gain?"

Her mouth twisted as if she had taken a bite of sour lemon. "There's more going on here than you know, Aidan. If the captain had another option, believe me, he would have taken it." She turned again, one hip on the bulwark, to face him. "It's only one raid. The circumstances must be fortuitous or the captain would not have agreed to it. Besides," her lips twitched with a touch of humor then, catching him off guard. "Haven't you heard? The *Arbiter* sails with us. Should be something to see, don't you think?"

His head whipped around to stare at the galleon where she sat at anchor across the harbor. "She's venturing out?"

The kind of metal that behemoth carried would certainly turn the tide in their favor, shore batteries or no.

If the Commodore could get her where she was needed...

"That's the tale I've heard, anyway." Her gaze drifted from the *Arbiter* to the *Chasseur*. She sighed, clearly unwilling to give the gunner more, but taking pity on him, nonetheless. "The Commodore's picked himself up a bit of intelligence. The place is a Dutch settlement on Bonaire. They've given it some typically unpronounceable name; Kralendijk, or some-such."

"What does the captain want with some blasted Dutch shite-hole?" Aidan never doubted his own courage, but he needed to know there was something worthwhile on the other side of such a leap. "I don't care about the Commodore, or this new guttersnipe from Port Royal. Why does Captain Maguire think there's any kind of good reason to sail after this Kral place or wherever?"

She shook her head. "I don't know. But if it's a new settlement it'll have everything they need to set up shop here. Supplies that will fetch a good price here or elsewhere, not to mention whatever coin they've brought along for their own trading needs. They'll have plenty."

"They'll also have an escort. The bloody republicans aren't in the habit of sending their voters off to die. They'll have at least a frigate in company."

Shanae smiled as if she approved of his thinking. For some reason, he found the expression irksome.

"They have a frigate, actually. But that's the Commodore's intelligence. Apparently the *Beschermer* has left station, chasing after a pack of Port Royal buccaneers."

Her eyes flicked back the *Chasseur*, but she said nothing more.

"Hart's a syphilitic arse." Aidan spat into the water below. "And I wouldn't trust him, Boothe, or the youngest powder monkey on that slab of rotten dock pine as far as I could throw them." His mouth filled with bile. "Even a fully stocked trader wouldn't be worth this trip, following him that far."

He felt himself starting to breathe heavily and tried to control his rising anger. "This will be the end of the squadron, Shanae, you mark my words here and now."

She looked for a long moment into his eyes, her own carrying a vague shine of surprise, it seemed to him. Then she shrugged, stepping away from the railing. "I've got to get the boat ready; Captain's been summoned to the *Arbiter*. Have you seen Perry anywhere?"

"He was in the forepeak before that bastard hove into view." Aidan settled back to the railing, glaring out over the shimmering water as if he could push the *Chasseur* back out to sea by sheer force of will alone.

"Rest easy, little jack." She managed to convey a world of condescension in the single pat she gave his shoulder. "The captain knows what he's about."

She was off before he could respond, which was just as well, as he had no idea what his response might have been. He trusted Captain Maguire. He had always trusted the captain, and always would.

That didn't make the prospect of a shore assault any more palatable, however.

"Do you mind if I share some of your shade?"

Aidan hadn't even really noticed the slide of the hauled sails' shadow until the calm voice intruded on his dark thoughts.

"What?" He turned to see the priest standing over him and tried to fight back a sigh.

Hunt was never easy to talk with at the best of times, and Aidan had noticed that the more annoyed he was before the conversation began, the harder it was for him to treat the man kindly.

It was never good policy to antagonize a crewmate but Hunt really made the issue difficult.

"Sure." He slid a step forward, making room in the sliver of shadow for the tall, gaunt man with the wild black beard.

Aidan tried to ignore him, going back to watch the motions of the *Chasseur's* crew as they dropped anchor and secured their ship.

"She's a beauty, ain't she?" The priest's voice was almost wistful, and Aidan had to glance aside at him to be sure they were both looking at the same thing.

The *Chasseur* loomed large in his mind, and in his fears, he knew. So much so that he had paid little heed to the actual ship.

She really was a beauty. A brigantine of a similar style to the *Bonnie Kate*, the similarities did not stop there. Her clean, crisp paint was green with gold trim, much like Maguire's ship, although the newcomer's colors were darker by far. The green was the deep green of jungle shadow, and the gold looked almost brown.

In a night action, the ship would virtually disappear into the surrounding shadows of the sea.

She truly was a hunter, made expressly to prey upon those unworthy of their own safety who chose to sail upon the waves.

The thoughts left a bitter taste on his tongue, however. He grunted, unable to conjure up the slightest sense of objectivity.

Chasseur was an interloper. It didn't belong in the squadron, it didn't belong on Tortuga, and it didn't belong in his life.

"Something weighs heavy on your soul, my son."

Aidan suppressed a sneer. He always hated it when the mooncalf called him that. There was no feasible way Aston Hunt was more than a few years older than him.

He decided not to deign to give the priest a further response and went back to his bitter contemplations.

"Would it be about the captain's plan to join the assault on the Dutch, by any chance?"

The man was insane, there could be no doubt about that. Whatever the Spanish had done to him in the dank hull of their ship, he hadn't come out the whole man he had been when last he said goodbye to the sun's light.

Hunt could go days at a time, floating through his own strange world, taking little heed to any of the events going on around him.

But then came moments like this, when he seemed to know exactly what was going on and focused on you with the intensity of the noonday sun.

Aidan grunted again, not willing to be drawn into another conversation about this fears that day.

Shanae had given him quite enough of that kind of claptrap, thank-you-very-much.

He felt Hunt settled down at the railing beside him, unwilling or unable to read the unspoken signals that made life aboard a small ship like the *Bonnie Kate* tolerable.

"Oftentimes, it is in the grip of our deepest fears that we achieve the loftiest heights."

That sounded more like the Anglican the man had once been than the crazed lunatic he was today.

But Aidan refused to lower his guard.

He grunted again, shifting his shoulder slightly as a further barrier to conversation.

"It might be that your soul senses some great test ahead for you, and you fear you will come up short before these peers whose esteem you regard so highly."

That stung a little. Aidan couldn't count how many times he had stormed the decks of a prey vessel or fought off a boarding action by a determined foe. And those few times the *Kate* had run afoul of a true fighting ship he had always kept his cool.

God's teeth, would the captain have elevated a coward to the position of gunner's mate?

He turned, then, teeth gritted, ready to spit out a reply.

The man's kind, empty eyes stopped him cold.

Giving a pathetic manikin like Hunt a tongue lashing was as rewarding as kicking an old dog.

Aidan shrugged, settling back against the rail, watching the crew of the *Chasseur* scurry about their tasks beneath the blazing sun.

"Fear is no great shame in a fighting man, Aidan Allen." The priest's voice had taken on a weightier tone that sent a chill up the gunner's back. "So long as the man meets that fear with a clear eye and a steady hand, that's courage, is all it is."

Aidan knew that. No flibustier worth his powder doubted the sense of a good dose of fear under the right circumstances. It was a tool that could spare your hide an unnecessary scorching just as much as it might persuade the prey to drop their colors before the decks were awash in blood.

And there was really little difference in assaulting some Dutch village as a well-prepared merchantman with heavy guns.

There was no way the captain would have agreed to such an action without sufficient information about the village's defenses.

Despite himself, Aidan felt some of the tension flowing from his shoulders at the priest's words.

He forced himself to turn, then, and look into Hunt's smiling face. "Thank you, Hunt."

The priest nodded pleasantly and turned back to look out over the harbor.

Several moments passed, and Aidan had almost forgotten the man was there, before he cleared his throat.

"Aidan Allen, there is a question I would put to you, if you were amenable?"

Aidan sighed and turned, cocking one elbow on the railing and raising an inquiring eyebrow.

Hunt seemed uncomfortable, almost unwilling to continue, but then bulled ahead.

Aidan found himself curious despite his former frustration.

"As you know, I am consecrated to the great Father of the Waves."

Aidan lowered his head.

"I have recently been considering my position, vis-à-vis the patron of us all."

He wanted to crack his forehead against the railing.

"As I have every reason to believe that I am the last living priest of Poseidon plying the waves of the world, I find this presents a pressing question."

Aidan opened his eyes, staring down into the translucent depths of the bay, trying not to laugh out loud.

"As I am the last; as there are no others…"

The topic might have been laughable, but there was no doubting the depth of apprehension in the man's voice. Aidan rose and turned, looking up into the watery green eyes buried between the wild beard and flying hair. He steeled himself, determined to try to take the man seriously.

"What is it, Hunt? You're among friends."

Maybe he was starting to come to his senses? Maybe whatever the bastard dons had done was finally unraveling, leaving this man to fight his way back to the light of sane day?

"Since there are no others, would it not be more proper for me to style myself a *high* priest of Poseidon?"

Aidan's head sank back to the railing.

"And more, though. Perhaps *the* high priest of Poseidon? I'm the only one, after all."

Chapter 10
1674 - Cayona Harbor, Tortuga

"This makes no sense!" He was ashamed at his loss of control even as his fist crashed down on the inlaid side table. But the Commodore had been so meticulous in his planning all these years. To throw everything away now, on the hopes of one foolish child's whispered intelligence, was maddening.

"Calm yourself, Boothe, or I'll ask that you leave." The Commodore sipped gingerly at the cup of tea he cradled in both hands, lifting his head to gaze out over the harbor.

"Sir, we have waited so long. You told the other captains we would be leading the squadron. The crew has withstood years of abuse from the others. If—"

Hart slapped his own open palm on the delicate table, then cursed as he convulsed, trying to keep his tea in the cup. "Damnit, Boothe!" He stood, looking down at the spreading stain on his white trousers. "Do I command this ship or do you? Do the hands? Are they in charge of the *Arbiter*?" The old man's blue eyes did not look thin or dimmed as they glared at him from above his glowing cheeks. "We will be shifting my flag to the *Chasseur*, and I'll hear no more about it!"

Boothe took a deep breath, trying to calm himself, but then snorted at the attempt and answered with a sweeping gesture of his own. "Commodore, for years we have avoided striking land targets. When the governor led his expedition west, you purposefully stayed away. You made a point of the need for the defense of the island and offered the squadron in the full knowledge that d'Ogeron would take the bait! And now, not only are we going to launch an assault on a land-bound mark, but with a fraction of the force he took with him, and now you tell me we're leaving our heaviest guns behind!" He snarled down at the smaller man, fists balled at his sides. "And I trust you remember how things went for d'Ogeron. The governor hasn't been the same man since."

Those blue eyes blinked slowly, the color returning to a more normal, sun-burnt pale as the Commodore visibly brought himself under control. "Boothe, you'll have to accept my word on this. Greene has no reason to lie. Kralendijk is going to be defenseless. A ripe plum ready for the plucking, and before any of those bastards out of Port Royal can take their shot, she will be ours."

That wasn't good enough, though. Boothe felt it in his gut. There was something more going on here, and it was his duty as first mate of the *Ultimo Arbiter* to give his captain, his Commodore, the best advice he could give.

"Sir, we know nothing of this *Captain* Greene." He packed every ounce of contempt he could bring to bear into the title. The man was too young to have earned it, and no buccaneer worthy of the name would grant any weight to such a title, bought and paid for with trader's gold. "You are sending all our strength south. We haven't sent a sail down that far in years. And yet here we are, about to—"

"About to cut years off my plans for this damned speck of mud, Boothe."

Boothe looked down at the polished deck, forcing himself not to shake his head. The old man's plans had been the driving force behind the squadron's actions for years, whether the other captains chose to acknowledge that or not.

Boothe had his own misgivings, however. Tortuga had experienced a golden age once, if you could use the term on such a God-forsaken little island. What were the chances that power could return after it had flown?

"With the resources we will bring back from Kralendkijk, d'Ogeron will have no choice but to offer us a seat at his table. The man is old, he's played his hand." Now the old, familiar, wheedling tone had entered Hart's voice. Boothe always hated that. It made it hard to maintain the confidence and esteem he always tried to hold for the Commodore.

"Even with his ear—"

"We will have more than the governor' ear, my friend." Hart had clearly taken Boothe's moderated tone as a sign that the conflict was over, and his relieved smile was another blow to his regard for the man. "d'Ogeron will be returning to France sooner or later. I mean to see that it is sooner, and I mean to take his place."

That brought Boothe up short. He had always assumed Hart meant to accept the governorship of the island one day, but that was a distant, unseen future. He watched the old man return to his seat, and then collapsed into the chair opposite.

"Convincing the governor to leave is one thing, sir. But how will Paris feel about an Englishman taking up residence in the governor's manse? I can't imagine they won't be sending a replacement of their own."

The supreme confidence in the Commodore's smile was disturbing, but Boothe couldn't have said why. "I'm no Englishman, Boothe, not here. You know that. Have I taken the king's offer? Have you?" He shook his head, taking another sip of tea. "No, as far as Paris is concerned, we are buccaneers first, and Englishmen a distant second, if that suits their needs."

"Buccaneers, aye." Boothe was lost, now, and it was not a comfortable feeling. "Which the French hold as even lower than the English."

Hart completed his latest sip, shaking his head. "Not when it is politically expedient not to be. d'Ogeron will be returning to Paris with much of the treasure we take from the Dutch, and instructions to distribute it liberally. Gold has always had a sanguine effect on the wheels of power, Boothe."

That didn't sound like the governor he knew, but Hart would never have made such a claim without first being certain of the old Frenchman. "And, because you're bribing them..."

Hart's smile widened and he leaned back in the chair. "Bribing them? Please, Boothe! I will merely be sharing the wealth of the New World with a faction in Paris that has not yet tasted the sweetness of such largesse."

"And the promise of more." As the Commodore's plans took form in his mind, Boothe was alarmed to note his concern had not ebbed at all.

The old man really thought they were within striking distance of reestablishing Tortuga as a haven for buccaneers throughout the region.

"Port Royal won't be happy." The balance of power in the Caribbean was ever precarious; Tortuga was a fulcrum upon which the Spanish and the English had tottered for many years, the French balanced between. With the rising power of the English in Jamaica, shifting the attention away from the small French colony, the Brethren had dispersed, all but eliminated as a factor.

But if they were once again offered a place of their own...

If Hart were able to truly create a pirate kingdom, independent of direct French control...

"They'll all be gunning for us, sir. The English, the dons."

The grin that swept across the Commodore's expression took years from his weathered face. "Don't forget the Dutch, upon whose backs we will take our first, fledgling steps!"

Adding another enemy to the list did not seem to be something to celebrate, but Boothe tried to summon up a smile nonetheless. He could sense which way the wind was blowing, and knew when the time had come to stop beating against it.

There were other concerns that he might have better luck addressing with the old man today.

"But leaving the *Arbiter* behind—"

Hart's grin faltered, and his eyes darkened. "Boothe, you know better than almost anyone that she's not going to leave Cayona Harbor. And you know better than anyone but me and Poza why."

Boothe grimaced at the mention of the *Arbiter's* carpenter and glanced out the window with a slight nod.

Hart took pity on him, then, which was not a comforting feeling at all. "She's a strong ship, Myles. She'll sail again, when she's damned good and ready. But that time is not now."

The grin returned, and Boothe felt his stomach lurch.

"Besides, Kralendkijk will be an easy nut to crack. They won't have had time to shift defenses ashore, and we're bringing plenty of hands. The *Beschermer* is gone and won't be able to return in time to stop us."

And so, we come full circle. Boothe forced himself to nod as he stood, settling the mask of calm acceptance over his misgivings. "Sir. If you don't mind, I'd like to check with Teddy if we're going to shift fighters to the other ships." Theodore DeVillepin was the first gun captain aboard the *Ultimo Arbiter* and had been in charge of the small arms and close-in training of the crew for about a year. It had been Boothe's idea, and he liked to keep an eye on the progress.

"Certainly, certainly." The Commodore stood up, his own smile firmly in place, and escorted his first officer to the heavy oaken door.

"Be at ease, Boothe. *Chasseur* is a good ship. She'll suit us well in the action, and if Greene proves to be intractable, by the time we return to Tortuga, we won't need him anymore. Aboard his ship, we'll be perfectly positioned to see that he's got nothing nefarious planned."

Boothe nodded, passing through the door without another word.

For some reason, that last reassurance had left him feeling even more at sea than before.

*****

The deck of the *Arbiter* stretched out before him in all its gleaming, polished glory. She was a beautiful, powerful ship; one of the most powerful in all the Caribbean.

And she would remain at Tortuga when the squadron ventured forth on this crazy scheme.

He bowed his head. He had known she was never going to lead the others south. After his years aboard, the Commodore was correct: he knew as well as anyone what she was capable of, and without months of attention to her neglected interior, she would be sorely pressed to sail once around Tortuga, never mind making the run down the Windward Passage and out into the Greater Antilles.

But he had been caught up in the crew's excitement, nonetheless. Even the crews of the other ships had been excited at the prospect of seeing the might galleon emerge from the harbor at last. No, it had been years since a buccaneer crew had had the audacity to put out in a ship so large. Beyond the static defenses of an established harbor, every major power in the region would seize upon the opportunity to take such a prize away from the Brethren. It was against the established order for the English or the Spanish to let the buccaneers keep her if they were given half a chance to rectify the situation.

The Spanish, in particular, who had lost her so many years ago, would be eager to turn back the clock.

But despite all of that, he had allowed himself to believe the Commodore would sail out, in company with the rest of the squadron, one of the most powerful buccaneer fleets the world had ever seen, and reestablish themselves as major players in the tangled game of politics and violence that marked the European expansion into the New World.

He sighed, settling his broad-brimmed hat over his head to shield himself from the sun, and moved out onto the main deck.

Perhaps, if this action proved as profitable as Hart thought it would be, there might be enough gold to set some aside for refitting the *Arbiter*.

A pirate kingdom would need such weight of metal, after all, if she were to make a stand before the Powers of the world.

The words felt hollow, but he clung to them, nonetheless, even knowing the danger of such self-delusion.

Teddy DeVillepin was standing upon the forecastle, arms folded over his broad chest, long black hair blowing fitfully in the warm breeze. He stood with Zachariah Rees, the ship's quartermaster, white-blond hair tied in a neat queue down his back. Overhead, tugged by that same breeze, a triangle of sailcloth had been tied to the foremast and a couple of pins along the rails to provide some small protection from the savage sun.

DeVillepin had served the French for years before a misunderstanding with his gun captain had brought him, ultimately, to the life of a buccaneer. Rees, nominally Boothe's second, had been born to the path and never looked back.

Teddy's pale brown eyes reflected the bright sunlight as he grinned down at his advancing first mate. "Boothe."

Rees turned at the greeting and nodded as Boothe ascended to the forecastle deck.

The Commodore kept a tight ship, for a buccaneer, but some official niceties would be forever out of reach, he knew.

"Teddy. How goes the work?"

"The work continues." The man's broad shoulders shrugged as he turned to look out at the scattering of hands clinging to what little shade they could find on the stretched expanse of the galleon's main deck. "They're blood thirsty enough, but just try to push them in the heat of the day and you'll soon see how highly they rate the actual practice itself."

He sounded bitter, but there was a resigned cast to his shoulders.

Boothe had noticed that most of the former navy men who had turned buccaneers, no matter what nation they had started off serving, tended to share that strange combination of bitter resignation.

He had felt it himself, on more than one occasion.

Still, these were the men and women they had to work with, and these were the conditions under which they had to perform.

"And the arms?" He looked to Rees, who was in charge of the general supplies of the ship.

The man's cold blue eyes sparkled. "The Commodore has never stinted on weapons, you know that. They'll have everything they can carry aboard the other ships, to bring to bear against the Dutch."

"They'll be ready?" He took a glance around the deck himself, trying to appear casual.

DeVillepin's bark of laughter was more bitter than resigned. "They'll be as ready as they will be." He turned somber as he turned back to Boothe. "Heading south on their own ship would have stiffened their sails a little, I won't deny."

Rees nodded, but with more wistful longing than hope.

Boothe looked down, making a show of studying his finely worked boots. "Yes, well, that can be said of more than just the hands, I assure you. But the Commodore has his reasons. The *Arbiter* needs to stay on Tortuga, for now. The governor—"

"The governor is a syphilitic whore's get, Boothe, and no one, from the lowest powder monkey to the council of captains, cares what he wants or feels he needs." The big man's eyes narrowed. "We're all putting a lot of trust in this action. Most of the lads and lasses have never been this far abroad before, never mind attacking a land target."

"Never mind riding as cargo aboard other crews' ships." Rees muttered.

DeVillepin nodded. "Nerves are high and leaving our best ship behind is a mistake even the slowest mooncalf among the lubbers can see. The hands need to know why."

That irked Boothe, and he made no effort to hide it. "Why what? The Commodore was rightfully elected to lead this ship and elected by the captains to lead the squadron. If the men have lost confidence, they can call for a vote. But I promise you, it won't go against the Commodore. He has the backing of the mates and masters, he has the backing of the other captains, and he has the backing of most of the hands as well."

He didn't like the smile that crept over the other man's face at that. "And how, exactly, would you know what the hands think? Mr. high and mighty first mate, who never deigns to join the hands at any honest work as he oversees the lord's demesnes from on high?"

Rees looked alarmed at that, putting a hand on the big gun captain's shoulder, but DeVillepin leaned in, arms still folded but threatening for all that.

"If this action goes south there isn't enough good will among the hands to see you all back into port afterward. They will trust you all only so far. You might want to keep your boots nearby, should things start to turn dark down on Bonaire."

Boothe glared into the taller man's face for a moment, but then looked away with a snort he hoped conveyed his own bitter resignation. "Just do the work, Teddy. We'll see to the rest."

He didn't wait for a reply, but instead slid down the ship's ladder back to the main deck and moved toward the towering poop deck. He ignored the men and women he passed, DeVillepin's words still echoing in his mind.

Was there a danger of mutiny aboard the *Arbiter*? He knew he sometimes tended to take the loyalty of his crew for granted, given that they were the flagship of the squadron and undoubtedly the most powerful ship in the region. Who in their right mind would be unsatisfied with such a berth?

But the fact that the *Arbiter* had not left Cayona Harbor in years had eroded much of that status, he knew. He needed to keep that in mind.

Next time he spoke with the Commodore, he had to try to convey to the man there might be unrest. Maybe they could take the ship around the island once, maybe fire a broadside or two into the jungle, let the men hear the roar of the cannons, feel the grit of powder smoke sweep across the deck. That might remind them of where they stood.

Something told him the Commodore would be against even such a benign, brief journey.

How realistic was the gunner's threats, though? If they couldn't take the ship out, even for a day, something else would have to be done to keep the crew in line and loyal.

He refused to believe the situation was as bleak as DeVillepin had suggested. He would know if the hands were that close to rebellion, wouldn't he? He wasn't so distanced from the hands as all that. He spoke to many of them every day. They would let him know if they were dissatisfied.

Buccaneers were notoriously lacking in restraint or respect without the immediate threat of enemy action. Someone would have approached him if they were losing faith in their Commodore.

He had to believe that. He knew the other crews looked askance at the *Arbiter*. Hell, even the other captains and mates shared a benign sort of contempt for the flagship and her crew. But he had always felt that this was as much jealousy as anything else.

In his mind, it was always the *Arbiter* first and foremost, and the rest could follow or hang, as they wished.

But if the gunner was right? If the men and women of the galleon shared that contempt, and he was alone with the Commodore and maybe a few of the other masters and mates, what then?

He tried to run through his fellows, to assure himself of their loyalty. Rees was Hart's man, without a doubt. But the sailing master, Mao? The Commodore had stolen him away from Maguire and the *Bonnie Kate* years ago. The man seemed to fit in well enough. He and Boothe had shared many a drink on a warm night.

Damn DeVillepin, anyway! He'd be second guessing the loyalty of every last man and woman on the ship before he was done.

There would be time to shore up the support of the crew when they came back from the raid on the Dutch colony. Their blood would be up, their pouches full of gold, and who knew; if the Commodore's wider plans came to fruition, they might even be the lords and ladies of a new pirate kingdom.

Their loyalty would be set in stone, then.

And if things on Bonaire proved to be a little harder than the old man hoped, there would still be time, and means, to take action and reassure the crew of their own security.

Either way, there was still time.

Chapter 11
1674 - Cayona, Tortuga

Maguire stopped before the prim little building and took his hat off to wipe the sweat from his brow. Walking the cobbles of Cayona's streets was always treacherous, scanty and poorly laid as they were. The afternoon's rains had done nothing to alleviate the heat, only adding a horrible weight of moisture to the air.

It had been over twenty years since he had last seen his native Ireland. He thought of himself as much a creature of the Caribbean as any man or woman sailing her waters now.

Except on night's like this. This wet, oppressive heat in the dark of the night was as alien to a son of Eire as anything he could imagine.

It always served to remind him that he was a stranger here no matter how much he wished otherwise.

The dark wood of the Daucourt home was well-maintained by the standards of Tortuga, and the fact that the street was clear of glass, broken pottery, paper, or the other detritus of the adjacent harbor was a testament to Cedric Daucourt's fastidious nature and command of the local creatures rather than an influence of Governor d'Ogeron's.

Maguire cleared his throat, stepping up to the red door of the tidy home and rapping quickly, his hat still in his other hand.

The door opened, the round, smiling face of Cedric's wife, Emmeline, brightening at the sight of him.

"Captain Maguire!" She stepped back, making room for him to enter her home. "We were worried you wouldn't come! Please, follow me. Cedric is with the others in the study."

That brought a slight crease to Maguire's brow. "The study? Not the dining room?"

Wealthy merchants like the Daucourts often entertained well-off visitors to the islands, taking great pride in their status as a public house frequented by such guests whenever they had laid in the supplies, ale, and other drink to entertain them.

But the Daucourts almost always did that entertaining in the spacious dining room off to the right. Maguire could only remember one or two times since first coming to Tortuga that they were in the study.

"Cedric thought it would be appropriate, given the gravity of tomorrow's grand adventure."

The woman's smile was conspiratorial as she spoke over her shoulder.

Someone had been telling tales, he realized.

No one was supposed to know the squadron was leaving tomorrow, never mind that it was set on anything like a *grand adventure*.

His initial reaction was that he would have to find out who had been spreading such interesting stories.

His second reaction arrived with a bitter twist of his lips. It wasn't his responsibility to police such behavior. If the captains and the Commodore were hell-bent on such a venture, they could bloody well keep their own secrets.

He had been putting a brave face on his own feelings about the Bonaire action in front of his own crew, but his misgivings had only been building during the weeks of preparation. And when the Commodore had finally announced that the *Arbiter* herself would be staying behind, his suspicions and fears had only intensified.

But the other captains had been convinced, and he would be damned if he left the men and women of the *Kate* out of any action so important to their future.

At least, if they accompanied the others south, they would be on hand if things went poorly.

But his frustration with the other captains was still a heavy weight in his gut, and he wasn't quite ready to set that aside just yet.

He had almost declined the invitation to meet at Daucourt's, but felt that he owed it to his friends to hear them out one last time, and try, at least, to mitigate the potential damage that might be caused to the squadron if things were completely left to the devices of Hart and his new young protégé from Jamaica.

Emmeline led him down the narrow hall and to the open doorway into her husband's study, where she left him with a demure nod and a shy smile.

Maguire stood in the doorway for a moment, looking in, and he could see why Daucourt had chosen the room for this particular gathering.

The furniture must have cost a fortune to shift from all over the region to this little room. Elegant chairs that would have done the governor's mansion proud for all their mismatched vulgarity, were strewn about the room. Along one wall were shelves of books, while charts and maps graced others, and small, narrow windows looked out into the darkness of the island's night.

Lounging in those seats were his fellow captains, barring, of course, the great man himself.

Sasha had folded her tall, lanky form into a yellow, wing-backed chair, a glittering crystal goblet held lazily in one hand. Bastian Houdin, smile firmly in place, was perched on the arm of an elegant brocade loveseat in which the huge form of Thomas Hamidi lounged as if it were a camp chair. The captain of the *Chainbreaker* looked entirely at ease, his dark face peaceful, the flash of his bright teeth gleaming from the nest of wiry beard sweeping down from his high cheekbones. In a large, almost throne-like chair Cedric Daucourt sat upright, a delicate wineglass in one hand. The man's thinning hair was combed up and over his domed head, a bright scar on his left cheek reflecting the glow from the fireplace in shiny knots and shadows.

The fire was to keep the damp out, he knew. He also knew that the heat from the blasted thing would mean he'd be sweating like a galley slave all night.

It all looked much as he had expected since Emmeline had told him they would be in the study, except for the last figure in the room, standing uneasily beside the mantle, a goblet held forgotten in his hand as he stared at one of the charts framed upon the wall.

Captain Fowler of the frigate *Jaguar*, long gray hair tied back in a neat tail, stood as stiffly as if he were on an admiral's quarterdeck, not deigning to acknowledge the others as if he was in attendance under duress.

Which was strange. Maguire knew well that none of the other captains would care to force Fowler's presence upon themselves for any reason.

It was, of course, Sasha who noticed him standing in the doorway first.

"About bloody time." She smiled to take the sting out of the words and unfolded from the chair, moving to a long, polished sideboard to pour him a drink without asking.

"Captain Maguire, you've come!" Daucourt smiled as he stood, moving forward to take Maguire's hand. "I was hoping you would join us."

"The Commodore's not with you, by any chance?" Bastian Houdin was in his cups; Maguire could tell from the man's warm, fuzzy speech. "We saved him some wine, I think, just in case?" The man's grin was impudent, and he made no move from his comfortable perch to search for the wine or approach Maguire for a greeting.

"I believe Commodore Hart is with our fearless governor this evening." Maguire accepted the glass of whiskey from Sasha with a nod of thanks. She knew him so well.

"The governor." Bastian sniffed. "Promising away all our shares, do you think, so the man will bless our venture with one of his supercilious gallic half-smiles?"

"Whatever keeps him from my sight, has my thanks." Hamidi's deep voice rumbled through the room like distant thunder, and his words gave Maguire some hope.

There was no turning the squadron from their appointed course now, but if there was sufficient ill will toward the Commodore among the masters of his ships, maybe a potential disaster could be mitigated, at least.

"Without the Commodore we'd all be scattered across the sea, scratching for scraps amidst the countless other buccaneer crews trying to make a living on these God-forsaken waters."

Fowler's scowl was as deep as ever, and he glared at Maguire beneath lowered brows.

"Are we going to be fighting over this old ground again, with such a *grand adventure* before us?" Bastian chuckled as he tossed the remains of his drink back.

"Without him, you'd be up in the hills sawing logs." Fowler's blue eyes looked almost black in the low lighting, and Maguire remembered the last time these two almost came to blows.

That was a bit more tension than even he had been hoping for.

He stepped into the room, putting a hand on Cedric's shoulder with a smile before turning to the others, trying to appear as casual as he possibly could.

"It's not like you all to air our dirty laundry in the public square." He gave a look toward Cedric, then smiled to ease the man's obvious concern. With the Commodore up on the hill, any word that had not yet spilled of their intentions would be long gone by morning anyway. And he liked the merchant, besides.

"Well," he continued. "I'm not sure about sawing logs, but we'd certainly be in a weaker position, no doubt about that." He could afford some small charity toward the Commodore at the beginning of the evening's discussions if it meant possible concessions from Fowler later. "We should not forget the man's foresight in all of the many changes the Brethren have endured over the recent years."

"Indeed." Fowler looked at him again with suspicion but nodded. "It seems all too easy to forget how many other crews have been scattered, either to other ports or off the sea entirely, when we have a little too much cheap rum in our bellies."

Bastian grinned again. "It's wine, actually, and quite good." The little Frenchman nodded at Cedric, who looked hardly put at ease by the gesture.

"Captain Maguire, we were just discussing the Dutch in the southern seas, and what you think they're appearance might mean for the future of Tortuga?"

The future of Tortuga had looked bleak for over a decade now, but Maguire had no interest in dampening their host's enthusiasm, no matter what the topic. "Well, sir, I hardly think they will pose any great threat to the already-established powers in the region. I hardly think, unless the republicans can all agree on a unified foreign policy that has less to do with spreading haphazard colonies across the Caribbean and more to do with challenging the status quo."

"They're hardly a factor now, sir." Fowler smiled stiffly at their host. "And they will be even less so by the time we return."

"One colony either way won't make that much of a difference." The small sofa creaked ominously as Thomas shifted position, his heavy forearms resting on his high knees. "Ultimately, what care we for these great nations and their pathetic games? We exist in the spaces between their momentous decisions, in the pauses for breath and in the silence before the storm. Dutch or Spanish or English or French, they are all the rightful prey of the Brethren."

"Surely you do not count the French in that list, Captain Hamidi?" Cedric looked even more uncomfortable. "Governor d'Ogeron has ever been a friend of the Brethren of the Coast, as have the people of Tortuga, certainly?"

The huge black man shrugged. "True friends are few and far between, sir. But I count you among them, of course."

That didn't seem to settle the merchant's nerves, and Maguire could tell that Thomas wasn't overly concerned.

The mood of the room was dark and heavy, not the light, rushing excitement of a coming adventure. Perhaps he had misread his fellow captains, and their commitment to this foolishness was not as strong as it had appeared?

"Regardless of the relative power of the Dutch, assailing a colony from sea is no laughing matter." Maguire swirled the whiskey in his glass. It was several orders of magnitude better than anything he would have spent money on for himself, and he was determined to enjoy it, no matter the setting. He tilted his head as he spoke, not looking up. "This Kralendijk hardly seems land worth dying on."

It was Sasha who responded, which hurt more than he would have expected. "We won't be dying there, Eamon. They're nearly defenseless. Port Royal has lured the *Beschermer* out of position. As Thomas said, we live in the spaces between. In this moment, we live in the space between the English plan to strip the colony of its protection and their ability to take advantage of that vulnerability."

"We'll be in and out before either the English or the Dutch know what has happened." Bastian looked as happy as he ever had again and moved to the sideboard to pour himself more wine.

"All the wealth and supplies to establish an entire colony will fill our holds on our return voyage, Maguire." Thomas's eyes glittered from the shadows beneath his lowered brows. "Port Royal, Santo Domingo, Maracaibo, the waves we set in motion with this action will reach every corner of the Caribbean."

"And they will all know who struck the blow." Fowler nodded, a reluctant ally in this old argument.

Maguire sighed, forcing his shoulders not to slump. "Can you not see the risks? You all speak of these things as if they have already come to pass. As if you already know the *Beschermer* is gone, the gold is ours, and the day is won. Aside from the fighting you know lies ahead, how do we *know* about Kralendijk? How do we *know* about the *Beschermer*? How do we *know* about anything at all that is happening on Bonaire?"

"Your dislike of the English is well-known, Maguire." Fowler growled from his place beside the mantle.

"And well-earned." Thomas offered with a nod.

Fowler continued as if the giant had not spoken. "But the Commodore trusts this Greene's word, and his intelligence, and that's good enough for me."

"I wouldn't trust the man as far as I could throw him from a decent height." Bastian resumed his perch on the arm of Thomas's wide loveseat. "But enough gold will go a long way. And aside from our recent windfall, it's been a while since we've seen anything like enough gold."

"And enough gold will buy more than baubles, Eamon." Sasha seemed to be looking at him more intensely than the others, as if trying to convince him of the weight of her eyes.

It had been a long time since that had been the case, however.

"Yes," rumbled Thomas.

"Enough gold can buy validation; it can buy safety..."

"It can buy freedom."

Maguire was starting to tire of this constant feeling of isolation and denial. They had sailed with him for more years than any crew he had ever had. Sasha had been with him for as long as he had sailed the waters of the Caribbean. Could he have known them so little?

"Can it buy you the loyalty of your crews?" He knew this gambit for the desperate last-ditch effort it was, but he knew of no other way to try to force them to see reason.

"It certainly can." Hamidi rumbled.

"What does that mean?" Sasha's response rode over the big man's voice. "Are you suggesting our crews aren't loyal?"

That seemed to get their attention. Even Fowler looked at him with searching eyes.

But that was the problem with the gambit. What did he have to support such a charge, beyond vague fears and jangling instincts?

"I've heard nothing specific."

"*Nothing specific* seems like a thin fog to hide such a ship in, Eamon." Bastian's grin had slipped, and his eyes were dark. "Are you suggesting we can't trust our crews? Or is it more that we can't trust your impartiality?"

He sighed, tossing down the last of his whiskey. "I've never been convinced this is our best course of action."

"And yet we have been." Thomas stood, nearly having to bow his head in the confines of the room. "The lots have been cast and counted, Eamon. You lost. Your only option now is to join us or to stay behind."

"And I hope you won't do that." Sasha took the glass, but Maguire shook his head to another dose.

"None of us are blind to the potential dangers of a shore action, Eamon." Fowler sounded as if the concession pained him. "And none of us are fool enough to want to sail into this any weaker than we must."

That set them all grumbling, and Maguire nodded ruefully. He didn't believe anyone in that room, with the possible exception of Cedric Daucourt, had truly thought the *Arbiter* was going to accompany them south, but confirmation of that had been a blow to the overall morale of the squadron all the same.

"But you can't scare us into changing course now, man." It was always unnerving to hear Fowler speak as one with the other captains.

"But Port Royal—"

"Is no place for my crew, Eamon. I have said." Hamidi settled back onto the lounge, forearms on knees.

"Nor mine." At least Sasha had the grace to look like she regretted having to say it.

"Much of my crew is French, Eamon. They have no desire to take Charles's coin, and might well not find Port Royal hospitable, anyway."

Fowler looked uncomfortable but turned back to focus on the glowing embers in the fireplace. He was the Commodore's man; the first to sign on to this venture and the last to betray it.

Each had their reasons, he knew. But he had had to try. He had worked so hard, preparing for the day when the shift to Jamaica would make sense for them all. If they started down this path now, would they be able to change course later?

"With the haul you think we could be bringing back from Bonaire..."

"We could try to make a place for ourselves in someone else's land on Jamaica, or we could build a kingdom for ourselves right here." Sasha's voice was brittle, and he could see the light hardening in her eyes.

He shook his head. "Greene—"

"Is a new brother, welcomed into the Brethren like all the others before him, or he is a means to an end to be discarded when he proves himself of no more value." Hamidi looked away, his tone also brooking no further comment.

"We will all be watching him. Have no fear of that." Bastian was ever the peace-maker among the squadron's lords and masters.

"Why do you think Hart will be flying his flag from the *Chasseur,* with his chosen men?" The captain of the Jaguar asked. "He will have the fighters of the ship outnumbered from the moment he boards, and they will all keep an eagle's eye on the lad throughout the journey and the action at its end." Fowler shrugged. "If anything untoward occurs, it will begin with the little pissant's death and end with us all the richer anyway."

That didn't entirely make sense, but he could see that they were committed. For weeks now, Maguire had felt that his only role within the squadron was to mitigate the damage the Commodore's blind allegiance to this plan would cause.

It was frustrating to be back here once again. He had hoped, away from the ships and the Commodore, the other captains would see more sense in his words.

But perhaps they were right? Perhaps his time at Port Royal, and the whispered rumors of the Greene family's ruthless work in the forced trade, had poisoned him to the possibilities.

He glanced around and saw one last chair empty in the corner. He moved to it, drifting into the shadows for a moment, and dragged it back into the ruddy light from the dying fire.

"Well, if you're dead set on the course, who am I to further dampen the evening?" He eased himself into the velvet softness of the seat as the others visibly relaxed at his words. He thought about getting himself another whiskey but decided to abstain.

He had a feeling he would need all his wits about him on the journey south.

*****

The *Bonnie Kate* was quiet as the jollyboat pulled up alongside with the muttered call and response of an alert sentry.

Say what you might about buccaneers; the crew of the *Kate* knew their business and could sense when their captain would be brooking no lollygagging.

Before he was even up and over the side, Shanae was beside him, a look of mixed concern and curiosity clear on her dark, refined features.

"Leaving as the Commodore intends, with the morning tide." He took his hat off and combed fingers across the rough stubble of his shaved head.

There wasn't much tide to speak of in the small harbor of Cayona, but it still made for a good time to coordinate the movements of the entire squadron.

His first mate nodded, and he noticed others standing behind her. His master gunners, Allen and Sanz, stood there with several members of their crews. Most of the hands would be getting what sleep they could belowdecks and in whatever nooks and crannies they had found above on a warm, humid night like this.

"Shanae, I want you to take command of the guns as we run south, and when we arrive at Bonaire." He paid little attention to the looks the others exchanged as he moved past them, making for his cabin.

If Greene tried something, and the sailors of the *Arbiter* accompanying the Commodore aboard the *Chasseur* were not enough to forestall them, he would be demanding the very best performance from his guns in whatever action ensued.

Aidan Allen and Isabella Sanz were excellent, and he would put them against any other gunners in the squadron.

But if they were about to be dropped into the drink as surely as he felt, he needed his best guiding those guns.

Behind him he heard the gunners mutter something between themselves. The tones were rye rather than angry, although he could not make out the words.

Shanae snapped out a response that made him smile despite its matching lack of sense.

She'd want to be with him on the quarterdeck, not in the waist guiding the working of the guns.

And she had every right, too.

But this feeling of misgiving would not ease. Something was wrong with this entire affair. And when that flaw in the Commodore's plan revealed itself, he needed Shanae watching his back.

Howard Pyle's pirates attacking a treasure ship

Interlude 3
1661 – Aboard the Chainbreaker, *Cayona Harbor*

"So, you're Maguire's girl." The voice was deep and rumbling, and the girl squinted up into the blinding sunlight to see a blurred, massive shape looming above her, reaching down to help her up the side of the smaller ship. She was lifted quickly through the air and deposited on the deck unceremoniously.

She looked defiantly up at the towering figure of captain Thomas Hamidi, the escaped slave turned master of the buccaneer sloop *Chainbreaker*.

The enormous man and the skinny girl could have been relatives, her skin only a few shades lighter than his own. But she glowered up at him, hands on hips, and eventually he raised his own in surrender.

"Never fear, little one. Aboard *Chainbreaker* we do not speak this way. You are your own, and no other's." He turned to gesture with a sweeping arm the confines of the small ship. The crew that looked appraisingly back at her.

Every ship of the squadron carried dark-skinned hands. There were buccaneers from the Barbary Coast, there were escaped slaves and freedmen from the Caribbean region whose families had been here for nearly a hundred years. There were even Carib and Taino men and women who had forsworn their island villages to sail the bright turquoise waters.

But each of those ships' crews were a mix of darker skinned hands and the men and women from Europe and even a few from as far away as the Orient.

Every face looking at the girl as she stood in the waist of the sloop was dark of skin and bright of eye. These were the escaped slaves of the *Chainbreaker*, each one holding a bloody grudge against the flesh merchants and any who benefited from their trade.

They looked at her with open appraisal. The story of the girl Eamon Maguire had saved from the slaughtered slave village all those years ago was commonly told throughout the squadron. Many thought the Irishman a fool, but aboard the *Chainbreaker* he was more fondly regarded.

The girl straightened her back and returned their gazes with an imperious one of her own.

Hamidi's smile was as broad as his shoulders, his teeth gleaming from the tangle of his beard, as he looked down at her.

"You are a fierce one, aren't you, little tigress?" He gestured, and a shaggy haired young man came forward, his golden eyes regarding her curiously. "We are no enormous ship of the line, like you are used to," his words were amused, but the light in his eyes took most of the sting from them. "We have but one master gunner, and he is young."

The captain cuffed the man across the back of his head, setting the tangled locks of his hair swaying. "Cassius is the best master gunner in the squadron, Tigress, on that I would stake my life. Do not let his youthful lack appearance fool you. He is a natural at the maths required to lay a shot into any target you could name. I have no doubt Captain Maguire will be well-pleased with your learning while you are among us."

Cassius, the gunner, was staring at her like so many of the others since she had come aboard moments before. "Why are you not learning from the gunners aboard your own ship?"

That seemed to catch both the girl and the big captain by surprise. The girl looked, without seeming volition, off the aft starboard quarter of the *Chainbreaker*, and the others followed her gaze, to watch as the vibrant green hull of the *Kate* beat out toward open sea, her sails luffing in the fitful wind as the crew scrambled among them, setting them in order.

"Off to Port Royal again, is he?" Hamidi leaned down closer to the girl, almost as if the words were meant only for her. They seemed to contain more sympathy than his earlier speech.

The girl nodded; her gaze still locked on the receding ship.

"I'm sure he's got his reasons." Hamidi sounded doubtful as he straightened.

"Nonetheless, Cassius will get you settled, and perhaps familiarize you with the various guns we carry? I know the *Kate* bears a bit of heavier metal, but I think you'll find the principals are the same."

The girl nodded, still looking off toward the horizon, a rucksack of her belongings dangling from one hand.

"You can set your things in the orlop. Tonight, when it's time to sleep, you can either string a hammock down there or grab some deck space, whichever you prefer."

The young man's voice was neutral, but something ugly flashed behind the girl's eyes. "I'll toss these down there and fetch them when it gets dark. I'll sleep on the deck."

He shrugged. "Looks like the weather'll stay fair enough. If we get any rain, belowdecks'll be tight, but we'll manage."

She glanced at him askance and nodded. "I'll manage."

Their eyes locked for a moment, his gold, hers a deep black. "Alright, then."

Her bag tossed into a corner of the dark orlop deck among the casks, crates, and barrels of the ship's stores, she followed the young man toward one of the two six-pound guns that served as the sloop's main armament to begin an education on a topic she had been learning about since she was five.

*****

The girl's eyes gleamed even as the acrid cloud of white smoke enveloped her and she leapt aside, letting the galloping gun carriage exhaust itself on the rope stays, the roar of the cannon echoing in her ringing ears.

She moved gracefully to the rail and peered through the coils of gun smoke and whooped like a crazed child when she saw the barrel that had been floating far off across the little cove was nowhere to be seen.

Bits of white splinter and a raging swirl of seafoam was all that remained of her latest victim.

"Well done!" Cassius grinned beside her, locks swaying as he shook his head in disbelief. "You didn't even need a ranging shot!"

She smiled back at him, then turned to lean casually against the bulwark, head tilted at an impudent angle. "Just a natural, I guess."

He laughed. As much as it might have rankled another teacher, he always seemed to take great satisfaction in how quickly she had learned the gunner's trade.

The girl had spent hours every day working with the different gun crews. From both the small four pounders to the six pounders and the swivel guns mounted fore and aft, she knew each weapon by now; the quirks and idiosyncrasies that might make one gun throw short, another wide.

No matter what crew Cassius set her to, she could generally hit a target at a decent distant within two or three shots.

Most of the time, of course, their work was theoretical. There wasn't enough powder and shot available to let a reckless girl fling iron up and down the harbor to her heart's content.

But she was a natural. There was no other way to explain how she could connect a cannon and a target. Cassius Black had been with the captain for over ten years, working first as a powder monkey hoisting bags and balls up from the magazine in the center of the orlop to the guns on deck, then onto the crews themselves, and then to the lofty position of master gunner.

A crew as small as the *Chainbreaker's* meant that casualties hit hard. The men and women aboard needed to serve in more positions, know more about the ship in general and the many tasks that kept her afloat and moving, than on bigger boats. As senior members were lost to action, disease, or the other ships, who all coveted the strong, independent crew of Hamidi's sloop, those left behind were constantly shifting into new positions, rising faster than their counterparts on other vessels.

But Cassius had never seen anyone with the instinctual ability to lay a gun this girl showed.

- 124 -

He patted her on the back and gestured for her to step away from the gun as the crew prepared for another shot. "Two more, I think, before the captain will want us to make ready for our return. Captain Maguire should be in port already. You don't want to miss your own ship, if he's heading back out soon, do you?"

The question seemed casual enough, but the girl looked sideways at him, as if she had detected something more in the words than their surface meaning.

From the way Cassius moved quickly off, she might not have been wrong.

*****

Chainbreaker sliced cleanly through the short chop of the Coastal waters around Tortuga, the sun setting in a blaze of crimson glory before them. The girl's dark hair streamed out before her as she stood beside Captain Hamidi, who had taken the tiller as he often did, setting his sailing master, Billy, off to one side.

He had summoned her to the low quarterdeck after they had moved out around the western point of the little bay and into the relatively open sea beyond. The sloop was moving at a sharp angle with the wind, which felt strange to her experiences with the more classically rigged brigantine, but it was obvious the big man knew his business and was having no problem maintaining a pretty speed.

"Cassius is very impressed with your work." The normal hush of a vessel running with the wind meant that the man's normal, gravelly voice provided enough volume to be heard without resorting to his ear-splitting battle cry.

The girl smiled and nodded with a shrug. "I like to hit things."

The captain laughed. "I don't doubt it, Tigress. I spoke with Captain Semprun and her gunner, Corine? They both warned me about you."

The girl smiled but made no other response. Her gaze shifted slightly, as if unsure where the giant was going.

"Yet no one aboard the *Kate* knows of your training regimen. Even Captain Maguire says he does not know where you work with your blades and pistols?"

Another shrug, her expression sharpening.

The captain looked down at her from the corner of his eye, then laughed with a deep, open boom that echoed across the deck like a gun.

"Never fear, Tigress, your secrets are safe with me. I have spoken at length with the mistress of the *Syren*. I'm familiar with her strange thoughts on the minds of sailors. You can do much worse than emulate her practices."

For several minutes neither spoke, and the *Chainbreaker* continued to move toward home with a crew tired from the continued exercise their captain had forced upon them during their sojourn away.

"I believe young Cassius will be sorry to see you go." The captain said this without preamble, and the girl jerked at the words. She glanced forward, to where the master gunner was leaning out over the bows, watching the rush of water sweeping under the ship.

She didn't seem to know how to respond. "I will miss everyone. My time here has been enjoyable."

The captain nodded; eyes still fixed on the horizon. "I was angered to hear of the events you went through aboard the *Arbiter*." His voice had hardened for a moment, and the girl's spine stiffened. She had never spoken about the attack, or the first time she had killed. But she knew the tale must have spread through the squadron as such juicy scuttlebutt always did.

She had had to fend off unwanted advances since, for sure. But no one had ever pressed her to the point of murder again, either.

"Thank you." Her words were icy as she nodded once. He nodded back, and silence lowered once more over the crewfolk manning their stations nearby.

"Cassius will not be the only one among us sorry that you are going." The girl looked up at the enormous man and started when she saw that he was looking down at her at last. "*I* am sorry that you will not be staying with us."

Cassius had made the offer the night before, as the ship was settling down for the night, fiddles set aside, hammocks rigged, and the watch moving casually toward the rails to settle in for their shifts. He had not pressed her for an answer, actually walking away before she could even put together any kind of response. But here, beside the wheel of the *Chainbreaker*, heading into the glorious sunset before them, the captain made the offer seem far more important.

"There is nowhere in the squadron where you would find a more fitting home, little one." His voice was low again. "Maguire, Houdin, Semprun, hell, even Fowler, they are good captains. They are good folk in the mold of the Brethren. But you belong with your own."

He looked down at her again. "You belong with us."

The girl looked away, out over the glittering waves with their red-tinged diamond tips. She took several breaths, her eyes narrowing, though whether against the glare or something else would be impossible to say. Her face was rigid, as if carved from dark mahogany.

"Thank you." The words were flat. "Thank you for everything, captain." He looked away at the empty tone, and the girl jerked, almost as if she had been about to grab him by one tree-limb arm.

She looked back out over the ship and the horizon beyond, and the silence stretched with the waves beneath them.

"I would be happy here." The words spilled out, now, as if they had been held in for a long time. "I would feel like I belonged here." She nodded as if having a debate within her own mind before continuing. "Captain, you have made me feel more welcome aboard your ship than I have felt anywhere but the *Bonnie Kate* for as long as I can remember. I have enjoyed my time with you and your crew." She smiled shyly. "Especially with Cassius."

Then she straightened, and her smile faded into a look of firm resolve. "But I belong aboard the *Kate*. I have a place there I earned through nothing but my own work, my skill, and my mind. Your ship would be a warm home, I know. And your offer will comfort me always. But I *have* a home. I have a family. And I need to return to them. No matter where I came from, they are where I belong now."

Hamidi nodded. "Wouldn't you rather serve with your own people?"

She looked genuinely confused at that. "I serve aboard the ship of a good man, Captain Hamidi. I serve with men and women of every imaginable background and hue. And every one of them respects me for who I am and who I have become and what I can do."

She sighed, but her shoulders were rigid. "The *Bonnie Kate* is my home because I have made it my home, and for no other reason. It is the place I have earned, and the place I belong."

When the captain smiled down at her, she found herself momentarily confused.

"Well done, Tigress." He reached out and patted her none-too-gently on the back of the head with a little laugh. "Only you define your place in this world. You don't let anyone else tell you where you belong or what or who you should be."

The girl's face seemed to waver between a smile and a frown, finding an unhappy middle ground that owed its shape to both.

The captain looked down one last time. "But if you ever do need another home, you have one here."

She nodded, then looked away, back out at the blazing sun even now disappearing below the horizon.

And as the dark blue of the night sky raced up behind them, the crew of the *Chainbreaker* looked toward the dying light of day and the safety and comfort of their home port.

Chapter 12
1674 ~ Approaching Kralendijk, Off Bonaire

The crash of cannon fire flattened the seas to starboard as Shanae ran from gun to gun, sighting through banks of acrid smoke. All around her the chaos of battle reigned as the crew aloft and running along the decks struggled to bring in the sails, responding to Captain Maguire's bellowed commands.

The top third of the foremast was already hanging by her shrouds, cut through by a lucky shot early in the engagement. As the crew tried to cut the wood and lines away from above, guiding the shattered mast top over the side, others were trying to keep the ship on an even keel, shifting the sails to compensate for the loss of the fore topsail, mainsail, and jib.

The strike had been a lucky one, and one they were not prepared for.

The Commodore had sent *Chainbreaker* and *Laughing Jacques* ahead, approaching the colony from east and west to be sure the *Beschermer* had, indeed, been lured away. The frigate had been nowhere in sight, and signals back to *Chasseur* had then been relayed to the *Jaguar*, *Syren*, and *Kate* to move in toward shore while the Commodore and the newest member of the squadron stayed back to provide a second wave of attackers should the need arise, as well as a keen eye out to sea in case the Dutch frigate was lurking just over the horizon, waiting to spring a trap.

All had been running according to the Commodore's plan, as most of the crew aboard the *Kate* prepared for the landing, her extra longboats already rigged alongside. On the other ships the scene was much the same, she was sure.

Until the first crack of gunfire from the shore announced that all was not as it seemed.

As best she could tell from those first hectic moments, the Dutch must have transferred several of the *Beschermer's* guns to shore emplacements, hidden behind berms of sand and piles of palm fronds. From the sound of the shots they had to be twelve pounders at least. The blasts sent the fronds swirling away, many trailing streamers of smoke and embers, revealing the positions of the cannons and their crews. She could just make out frantic movement through the smoke; preparations for a second volley.

Their foresight gave her a moment's pause. If they had thought to leave coastal batteries behind, what might they have taken with them, to protect from more determined predation?

But the moment had too much to demand of her, with the enemy's newly realized capability, and she off left her speculation, trying to assess the status of the squadron.

The first volley had been more of a psychological blow than anything else, stunning the sailors preparing for an easy assault on unprepared civilians. One shot had struck the *Laughing Jacques* a glancing blow off her bow, the impact echoing back across the other ships, splinters tossed into the bright blue sky as somewhere aboard the little sloop someone started to scream a terrible, high-pitched cry.

Shanae had still been trying to fathom what was happening when the second volley from shore, this time more ragged and poorly timed, crashed out. The ball that had struck their mast had flown with that fusillade, giving the crew of the *Kate* more to worry about than their own surprise.

After that, things had devolved quickly into a pattern more familiar to them all, despite the fact that their targets were shore batteries and not other sailing ships. She had bellowed to her crews, many dropping long arms, cutlasses, and axes to take up their positions around the guns.

She had taken a moment to thank God Captain Maguire had insisted the guns be carrying a battle-weight of powder and shot for the duration of their journey. She knew it had been in case Greene had meant to betray them in route to Bonaire. The betrayal had never manifested; but it meant her crews were ready for this new development.

Aidan and Isabella had the gun crews sorted in good order, and she rushed down the length of the main deck, directing the fine aiming of the weapons as Maguire brought the ship sharply about, presenting her broadside with an unobstructed view of the shore.

It appeared that the guns of the *Beschermer* were positioned to the right and left of a rough boat ramp the colonists had established for the unloading of their supplies. The two positions were well-placed to fire upon attackers approaching from the east or the west, with a wide overlapping kill zone directly in front of the small cluster of huts. A kill zone into-which the squadron had just so blithely sailed.

She did not wait for the shore batteries to fire again to fix their positions in her mind, but rather had her crews aim for the center of the billowing white clouds still obscuring the positions. Aidan and Isabella provided further guidance to the two pairs of nine pounders fore and aft while she focused on the center two.

The two three pounders on the quarterdeck had not been prepared for use during the journey and would be of little use at this range, anyway.

Shanae's first broadside had been close on the heels of the enemy's second volley, and aside from the frantic scrambling she caught through the swirl of smoke, seemed to have little effect.

They were too far away to use grapeshot, although each cannon had one of the sacks ready in case they had been forced to use them on the *Chasseur*. Still, she could imagine the slight impact the round shot was going to have on the sand embankments that hid her targets.

Unless they got lucky and skimmed a ball over that berm and into the emplacement, their assault on the colony was going to be bloody and short-lived.

She patted Costa, a vicious card-sharp and keen eye with a cannon, on the back to encourage him to keep his crew firing, and then sprinted for the forecastle, dodging sailors and dangling rope and sailcloth as she ran.

There were several still forms on the deck, but she didn't take the time to look at them. Plenty of time to count the dead when they were all done; and if not, it wouldn't matter.

She scaled the forecastle ladder at a run and stopped herself at the base of the damaged mast, snapping out her spyglass and scanning the shore. From the flashes that stuttered through the artificial fog, she figured there were three emplacements to either side. With the speed of the *Kate's* approach, even after she slewed around, they were leaving the right-most cluster of cannons behind, moving up on the far emplacements at a dizzying pace.

Before her she could see the *Jacques* heading out to sea, a section of her mast caught in a net of rigging and tattered sail. The Dutch must be firing bar or chain shot to have gotten so lucky twice so early in an engagement. The smaller cannons of the sloops would have little effect on the battle, though, as long as the Dutch gun crews were able to hide behind their piled sand.

She slid the circle of her vision back across the beach, over the ramp and at the gun emplacements she had just targeted.

She was looking right into the revetments. The berms were hasty works, only covering the front of the positions.

She could clearly see the crews scrambling to reload.

She collapsed the spyglass as she turned and leapt onto the main deck, taking the impact with her knees and leaning into a dead run aft. She dodged where she could and bulled over anyone too slow to move.

"Captain!" She cried, her eyes narrowed on Maguire, standing beside Ruiz, the helmsman. "Captain!" She didn't try to gesture toward the revealed guns, focusing instead on scrambling up the ladder and sliding to a stop before her captain, bare feet slapping on the burning wood of the deck.

"Captain, haul wind and head for shore here. I'll silence the batteries to starboard." She pointed, then, and he followed her indication into the smoke, then turned to her with a dark look.

"And the guns to port?"

She shook her head. "Signal to *Syren*, sir, or *Jaguar*." She tilted her head toward the frigate towering behind them. "If Fowler hauls at the same time, he'll have enfilading shots on the port batteries as we take on the starboard."

He looked around, face darkening further. The Brethren lacked the more nuanced codes of the established navies, but there had to be a way.

He nodded. "Get your crews ready. I'll give you the shot."

She was gone before he was finished, sliding down the polished rails of the ladder and hitting the main deck hard. She called the two master gunners to her and they came without question, leaving their crews to prepare for the next broadside.

"Hold fire until the captain brings the ship back around." She pointed toward the distant cluster of gun emplacements. "We're going to have clean shots, but probably only enough time for one volley."

Aidan had already turned, shouting orders to his crews to hold their fire. Isabella's aft gun crews were nearer and had paused when they saw the first mate and gunners' mates shouting over the sounds of battle.

Standing between the two centermost guns, Shanae looked back to the quarterdeck, waiting for the captain's signal. He waved to her once, brought his hand sharply down, and the deck slewed beneath her.

She spent a moment worrying about how much freeboard they might have under them but dismissed the concern with a shake of her head. Others could worry about that. The captain had tasked her with the guns, and she had more important things to occupy her mind.

She had the guns aligned with the sandy berm when the ship turned, rushing now straight toward shore and the other batteries. They were racing right into the teeth of three heavy cannons, but she couldn't spare them a moment's notice.

She ran down the length of the ship, putting a last adjustment to the guns with an eye toward each weapon's peculiarities. Finally satisfied, with the rush of the surf rising up all around her, she took one brief glimpse out of the corner of her eye at the looming shoreline and the positions set there and then, squinting into the distance, paused one last moment and screamed.

"Fire!"

All six guns crashed against their cradles, throwing white smoke rolling out over the water.

Just before the scene was entirely swallowed by the cloud, she watched as the earth all around the Dutch guns leapt into the air, throwing bodies, cannons, and supplies in every direction.

A curtain of acrid smoke swirled across her vision, shielding her from a bright flash on shore. A mighty, thunderous roar erupted behind the white bank, a hellish orange blooming within, and as the detonation echoed away, it left behind it the thin, despairing cries of wounded Dutchmen.

A great shout arose from the gun crews, taken up by the men and women in the rigging and working on the deck all around. She glanced up at Maguire with a grin, but he wasn't watching the main deck. His head was turned off to starboard. She followed his gaze, her eyes widening as an enormous shadow pulled out of the smoke.

Jaguar was almost never unleashed from Cayona Harbor. She displaced too much water for shallows work; too slow and ungainly for the smash and grab actions the squadron usually employed. When *Jaguar* did sail out in company with the others, she was usually used to intimidate and threaten, not in direct action.

Before that day, Shanae could not have said if she had ever even seen the frigate fire a broadside in anger.

She knew now that she hadn't. It was not a sight she would have so easily forgotten.

Fowler dragged the big ship's bow around much as Maguire had done with the *Kate*. The frigate heeled over sharply, and Shanae had the sudden thought that the ship must have dropped an anchor or a weighted sail off the far side, to turn so sharply.

The broadside thus presented was like a vast brown wall with cream trim, plowing through the streamers of the *Kate's* own broadside; it looked far too large to move in such a way.

The Dutch gun crews knew where the threat lay, which explained why Shanae had not been dodging round shot as she prepared her own guns. The three shore pieces were firing at a desperate speed at the frigate, but their speed was harming their aim, even at the broad wall rushing at them.

A rail along the towering quarterdeck shattered, spraying the crew there with splinters. A ragged hole appeared just behind the peak, below the forecastle, with a crashing ring of impact. Several of her sails tore, holes appearing in some while others just flew apart with the strain.

But none of the shots were enough to slow the frigate's inexorable advance.

Nothing could have stopped it by that point.

And then the big ship's broadside, with a clear line of fire to the cannons behind their raised sand berms, erupted.

Two rows of cannons, from the gun deck and the main deck, bellowed their rage at the pathetic battery on shore. A veritable fogbank rolled over the *Kate* and onto the beach, obscuring everything beyond arm's reach.

Maguire's voice cracked out over the echoing thunder and the explosive detonations that followed, and the crew scrambled around her.

Shanae looked around, trying to decide on her next course of action, when she realized what the captain was doing.

The crew was pulling on the anchor lines attached to the boats.

Maguire was making ready to launch his assault.

*****

They were pressed tightly together in the jolly boat as the hands to either side rowed for all they were worth. Shanae checked the give in her holster as best she could, cursing the spray of surf as it flashed in the sun all around.

The shore batteries were silent, but that didn't mean the Dutch were finished. They had already put up more of a defense than any of them had expected. Captain Maguire was shaking with rage, as he had been since the signals from the *Chasseur* had indicated the Commodore's desire for the landing to continue.

Laughing Jacques was still out in the open water, trying to make sense of the wreckage of her mast. *Chainbreaker* had emerged from the smoke behind *Jaguar*, Hamidi holding back, waiting to see what Fowler and Maguire would do.

Syren was probably on the other side of the big frigate, as she couldn't see the blue brigantine anywhere else.

At first it had seemed like Maguire was going to refuse the suggestion, but *Kate* had lost several hands in the approach, and she knew he was loath for them to have fallen for nothing. Fowler was dropping boats all along the length of *Jaguar's* side, probably an equal number to starboard, hidden by the ship's hull, and they were filling up fast with men and women eager to get some of their own back from the Dutch.

Maguire would never have let members of the squadron rush into an enemy position alone, and so he had begrudgingly given the signal for his own crew to take to the boats.

He had started to order her to stay behind, maintain station, and prepare for a hasty retreat, but she had glared at him and he stopped before the first words left his mouth. Mathias Sylvestre, the quartermaster, had been given the unenviable task of staying behind, and she had nodded to her captain in thanks.

The bottom of the boat ground against the sand of the landing and the buccaneers leapt out, rushing through the still-swirling smoke of the destroyed batteries. They crouched low as they ran for the ghostly shadows of huts on the far side, clutching long guns and pistols close to their chests, cutlasses and the heads of short spears gleaming in the fitful sun overhead.

The sharp crack of gunfire was a new and horrible surprise, punctuated by two of the *Kate's* sailors spinning down into the wet sand.

It was hardly a disciplined volley, but the sounds of rifles and muskets rattling off from the village was a further unwelcome development, and the buccaneers dove for cover, scrambling behind the berms and scattered wreckage of the batteries.

Off to the right several boats worth of *Jaguar*s were scrambling up the shore. Two of them were wrestling with a swivel gun and a heavy iron stand.

Behind her, breathing heavily, Fabien Astier, the giant from the Marie Lajoie, crouched; her self-appointed bodyguard.

At the crest of the sand rise that hid them from the Dutch, with spouts of sand leaping up at irregular intervals, Shanae looked back to Maguire with a question in her eyes. Were they going to do this?

It didn't appear that the colonists, or marines, or whoever was defending the village, had a good field of fire down at the ships due to the angle of the beach.

They could be back on the ship and pushing for the open sea before the Dutch came out of their huts.

Maguire's eyes shifted from side to side as he thought. The *Jaguar*s were getting into position to the right. Off to the left there was movement, but she couldn't see through the drifting smoke and glaring sunlight who it was. Perhaps that's where the *Syren*s were?

"We're going to have to move sooner or later. We can't stay on this beach all day." She scuttled in close to Maguire and muttered into his ear.

The captain nodded, then looked over at the *Jaguar*s. Fowler was with them, his flamboyant hat easily visible. Maguire was wearing the black kerchief wrapped around his shaven head that he used for battle. He claimed it kept the sweat out of his eyes but didn't attract undue attention.

Fowler followed a different philosophy altogether, with glittering gold trim and bright white feathers sparkling in the sun.

A few more feet further up the beach and some Dutchman was going to relieve him of that hat.

Maguire looked back over at her and nodded. "We need to go."

There was no pattern to the incoming fire. No beat they could use to ascertain when the enemy was reloading their weapons. Whether that was by design or the result of poor training was unimportant.

No matter when they rose for their charge, they were going to take shots.

Each of them made ready for the charge, checking powder, shot, and blades. Astier hefted the enormous wooden hammer he had chosen, his face as calm as she had come to expect.

"Send someone around to either side—" Shanae began to suggest, when a loud cry echoed from off to the left.

"The sea comes for us all, you fools! Embrace her!"

She closed her eyes, shaking her head.

"The priest." Maguire grunted. She wasn't sure whether it was in disgust, annoyance, or wonder.

"All praise the lord of the waves! Bow down before the rising tide, you land-chained lagards!"

Shanae rose, still in a half-crouch, trying to keep her profile low, but her eyes widened as she watched Aston Hunt making a mad dash across the wreckage-strewn yard in front of the small village.

The man's hair was wild, as always. His beard was bouncing on his chest in a dizzying dance. In either hand he held a stout bar of heavy spar entwined with seaweed.

And he was grinning like a madman.

Around Hunt rushed others she recognized as the port watch from her own ship. Filip Carita, Martin Tenorio, and Anna Green, all shouting along with the madman, clutching short boarding guns. Tian Rodier, his black skin shining in the Mediterranean sun, held a huge pistol in either hand, smoke rising from them as he roared his defiance.

"Or that might work." Maguire smiled for the first time since the assault had begun.

That made her think for a moment. Things were not supposed to have gone this way.

Maguire must have realized that long before she had.

Undoubtedly, he intended to see that someone answered for the discrepancy.

The Dutch long arms shifted their aim to Hunt's party. She could almost feel the enemy's eyes moving away from her, taking their lethal intent with them.

It felt very much like freedom.

She rose to her full height, pulling a pistol and a cutlass, and began to charge for the huts. Astier was silent, right behind her.

She could hear Maguire beside her, his own finely crafted sword high in the air.

The village was small, with only a handful of huts scattered around a wide clearing. The Dutch were obviously intending to spread out from this center. In fact, as she scanned the ramshackle structures for targets, she realized there must be a gathering of women and children somewhere in the jungle nearby. She knew a moment's pity for the noncombatants. Battle must be terrifying for those whom life had not prepared for it.

The musket fire was rattling out from the huts nearest the beach. Hunt's flanking attack had distracted them, allowing the men and women of the *Kate* and the *Jaguar* to rush toward them, but now their attention was scattered across the advancing front. Buccaneers all around her began to fall.

She knew a rush of anger. If her story ended here, on this god-forsaken beach so far from anywhere she might call home, for little more than the hope of a small pile of gold that seemed more and more likely to be a fairytale...

The priest's attack crashed into the huts off to the left as men and women with axes and cutlasses rushed through the open doors, dived through the windows, and the two lines devolved into a whirling, violent churn.

"Come on!" Maguire was ahead of her, running toward the largest hut, situated in the center of the little village. Shanae pushed harder, digging her feet into the sand to keep up with her captain.

Astier, silent as always, started to pump his mighty legs harder, pulling equal with her, then moving ahead.

To the right the larger force of *Jaguars* had slammed into the huts there, silencing those Dutchmen as well.

Without stopping, Maguire crashed through the thin door of the big hut and slid to a stop in the middle of the single chamber.

By all rights this would be where they might find the treasure and supplies they were expecting.

This was where they should find, heaped up in neat, regimented piles, everything they needed to complete whatever grand scheme the Commodore had in mind.

Shanae slowed to enter with a little more caution, stepping up beside Astier as he, too, scanned the room. As her vision adjusted to the interior dimness, she realized the hut was almost entirely empty.

Before them were several crates and boxes and a single strongbox that could not have held a single month's pay for a naval sloop.

There was nothing worth the losses they had already sustained.

Maguire stood, his shoulders heaving, weapons dangling at his sides, staring incredulously at the meager spoils. She looked at him, taking in the tightening of his eyes, the rising color in his pale cheeks, and felt an answering anger within her own chest.

Then she saw the movement behind her captain.

A defender had been hiding behind an overturned bed in the corner to the left of the doorway. He stood now, struggling to free a long musket from the tangle of sheets that had covered him.

Astier spun, eyes tightening as he saw the Dutchman, and raised his giant mallet with a silent snarl.

She cried out, rushing toward the man, her pistol rising.

Maguire flinched at her shout, looking not toward her but around them for the threat, his own pistol rising.

It was going to be too late. The long barrel was free, and it was coming into line with Maguire's head. Astier wouldn't make it in time, robbing her of her own shot.

Shanae shouldered her captain aside as the confined space of the cabin filled with a crashing roar and a choking, acrid fog.

There was a strange floating sensation. It was as if she was drifting in warm water, and someone had pulled on her head, sending her scudding backward in a slow, leisurely arc.

She was confused. What had happened to the sound? Everything was muffled; distant.

The interior of the hot, close hut had been dim, but had it been this dim?

Was it getting darker?

She tried to understand why she was taking so long to drift to the ground.

Why was her head suddenly so warm?

Her body continued its slow, languid fall, pulled by the head toward the soft sand of the hut's floor.

She tried to ask what was happening, but her mouth did not respond. No sound emerged.

She couldn't talk.

She felt like that should alarm her, somehow, but it didn't.

She wasn't scared at all.

She was confused. What was happening? Where was Captain Maguire?

She thought about the Frenchman, Astier. She didn't know why.

She thought about Aidan. She thought she knew why, although she would never admit it.

And with his face swimming in her darkening vision, she knew nothing else.

Chapter 13
1674 – Greater Antilles, In Route to Tortuga

The *Bonnie Kate* was eerily silent the entire voyage back to Tortuga.

Captain Maguire kept to himself, pacing the quarterdeck at odd hours, but spending most of the journey in his cabin, where Shanae was being kept, looked after by the ship's surgeon, old Maia Burton.

Fabien Astier, the silent Frenchmen from the fluyt, had stood guard outside the companionway to the captain's cabin the entire time, heeding no call to step down, even to eat or sleep.

Aidan hung from one of the stays, his hip resting on the rail over the bow at the forecastle.

He remembered standing there a thousand times before with Shanae.

His cheek twitched, and his eyes tightened once again.

He told himself it was against the blazing heat of the tropical sun.

He lowered himself to the deck and rested his back against the foremast. There was plenty of extra canvas for rigging a sun shelter if he had wanted one, but that seemed like too much effort.

Plenty of canvas now that they were down three sails.

The *Kate* had been savaged by the heavy guns of the Dutch in front of Kralendijk. The pumps were still needed every other bell to keep the ship on an even keel. One shot had holed her just at the waterline on her starboard bow, and the shot plug the ship's carpenter, Hector Fraga, had put in position was barely keeping the water to manageable levels now that they were making their best speed for Tortuga.

He flinched as his mind began to burn, remembering why they were making their best speed for home, and he forced it onto less familiar paths.

Like the burning anger they had all felt upon discovering the pathetic haul from their disastrous raid.

Reason argued that there was no way Greene could have known the Dutch frigate was going to leave half a broadside behind to defend the colony or take most of the treasure with her when she rushed off after the Port Royal ships threatening them.

Aidan still wondered, to himself, if that was the case or if the gold and supplies might have been just a few yards away, thrown into the jungle by the Dutch as they realized they were being attacked.

The squadron had taken a severe beating, none of them escaping without damage.

Well, none of them besides Greene's *Chasseur*. But the newly-minted captain and his ship, carrying the Commodore and a sizable contingent of the *Arbiter's* crew packed aboard, had been holding back as planned, and so, objectively, it made perfect sense that they would have been well out of the fighting until Shanae's plan had silenced the guns.

Thoughts of those terrifying moments, slewing to starboard with what must have been mere inches between the ship's keel and the bottom, in the teeth of the Dutch guns and laying in her fire with precision he knew he himself could never have matched, had him thinking about her all over again.

They were all thinking about Shanae, though, to be fair. Not a man or woman aboard the *Kate* doubted that it was the first mate that had saved them from the humiliation of retreat before the lubbers of Kralendijk, or the even greater disgrace of being sunk at the feet of their budding colony.

And now she was in the captain's cabin, on death's door, her head laid open by a cowardly Dutch bushwhacker who had by all accounts been gunning for the captain himself.

Aidan could feel his teeth grinding together. The entire encounter had the feeling of a trap, although he could never have said how it might have been pulled off, or why.

All the crew of the *Kate* knew was that the raid had not gone according to plan at all, and that the haul had been pathetic. The promise of handfuls of gold was not going to come to pass, and they didn't blame their captain on that for one moment.

Every one of them blamed Commodore Hart. And Aidan Allen was right there alongside them.

He had to believe that a similar sentiment was darkening the other ships' morale as well. No number of extra portions of rum had quelled their disappointment, frustration, and mourning entirely.

Kate had lost five men. He knew from speaking with Cesar Japon that the *Laughing Jacques* had lost twice that many. When *Syren* had lost her foremast completely, three women had been swept overboard and lost. Three more had been killed in their sweeping attack on the left side of the village.

Chainbreaker had not lost as many, but they had taken three direct blows to the hull, two below the waterline; the ship was having a hard time staying afloat and was falling farther and farther behind the rest of the squadron as they limped their way home.

Once all the repairs were made, the dead crewmen's shares paid out to their families, and the governor's cut taken off the top, he doubted there would be anything left for the rest of them.

Aidan lurched to his feet. He couldn't give in to the despair and anger that he knew was swirling through the crew.

He had survived his first shore engagement. He knew that on some level, that should have elated him. He had been terrified to take the fight onto the land. He remembered well the weeks of hell that had led up to Bonaire.

In fact, under different circumstances, he would have been ashamed to remember how thoroughly that fear had unmanned him.

But then he would remember that he had survived, and he would want to celebrate.

But he wanted to celebrate with Shanae.

He wanted to apologize to her for the bitter shadow he had cast over the ship, for how his own sense of doom had colored every interaction they had had for weeks.

But he couldn't do that. He couldn't stand before her, head bowed, and accept the good-natured contempt and sarcastic absolution he knew she would be more than happy to dispense.

He was only allowed to see her for a brief period each day, having no practical duties that would bring him to the captain's cabin. Everyone aboard the *Kate* wanted to check on the first mate, and he had no special claim of his own, other than their friendship.

And everyone aboard the ship was Shanae's friend. That was something he was only now realizing. He had always assumed they were closer than most of the others, but as he spoke with them, and as the leagues rolled by beneath them with no change in her status, he realized how important she was to everyone.

The looming threat of being out on the open sea where the British navy, the Spaniards, or even the missing *Beschermer* might find them, was doing nothing for the spirits of the crew.

Aidan hopped down from the forecastle and grunted as he nearly collapsed to one knee. How the hell had she done that during the battle? He rubbed his leg and cast a rueful glance back up at the raised foredeck, shaking his head.

The guns were all stowed for the journey, unused powder and shot back in the magazine. The captain clearly wasn't expecting further action. *Chasseur* was too far ahead to have anything to fear from the *Kate*. The Commodore's flagship was making excellent time rushing home, undamaged.

No doubt to give a favorable shading to events on Bonaire to d'Ogeron, Aidan thought with a bitter twist to his lip.

He hauled himself up the ladder onto the quarterdeck with a casual glance around to make sure the captain wasn't on one of his brief visits to the wheel, then walked to stand beside Ruiz, standing with a single hand on the polished rim, looking grimly back at the sea behind them.

Their lack of speed was giving the churned water plenty of time settle, rather than the narrow wake they were accustomed to leaving.

"How is she?" The old Spaniard's accent was still thick enough to make understanding him a bit of work, but the concern in his dark black eyes would have made his meaning clear no matter how garbled his English.

"The ship? You'd know better than I would, Martin. I haven't spoken with the captain or Fraga all day."

Aidan thought he knew what Martin really meant, but his mind still shied from the topic.

The old man gave him a sour look, stroking his salt-and-pepper goatee with his free hand as he shook his head. "You fool no one, *joven tonto*." His gaze flicked at the deck beneath them. "And you do her no favors, pretending to callousness."

Aidan looked down at his feet, suddenly unwilling to meet those black eyes.

"I don't know that either."

He felt odd whenever one of the older crew read him this well. If Shanae was, in fact, friends with so many, and he was just one among that throng, what did the depth of his concern for her say about him?

He hadn't felt this way since his first blush of boyhood infatuation.

He had known many women since then, as well. He was no callow youth. He was certainly not pining away after the first mate, no matter what any of these gray hairs thought.

But he felt another stab of guilt as Martin looked at him.

"I haven't been in to see her yet today."

The man's expression softened. He shook his head again, but this time there was less judgement in the action, and more pity.

Aidan wasn't sure that made him feel any better.

"The guns are stowed. Your crews are seconded to the pumps or the rigging or Fraga's watch. Why do you not go down now? You can come back up here and tell me, when they send you away."

Those last words were close enough to the caustic humor he would expect from a member of the *Bonnie Kate's* crew that it managed to set his mind a bit more at ease; at least enough to smile.

"You know, I just might do that?"

He didn't like going down when the captain was in residence. It was awkward enough entering the man's inner sanctum under old witch Burton's eye. But with the sailing master's word as permission enough, and nothing else pressing for his attention, with a shrug he moved back toward the ladder, patting Martin's shoulder as he passed.

"I'll be up shortly. Miss Burton doesn't let me stay longer than half a bell, anyway."

The sailing master laughed. "That old *bruja*. She gives you any trouble, you send her up here. I'll keep her distracted, so you get a good and proper visit."

Aidan grinned back as he turned to go down the ladder.

Not that he was going to tell the ship's surgeon any such thing.

He nodded silently to the hulking Astier by the hatch. The man acknowledged him with a shallow nod of his own as he passed. Aidan wasn't at all sure how he felt about the newcomer's obvious obsession, but he couldn't think of a better man to guard Shanae, so passed off the feeling as petty jealousy.

Not that the brute had done her much good on Bonaire, he thought with a sour scowl.

In the cramped companionway outside the captain's cabin he was brought up short outside the door as the surgeon herself backed through hastily, almost bumping into him.

Maia Burton spun around as she sensed him there, glaring up at him with her one good eye.

"What d'you want?" She bristled, and he prepared himself to be turned away once again.

"I was just going in to see—"

"Burton, who's that?" The captain's voice was strained but recognizable.

"Gunner Allen, sir." The old woman whispered through the half-closed door with a voice that would have scraped barnacles off the hull. "I'll see him off, Captain."

"No." The word was low, but clear. "Send him in."

Aidan had already been turning away, nodding to the surgeon. When he heard the captain's statement he stopped, not at all sure he wanted to go in, now.

The captain's voice had sounded rough. If he hadn't known the man as well as he did, he would have said it was the voice of a broken man.

"You heard the captain, gunner." Burton opened the door wide. "Hop it."

He nodded again, squeeze past the solidly built matron, and moved into the captain's quarters.

The door eased shut behind him with a solid click, and he felt as if he'd been sealed into a cell.

The room was dim despite the harsh noonday sun overhead. The windows had been covered over with several layers of sailcloth. The chamber was warm and stuffy without the breeze that usually circulated through.

Shanae was on the captain's own cot in a far corner, nearly lost in shadow. In a chair pulled up beside the bed sat the man himself, holding the woman's still hand in both of his. The room was in disarray around them.

The captain didn't look up as he approached. Looking around, he saw a chair off to the side and slowed. On almost any ship it would have been unthinkable for anyone on the crew, even a mate, to help themselves to such an amenity without first being offered. Even on a buccaneer ship, most captains would probably see it as obnoxious at best, and at worst, a challenge to their authority.

After another moment's hesitation, Aidan slowly gripped the back of the chair, watching the captain for a reaction.

When there wasn't one, he slid the chair gently across the deck toward the bed, still watching Maguire's face.

The man didn't move, his gaze lost in the middle distance above his first mate.

Aidan settled slowly into the chair across from his captain and then nervously shifted his gaze from the distracted man to the face of his friend, lying still and pale on a pillow wrapped in white cotton.

Shanae looked like she had died, her skin was such a ghastly hue. For a moment Aidan was ready to leap up again, thinking she had indeed passed, and the captain somehow hadn't noticed, or was now in desperate denial.

But her chest beneath the heavy blanket rose and fell, if barely, and he breathed a sigh of relief. The motion was almost imperceptible, but it was there, and he wanted to slouch down into his chair at the rush of emotions that swept over him.

He stared into her face for a very long time. Over the pallor that marked her weakened condition, her normal, dark complexion was almost completely lost in the gray pallor. The shadows had made it hard to notice, but as the sun-glare faded from his eyes and he became accustomed to the half-darkness of the enclosed cabin, the drastic changes in her appearance were easier to see.

Her head was wrapped in a blazingly white linen bandage, but there was already an alarming shadow forming within it, just over her left temple.

The Dutch shot had glanced over her skull at an oblique angle, or she would have been struck instantly dead. The man had been aiming for Maguire, they said, as she knocked him aside, trying to throw them both out of the musket's path.

The priest had been coming through the door when it happened and said she had been senseless before she hit the sand.

They said Hunt had gone insane at the sight.

More insane than normal, that was.

He had bludgeoned the Dutchman to death with his heavy staff, not stopping until Fabien Astier had pulled him away.

Every ship had lost people on the raid. Hell, there were several holes in the *Kate's* own compliment that would have to be filled when they returned to Tortuga. But none of those losses had struck quite so hard as Shanae's fall.

Many of the crew were already mourning her passing, speaking of her in the past tense, in hushed, revered tones.

He refused to indulge such morbid fancies, however. She still breathed, and as long as she still drew breath, he chose to hope she might come back to him.

To them. He hoped she might come back *to them*.

"How is she?"

He could see how she was, and that she wasn't good, but he wanted to break the silence and there was only so long he could stare at her still, peaceful face without troubling thoughts invading his mind.

And if he was going to be honest with himself, the captain's continued silence was weighing on him.

The captain did not seem to hear, so after waiting another few heartbeats, he cleared his throat and made another attempt.

"Captain? How is she?"

Maguire shook himself slightly, glancing very briefly at this gunner's mate, then back down to Shanae.

Aidan thought for a moment the captain wasn't going to respond. But then the man shrugged; a forlorn, alarmingly hopeless gesture.

"She is as she has been, Allen." The captain's voice was dry. It made the gunner crave for a sip of water.

Or something stronger.

"She hasn't moved since we found her after the fighting, lying there in her own blood."

It wasn't like the captain to wax morbid like this. The way of the Brethren of the Coast was a bloody one, and although it was only proper to mourn those who fell along the path, such a display as he was seeing now, especially from a captain as highly regarded as Maguire, was disconcerting.

And it was all the more disconcerting because he felt exactly the same way.

Each time he had visited Shanae before, only the surgeon had been in attendance. The captain had been on deck.

He now wished he had decided to come another time this visit as well.

It was hard enough to maintain his composure as things stood. Now, with Maguire's despair on full display, he found something rising in his chest he knew would be hard pressed to force back down.

There was so much he wished he had said to Shanae. So much he wished he had done.

The thing rising within him shifted toward anger.

There was so much he wished he *hadn't* done.

"If she dies, it all dies with her."

The words were whispered, barely heard. In fact, as Aidan looked up, gaze narrowing in confusion and doubt, he started to wonder if had heard them at all.

"Captain?"

This was starting to feel like a dream. No, it was starting to feel like a nightmare.

"If she dies, each and every one of us is doomed." The man ran both hands over the stubble of his scalp and then over his face, into his beard, lowering his head until his elbows were on his knees. "She was the key to it all."

Aidan understood the words, but they made no sense. The words reeked of histrionics. He felt like he had stumbled into some strange pantomime, where the rules he had lived by most of his life no longer held sway.

He was about to ask the captain if he might get him a drink, when the man raised his head and looked directly into his face.

The captain's eyes were bright and clear.

"The squadron cannot last as we are, Allen. The Brethren cannot last as we are. Tortuga, Port Royal, English, French, Spanish, we will eat ourselves before we have a chance to make a mark on history beyond some pathetic romantic notion." He nodded down to the woman lying still and pale on the bed before them. "The only hope of making something lasting out of this hell hole requires people like Shanae to take up our banner. It won't be old relics like me or the Commodore, or even the younger captains."

He shook his head, once again locking his gaze on something hovering over the bed that only he could see.

"She is the best of us. Her very blood argues for it. She could blaze a path forward that even history will not be able to ignore." His voice seemed to vibrate, and although Aidan could only garner the barest sense from the words, they made him want to believe.

"But without her it won't matter whose path we try to follow; my path, the Commodore's path, the English path, the French path. We will be diluted and weakened until there is nothing left of us at all but a sad shadow of what might have been."

Aidan wanted to reassure the captain that she would be okay, but how could he do that? She looked like she was at death's door as it was. And the man's strange words only made the whole thing worse, more surreal.

"It can't end like this." Again, the words were low, no longer intended for him, if anything the captain had said had been.

"It can't end like this." He repeated.

Aidan looked at the distraught, distracted captain and down at the pale, still face of the woman before them.

Although he didn't understand what the captain meant, he couldn't help but feel the same.

Chapter 14
1674 - The Lazy Dog, Cayona

The usual sounds of revelry that would be pounding through the floor from the common room below were nowhere in evidence, for which Maguire was duly thankful.

The Lazy Dog was an exemplar of its type: a tavern that catered to the middle-ground of the buccaneer crews. The experienced sailors, the mates and masters, even the first mates and quartermasters frequented the place whenever they had the time and coin.

Often, they didn't even need the coin, as either Andre Marchette, the barman, or Severin Serre, the owner, were quick to extend credit to any of the Brethren who were known to be in good standing. During the entire reign of the Commodore there was one thing a tradesman in Cayona town could count on: even if a sailor was low on coin one night, he would be flush again eventually. And the captains kept a tight enough leash on their people that no one was allowed to run up an unpaid debt with impunity.

He was thankful he had maintained such a good working relationship with Serre and his family, now. He would have felt terrible, had he not been able to care for Shanae under the circumstances.

He tapped the back of his head against the wall of the small room, pressing his temples with his thumbs, fingers wrapped against his slick, shaven skull. On the bed before him, beneath clean sheets and blankets that would have made any other patron of the establishment jealous, Shanae rested uneasily.

She had yet to wake, but old Burton claimed she was much stronger than she had been. The wound was healing as it should, there was no sign of corruption, and even he could see that the girl's breath was stronger and steadier than it had been.

She was clearly on the mend by nearly ever metric he could apply or understand.

She just wouldn't wake up.

A part of him wished the sailors below would go back to their old, rowdy selves. Maybe the crashing rhythms of the music, the rush of laughter and the raucous chatter would have roused the girl from whatever place she had retreated into at her wounding.

That was part of the reason he had politely declined Cedric Daucourt's invitation, when the merchant had learned of his first mate's situation.

Daucourt's was normally reserved for captains only, and it was a mark of his high regard that he would not only invite Shanae to enter his home, but to stay there as a guest while she recovered.

But he had wanted her to be around her people, not isolated and alone among strangers. He knew she frequented the Lazy Dog often, and if she woke up, he wanted her to be in a familiar environment.

When she woke up, he corrected himself.

When she woke up.

Maia Burton had left no doubt that the girl could not stay on the ship. Her cramped little cabin, baking under the unseasonably hot sun, was no place for a sailor to recuperate from a head wound. She needed to be ashore, in a bed that didn't move, away from the damp, and where the doctors of the town could be summoned if things took a bad turn.

That was as alarming to him as the injury itself; Burton had little faith in land-bound doctors.

Maguire had taken to spending at least two bells in the afternoon with Shanae each day since their return. Things in the squadron were not smooth, and he could ill-afford time away from his crew and the other captains, now.

Morale was lower than he had ever known it. His assessment of the haul from Bonaire had been optimistic, if anything. By the time they had paid out the yards for the repairs to the ships and gave the governor enough to keep him sweet despite the disappointing outcome of the raid, there had been almost nothing left to distribute to the crews.

He, himself, had taken nothing, passing on his own shares so that they would see at least a little coin in their pouches. He assumed the others had done the same, and knew that Sasha, at least, had even withdrawn a small fortune from Chartier's to give the women of the *Syren* a little more to distract them from the loses they had suffered.

He thought once more of his own situation, and wished he had the free coin to do the same.

He was equally sure that Fowler had *not* passed along his shares to the crew of the *Jaguar,* but to each his own. The politics of the Brethren was fast and vicious. If the men and women of the frigate decided their captain was being parsimonious with the booty, he could be swiftly replaced. However, by the code they all lived by, there was no requirement for largesse under circumstances such as those that currently haunted the squadron.

Still, it would have put a smile on his lips if someone aboard the *Jaguar* had called for a vote of no confidence.

He leaned over the bed and reached out with a wet sponge, squeezing a little water onto Shanae's cracked lips. The poor girl was going to waste away before she ever—

She convulsed in a spasm of coughing, her face darkening as she curled up around her chest.

Maguire dropped the sponge and lurched to his feet in a panic. Was this it? Was this the end?

He stared at her struggling body. Her arms were wrapped around her sides as she rolled first one way and then another, trembling with the shaking of her cough.

He moved toward the door, trying to remember where Burton was supposed to be. Was she downstairs? Was she back on the ship?

Life aboard the *Bonnie Kate* had continued, as well, and they all had duties no matter what condition the first mate might be in.

But as he turned back to her, wondering desperately what he should do, he stopped.

She was still coughing, still rocking back and forth, but there was a flash of blue just beneath the bandages.

Her eyes were open.

They flashed around the room, flitting from one point to the next, clearly not focusing on anything, a growing panic in their depths.

But she was aware. She was awake, and she was aware.

He dove back across the room, taking her by the shoulders, trying to ease the shaking.

"You're alright, lass. You're going to be alright." He had to stop himself from shouting as he felt the smile distort his features. "Jesus, Mary, and Joseph, you're going to be alright."

She let her sides go and grabbed his wrists with a desperate strength, staring imploringly up into his face. Her lips moved but no sound emerged. The left side of her face contorted in pain and one hand went to the wound, flinching back as it encountered the bandage. Her look grew more frightened and she gripped him even harder.

"You're going to be okay, lass. Thank God, you're going to be okay."

*****

She settled down over the course of what seemed like forever, but eventually, she eased back into her pillows, her breathing calmed, and she was able to make her wishes known.

The first thing she wanted was something other than water to drink.

He fetched some small beer from the pub downstairs. The crew had erupted with questions as soon as he appeared at the top of the stairs. He tried to answer even as he forced his way toward Marchette behind the bar. The short fat man was standing with Nadine Berthelotte, one of the serving girls of the Lazy Dog, and both of them were staring at him as if a revenant had erupted from the upstairs room, descending upon them with the fury of God.

In the end, he had to stop halfway to the bar and respond to the crew's barrage of questions. When he told them their first mate was awake, the roar was fit to shake the tiles off the roof.

Back up in Shanae's room, he helped her to sit up and sip the beer, and then gently clapped her on the back over and over again when the drink brought on another bought of hacking cough.

Eventually, she was able to get enough of the fluid down that her immediate need was lessened, and she breathed easier, if with shallow breaths, for the first time since awakening.

"What happened?" The words were soft and reedy, a shadow of her usual voice.

It reminded him of a much younger girl, and that twisted in his chest as he tried to reassure her everything was alright.

"The haul?" He hadn't even begun to reassure her about her own health, and she interrupted with questions that bore more import, as far as she was concerned, on the squadron as a whole and upon the *Kate* in particular.

He shook his head. "Plenty of time to talk about that later, girl. You need to gather—"

She shook her head, wincing at the sudden stab of pain, but then shaking it again, as if in defiance of her own weakness. "The Dog, yes?" She looked around, taking in the shanty room's sparse decorations and amenities. "How long?"

He shook his head again, not wanting to burden her with all this now. "Shanae, love, you've got to relax. There'll be plenty of time—"

"That bad." It wasn't a question, and the look she gave him stopped him short. "You can't protect me, Captain. If the action went poorly, there are things we must do. Things you've had to do alone. We need to be sure of the crew. I think—"

"Don't teach your grandmother to suck eggs, girl." He was frustrated, more at his inability to protect her than her single-minded focus, but his relief at her sudden awakening was making it hard to regulate his emotions that finely. "I was captain of that barge long before you were born, let's not forget. Things weren't going to fall apart just because you decided to take a bit of a kip in the middle of the work."

She started at that, almost rising to his taunt, but then settled back, satisfied with a glare that conveyed all the heat she required.

"I promise you, girl, there'll be world enough and time, once you're feeling better." He reached around for a bit of lamb from the plate Nadine had given him and tried to get her to eat it. "You need it. You've been out for longer than you'll want to hear; nothing but sugar water and lemon juice. You must be starving."

She started to deny that, he could see, but then, with the bit of dry meat hovering before her, mesmerizing her, she just nodded and grabbed for it.

The next few minutes were spent ravaging the plate. He went down for another, and two more beers, that they might share a toast to their good fortune and turned away several of the crew who wanted to come in and see her for themselves.

There would be plenty of time for all the nonsense they had in mind when she was stronger, he told them.

Besides, there was something else they had to speak about, first.

In the end it took three plates of meat and vegetables to sate her hunger, and by the time she had started in on the third, she was alternating between cups of water and watered wine.

She listened carefully as he told her about the final parts of the battle on Bonaire, and the subsequent disappointment as they dug through the village only to find the lion's share of the treasure and supplies gone.

"It was in the jungle. Had to be." She said around a mouthful of goat. She looked at him with a dark expression. "You should have known that."

He nodded. "It probably was. But we couldn't spare the time to look, after we'd torn the clearing apart."

She paused in her chewing, looking up in thought, and then nodded. "The *Beschermer.*"

He responded with a nod of his own. "No telling when she might return."

"Enough of Greene's intelligence was wrong, you couldn't take any chances with that."

He described the damage sustained by the squadron, and her blue eyes darkened.

"It's all being repaired now." He smiled ruefully. "We brought away enough for that, at least."

"But not enough to put me up at Daucourt's, eh?"

He paused, then gave her a sour look as she grinned.

"Morale must have taken a blow." She went back to eating.

"It isn't good. The *Kates* are well enough, and Sasha's got the *Syrens* doing well. I think Bastian and Thomas have kept their people happy enough. I don't know about the *Jaguar*, and no one's seen much of the Commodore since our return; Boothe's been taking care of most of the ship's day-to-day. He hasn't seemed none-too-pleased."

She took that in, not seeming surprised by any of it. "I assume we've drummed Greene out? Did he even make it back to Tortuga?"

He hesitated. He was still processing this himself and didn't want to risk her recovery by upsetting her too much. Still, he knew how she would react later if she found out he had kept something like that from her now. It wasn't worth it.

"He's still with us." She looked like she had just bitten into a poisoned apple, opening her mouth to bellow or curse, and he raised a single hand to forestall any such outburst.

"He made a good enough case that the intelligence was good, and that it was just that the Dutch were better than they had any right to be. Hart believed him, as did Fowler." He shrugged, trying to seem casual about the whole thing despite his own misgivings. "The others are willing to extend the benefit of the doubt. The Commodore claims he's still an asset to the squadron, that his connections at Port Royal could mean another big chance downwind."

"You have connections at Port Royal." Her lips were twisted with bitterness. "He never seemed to give you much weight for it."

Maguire shook his head. "Lass, as I'm sure you know, it's complicated. We're buccaneers; it's always going to be complicated."

"I'd thought he'd be gone. I'd thought there might even have been a vote of no confidence against the Commodore. What's happened to the courage of you captains while I've been asleep?"

She still looked wan and weak, but the color of her anger, flooding her cheeks and flushing away the pallid remnants of her illness, gave her the illusion of health and strength.

"Shanae, I think that's enough for now." He took the plate away; there wasn't anything left on it anyway. "You need to rest now that you're back among the living. I'm going to let some of the crew come in and see you for a bell or so, but then you need to get some sleep. Good, natural sleep and more of this food is the only way for you to get back into fighting fiddle."

"I don't need—"

He turned back to her, raising one hand, and her voice faded away at the look on his face. "We need to talk before that happens, however."

She looked puzzled, then suspicious. "About what?"

He had tried to have many serious conversations with her over the years, trying his best to navigate the waters between father and captain before he gave that up as a bad job, and decided being the best captain he could be would be better than being both a distracted captain and a bad father.

The remnants of that time were these looks she gave him when he did still try to wade into that vague, questionable space.

But this was too important to shy away from on some vague fear of embarrassment.

"You could easily have died on Bonaire." He made the statement as blunt as it could be.

She started to deny this, but he shook his head and continued.

"You could have died there. You *should* have died there, after the maneuver you tried to pull." He heard his voice tighten, could feel his body starting to vibrate with remembered fear and anger. "You can't do that again."

That look of reflexive dismissal crossed her face again and she raised her hand to wave his concerns away, but he caught it, held it in both of his own, and leaned in to look directly into her eyes.

"You can't do that again. You can't *ever* do that again." He searched her face for any sign she understood the gravity of his words and was frustrated by the casual levity he saw there. "This is no jest!" He stood over her, not letting her hand go. "When I die, *you* must be ready to take my place on the *Kate*! You know that! We've spoken of it often enough!"

She shook her head, pulling her hand away. "*You've* spoken of it often enough. Your typical Irish morbidity, I've always felt. You've got many years yet in you, captain. And your first mate certainly can't stay out of the action and remain affective. This is not a talk for today."

He went to one knee by her bed, refusing to let her dismiss him now. "No. Today is exactly the time we must talk about this. When I pass, you will be the captain of the *Bonnie Kate*. You're the only person I would ever want captaining that ship after me. The squadron will need you as well. At least, Bastian, Thomas, and Sasha will need you. If I fall before this work is done then so be it, so long as the four of you remain."

He glared into her eyes, trying to make her understand. "You are going to be more important than me, Shanae. Whatever happens, *you* must live. You cannot throw yourself away trying to protect me. If you die and leave the rest of us behind, no matter the cause you died for, your death will have been in vain."

He searched her face for any sign that she understood, and for a moment, he hoped she might at least have glimpsed the weight of the moment.

Then she smiled. "I'll just skip on down to Daucourt's and get myself some dresses, then, shall I?"

He sat back on his heel, mouth tightening, but she wasn't done. "Or would it be the lumber trade you'd like me to put my hand to, until you pass on into the great beyond?"

"What—"

"We're buccaneers, captain. We are the Brethren of the Coast. We live and die by the sword and the gun, and our lives will never be peaceful or calm." She shook her head. "Would you even *want* them to be? We live on the edges, you've told me countless times before. We live on the verge, where a man or woman makes their own destiny, not living at the whims of some eejit born to his privilege rather than earning it."

He stood, looking down at her. "You've learned your lessons well, lass. Just not the ones I'd hoped."

She shrugged, settling back into her pillows. "Well, you were the school marm, Captain. If I learned the wrong lessons, perhaps you sent me to the wrong teachers."

He shook his head. He had said his peace. She had just awakened after too many days standing at death's gate. Hopefully, his words would find a purchase as she ruminated on them in the days and weeks ahead.

Or he'd have to have this conversation again. He wasn't willing to set that possibility aside, either.

"I should have sent you to someone to learn prudence. Or at the very least, respect."

Her smile got wider, and she looked like her old self for the first time since opening her eyes. "Well, I don't know about respect, but I'm sure Nadine would have had a few things to say to a young girl concerning prudence, at least."

There were times, blessedly few and far between since she had grown, that he still felt like he wanted to reach out and cuff the girl.

She grinned through a fall of tussled brown hair, as she often did in such moments, and the urge faded away.

Mostly.

*****

He went downstairs and was surprised to find the entire common room packed with what seemed like the entire crew of the *Bonnie Kate* and a hefty contingent from the other ships as well. Word of her awakening must have rushed through the streets and down to the harbor like a tropical flash flood. He even saw a few *Jaguar*s and *Arbiter*s looking up at him as he came to the top of the stairs.

He searched the crowd for one face in particular and crooked a finger at him when he noticed the man hovering just at the bottom step.

Aidan Allen hardly attempted to maintain a dignified pace as he lurched toward him, his hat clenched in his hands. Behind him Aston Hunt followed as if he was the master of the house.

Maguire smiled and made no fuss as the two men passed him, and he gestured toward the small room at the end of the hall.

"She's still weak; don't let her usual bad attitude fool you." He stopped them outside the door. "We're going to go in, you're going to assure her that you're both alive and well, and that the world has not ended while she was away from us, and then you're going to have to take your leave, no matter what she says or does."

Aidan tried to maintain a serious face, nodding at the instructions, but the madman the crew called the Priest pushed past him with a shrug and entered the room first.

By the time Maguire had followed, Aston Hunt was standing by her bedside, holding the small vial of seawater he wore around his neck over her, sprinkling her with the fluid.

"The lord of the waves is not done with you yet, girl!" Maguire was always surprised how powerful the man's voice could get when he was acting out his role as priest of Poseidon.

He stopped himself. Aidan had informed him, weeks ago, that the man had given himself a promotion after coming to the realization that he was the only priest of Poseidon left in the world.

Shanae was being blessed by a high priest. *The* high priest, in fact.

He smiled.

Aidan Allen was standing at the foot of the bed staring at her, a glazed, silly grin on his face that made him look far more the fool than the actual fool was looking, going on and on with his blessings from the Master of the Waters.

Maguire looked down at Shanae and then up at Allen again. She was smiling at the two men, laughing as Hunt's benediction grew more and more grandiose.

He wondered, not for the first time, how she could miss the adoration the crew felt for her. She saw it as just the fondness of fellows-in-arms, he knew. But looking again at Aidan Allen, and even Hunt, he knew it to be so much more.

When the time came, whether she wanted to face it now or not, she might not be ready, but the crew would be.

He needed to be satisfied with that, for now.

Chapter 15
1674 ~ The Lazy Dog, Cayona

"Make way, Boothe!" He jerked out of his dark reverie and looked up to see an arc of faces looking down at him, half-hidden in the murky darkness of the Lazy Dog.

Boothe had been working diligently through the tavern's poor wine selection in a dark mood for so long he had lost track of the time. He had come in thinking to go up and see the girl, Shanae, but his courage had failed him at the foot of the stairs. He had shifted course to an abandoned corner of the dais behind the quarterdeck rail, called to Nadine for his drink, paid her enough to ensure a steady resupply. He had not moved since.

He had thought, for a moment, of bringing Zachariah Rees with him. His quartermaster's icy glare and caustic observations would have made the time pass more quickly.

But he hadn't come up the hill to make time pass quickly. And had he followed his intended course; the quartermaster of the *Arbiter* would not have been a fitting companion for the final leg of his journey.

He glanced out one of the cloudy, narrow windows. There was no light outside, and he had left the *Arbiter* just after six bells in the afternoon watch. He frowned down into his cup.

He had been lost in thought in this fetid darkness for over three hours.

He looked up again as one of the figures around the table cleared its throat.

"We mean to sit, Boothe. If you want to be alone, about a hundred yards due west into the jungle will see that out a treat."

He recognized the voice, now that he was focusing on it.

"Sylvestre." The quartermaster of the *Bonnie Kate* was glaring down at him, but he didn't much care. "And who else have you brought with you?" He looked owlishly at the others. The old sailing master from the *Kate*, Ruiz, stood at his quartermaster's shoulder, the priggish Spaniard's distaste clear from the twist of his lips. The Amazonian quartermaster of the *Syren*, Renata Villa, stood with her massive hands on her hips, the tavern's lanterns gleaming off her shaven pate. And beside her stood a vision so ludicrously opposed to the big escaped slave girl's that it might have been part of a traveling show; the short blonde who served the *Syren* as its master gunner, stalky and belligerent at the best of times. What was her name? Beauvais?

The muscle-bound form of Cassius Black, one of the best gunners in the squadron and a vocal member of the *Chainbreaker's* crew, stood at the far left of the little group, his golden eyes inscrutable. And at the far end of the arc stood Cesar Japon, *Laughing Jacques'* quartermaster. Boothe had always thought the man had put too much effort into projecting a contrasting image to his jovial captain, but staring up into the long, cynical face, maybe he came by his pessimism honestly.

"Can I help you all?" He found speaking a little harder than perhaps it should have been and spared a moment to wonder exactly how much damage he had done to Severin Serre's pathetic wine cellar.

The group settled into chairs around the table, Black reaching back to pull one from nearby.

The place had been subdued ever since the squadron's return from Bonaire. Whether that was due to the buccaneers' lack of coin or their damaged morale, he didn't know.

Of course, if it was due to lack of coin, it would wrap in their morale soon enough.

"We want to know what the Commodore's next move is supposed to be." Sylvestre seemed to have been chosen as the group's mouthpiece.

"I don't know shit."

That seemed to catch Mathias Sylvestre and his little cadre of masters off-guard.

"What do you mean, *you* don't know shit?" Black's voice was a dangerous rumble as he leaned in over the table. "You're the flagship's first mate."

Boothe laughed. He didn't like the bitterness he detected there, but he was beyond caring enough to hide it. "Commodore Hart has more important people to spend his time with than me, I'm afraid. Perhaps you all could call on the man himself? He might be on the ship, but you've a better chance of finding him at the governor's manse. D'Ogeron is a lively conversationalist. Or you might want to talk to Greene. Captain Greene has the Commodore's ear these days, I find. They'll be able to answer your questions." He glared at each of them. "As for me? I don't know shit."

He looked down into his empty cup, and the lack of wine felt suddenly more tragic than it might have seemed a short while ago.

"We don't want to talk to Greene, we want to talk to you." The man's dark skin had somehow gotten even darker. "This isn't something the captains need to hear right now."

He didn't try to hide the snort of disgusted amusement that bolted through him at the words.

"How stand things on the *Arbiter*, Boothe? What's the spirit of the crew?" Renata Villa adjusted her long legs beneath the table, the clatter of her tribal jewelry a strange counterpoint in the subdued room. "We're serious. Something needs to be done; if not by the Commodore, then we might have to take it into our hands."

He blinked at her, then around at the others. "What are you talking about?"

Japon spat into the rushes on the floor. "How long have you been this drunk? We refer to nothing short of the fate of the squadron."

"There are rumblings of calls of no confidence." Beauvais, the little gunner, dropped a double fistful of tankards onto the table after a brief journey to the bar. "They're angry, Boothe. The crews are furious, and they blame the Commodore."

"Maguire and Semprun passed their full shares on to their crews. They even took gold from Chartier's." Sylvestre shrugged, looking over at Black and Japon. "I think Hamidi and Houdin did similar?"

The big gunner nodded, while Japon stroked his dark goatee with a shrug. "Captain Houdin was generous as well, yes."

Boothe tried to make sense of what they were saying. He had heard many of the captains had not taken their shares from the Bonaire venture, passing on to their crews what meager gold had remained after repairing and refitting the ships.

But pulling from their accounts with Chartier's? Why would anyone do that?

"And even with all that, the crews are restless." Sylvestre put down his tankard and wiped the back of his hand across his mouth. "Times have been lean, Boothe. You know as well as the rest of us. The Bonaire action was supposed to conjure up a bit of the old days."

"To hell with that, it was supposed to bring things back exactly to where we once were!" Beauvais slapped her small hand on the table.

"*Better* than they were!" Ruiz growled. The sailing master was easily the oldest buccaneer at the table. "Few of you remember the times you think of now as golden here on Tortuga. Even then, this was no paradise. Competing captains, competing crews, governors flitting though so quickly you could hardly keep track. Possession of the island changed on nearly a daily basis. That was our reality before the scattering of the Brethren."

"But it was better than the pea soup we have now." Japon finished for his fellow Spaniard.

Ruiz nodded. "It was. And better still would have been making Tortuga a pirate kingdom in its own right with the treasures of Bonaire."

Boothe shook his head to clear it, but they wouldn't leave off.

"Captains may lose their ships over this." Sylvestre, again. "The crews have had enough. They went south believing they were working toward a better day. The outcome, and what followed, have them wondering why they would continue to follow the captains."

"And the Commodore." Cassius Black growled.

"We have already lost many men to the lumber trade." Japon took another sip of his drink. "I know *Chainbreaker* has suffered similar losses." He looked to Sylvestre and Renata Villa. "What about you two?"

Villa shook her bald head. "None of the *Syren*s has taken to the shore yet, but fewer women join the trade as it is."

"No one from the *Kate* has gone inland either, as far as I know." Sylvestre tactfully left out how Maguire and Semprun had paid out of their own private accounts to keep their people happy.

Boothe wondered how much longer either would be able to do that.

"I don't know what you want me to do about this." He waved vaguely toward the waterfront down the hill, and then toward the governor's manse, somewhere behind the tavern. "I truly don't."

It was so unfair. He had fought the Commodore every step of the way on this, and now *he* was the one who would have to defend it?

If Shanae Bure had made it back to the island on her own two feet, he would be dealing with *her* right now, he had no doubt. But Shanae would have had little trouble keeping her own crew in check.

That made him wonder about the *Arbiter* and the *Jaguar*. Were they shedding crew as well? He knew damn well that neither Hart nor Fowler had foregone their own shares in the pathetic bootie from Kralendijk. If the men and women from the smaller ships were abandoning the buccaneer path, what must it be like on the galleon or the frigate, below decks?

"Does the Commodore have a plan?" Beauvais leaned toward him, rising out of her chair to extend her reach. "You have to give us something to offer the crews, to give them some hope that this isn't the end."

Villa nodded her bald head. "If he doesn't have a plan to preserve the squadron, it will dissolve before the end of winter."

The ships wouldn't have been heading out into the open sea now anyway, he reminded himself. Winter was no time for reaving, no matter how desperate the buccaneers were to fill their purses or their gullets.

But winter was also the time when the men and women found other opportunities more enticing. Each spring there were fewer men and women willing to take to the water. There were always those who headed inland to the lumber trade or settled around the harbor employing the skills and trades they learned at sea in a safer, more stable environment.

He had no doubt this lot of malcontents was correct. If Hart had no plan to recoup his loses on Bonaire, those numbers were going to go so high, they might not recover.

And that didn't address the fact that some of the crews might elect totally new captains and officers, and those men and women might take it upon themselves to strike out on their own, winter or no, with no regard toward the alliances and bonds Hart had spent years building.

He shook his head again. "Honestly, I don't know."

Hell, he wanted to spit; none of them were supposed to know about any of this. The plan to basically buy the island from d'Ogeron with the spoils from Kralendijk was no closely-held secret, but it wasn't something he or Hart would have discussed openly.

And since they're return, following the disaster at Bonaire, he had felt utterly abandoned by the Commodore. He understood there were many fires that needed putting out, regarding the governor and the merchants and vendors of the harbor and the squadron's precarious financial state. But whereas he would have been working with the man on such situations in the past, he was more often relegated to overseeing the day-to-day running of the galleon while Hart worked on these other concerns ashore, oftentimes with Captain Greene in attendance.

And there was not much work to the day-to-day running of the *Ultimo Arbiter*.

"Boothe, we need something to bring to our people." Villa was looking at him with more concern than anger, now, and he found that oddly more troubling.

"If not tonight, then soon." Ruiz, on the other hand, obviously had little sympathy for the first mate of the *Arbiter*. "We'll continue to lose people as the winter deepens, and if there's no hope to offer, we'll lose ships next."

He wondered who they thought they would lose first. He knew the *Bonnie Kate* would never go, not so long as Maguire was alive. And he doubted Semprun would allow her ship to be taken out from beneath her, and she would never abandon Maguire.

He doubted *Chainbreaker* would run. Where would she run to? Hamidi was a proud man; as proud as only an escaped slave can be. But a ship full of such men? There would not be many friendly ports open to her. He might be bold and brave on Tortuga, but there were times, when he wasn't feeling particularly charitable, that Boothe wondered if Hamidi and his crew had any options at all, should the little island become untenable.

Houdin and the *Laughing Jacques* were another matter entirely, of course. As the fortunes of the French in the West Indies waxed and waned, there would be more or fewer friendly ports for a French ship, but the *Jacques* wasn't a French ship, not really. She was more in the mold of the *Kate* or the *Jaguar*. Mongrel crews devoted more to the Brethren than to any other allegiance.

The *Jaguar*. Fowler was a vicious commander, pushing discipline to the very edge of buccaneer tolerance. And he was tightfisted with the booty, as this recent business with Bonaire had shown.

Might they lose their frigate over this mess? The most powerful ship in the squadron, second only to the *Arbiter* herself?

If the *Arbiter* could even leave her moorings.

"I'll see what I can find." He muttered the words, cursing the drink he had taken onboard. Sober, he probably would have been able to extricate himself from this ridiculous conversation long ago.

Sylvestre nodded, as did most of the others, save Japon, who just continued to glare. "That will have to be good enough, for now. But if the captains have to get involved, this might not just mark them."

"We may be seeing a new Commodore, before all this is over." Japon's glare deepened.

Boothe forced himself to nod, then leaned back with exaggerated relaxation in his chair.

He ignored as it creaked ominously.

"And what brought you lot up the hill, other than this little tongue-wagging session? Any other scuttlebutt you'd care to pass along?"

They all straightened as if recalled to more important duties.

"We came up to look in on Shanae." Sylvestre looked around at the others. "And I think we should continue on upstairs, now that we've said our piece."

They rose as if they had drilled the maneuver all afternoon, moving in a tight group toward the stairs.

"You're welcome to join us, First Mate Boothe." Renata Villa's tone was kindly, at odds with her earlier tone.

When Boothe had trudged up the half-cobbled hill to the Lazy Dog it had been with just that purpose in mind. But as he looked from the other mates up the stairs and back, he felt his earlier reticence dig in even deeper.

He wasn't afraid of Shanae; not at all. But for some reason, the thought of seeing her laid up, head wrapped in bandages and still recovering from her wound and the subsequent illness that had struck her down was enough to freeze his limbs.

"No, thank you." He settled back into his chair, lifting his cup to find it disappointingly empty. "You go on ahead. I'll stop by another time. The room will be overcrowded as it is, with all you lot shoved in."

They moved upstairs, Villa giving one last, appraising look over her towering shoulder, and they were gone.

He watched them disappear around the corner upstairs and then sighed.

He would have liked to join them, he realized. He would very much like to see Shanae again. To speak with her, perhaps alone, without all these others about.

But still, somehow, he knew he wouldn't.

With a sign he signaled to Nadine for another bottle. The girl nodded to him, with a quick glance up at the windows to Serre's office up behind him, on the faux quarterdeck, and she nodded again. He sat back, closing his eyes. He knew the publican would keep the wine flowing. Not everyone was losing faith with the Commodore.

Not yet, anyway.

Was it possible the squadron could be so frail a thing? One bad action and they might shatter like poorly tempered steel?

But it wasn't just that one action, was it? He couldn't fool himself. Not like this. The Commodore had forestalled their shifting to Port Royal for years with the hope of something more on Tortuga. And no matter how they had tried to keep it under seal, enough of the buccaneers in the squadron had known that Kralendijk had become the lynchpin of that hope.

The disaster that had struck them there, between the cursedly efficient Dutch and the squadron's fear of the *Beschermer,* had put an end to that plan. Even he, privy to most of Hart's intentions and machinations, was not entirely sure what might come next.

All he was sure of now was that there would be no improvement in their current situation. Tortuga would continue to be a safe haven for them, but hardly a prosperous one.

Their hopes of creating something wonderful here would be put off yet again, if they had not been entirely lost.

Maybe Maguire had been right all along. Maybe focusing on building up their status locally, filling their coffers and heading for Jamaica, would have made all the difference by now.

Hell, they might even have been able to do that with the booty from Kralendijk.

If there had been booty from Kralendijk.

He sighed, nodded his thanks to Nadine for the new bottle, and leaned over the cup as he poured, so as not to lose any in the transfer.

Tortuga was home, and it would continue to be home, whether that was for the best or not, for the foreseeable future.

He took a sip and stifled a cough.

He thought again of Rees with a sour twist to his lips.

He wondered if the wine was any better in Port Royal.

Chapter 16
1674 / 1675- The Lazy Dog, Cayona

He ignored the shouts and screams. His ears rang, but none of it could penetrate to the unsettled core of ice in his chest.

Aidan waved away the beckoning hands, smiling at Nadine as she sashayed through the bustling mob, sparing him a moment's warm grin.

He ignored the hopeful gleam in her eye. He hadn't been by to spend time with her in so long he might have forgotten how long it had been.

Except he knew.

Since he had returned from Bonaire.

A lot had become clear to him, running south with the Squadron and then fleeing back to Tortuga again after their questionable victory.

He was still working a lot of those things out in his mind, but of all of them, he was most clear on the thoughts regarding his once rakish attitudes.

He didn't know what to make of it. His casual approach to the temporary pairings that marked most of the crews' relationships had never seemed wrong to him, or something to be ashamed or proud of. Men and women shared time together, sometimes a long time, sometimes more brief encounters. He had certainly never wanted for companionship.

But ever since Bonaire, he had had no time for any of that.

He knew this was not a common reaction to the events down south. If anything, the squadron was even more fevered than before, as the buccaneers struggled with their grief and fear in a time-honored tradition that celebrated life and denied the sway of death.

For him, however, there always seemed to be something more pressing to see to.

Isabella had been the first to note it, but as any healthy pirate woman, she had laughed at his reticence and sought solace elsewhere, bearing no grudge, he hoped, as she went.

He moved toward the stairs, not looking too closely at the revelers as he passed.

He wasn't really interested in the celebration, but if the right people summoned him, he'd be hard pressed to brush them off as readily as he had Nadine.

He just wanted to get upstairs.

As he came to the foot of the staircase a glimpse of movement above caught his eye and he looked over. The windows that looked out over the room from Severin Serre's sculpted quarterdeck office was partly open, and he saw the owner of the establishment standing there as if he often did.

But this time he was looking over at Aidan, and when their eyes met, he nodded knowingly, as if he had seen into the gunner's mind, into the chaos of his thoughts, and understood.

Aidan smiled awkwardly, hoping fervently that the old man didn't possess such powers, and with a shallow nod, took the stairs two at a time, moving above the warm, humid fug of the common room and breathing a silent prayer of thanks as he escaped all of the eyes, and the volume dropped to less-painful levels.

He stopped at Shanae's door for a moment when he heard muffled voices from within, but before he could hear anything, or be tempted to listen, he knocked.

Shanae's response was muted but unmistakable, and he pushed the door open, slipped inside, and eased it closed as quickly as possible, not wanting any more noise than necessary to invade her quiet sanctum.

Only days after she had awakened on this very bed, she had succumbed to a terrible fever that had him and the entire crew of the *Kate* worried all over again. Old Maia Burton had tried to assure them it was nothing, just a passing malaise, but after having come so close to losing her already, there wasn't a man or woman aboard that was willing to take any chances.

Burton had stayed by Shanae's bedside day and night, as had Aston Hunt. That madman had muttered prayers to the Lord of the Sea, sunshine and rain, for over a week, until the fever had finally broken, and their first mate was fit to smile once again.

There was a great deal of speculation below decks on the *Kate*, whether Burton or the priest had had more to do with her recovery.

But Shanae was still weak. Between her wound and the fever, her body had been ravaged. She was barely a ghost of her former self. Her breath would grow short at odd moments, and her strength could flee at any time.

It made visiting her both a relief and a trial, as she seemed to refuse to get better as fast as any of them might wish.

Aidan was unsurprised to see that it was Hunt sitting at Shanae's bedside, the little bottle of sea water clutched in one hand.

The man turned his unsettling green eyes toward the master gunner, lips twitching into something that might generously be considered a smile within the nest of tangled black hair. His tall frame was folded uncomfortably onto a small stool, leaving the two chairs that had been carried up from the hall below empty in the far corners.

"Aidan." Her voice wasn't a whisper, exactly, but it still lacked the strength he even now expected, each time he visited her. "Took your own sweet time, I see."

He tried to summon a smile, but it was harder and harder as her convalescence dragged on. Burton had tried to assure him she was on the mend, but it was too easy to see something more ominous in her short breaths and tired eyes.

"It's New Year's Eve, darlin'." He put more effort into the smile. "A man's got a lot of claims on his time, bidding adieu to the old and ringing in the new, and all."

Even as he said it, a distant swelling of sound from below marked a high point in the night's revelries.

She nodded, her head rolling to the side to look back at Hunt. "I keep telling Aston to go down and spend a little time with the others, but he won't leave."

Hunt looked offended. "Abandon my Lord's chosen champion in her hour of need? Never!" He struck a dramatic pose that would have done the stage of a London theater proud, despite the awkwardness of his crouched position.

She smiled, and Aidan nodded to himself.

That was just the kind of odd display she had always tolerated better than him.

He pulled one of the chairs across the room and to the side of the bed opposite the lunatic. "I wanted to see how you were faring before I dove into my cups for the night."

He tried to sound casual and amused. To his own ears, he failed.

"I heard you haven't been drinking nearly your fair share, lately, among other things." She teased him, looking up from beneath the fall of her shining dark hair. "You've not gone serious on us in your old age, have you?"

That was a little disconcerting. Who had been talking about him with her? And who had noticed that, along with his lack of romantic interest, he had taken to drinking water and small beer far more often than wine or rum or any of the other spirits the squadron had acquired in its adventures?

Then he shifted his gaze to Hunt, who squirmed a bit, turning to look out the window as if something very interesting had caught his attention out in the darkness of the tropical night.

"It wasn't just him." She reached out and brushed his hand with her own. He almost jerked back from the contact.

"Well, not that it's anyone's concern, but I've been kept quite busy of late. Without you around, the captain's been leaning very heavily upon me."

Hunt scoffed. "Leaning on Sylvestre, you mean? Or perhaps you meant Ruiz? Or Isabella? I haven't noticed him being particularly concerned with your whereabouts."

Aidan wanted to slap the man, but knew better, especially in front of Shanae, invalid or no.

The work he had been doing for Captain Maguire had been sensitive. The ice behind his heart gave another lurch.

He wanted to tell Shanae.

He probably would have, if the priest hadn't pricked his honor.

He almost certainly would have, if the man hadn't been there at all.

And so, in a way, he owed a grudging thanks to the man. He had no interest in breaking trust with the captain.

He looked away, then noticed that Shanae was staring at him. He shifted in his chair, forcing himself to smile.

A slight line appeared between her eyes; the one that came when she was thinking heavily about something.

It felt as if she were looking directly into his mind.

Had he become that transparent? Could just anyone see his thoughts, now?

Her face darkened, and she opened her mouth to ask him the question he had dreaded since deciding to come straight here from his last meeting with the captain.

He panicked. He wanted to run, to flee before she could ask him. He opened his mouth to forestall her, when the door crashed open. Sefu Barasa, the short, stocky quartermaster of the *Chainbreaker* came rushing in as if taking a prize in open battle, a small crowd of the squadron's middling high and mighty rushing in behind him. All of them were laughing, flushed with drink and none-too-steady on their feet.

Mathias Sylvestre and Martin Ruiz at least had the presence of mind to look embarrassed to be involved in such an assault, while Axel Perry, the *Kate's* young boatswain, looked as if he could not have said where he was at all. The vicious little blonde gunner from the *Syren*, Corine Beauvais, had an impish grin on her thin lips as if she had caught someone doing something wicked. A lanky man he didn't recognize stood near the back of the group, a look of placid happiness overlaying glazing hazel eyes and stubbled cheeks despite the livid scar that ran diagonally down over his nose, from right to left.

Behind them all, looming darkly like an accompanying spirit none of them could see, was Boothe, the first mate of the *Arbiter*.

Boothe looked out of place in his finery, but even more so because of his clear eyes and distant demeanor.

The man gazed around the room, taking in the sparse decorations, the tall mooncalf crouching in the far shadows, and Aidan's own form, sitting up in the chair opposite.

"Eight bells in the first watch comes fast upon us, First Mate Bure!" Barasa glared down at Shanae, swaying slightly. "You can't expect we should let such a significant moment slip you by without comment!"

Corine Beauvais nodded vigorously. "Damned straight. You shouldn't have lived to see 1675, girl. We'll certainly be celebrating you scarpering out on the Grim Reaper, and you'll be doing it with us!"

Already, from beyond the darkened window, Aidan could hear the distant popping of small arms, swivel guns, and even the booms of light cannons. There would probably be the whistle-pop of rockets, too, as midnight approached.

He looked at Shanae, wondering if this was too much for her. But she was grinning broadly, blue eyes shining bright, and he sighed.

"You need a full glass, lass!" Barasa looked around as if there might be one floating somewhere around his head, then laughed at his inadvertent poetry. "Glass, lass!"

The others laughed with varied levels of enthusiasm, as the man with the close-cropped brown hair and the horrid scar passed forward a gem-encrusted goblet that looked almost as out of place in the shabby little flat as Boothe did, still haunting the back of the group.

"There she be!" Barasa grabbed the cup. "Fit for a princess, no?" He brandished it like a cutlass before bringing it back toward him, glowering down into its empty hollow like a child. "Where'sa rum?"

With a look that seemed almost apologetic, Sylvestre handed a small clay jug over to the dark-skinned quartermaster.

"Mistress Burton said one glass wouldn't go amiss, ma'am."

Shanae laughed. "It's okay, Mathias. And you need not be so prim, tonight of all nights?"

The man tried to conjure up an answering smile, but Aidan, for one, didn't think it was overly effective.

They provided Aidan and Hunt with wooden cups of their own, filled from the same jug.

Barasa handed Shanae the goblet with exaggerated care.

"To the squadron!" He bellowed, hoisting his own cup with far more vigor once she had taken the other.

"To a better year than 1674!" Someone in the back shouted, but Aidan couldn't have said who.

"Bugger 1674." Corine spat on the floor.

"And good riddance to ya." That was Perry, his young face twisted in bitterness.

The mood of the little group darkened at that, but then Barasa roared again. "No! Tonight is a night of hope! We look forward, tonight, to the realization of all our hopes and dreams, and the rising of tomorrow's sun on a kinder, more just world!"

The scarred man snorted. "It strikes me the likes of us best not be praying for a just world, Sefu. In a just world, we'd all be dancing the hemp-en jig. We're pirates, remember?"

Barasa made a sound that would have done a broaching whale proud. "In a just world, we each take and keep what we can, and the devil takes the hindmost!"

That cheered them, and nearly as much drink made it down their throats as got splashed across the old wooden floor.

Aidan wished he could join them.

But they didn't know what he knew.

*****

By the time the riotous mob left, Shanae seemed to have truly forgotten the course of her thoughts.

Aidan breathed a silent prayer of thanks but kept his face under rigid discipline.

Given half a chance, she would find the scent again, and he would be lost.

Hunt had gone with the others when they retreated back down to the common room to gather up fresh supplies. They were alone, and he found that more disconcerting than he had expected.

He tried to watch her without seeming to watch her. Her eyes were drooping with exhaustion, and he knew a pang of guilt. He should really leave her alone so that she could sleep and continue to gather her strength.

But he couldn't bring himself to say it, for fear she would agree.

She seemed to feel his gaze and looked up, teeth flashing in a thin smile.

The room seemed to brighten painfully.

"Something on your mind, gunner?"

And with that, all of a sudden, there seemed to be nothing on his mind at all. Or in his mind, for that matter.

He stammered a reply, looking away. He wasn't even entirely sure what he said, only that he needed to distract her from the electric moment he had felt when their eyes met.

He shrugged, pushing his chair away from the bed. A hundred reasons he needed to rush back to the ship came thundering into his mind at once.

None of them made any sense, a bell into the new year, but he was doing the best he could.

There was a more subdued knock at the door and with a glance to heaven he launched himself out of the chair.

"I'll get it."

He hadn't even gotten the words out before Shanae had finished, "Enter!"

Captain Maguire eased the door open, and the ice in Aidan's chest shifted yet again.

Whether the captain was here to relieve him of his burden or be sure he still carried it, he didn't know.

"Ah, good. You're awake." He went directly to Aidan's chair and sat own, giving the master gunner only the slightest nod of acknowledgement in passing.

"Happy New Year, Captain." She smiled up at him, an almost imperceptible tension in her bearing.

"I trust the crew has taken it easy on you?" He took her hand with a smile and gave Aidan a mock-serious glare. "We need you in fighting trim as soon as can be."

"Never, sir." She patted his hand with her free one. "I'll be ready when you need me."

Aidan went around the bed, looked at the stool Hunt had been perched on, and then turned to draw the other chair closer. He kept his gaze away from the first mate, not trusting his own face.

But he saw the answering discomfort in Captain Maguire's expression, and felt that maybe, just maybe, this fresh new hell would be over soon.

The captain cleared his throat. "That is something we should discuss." He looked directly at Aidan, eyes tightening as if trying to read him, then turned back to Shanae. "It looks as if we're going to be heading out sooner than we anticipated."

Aidan didn't even try to mask his relieved sigh.

Shanae's brows lowered dangerously. "What does that mean? Raiding season's over. You're surely not going to be taking some of the ships out *now*?"

The weather had been mild, for winter, with only a single bad storm so far lashing the islands with its fury. But there was no telling how long the calm would last. And most of the Brethren were of the opinion that a mild start to winter could only presage the season's striking with a vengeance later.

"Well, we're not taking *some* of the ships out." Aidan started at that, looking at the captain in wonder and a building sense of relief.

"We're taking them all out."

And there it was.

"When?" A dark suspicion began to dawn in the woman's eyes.

Maguire looked away but continued speaking. "It's been decided that we can't wait. We'll be leaving tomorrow. The crews should have recovered from the night's celebrations by the noon tide."

"Tomorrow." The word was flat as she pushed it through her gritted teeth.

Maguire looked back at her. "It could be exactly what we need to make up for the Bonaire raid." If Aidan hadn't known better, he would think the captain was nervous about Shanae's reaction.

"*Who* decided?" Her face had tightened, her eyes were narrow, dangerous slits.

"What?" Maguire's words faltered, as if he had lost the thread of the conversation.

"You said 'it has been decided'. *Who* decided?"

The captain waved that away. "Everyone. The captains in council. Commodore Hart—"

"Greene?" She spat the word, and Maguire slumped back into his seat.

"The information did come from Greene, yes. But the captains agreed—"

"Kralendijk came from Greene, too." It wasn't an accusation, exactly, but Maguire recoiled from the words all the same.

"The others believe this is different." His voice took on a pleading tone. Aidan knew the captain had agitated against the attack. He had been furious upon returning to the *Kate* from the galleon. He wondered why the man wasn't telling Shanae any of that.

"Different how?" Shanae's voice was low and dangerous.

"It's a treasure ship, Shanae. A Spanish treasure ship. It's the fecking Holy Grail, and with its scent in their nostrils, there's no turning the captains away." The captain's shoulders had slumped in defeat.

"A treasure ship. How does *Greene* know anything about a treasure ship?"

"It was spotted by a sloop out of Port Royal. She must have been cut away from their fleet in the storm last week. She was damaged, listing badly, but still had enough fight left in her to see the sloop off."

"And why haven't the Port Royal Brethren seen to her?" The suspicion in Shanae's voice was like a physical chill sweeping through the room.

The captain lifted his chin. "There's no single captain in Jamaica capable of commanding a force big enough to threaten a galleon. They're trying, but they're fighting over everything from which ships can go to who will be in command."

"Greene says." She spat.

The captain nodded; eyes unwavering. "Greene says."

"Tomorrow." This time, she almost whispered the word.

Aidan had enjoyed the growing confidence the captain had shared with him during Shanae's recovery, but suddenly he felt like nothing so much as an intruder peering in on an intimate family argument.

"Tomorrow." Maguire agreed.

Shanae lurched forward in the bed, trying to push herself up.

Aidan bent toward her, hands outstretched, as if he could stop her or support her despite the distance separating them.

"What are you doing?" Maguire was much closer, and instantly at her side, trying to ease her back onto the bed.

"I'm going with you, of course." She muttered, trying to shake off his hands.

"You most certainly are not." He pressed her back down, gently. "You're in no condition to leave that bed."

"I'm going with you." She repeated the words as if she hadn't heard him.

"Shanae, you're in no condition for a fight right now." He straightened, his eyes pleading. "I'm going to need you in top form when we come back. Success or failure, nothing is going to be the same for the squadron after this."

That was true enough, but seemed to carry little weight with Shanae, who tried to rise again.

The captain's tone hardened as he straightened, looming over the woman.

"You're in no fit state to serve aboard a vessel in hot action, Shanae. You would be more of a hindrance than a help, and I can't take that chance."

Aidan felt himself shying away from the words, and they hadn't even been directed at him. He turned to look at Shanae, who had recoiled as if slapped.

Tears of rage shined, unshed, in her eyes. But the truth of his brutal, blunt words seemed to have reached her where his gentler pleadings had not.

She nodded, but she didn't say anything, her lips pressed into a hard, angry line.

Captain Maguire nodded, clutching his hat in both hands.

"Be well, Shanae. I will need you when we return."

She didn't respond, and as Maguire left, nodding silently to Aidan as he went, she glarred daggers at the man's back, and then at the door after he eased it closed.

Aidan stared at her as intently as he would watch a powder keg on a burning deck.

The tears were there, but she refused to let them fall. Her gaze shifted, at last, from the door to him, and the expression did not alter one bit.

"You knew."

He opened his mouth to reply but then closed it again.

He had known. There was no other response he could make.

He just nodded.

He would have sworn her eyes could not have darkened further, and he would have been wrong.

The door burst open once more and Hunt came stumbling in, a glorious smile on his empty face.

The lunatic stopped at seeing their expressions, though. The smile faltered but didn't fade completely.

"Have you not heard? We shall bring the Lord's vengeance down upon the despicable dons!"

Aidan looked at Shanae out of the corner of his eyes. Her face had darkened dangerously.

Then the Priest's smile faded.

He looked from Aidan to the bedridden woman and back.

"What has transpired here?"

Shanae looked away, every muscle of her face and neck taut.

Hunt took another step into the room. "What is it?"

Aidan approached him; one hand raised in a mollifying gesture. "The first mate needs some sleep, Hunt. We can come back tomorrow—"

At the word she jerked as if he had slapped her, and Hunt pulled away.

"Tomorrow? There is no tomorrow for us here." He seemed confused, but his excitement began to bubble up again in his voice. "Tomorrow we leave for—"

Again, Shanae flinched.

Hunt's words stumbled to a halt.

"You're not coming?" He sounded like a lost child, and Aidan wanted to slap him.

Shanae shook her head, still not turning toward them.

"She's not fully recovered, Hunt." Aidan took the man by the shoulder and tried to steer him toward the door. "You know she's not well enough to sail, yet."

"No." Aidan stepped back, feeling the madman's body tense beneath his hand.

With a strength he wouldn't have expected, Hunt repeated the word like the snap of a pistol.

"No."

That brought Shanae's head around, and she stared at the priest with an expression that did a fair job of combining furious anger and surprised confusion.

"You cannot be left behind on land as we seek vengeance against the foe." Hunt was shaking his head violently back and forth. "You cannot be left behind. You must be aboard. You must be with us." He was snarling.

"No."

Without another word, the man spun on his heel and lurched from the room.

Aidan stood there, staring out the open door for several heartbeats before looking back to Shanae on the bed. She looked up at him, much of her anger submerged behind the rising tide of her confusion.

"What?"

Aidan shrugged, looking back to the door.

"He really wants you to go."

And with those words, her anger returned.

Aidan retreated, knowing there was nothing more he could have said to settle her rekindled fury.

He would be sure to see her tomorrow as he made his final sweep of the town for crew who missed the morning's muster. He would say his good-byes in the light of day.

Maybe her anger would have lost some of its heat by then.

He shook his head as he went down the stairs.

Sometimes it just didn't pay, trying to fool yourself.

Chapter 17
1675 – The Lazy Dog, Cayona

"It's your turn, girl."

Shanae nearly snarled at the word, then looked up from her distracted musing. She glanced back down at the cards arrayed before her, glared briefly at her hand, and then tossed it onto the table.

"I'm done." She pushed herself gently back, reached out for her tankard of small beer, and rose to a chorus of good-natured complaints.

"My eyes are starting to cross, trying to put tricks together. I've every right to abandon between games, as you well know." She reached into her pouch and dropped several coins onto the table. "You can fight over who gets to keep that."

She moved gingerly through the common room of the Lazy Dog toward the bar. The place was nearly empty save for a few members of the *Arbiter's* crew who had either elected to stay back with their ship or been selected by the Commodore.

Renee Boudot stood behind the bar, staring listlessly out a small side window at the lashing rain, not considered in the least with the possibility that Severin Serre might be watching from his quarterdeck offices.

Serre was just as likely to be staring out a window at the rain as well. With the entire squadron gone, there wasn't much for any of the stragglers to do.

The winter storms had struck only days after the squadron left on their foolish quest. It was as if Hunt's Poseidon had decided to punish them all for the Commodore's hubris.

"Nadine upstairs?" Shanae settled her elbow onto the bar and pushed her empty tankard across the polished wood.

She had become much closer with the serving girls since the squadron's departure. Andre the barman and Severin the owner were nice enough, but they seemed intimidated by her for some reason, and so were on their very best behavior whenever she was around. Severin, for his part, almost never ventured from his office these days.

It was enough to send her screaming back up to her room, and she wondered what had cowed the two men so. Had Captain Maguire been making threats on her behalf? Or Aidan, maybe?

But the girls were a different story; more than willing to treat with her as an equal.

And she hadn't yet been able to convince herself that any *Arbiter* left behind was truly worth her time and attention, besides.

"Feeling under-the-weather, poor lass." Renee was a decade older than Nadine or Shanae, but other than the gray in her faded red hair, it was hard to tell.

A crack of thunder shook the rickety walls, and Shanae grinned. "Well, we're all a bit under this weather, anyway."

She was trying to keep things light, but knew she was only meeting with slight success.

The squadron was more than a week overdue, giving them the most liberal timeline for success or failure.

She had begun to fret after the first couple of days, as her anger faded, replaced by growing concern.

Greene was a menace, his only action a dismal failure, and it was too soon to be throwing the entire squadron back into the fray.

Well, the entire squadron except for the *Ultimo Arbiter*, of course. Never her.

The crew the Commodore had left behind were growing agitated as well. Although the Lazy Dog was usually reserved for the mates and masters of the squadron and their guests, with each passing day the ships stayed away, the more common crew were appearing at the door and not being turned away.

Severin needed to make money somehow, after all. With most of his usual customers gone, he couldn't afford to be particular.

Winter's arrival, even in the usually-quiet Caribbean waters, meant, there had been precious few ships moving about, either, and those that had come into port down below had been tight-lipped about anything they might have seen out on the open seas.

She had done her best to ply the men and women who came in out of the roaring weather with drink and even coin, but you couldn't buy what wasn't there.

No one had seen hide nor hair of the squadron. There had even been a couple ships out of Port Royal who might have known Greene if she'd thought to ask. But as the days stretched on, she was less concerned with blame and more with the whereabouts of her friends.

The first week of her isolation had dragged, with only Nadine and Renee for company as they came up to bring her food or change her bandages. She had asked after those she knew had been left behind, but the serving girls knew little about the internecine politics of the squadron and paid almost no attention to the frictions of the moment.

She knew Myles Boothe had stayed behind, ostensibly to command the *Arbiter*. She hadn't seen him, though, and to the best of her knowledge he remained aboard the galleon, hardly coming out of the Commodore's cabin for days at a time.

Most of the galleon's gunners and best fighters had rounded out the crews of the smaller ships, leaving only a few behind. And those not the finest specimens of the sailor's craft.

She still didn't know if those who stayed had chosen their own fate or if they were out of favor with the Commodore. She had been playing lanterloo with them for over a week now, keeping her victories mild and far between to keep the talk flowing. But other than the usual bitter grumblings of *Arbiter*s left behind during an action, she had detected no unusual resentment.

Everyone wished they had been out with the others, to be on deck when the squadron claimed the most elusive prize of all: a Spanish treasure galleon.

But, oddly enough, Shanae had had no luck hearing any more about that ship, either, from the sailors and mates that came through.

No word of the Tortuga squadron; no word of a missing treasure ship. Her suspicion of Greene's lack of value grew with each day they didn't return.

But her concern grew as well, and that began to overshadow everything else.

She thought about going back up to the close confines of her little garret room and decided she couldn't face the isolation again so soon.

She had no interest in the card game, but she needed the company of Brethren.

Even if they were just *Arbiter*s.

"We'd have heard something if it went south." DeVillepin, the one master gunner of the galleon to stay behind was a broad man, with a long black queue laid down his spine and dramatic, pointed goatee. "I've faith the Commodore will bring them all back safely."

"I don't know, Teddy." Shanae was unfamiliar with Efrain Gallo, the *Arbiter's* newest boatswain, but she had quickly come to consider the man a coward. Considering the heat the squadron had been sailing into, she was just as glad he had been left behind.

"They should have been back long before now. What if that's it? What if they're not coming back?"

The words echoed her own worst fears, but she put a brave face on as she settled back into her recently surrendered chair. "With the heavy weather we've been getting, it's no wonder they're late."

Teddy DeVillepin nodded, his black tail bobbing. "They could have easily been blown a hundred miles north. They'll be beating back here even now, Efrain. Don't you fret. You'll get your lubber's shares."

If the fabled treasure ship held even a fraction of what they hoped, even a lubber's share of the spoils would be well worth the weeks of wrenching worry and uncertainty for most of them.

For her, the treasure was the least of her concerns.

"But what if you're wrong? How much longer are we going to sit around here waiting?"

Another *Arbiter* at the table, a common sailor named Sidney Day, nodded violently. "Boothe won't say, but we've got to be close to running out of food. Victualers ain't gonna be extending no credit to the old girl without the comfort of the squadron bobbing off their quays."

She sipped her beer and glanced at the men over the dull metal rim of her tankard. She wiped her lip with the back of her arm and then leaned forward, mindful of her weakened state.

"Just what would you be suggesting, Gallo? If we're alone now, that is."

DeVillepin shot her a look, but then glanced away as if he didn't want to catch her attention when she was focused on the young boatswain.

Probably a good idea.

The boy shook his head, unaware of the others pulling back from the table as if he'd just coughed up a plug of blood.

"We could sell the galleon. Ought to fetch us enough per man, we could get land somewhere else. Maybe Port Royal? Maybe somewhere else. Each to their own, as far as that's concerned, I say."

"If you're so anxious for your next meal, you could always head inland and pick up a saw."

The others laughed, but Gallo's chin rose a degree, and his eyes hardened.

"I could, at that. But I'd rather have some gold in my pockets and make a go of it somewhere else. Somewhere a little less French, if you don't mind my saying."

Judging from the boy's accent, he could have hailed from anywhere within a league of the East End of London, but not much farther.

"And who do you imagine would buy the *Arbiter*?" She leaned back, fascinated despite herself. She knew the others thought she was baiting the boy, but she found herself truly distracted for the first time in days, and that was worth its weight in gold.

The boatswain shrugged. "I don't know. Chartier's, maybe?"

Several of the older sailors laughed. "You're not going to get a counting house to take on that kind of burden." DeVillepin was looking at the boy with something like pity in his eyes.

"Won't be anyone willing to take on that kind of burden." That was muttered by another sailor at the far end of the table, a man named Sanz.

She wondered what, exactly, he meant by that. Why, if they were fantasizing about selling their ship; a ship that hardly belonged to any of them, truth be told, they weren't considering sailing it to a better market was beyond her.

If you sailed a galleon like the *Arbiter* into Port Royal with an eye toward selling her, you could be rich in a heartbeat.

Given that, they could sail anywhere they wanted and set themselves up as an independent buccaneering crew. With a ship like that? There was hardly a shipping concern in the New World that might hope to stand up to a galleon in fighting form.

But then, she wasn't in fighting form, was she.

Shanae knew next to nothing about the *Arbiter*, other than the fact that she hardly ever moved, other than shifting anchorage occasionally. And she hadn't even done that in years.

She mused on the many possible reasons for this as the game played out before her. Hand after hand cycled through. Occasionally the men would look to see if she wanted to be dealt back in, she would shake her head with a smile, and they would go back to trying to steal each other's money.

The many mysteries of the *Ultimo Arbiter* had hovered over the squadron for years; far longer than she had been alive, she gathered. And she had to admit she found the whole affair less interesting than maybe she should.

But as had been the case for weeks now, nothing could distract her for long from worrying about the *Kate* and the other ships.

What if they were lost? What if she had seen Maguire and Aidan and the others for the last time?

She had no massive ship to sell; buyers or no.

If she was now, for the first time since she was a child, on her own, what might that look like?

She loved the open sea. She loved the feeling of a solid ship beneath her bare feet and the roar of the guns as the trusted men and women around her sailed, all together, into the very teeth of hell.

She loved the life of the Brethren, where you survived on your abilities, your allies, and your native wits.

She wasn't at all sure, however, that she would want to continue on that path without the men and women she had shared that life with.

She rose again, pleading a headache with a gentle finger to her temple, and made for the stairs.

Outside, the storm continued to rage against the thin roof, and thunder rumbled off to the west like distant cannon fire.

Up in her lonely little room she pulled a chair to the window and sat down, resting against the sill and staring disconsolately out over the harbor, nearly lost in the mist and gloom and sheets of dirty rain. There were only three ships moored there, other than the vast, shadowed bulk of the *Arbiter*.

They'd be back. They had to be back. There were a hundred entirely plausible reasons they would be late during the heavy season.

And many of them would see her friends restored to her any day now.

She sighed, annoyed to find that her pretense of a headache seemed to have summoned the real thing.

She moved from the chair to the bed and eased herself down onto her back, resting her head against the cool pillow.

Perhaps she would rest.

Perhaps, when she woke, they would be back.

They would be back, holds stuffed with Spanish treasure, and whatever the next phase of the plan might be, they would embark upon it, all of them together again.

The commodore's plan or Captain Maguire's plan, it didn't matter.

They would all be together again.

Sleep, either despite the pounding pain behind her eyes or because of it, was a long time coming

Chapter 18
1675 – Entering Cayona Harbor, Tortuga

"Captain, I'm not sure we're going to clear the shallows at the mouth of the harbor."

Ruiz's voice was calm, but it had a brittle quality, just beneath the surface, that Maguire wasn't used to from the old Spaniard.

He cursed under his breath and forced himself to walk calmly to the taffrail and glare down at the serene-seeming swells of the Caribbean.

The damned waters hadn't been this calm in weeks.

It had been a bad voyage; and the *Bonnie Kate* was in bad shape. So much of his attention had been focused on getting them home, he hadn't even considered this new development. The *Kate* wasn't so shallow as *Chainbreaker* or *Laughing Jacques*, but she generally didn't have to worry about the challenges of navigating the mouth of Cayona Harbor like a deep drafted vessel.

He spat over the side, thinking of the Commodore with a dark, baleful look at the horizon.

Curse the man, anyway. Curse him and his tragic combination of ambition, naiveté, and charisma.

Of course, Hart was beyond his curses, now.

And that just served to emphasize Maguire's feelings of impotent rage.

"Make for the center of the channel, Martin. You know the place." He spoke calmly over his shoulder to the sailing master. "If you're really concerned, we can heave to and allow *Jaguar* to take the lead; follow her into the harbor? Sarah Jolie has more practice than anyone, getting a heavy ship through there."

Ruiz made a face as if Maguire had offered him money for his mother. "We'll not be following *Jaguar* into port, Captain." He managed to make the frigate's name sound like a foul curse. "We'll manage."

Maguire hid the slight smile that managed to crack his dark mask.

It had been a challenge, maintaining his composure for the return journey. He knew the crew's morale hung by the thinnest of lines, and he wasn't about to take a chance with discipline now.

"Captain?" He turned to see Isabella Sanz and Aidan standing before him, hats and kerchiefs in hand. They're humble poses didn't fool him, however. The anger he felt churning in his own gut was echoed on their faces.

"Yes?"

He knew what they were going to ask, and he knew what he was going to have to tell them. But didn't know how he could without choking on the words, and every moment he gave himself to think of a more diplomatic response, the better.

"Sir, should we have the guns ready as we come in?" Aidan's voice was rough. There was a bandage over one eye, with the brown of old blood speckling the cotton.

"We can have *Chasseur* under them before they reach their moorings, sir." Isabella was nodding. "Greene won't have the leeway to maneuver in the harbor. There'll be no more shenanigans from him."

Aidan leaned in closer to his captain. "A quick signal to *Chainbreaker* and *Jacques* will see them set as well, sir. I don't doubt Captains Semprun and Hamidi would agree."

Maguire pursed his lips and turned back out to the horizon.

In truth, he would like nothing more than to wait for *Chasseur* outside the harbor with a wide smile on his face, and then blow Greene and his Port Royal crew to hell out where the wreckage wouldn't hamper the future operations of the honest ships of the squadron.

But who the hell knew what had really happened under the guns of the *Oscuridad*?

He couldn't kill Greene, let alone the men and women of his crew, without knowing that, first.

The squadron had taken a far-worse beating at the hands of the Spanish galleon than it had on Bonaire.

And the losses had been far worse, as well.

And whose fault could *that* be, if not Greene's?

But without piecing together the entire action, speaking with Sasha and Thomas and, yes, even Fowler, he couldn't very well open fire on another ship of the squadron without provocation.

Not that he couldn't claim provocation.

But now wasn't the time for the finer points of sea-lawyering. Between Kralendijk and this latest debacle, Hunt's god alone knew how they would keep the squadron together.

And as things stood, Chartier's had nothing for him but debt ledgers, now.

He rested his hands against the railing, bracing his arms and lowering his head.

He wasn't entirely certain there was even a point in keeping the squadron together.

"Captain, she won't know what hit her." He now had Isabella on one side, Aidan on the other. They were the proverbial shoulder-balancing voices of conscience, except that he had two devils, and no angel in sight.

He shook his head. "No."

He raised a hand to stop them from furthering their arguments. He could see they were angry; he shared their anger. But he needed them calm, at least by the time they went into the harbor, or all was lost anyway.

"We will need to meet in council, decide what happened, before punishments can be meted out." He raised his other hand as they both surged forward in response to his words. "I know. From the deck of the *Kate*, it all seemed pretty cut and dried. But until we hear more—"

"Sir, with all respect, it was cut and dried on the deck of the *Oscuridad*, as well." Aidan glowered at him. "There can be no question Greene went into the aft cabins with the Commodore, alone."

"In the middle of the boarding action, sir." Isabella's anger was palpable.

"And he was the only one to emerge." Aidan spat the words between clenched teeth.

Why were they so angry? He had no delusions about the way the crew of the *Kate* had felt about the commodore. He had hated the man and hadn't tried to hide it on his own ship.

It was the thought of betrayal, he knew.

It was the sense that Solomon Hart, no matter how much of a sniveling bastard he had been, had been one of *them*.

And he had welcomed Greene into the squadron. Had welcomed him, in fact, against the express wishes of nearly every other captain on the council, and the combined sentiments of the entire squadron.

And then, during the chaos and violence of a protracted boarding action, Hart had died, and Sidney Greene had come out unscathed.

Had, actually, ordered the scuttling of the big galleon before any of the other captains had a say.

How could they even know all the gold came away?

Maguire cast a quick glance around the quarterdeck. Everything was going as smoothly as could be expected, navigating a torn and wounded ship through a tricky series of approach maneuvers into port.

But Ruiz wasn't the only other member of the crew with them. And every one of them was straining to hear every word while doing everything in their power to appear intently focused on their own responsibilities.

"Come with me." He turned, his frockcoat flaring, and patted Ruiz on the shoulder. "Steady as you go. I'll be back up before the final turn."

"Aye, captain." The little Spaniard nodded to him, but his eyes were locked on the two gunners eagerly following on his heels.

Down in his cabin, he turned on them again, not trying to hide his own anger now. "The two of you know better than to sow dissension up there!"

He pointed to the low ceiling overhead. "You know the crew is hanging on by a thread. I know you're angry. Do you think you're the only ones? But if this crew falls apart before we can even drop anchor, what do you gain? How is your anger served then?"

They both had the good grace to look embarrassed, but there was a stubborn grit behind their eyes that never wavered.

"Greene will pay the price for whatever happened on the galleon." He tried to put every ounce of reassurance he could into the words, but they fell flat, even in his own ears.

Why couldn't they just blast the damned Englishman? There were those among the Brethren, he knew, who would have done just that.

But the Commodore had been trying to build something here on Tortuga. Hell, he had been trying to build something more than that himself.

And that fledgling dream, either dream, would die here, in the aftermath of the assault on the *Obscuridad*, if they weren't very careful.

"The captains will have to meet to discuss the situation and come to an agreement. If we just kill Greene out of hand, without giving him a proper hearing, we're no better than—"

"Pirates?" Isabella spat the word. "It seems like you're not wrong, captain. We are at a crossroads. We have to decide what we believe, what we want to be, and which direction we want to sail."

Aidan, at least, had the good sense to look away at that.

But then, if he had wanted obedient underlings, he would have swallowed his pride and taken King George's commission long ago.

"I need the two of you back up on deck in case anything else shakes loose when we come about." There were nearly as many holes in the crew as there were in the ship and her sails. It was a pretense to get them to leave, but it wasn't untrue, either. "I promise you, the council of captains will see that Greene pays for whatever share of this is his to own. Right now, I need to prepare myself for that meeting."

Aidan nodded, bowing a little, and backed toward the door.

Isabella, however, hesitated. "What if he's already gotten to the other captains, sir?" The anger was gone, replaced with genuine concern. "What if they're blinded by the Spanish gold? He who holds the gold..."

"We all hold the gold, Isabella. Don't worry. I have faith in the other captains. Well, other than Fowler, of course, but we've been working around him for years, so no worries on that score. Sasha, Thomas, and Bastian are good captains. Together, we'll see this ends straight for all of us."

She nodded, bowed in turn, and then he was alone.

He looked over to the corner of his cabin, to where the *Kate's* share of the Spanish gold was stacked in small, iron-bound chests.

How could it possibly be that they could come away from an action with so much gold, and still feel that they had come up short?

The price had been steep. If Solomon Hart had been another man, a better leader, maybe, or at least a more likeable captain, one could say the price had been *too* steep.

Kate had been battered nearly under. *Jaguar*, having presented the largest target as they made their approach, was even now in danger of sinking. Even Greene's *Chasseur* had lost a mast and taken several shots below the waterline.

The squadron had lost nearly a hundred men and women, too. Most to grape and scatter guns as they made their final assault.

But they had come away with the gold.

And they had sent a Spanish treasure ship to the bottom of the sea.

Would that victory, and that gold, be enough to buy their way into respectability on Tortuga? Without the commodore to shepherd that plan, was it even plausible? Would Governor Bertrand d'Ogeron treat with someone other than the commodore? What kind of private codicils might their agreement have contained, that had never been known by another living man?

The hours after they all returned would be fraught, he knew. But they had never been closer to achieving his own goal of an independent home for the squadron, for *all* the squadron, than they were at that moment.

If only they could agree on what to do about Greene.

*****

"I agree." Thomas's voice was the reassuring low rumble it had always been.

But there was no reassurance to be garnered from it now.

The council of captains was meeting in Commodore Hart's grand cabin aboard the *Arbiter*. This, in and of itself, was hardly auspicious.

Maguire had sent requests for a council to the other ships before the *Kate's* anchor had hit the sandy bottom of Cayona Harbor. His assumption had been that the other captains would be as eager to meet as he was. He had thought they might meet at Daucourt's at noon, or maybe even aboard the *Kate*.

Jaguar had taken a twelve-pound ball right through the gallery, and Fowler's cabin had to have been shattered by the impact. *Syren* had suffered a small fire on her quarterdeck, and so would probably be no fitting place for them to meet.

And there was no way he was going to board the *Chasseur* willingly.

But no matter where they met, he knew the others would want to gather soon, to begin the dispensation of the gold and to discuss the next steps they would take, either with the Commodore's plan or with something new.

But he caught, in the reply from each captain, a strange reticence to meet in haste. First Bastian had begged off due to injury, which was understandable. The man had been skewered by a foot-long splinter through his biceps when the *Laughing Jacques'* quarterdeck had taken a nine-pound ball through the bulwark. But then *Chainbreaker's* response returned as well, and Captain Hamidi regretted that he would be unable to meet due to overseeing the beginning of repairs.

Maguire's blood had chilled as he realized none of his fellow captains was going to make a move. It may have been his imagination, but his crew seemed to be more and more subdued as they realized the captains were not preparing to meet in emergency council after the costly battle and the loss of their commodore.

The men and women of his ship could only be wondering, now, what fate lay in store for the squadron.

He had put a brave face on for the crew, joking about the prince's ransom that awaited them.

But when he saw the boat putting off from *Chasseur* for the *Arbiter*, Greene's gilt-edged hat clearly visible in the stern, his concern had redoubled.

He had been planning on going to meet with Boothe to give him the news as soon as things had settled with the *Kate*, but Greene was beating him to it.

Were Boothe and Greene working together?

As it had turned out, it was nothing quite so mundane.

Boats had departed from *Arbiter* soon after Greene's arrival, but they were the black and red jollyboats of the flagship herself, not *Chasseur's* boat.

One of the small craft had gone to each of the ships in the squadron. Each had contained a letter addressed to the ship's captain. At least, he had assumed he was not the only one to receive such a message.

A summons, really, to the *Ultimo Arbiter*.

To meet in council.

He found himself wondering if these letters would be treated the same way his own messages had, but before he could even decide how he, himself was going to react, he saw a boat putting off from *Jaguar*, heading for the big galleon. Then Hamidi's unmistakable bulk, weighing down his own ship's boat, was crossing the harbor.

He had yelled for Axel Perry, his befreckled young boatswain. The lad had done nothing wrong, of course, but he had had to yell at someone.

Perry had been preparing to take Maguire across to the harbor so he could check in on Shanae, after it became clear his own call to council was being ignored. Nevertheless, by the time the boat was in the water, Bastian had already left *Laughing Jacques*, and Sasha's boat was being lowered down as well.

He couldn't be sure, of course, but the appearance was that Greene had snapped his fingers and the captains of the squadron had scurried in response.

He had not, of course. There was no scurrying in *his* motions. He needed to get to the meeting to stop the others from doing anything rash.

The buccaneers of the squadron would not stand for the man who had pushed their ships into the meat grinder to escape the responsibility unscathed.

That had been his thought, anyway.

Now, as he stood by the tall window of *Arbiter's* stern gallery, just off the cabin that had, until very recently, belonged to Solomon Hart, he couldn't believe how wrong he had been.

Isabella's words came back to him, flavored in his mind with his own bitterness. He who holds the gold…

And, somehow, *Chasseur* had come away with more gold than any other.

Not only that, but Greene had clearly been making his case to the others, through some channel he had not been privy to, long before the battle.

Fowler seemed almost eager to seize this chance to take control of Tortuga. *Jaguar* was ready to bring their word to any coast on the island. And there wasn't anyone in Cayona or beyond that would be able to ignore the wrath of a frigate's weight of metal.

The others had the decency to look ashamed as they agreed with statement after statement from the English popinjay.

But agree they did, and the future of the squadron was laid out before them as if it had always been the only, inevitable path.

D'Ogeron would be on his way back to France as soon as the weather broke. He would be taking an appreciable portion of the *Oscuridad's* gold with him. The squadron would functionally own Tortuga for as long as they could keep it. And with the remaining gold, they would most likely be able to keep it for a long time.

But this last proposal, made with the same even, quiet tone Greene had introduced each preceding proposal, made no sense at all.

"Why are we going to start specifically targeting the English?"

He couldn't believe he was saying that. The one group in the world he would be more than happy to target, and he was balking at the suggestion?

"Why would we specifically target anyone, other than the prey that presents itself?" He was struggling to rectify the vision of this Englishman suggesting that the squadron, effectively now, theoretically at least, the navy of a sovereign state in the New World, should be attacking the British Navy.

He looked back to Thomas, who seemed eager to take on this new task. "Thomas, why would you be behind such an idea?"

The huge black man snarled back. "The Spanish are open in their contempt. The French at least try to be objective. But the English? They follow their purses, allowing their mouths to flap on about equality and the nobility of man, but then turning a blind eye to all manner of dark practices."

The captain of the *Chainbreaker* smiled, and it was not a pleasant sight. "There should be a price for such hypocrisy."

Maguire shook his head. He would be the last to defend the English after what they had done to his precious Ireland. But it looked to him, anyway, that they were not better or worse in how they treated the Africans, both escaped slaves and those born free, as any other European power.

But it was obvious Thomas Hamidi's experience was different.

He turned to Sasha, but she looked away. "I'm sorry, Eamon. I can't ask my crew to wait until the sensibilities of Port Royal, or San Juan, or any other port develop enough to accept us." She looked up at him then, and there was a fierceness in her face he hadn't seen in a while. "We'll make a home that will accept us here, rather than wait for someone else."

"My friend," Bastian smiled. But then, Bastian always smiled. "The strength of the squadron has been established now, no? The Commodore's vision has proven true. Look to what we have accomplished together! Kralendijk? Now the *Oscuridad*? With the governor out of the way, who's to stop us doing whatever we want?"

Maguire shook his head. He couldn't believe this.

He wanted to shout at them. He wanted to remind them that the Commodore they now lionized in memory had died, alone and isolated from his Brethren, with only this strange Englishman in company.

But those words sounded petty, even in his own mind. They had made their choices. They were tired of waiting for someone else's dream.

He sighed.

Even if that someone else was him.

He looked at them again and was alarmed to see the tension hanging in the air. It was strung between them all like some nearly invisible web spun by some terrible, grief-feeding spider.

They were scared, he could see. And they were angry. But the obvious object of their anger had offered them the illusion of security, at least.

And sometimes even a pirate preferred security to vengeance.

He hoped the men and women of the squadron agreed with their misguided captains.

If the crews decided the people in this cabin were wrong, it didn't matter what they had voted on or who they had laughingly elected as the new commodore.

Any one of them, or all of them together, could lose their power and position tomorrow, at the whim of the Brethren.

It was the greatest strength of their path, this ability to change course when the common wisdom perceived trouble ahead.

But it was also the greatest weakness, when that common wisdom was subverted.

He rose, taking his leave with a last dark look at Greene.

The trouble was, how to tell when it was subversion, and when you were just plain wrong?

Chapter 19
1675 - Cayona Harbor, Tortuga

"Enter."

Aidan had warned her of the captain's mood, but she could sense his anger and frustration through the thick wood of his cabin's door, and she hadn't expected that level of rage.

Aidan often overstated the level of displeasure in those above him when reporting such things. She had never wondered after the why of it, until now.

She entered. The captain's small cabin was in its usual state of tidy disarray. There was nothing that would indicate a lack of cleanliness or care, but the chamber was definitely lived in.

And it was obvious that whoever lived here had been doing a lot of reading, lately.

And pouring over charts.

She tried to see what regions were of particular interest to the captain this time around, but she couldn't make anything specific out before he turned from the big table with a sigh.

She thought she had seen the shape of Jamaica on one of the charts, but she couldn't be sure.

"Oh, good. You're back." He didn't seem all that relieved, but she tried not to take it personally. He had visited her at the Lazy Dog soon after returning and had filled her in on the captain's council and everything that had transpired there.

It was hard to believe Hart was gone, even harder to believe command of the squadron had been handed over to that English poseur and his brigantine.

The man wasn't even shifting his flag to the *Arbiter*.

"Sir." She nodded, standing easy. "I'm sorry it took so long, but someone had taken to storing cordage and sailcloth in my cabin, sir. I had to have someone clear it away before I could settle back in."

He nodded distractedly. "Things got a little chaotic on our return voyage." He settled into one of the chairs around the table and pushed a small ledger across the polished wood. "What do you make of this?"

She took the book and flipped through it. Numbers. Columns of numbers, with headings above and along the left side, adding and subtracting from each other, going up and down as she went forward through the record.

"The squadron's accounts?" She looked at him through the fall of her bangs. There wasn't enough information on the pages to tell the full story; nor would the squadron's accounts be kept on the *Kate*.

"My own accounting of them, yes. As best I can recreate." He took the book back and opened to the last entries, handing it to her again. "This is from what the others reported, and what I was able to glean from Chartier and the other lubbers."

She looked again, and whistled a single, low note. The squadron's take from the treasure ship appeared to have been a king's ransom.

And almost all of it was gone.

He waited until the realization dawned, and then he nodded.

"If everyone is being above board, and within the limits of normal human greed I assume they are, then Greene's collected and distributed over 80% of the gold before we've even *begun* to discuss the apportionment of the treasure."

"Distributed it to who?" She settled into a chair across from him, sweeping off her hat and laying it on the table.

"Who knows?" Maguire shook his head again, turning to stare out into the bright, hot sunshine beyond the cabin's stern windows. "Repairs are underway, and provisioning. He had to have paid for those."

"That wouldn't account for half of the missing gold."

"I know. But then there's d'Ogeron. All signs seem to indicate he's uprooting his entire household, taking them back to France. That's going to cost a pretty penny."

She sighed and settled back in the chair, pointing to the ledger. "That's a lot more than a pretty penny, sir. For that much, we could have bought a brigantine or two out of English service."

He smiled, but there was a bitter tiredness in his eyes that leached the expression of any warmth. "Hell, with that much we might have even gotten the *Arbiter* off her mooring." It was his turn to sigh, and she didn't like the sound. "But I couldn't be that lucky, could I."

It was a statement, not a question, and for some reason, it scared her.

"Lucky, sir?"

He shot her a glance, then shrugged, waving her concern away. "Nothing, Shanae. Just the maunderings of a frustrated old man."

He stood, stretched, and walked about the cabin restlessly, reaching out to touch an object here or there. She saw he had unpacked his things as he often did when in port, and there were shells, small statues, and other bits of memorabilia scattered about. She noticed two small strongboxes in one corner that were not there before but dismissed them for the time being.

"Captain, what is it?" This strange, vague energy was growing more and more troubling.

"Our new Commodore flies his flag from a brigantine, you know." He said this as if it was news. The fact that it wasn't news to anyone, even to a first mate newly returned from shore, was just more unnerving behavior on top of all the rest.

She nodded, not wishing to take part in whatever strange pantomime he was descending into.

"That, of course, leaves our most powerful ship without a captain." He drew one hand along the flat of a wide-bladed Spanish dagger set on a small side table.

"Most powerful in some ways, sir, but not in most of the ways that truly matter."

But he didn't hear her. "We cannot leave a galleon of the Squadron without a leader to stand her quarterdeck, Shanae."

"Boothe—"

"Myles Boothe has, in no uncertain terms, let it be known he does not covet the captain's cabin of the *Ultimo Arbiter*."

She looked at him as a sickening fear began to dawn.

"No."

He glanced down at her, smiling wanly. "Yes."

She felt the blood drain from her face. "He can't. There's no way he could force you..."

The captain, shoulders slumped, slid back into his chair. His clear exhaustion was worse than anything else she had seen since coming back aboard.

"He can't, and yet, he will. I know it."

"*This* is your ship!" She stood, now, fist pounding on the table. "He has no right to take her from you!"

His smile was more a grimace of pain. "He won't. He'll just let it be known that that is where I should be."

Her anger was as bright as the late-winter sun. "Under what precedent could he possibly dictate to the crew of the *Bonnie Kate*? The Brethren do not bow to the dictates of *anyone*. A captain rules at the pleasure of her crew, until that crew decides she is no longer fit."

Something cold slithered into her belly. "The crew would never—"

"No." He jerked his head sharply. "No. The crew are loyal. They would never vote against me. But if we wish to remain with the squadron..."

She shook her head again. "Then we leave the squadron! They've all become lily-livered buffoons anyway! What do we need them for? Without them, we could go anywhere! We could go to Port Royal!"

He had always dreamed of creating a home for them all in Jamaica. She knew that. She glanced at the charts.

He had been thinking the same thing.

For a moment, hope soared in her chest, all the uncertainties and suspicions fell away.

Then she looked more closely into his eyes.

He looked away.

And it all came crashing back onto her again.

"The *Bonnie Kate*, alone, shifting to Port Royal would be one among many. We would have no esteem there, we would come with no treasure, no great victories; there would be no reason for anyone to take us seriously at all. We would have nothing."

She stood up, trying to deny the sick feeling rising in her chest. "We could take the king's paper. We could—"

"No!" He slapped the table, and it was far louder than her blow a moment before. "No. We cannot. There would be no place for you aboard a King's ship. No place for Isabella or Maia, either. Mathias and Martin would not be welcome there, nor any of the African crewmen and women. I will not abandon any of my crew here to save a few by taking them there."

His own frustration was almost comforting to see, after the glimpse of the despair that had taken him. "If Bonaire had worked out for us; if the *Oscuridad* raid had gone well, perhaps..."

He looked at the two boxes. "If we had gold with which to purchase a higher position in their councils."

The despair came rushing back in again. "None of that pertains, Shanae. We must live in the world God has created, and often it conforms less to our wishes than we would like."

She shook her head, sinking back into her own chair. "Then what happens to the *Kate*? You can't let Greene—"

"No." He was saying that a lot today. "Greene will never have a say in the governance of my ship."

Then he looked at her, and this time his gaze was fever bright. "Your ship."

She looked at him through narrowed eyes. She knew the words, of course. But in context of this conversation their meaning refused to impact her mind.

"I don't understand."

Now his smile was gentle, almost sad. "You will be the *Kate's* new captain, Shanae."

She shook her head. This made no sense at all.

"No. I can't."

He placed both of his hands flat on the table and leaned toward her. She leaned away.

"Don't give me that nonsense. Of course, you can. And you will. When the time comes, you will take my place, and you will captain the *Kate* better than I ever have."

Again, his words held no meaning as she struggled to understand what was happening. "The crew, they would never—"

"Shanae," his anger was back, and it was hot, but it was directed at her, and she couldn't understand why. "Shanae, you must leave off this childish attitude. The crew would never what, elect you captain? Of course, they would! In a heartbeat! You would be the most qualified captain between here and Port Royal and beyond. You *have* been for *years*. The only person who doesn't realize that is you, and we have run out of time for you to come by your confidence honestly."

She didn't understand what was happening. "The crew—"

"Love you. Love you better than they love me. And they will follow where you lead."

He stood and came around the table, reaching out to take her by the shoulders. "I need this from you, Shanae. I need an ally I can trust, now more than ever. You can no longer hide behind your age or your position as first mate. We navigate through difficult waters. I will need you strong, I will need the whole crew of the *Kate* strong if we are to come out the other side."

"The other captains—" The fear would not release her.

"Have no say, as you have already mentioned. Greene is not forcing me to take the *Arbiter*. He is forcing me to choose between exile and the galleon. With me aboard that beast and you in command here, we still have a chance to take some control of the future that rushes toward us. If we were to leave alone, we would be at the mercy of every buccaneer, every pirate hunter, and every navy ship plying the waves."

He sighed, going back to his chair. "Sasha may come around. Thomas may realize there is more hope in Port Royal than there ever could be here. Hellfire, even Bastian might take a moment to rise from the eternal jest of his life to see that a future under Sidney Greene would not be the future we have all been working toward. And if some, or all of them, come to their senses, then our situation could change."

Again, he looked like a gray, defeated old man. "Until then, all we can do is endure."

There was a roar from across the water. Voices raised in anger or joy, she couldn't tell, were echoing over the harbor from starboard.

Then another, answering shout came from port.

Then all around them, cries of excitement, it sounded like.

She turned back to her captain and was even more confused to see him shrink from the sound, glancing over at the two boxes in the corner.

"They have distributed the crews' portions, it would appear."

There was a heavy knock on the cabin door and, before Maguire could finish his summons, it opened. Mathias Sylvestre entered, his black and white striped hair floating in the mild breeze caught by the companionway outside.

"Sir, signal from *Chasseur*. Distribute the shares?" He glanced at Shanae sheepishly. "I had not wanted to disturb you, but the crew, upon seeing the other ships..."

The captain nodded with a sigh, pushing himself to his feet. "No, Mathias, you were quite right. There's no need to foster resentment among the crew by keeping it from them any longer."

The quartermaster nodded after a brief hesitation, then spoke quietly into the hall behind him. Four crewmen slid past, nodding to Shanae and dipping their heads to their captain. With a soft grunt or two, they lifted the strongboxes and took them back through the door.

"We'll be up in a moment, Mathias. I wouldn't want the crew to forget where that gold is coming from."

The quartermaster nodded again, then eased the door closed behind him.

The captain looked down at the deck. "Let's home there's already enough." The words were more senseless flotsam on the flood of his dark thoughts, indecipherable no matter how she might twist and turn them.

Sylvestre wouldn't have shown the gold before his captain joined him, but from the cheer up on deck, it was clear the crew knew the contents of the two boxes, nevertheless.

Maguire looked back to Shanae. "He cements the goodwill of the sailors with a more-than generous share, timed to coincide with a revel he will be throwing up at the governor's manse tonight, all masters and mates to be invited."

There was still bitterness in his voice, but a grudging respect, as well.

She could only shake her head.

He took her by one shoulder as they moved toward the door. "Never underestimate the power of a bellyful of food and rum, Shanae. More kingdoms have been purchased with such coin than all the gold and jewels in Egypt."

She was no expert on Egypt, but his words rang true. With such maneuvers, Greene would purchase the loyalty of the men and women of the squadron quickly.

If something wasn't done.

*****

She started as the scream split the night behind her. But then the voice trailed off into a cackling laughter, and she tried to relax.

Nothing in her experience was as chaotic and bothersome as a true, full-on debauch in the streets of Cayona.

Between their newly-stuffed purses and Greene's fete up the hill, the men and women of the squadron were truly cutting loose and losing all self-control.

A crowd rushed past her, several riding the shoulders of their crew-mates, all howling like devils released from hell.

She knew many of the most senior members of the squadron would most likely be in the Lazy Dog already, settling in for the night and eagerly looking to establish their new positions in the refined pecking order.

She wouldn't be welcome there much longer if she took the helm of the *Bonnie Kate*.

But she had lived in that dank little hovel for over a month, and it was the last place she wanted to be on a night of celebration like this, anyway.

Celebration for some, at any rate.

Shanae wandered the poorly cobbled streets like a ghost bemoaning a lost past.

Seeing Captain Maguire so broken by recent events, and contemplating taking over as captain should he lose his ship to the machinations of that cretin from Port Royal, would have sank any good humor. But this, based upon such a painful, costly victory for the squadron and such a violent shift of power within it, was already tenuous at best.

She was already more inclined to a surly, slow-burning anger than the high spirits of victory.

But given everything else that was swirling around these events, she could have hardly enjoyed the night no matter where she went or who she spent it with.

A man stalked toward her down the street, heading in the direction of the harbor below, and then stopped.

She looked up, ready to send him on his way no matter who he was but stopped when she saw him more clearly by the fitful light of a passing troupe and their lanterns.

Myles Boothe looked like hell warmed over.

His dark brown hair was disheveled and gleamed in the orange light with an oily sheen. His elaborate beard and mustache were disappearing into the growing stubble of his unshaven cheeks, his black eyes glittering from bruised pits.

"Boothe." She didn't know what else to say.

He looked up, and for a moment she thought he must be drunk, wandering from one wild celebration to the next.

But the look on his face immediately convinced her that she was wrong.

"Boothe, are you alright?"

He blinked at her, eyes narrowing, and then shook his head.

The man was acting as if he was drunk, or a cannon had gone off right next to his ear.

He shook his head again as if to clear it, opened his mouth as if to speak, and then shut it again with a click.

After one more awkward moment he pushed past her and continued down toward the waterfront.

She watched him go, avoiding the little clumps of revelers as he went, and then turned back up the hill.

She didn't move. She was caught by the sudden urge to return to the ship and try to get some sleep, but she didn't want to follow Boothe too closely. There had been a wildness to his expression that she misliked.

After a moment more, she turned back toward the harbor and began to make her careful way along the pitted roadway.

The cobbles were a little more uniform the closer she came to the harbor. As the buildings became less ramshackle, more permanent, comfortable structures, the warehouses that lined the docks looming up behind them, her footing was more sure, and she let her mind wander.

She had no interest in being captain of the *Bonnie Kate* now. She had never given much thought to her future beyond the moment. Captain Maguire had always been there, for every memory in her head he had been beside her. Even if she felt competent enough to stand the ship's quarterdeck, why would she try to imagine a ship without her captain?

But if Maguire had been outmaneuvered by Greene, if he was forced to abandon either all his dreams or his ship, and he chose the ship, what would happen?

It was a future she had avoided considering all her life. As it reared up before her now, more real than she would have ever wanted, it made her heartsick and ready to vomit at the same time.

"Shanae Bure!" The voice was cultured, British, but unfamiliar to her. She turned and started as she realized who it must be that had addressed her from the porch of Chartier's counting house.

The man wasn't tall, with a slight build that seemed only accentuated by the elaborate frockcoat he wore despite the heat of the night.

His fair hair, hints of red catching the lantern light of the porch, was tied back in a severe tail, while his well-trimmed beard framed a friendly if thin-lipped smile that failed to reach his cold, jade eyes.

Sidney Greene.

She had seen him before, of course; even met the man once or twice. But they had never spoken directly.

Until that moment.

He took the stairs with an unconscious grace that seemed to draw attention to the small sword at his side.

Most of the Brethren, in a friendly port, would leave their weapons on the ship as a show of good faith and to avoid unpleasant misunderstandings. However, it was not unheard of for captains to wear such jewelry as a counterpoint to their formal clothing. The Port Royal captain's fancy silver-chased sword fell more into that category than a clumsy, plain cutlass.

And yet his walk seemed to indicate that he was a man who might be more dangerous with the petite weapon than most other men with its larger cousin.

"Captain Greene." She kept her voice steady, standing as still as a cat ready to pounce or flee.

He stopped, looked at her for a moment, smile slipping. Then it came back, this time perhaps even a touch more genuine.

"I was going to tell you you didn't have to call me Commodore, but obviously you came to that conclusion on your own."

Her chin lifted an imperceptible degree as she made the conscious decision not to acknowledge his barb.

"I was hoping I could have a moment of your time." He came to stand beside her, turning down the hill as she was. "I was going to seek you out aboard your ship, but this happy coincidence has saved me the steps."

She shifted, putting her hands on her belt, near the long dagger she always wore. Only a fool would have confused it with a utilitarian tool.

"I have heard great things about you from your crew and the other members of the squadron." He tilted his head as he looked at her, and she felt as if she were being judged on some list of criteria she could not possibly understand. "Even the captains speak highly of you."

He looked down toward the waterfront and then back to her. "Were you heading down toward the harbor? I could accompany you, if you'd like."

She kept her face still. "No need. Was there something more?" There was no way he had stopped her on the street just to exchange bland pleasantries.

His smile darkened just a bit as he leaned toward her. "Have you considered when it might be a good time for you to take up the mantle of captain yourself? If half the things I've heard about you are true, I would be proud to have you sailing at my side."

She wanted to tell him she would rather never step foot upon a deck again. She wanted to tell him she would die before sailing under his command. She wanted to slap that self-satisfied look off his face, after all the violence and chaos he had brought down upon the squadron that had been her home nearly all her life.

But Maguire and the other captains had taught her too well.

She merely shrugged.

He searched her eyes for a moment in silence, then nodded. "Well, certainly something for you to consider, my dear. The path of the buccaneer is ever-shifting, as they say, and I wouldn't want your talents and abilities to go to waste."

He tipped his gilt-trimmed hat and wheeled on one finely-turned heel, making his way back up the hill, in the direction of the governor's manse.

She stood watching him, as she had watched Boothe, but this time, rather than feel sorry as she had for the one man, she felt a burning, visceral dislike for this one.

Chapter 20
1675 ~ The Windward Passage In Route to Port Royal, Jamaica

The *Laughing Jacques* was a miniscule little scow.

Boothe glared out at the northern horizon, hanging by one lackadaisical hand from the starboard shrouds amidships on the diminutive sloop.

He was not normally an impulsive man. In fact, he could probably count on one hand the number of times in his life he took an action that was not entirely thought out ahead of time and calculated with the very best of his not inconsiderable abilities.

Following Shanae Bure onto the deck of the *Laughing Jacques* on some fool's errand to Jamaica would probably send that count onto his next hand.

In fact, it was so ill-considered, it might entirely fill that hand and send him into counting his toes.

But what else was there for him to do? He was loath to squander his shares and his account on a room at the Lazy Dog. For one, he had a suspicion that monsieur Serre was charging him considerably more than he would have charged nearly anyone else from the squadron for the squalid little garret. For another, it was bad enough walking away from his position of first mate on the flag ship of the plucky little pirate navy.

If he wasn't the Commodore's first mate, what was he?

He had always assumed that, eventually, he would take command of a ship of his own. Maybe not the *Arbiter*. *Hopefully* not the *Arbiter*.

He would prefer a ship that could stir herself from her moorings.

But certainly, there would be a prize worthy of a faithful mate, eventually?

He had underestimated the power of tradition among the Brethren. Even an old salt like Hart was susceptible to the inertia of time. Once you accepted a role aboard the *Arbiter*, you were there until you moved up aboard the *Arbiter* or you died.

He wasn't sure when he had made that realization, or reconciled himself to his fate, but it must have been some time ago, judging from the shattering blow to his mind he had suffered when that structure had been overturned.

He sighed, then looked around to make sure none of Houdin's misfits had witnessed his moment of weakness.

He had never had much use for either sloop of the squadron; although you would have to be a fool not to give Thomas Hamidi his due as both a captain and a fighter. But the light ships were just too small to feel truly dangerous beneath his fee.

His mind knew they were far better-suited to most buccaneering work, but still, with their smaller cannons and lack of weight, he had always felt the sloops to be too ephemeral upon the waves to convey the kind of gravity and power he imagined a true buccaneer should command.

His lips twisted into a bitter grimace of self-loathing. A sloop would be far preferable to no command at all.

The fact that he should be thankful Houdin had allowed him on his little craft at all still rankled. He had no power with which to command or request anything from the squadron now. What was he? Nothing more than a shore-bound old comrade with no claim to anything beyond his account at Chartier's.

He sighed. This unexamined pressure in his own mind had driven him from Tortuga, he knew. And it had done so with such speed he hadn't even been sure they were headed to Port Royal until after they had cleared Cayona Harbor and turned the little sloop's prow westward.

And he still had no clear idea why they were heading to the English stronghold.

Shanae looked to be no happier than he did, which was obviously distressing the crew of the *Jacques*.

In fact, he was probably the only person aboard the ship, including her jolly little captain, who understood Shanae's current situation at all.

He knew squadron scuttlebutt claimed he had been offered the captaincy of the *Arbiter* and he had refused.

He wished that had been the case.

He wished he had been given the chance to show the courage of his convictions by turning that little bastard's offer down, spitting into his English face.

The truth was that Greene had not even spoken with him. News of the Commodore's death had been brought to him by messenger.

As had the information that he had been relieved of his position, the very next day.

The shock of the double blow had been more than he could have possibly prepared for. He had been numbed by the old man's death. He had never felt a great deal of loyalty for Solomon Hart, but he had served under the man for more than a decade. There was a certain comfort to that which might, to the untrained eye, at least appear like loyalty.

He had certainly been accustomed with the old man's presence, plans, and foibles.

His death had been a blow, obviously.

But then to be beached in that same moment of uncertainty.

He had never liked Greene. When he had tested the attitudes of the captains during that first meeting after the *Oscuridad*, he had known something was amiss. Rather than anger and resentment, there was confusion and a strange sense of something more like hope than the despair he had expected.

Then they had left with no further word to him.

And then, at six bells in the morning watch, the messenger had made her second visit.

And he had found himself cut adrift from the life he had created for himself.

He had wandered the rutted streets of Cayona ever since. He had felt like a ghost, haunting the locales and companions of his former life with no direct connection to them and no ability to reach them.

He had followed Shanae's angry progress from the *Kate's* boat, down the rickety dock to the Jacque's slip. Only the sloops were able to dock directly to the harbor's waterfront, and when there was a free slip, they always availed themselves of the privilege.

And so he had been standing at the foot of the boarding ramp when she stormed onto the main deck and past a chagrined Bastian Houdin, charging into the cramped belowdeck spaces without a word.

Even now he couldn't have said why he had followed her, but he attributed Houdin's shaken manner for the captain's lack of challenge when he did. He had allowed the former first mate aboard with a mere shrug and smile, and that had been that.

There was no place for him in Tortuga. There was no place for him anywhere. The *Laughing Jacques* was as good a place as any to find somewhere new.

Or to end it all.

He had had little of his gold with him when he came aboard, not having planned to be away.

He wondered how long it would be before Serre would decide he wasn't coming back, rifle through his things, and throw away whatever he didn't want to keep for back pay of the room.

If Boothe was lucky, someone would mention to the innkeep that he had left on the *Jacques*, and at least give him until the ship's return before consigning his few remaining possessions to the harbor.

If he *did* come back.

He'd had very little to live for, having had his position and his home taken from him. But this strangeness with Shanae, at least, was something to distract his mind and occupy his time, filling his hours with something more than the cold contemplation of his own demise.

He struck the rail with a balled fist. So far, she had given him nothing. And aside from a muttered reiteration of the ship's ultimate destination, Houdin had given almost as little.

He looked around the small deck. It was cramped after pacing the open spaces of the *Arbiter*, but he had to admit it was nice to feel the wind at his back once more, and to feel the bracing pulse of the seas beneath his feet.

Even if he *could* feel it a bit more than he would like.

Shanae was nowhere in evidence, of course. Houdin was standing at the tiller with his helmsman, Jean Martin, sharing idle conversation as the ship made her easy way westward.

He nodded to the two men, who gave him vague, uncomfortable looks before returning the gesture.

No one on this ship knew quite what to make of him.

Which was fair, since he clearly didn't know what to make of himself.

He moved toward the small hatchway leading beneath the vestigial quarterdeck and doffed his knit cap. All of his accustomed finery was still in the room above the Lazy Dog, just waiting for Serre to find it a new home.

In the claustrophobic confines of the miniscule cabin section, he hunched over in the shortened hall and knocked on the door to the cabin Shanae had been given.

He had not seen her since they left several days before. She must have been taking her meals in the cramped little cell.

He needed to speak with her. If this was just make-work, to get her away from Greene so she could calm down about what was happening to the squadron, he would be very put out.

He put his knuckles to the door and rapped once.

The response was muffled and dismissive, but the actual words were unintelligible.

He decided to play the fool.

"Shanae, are you in?" He rapped again.

This time, he could just make out a few words. They included several choice epithets and ended with "go away!"

He knocked again, with a little more force. "We must speak."

There was a grunt, the sounds of some shuffling and scraping, and the door jerked open just enough for one crystalline blue eye to peer out at him. The flesh around the eye was pale, the socket bruised. She was barely recovered from her ordeal on Bonaire, and already haring off on another adventure.

And she was none too pleased.

"Speak quickly."

He looked into the narrowed eye for a moment, then looked away. "I have no right to make demands, but if I know what our purpose in Port Royal is to be, I might be able to help."

Fine lines appeared at the corner of the eye.

She was smiling.

No, she was laughing.

At him.

"Our purpose?"

The door jerked open all the way. The interior was dark, especially with his eyes accustomed to the bright sun outside, but he could make out the disarray.

He did not know Shanae Bure well, but he would have been surprised if she turned out to be a messy person.

"*We* have no purpose in Port Royal, Boothe. You jumped onto the *Jacques* without my knowledge. We have nothing to do with each other. We have no connection at all, and I prefer it that way."

She had been angry through the door. Her single eye had radiated ire through the crack. Now, she was working herself up into a true fury. He could see the tightening of her face, the lowering of her stance. The stiffening of her muscles.

She could very well kill him right then and there if he wasn't careful.

"If you hadn't been such a coward, running from your responsibilities aboard the *Arbiter,* none of this—"

"No!" He slammed his fist into the door frame with a crash. The stout Old-World oak cracked.

So did his hand, but he wasn't about to let anyone know that.

"No!" He repeated, refraining from punching the ship again. "You do not know my battles, Shanae. *I* cannot know what you have suffered. I cannot know what burdens have been laid upon your shoulders by all this, but do *not* lay any of this at *my* feet. There is a viper in our midst, a creature with only a passing familiarity with the truth."

That stopped her, but only for a moment.

"Boothe, I've no obligation to deal with you. You've relinquished any kind of claim you may once have had over me. With your choice—"

"Damnit!" Again, he maintained the presence of mind not to further damage his hand, but the crack of his voice was enough to bring her up short.

"There *was* no choice, are you not listening to me?" He slumped against the doorframe and she moved back into the cabin to maintain the distance between them.

He was so tired.

"I was pushed out of my berth aboard the *Arbiter*. I didn't turn down the captaincy, not that it would have been Greene's to offer me. But he never even gave me the chance. The crew were quick to turn, as well. He must have paid them off or gotten to them somehow. Aside from Rees the quartermaster and a few other mates, there was no support. And when he let it be known I was being put ashore, there was no one to say him nay."

Her eyes narrowed again, but she didn't charge back onto the attack. "No one—?"

He snorted. "I had friends among the crew. Of course I did. Do." He shook his head. "I don't know. I thought I did. But there was nothing they could do. Or would do. Several of the most influential were already that bastard's creatures. I don't know for how long. I couldn't have made a defense if I'd wanted to."

She shook her head. "I don't understand. Why didn't you say anything? Why didn't you tell—"

"Who?" Now the resentment came rushing back up his throat. "The other captains? They were already hearing nothing but his grand plans for Tortuga. Hart's plans, but dressed in new clothes, with a more flattering hang. All but Maguire, and you know there has never been any great love lost between him and I."

Maguire had never hidden the contempt he felt for the first mate of a ship that never left port, and that contempt had made it extremely hard to appreciate any finer points the man might possess.

She seemed thoughtful, which was an improvement over the incandescent rage of a moment before. "I still don't understand, why…"

But she did understand. He could tell by the look on her face as the light dawned, that she was realizing the true danger.

"I know you'll tell me every Jack and Jill aboard the *Kate* is loyal to Maguire, but take it from me, Shanae, you cannot be certain of anything."

He was looking into her eyes, maintaining the contact no matter how much he wanted to look away.

He needed to convince her this was a real danger.

He needed her to trust him, to let him help her with whatever Maguire had sent her to do in Port Royal.

Because he had realized, standing in that door aboard that tiny little ship, this was all that was left to him. Maguire was a cunning rat. The man would have plans in place; plans to deal with just such a problem as Greene.

And Boothe *very* much wanted to deal with Greene.

"I don't understand how this all fits together." She sank back onto the bunk behind her, and after a moment, he followed her into the dark cabin.

Inside, it was close and humid. He looked around, found a lantern, and turned up the wick. When the warm orange light bathed the tiny space, he turned around, keeping his elbows in close to his sides, and closed the door after checking the short companionway.

There was no one nearby.

"How what fits together?" He asked when the door was closed, and they were shut off from the rest of the ship.

He could already feel the heat rising, the sweat prickling along his back and legs. They needed to finish this conversation up quickly or he was going to pass out.

"Why beach you and offer the ship to Captain Maguire?" She wasn't looking at him, but at the warm brown wood of the wall, a line of confusion or concentration between her eyes.

"He offered the *Arbiter* to Maguire?" He had known something like this would happen, but it hurt, even now, to hear it.

She looked up at him. "Yes."

He shook his head. "Why would he take it? Who would helm *Kate*?" He knew, even as the words escaped his lips, from the look on her face.

"Ah." He tried to find other words, but they failed him. "Congratulations?"

She gave him a sour look, and then went back to staring at the wall. "What does he gain, shifting Maguire to the *Arbiter*? The captain's his biggest obstacle to controlling the squadron. Why give him the flagship?"

It was his turn to look away as he tried to find a comfortable position leaning against the wall. "It's not the plum assignment you might think, girl."

"Don't call me that." She hadn't even thought about saying it, he could tell. Her words cut like razors and dripped with scorn.

He felt just a little bit smaller.

"I'm sorry." He mumbled, then went on. "The *Arbiter* is not the healthiest of ships. Moving Maguire aboard her would conveniently isolate him from the others."

She looked up; lip curled dismissively. "She can't leave her moorings as she is, I know. I'm not a fool. But if there's any captain on Tortuga today who can get her moving, it's Maguire." She shook her head, back to staring at the wall. "It feels like a mistake to me."

He wanted to tell her why it wasn't a mistake. He wanted to tell her why moving her captain to that decrepit ship would have effectively removed him from the squadron's power struggles all together.

But some faint vestige of loyalty kept his mouth shut. Loyalty to either the ship or to his dead commodore's memory, he couldn't have said.

"And you're to captain the *Kate*?" He could understand her ambivalence, but eventually she would come around and see it as the honor it was. It could well take the sting off what had been done to Maguire.

Greene might well have purchased Shanae's loyalty as well.

He couldn't let that happen.

"Why Port Royal?"

She sighed, looked up at him suspiciously, and then shrugged. "I don't even know, really. So, I'm not at all certain why I can't just tell you."

That didn't clarify things at all.

"I'm sorry?"

She shook her head. "He needed to contact some captain in Port Royal. Some friend of his from the old days. It wasn't a name I recognized. Lachlan?"

Boothe started, nearly hitting his head on the low ceiling. "Porter? Captain Lachlan Porter?"

She nodded. "That's him. Some old friend of the captain's. He sent us to reach out. Said this Lachlan might be able to help. Might know things."

Lachlan Porter had been a member of the squadron when Boothe first joined. He and Maguire had always been close, that much was true.

When Porter had shifted to Port Royal, one of the last buccaneer captains out of Tortuga to do so, it had come as a surprise to many of his mates that Maguire didn't follow.

"What could he want with Porter?" Boothe hadn't known the man was still sailing, never mind following the path of the Brethren. "Does he still sail that brigantine of his? What's one more ship going to do?"

She shook her head again. "I told you, I don't know anything else. We're supposed to find this Lachlan and explain the current situation on Tortuga. Captain Maguire said we were then to follow the man's advice, whatever it might be."

Boothe settled back against the wall again, sopping the sweat dripping down his face with one sleeve. "And you've been hiding in this cabin because...?"

She gave him another sour look. "I don't know what to tell anyone on this ship. I don't know what I'm supposed to say, I don't know what I'm not supposed to say, and I'm—"

The flow of her words had been angry and fast and then cut off abruptly.

He thought he knew what it might be. "You wouldn't be able to help him, staying back in Cayona, Shanae."

She glared at him, then shrugged. "I won't know, though, will I?" He shook her head. "How am I supposed to know what I might or might not have been able to do if I'm not there to do it?"

"You're doing what he wants. What he thinks will help. And when you return, whatever happens, you'll have the *Kate*, and you'll be able to set your course with a better sense of the battlefield."

He didn't want her to lose sight of the fact that this was very much a fight.

Not that she seemed likely to do so.

"I don't want the *Kate*!" She lurched out of the bed and they were standing nose to nose, forced together by the confines of the cramped space.

That was it, then.

"You don't have to be afraid." He didn't know what to do. He wanted to reach out and grip her shoulder, but he was fairly certain, having seen her fight, that such a gesture would end up with him sailing over the bed and into the far wall. "You'll make a great captain. Every—"

"Not like this!" She shoved him into the corner, probably for lack of anything else she could do, then sank against the other wall, her shoulders pressed to the old wood. "Not like this."

He looked away. He could understand that.

The silence stretched on into an uncomfortable void, and eventually he couldn't take it anymore.

"Will you let me help, when we get to Port Royal? I've been there before. I'll be able to bring you to where we might find Porter."

Her lips pressed together in an expression of annoyance. "We shouldn't have any trouble finding him."

She had said 'we' several times, he realized then. He had assumed she meant Houdin and his crew.

But she had said she hadn't confided in them at all.

"We?"

She nodded. "Captain sent Hunt with me. I haven't seen him since I boarded, but he's here somewhere. Probably down in the orlop, or the bilge, on a ship this size, as close to the water as he can get."

It took him a moment to place the name. Hunt ... Hunt ...

"Aston Hunt?" He couldn't believe it.

The madman? The *Kate's* notorious lunatic priest?

What was Maguire thinking?

"Yes." She was smirking at him. She must have followed the thoughts coursing through his mind and watched as he came to his conclusion. "Captain likes to have him watching over things."

Boothe's eyes narrowed. "Maguire doesn't hold with such nonsense, does he? I thought he was a good Catholic lad—"

"The captain's a papist, right enough. But there's no denying that Hunt's perceptive when it counts. And he always seems to be where he needs to be when he needs to be there." She looked away. "Besides, there's no telling what Greene might do with him, when he doesn't have Maguire's protection anymore. Anyway, Hunt's been to Port Royal many times, as has almost everyone else aboard the *Bonnie Kate*. He should be able to get us to One-

Eyed Jack's without much trouble."

Boothe's brows slid down at the name.

She looked up at his expression and her own face darkened.

"What? Have you heard of it?"

He nodded.

"Yes. And believe me, when you find it, you're going to want to have more than some crazed priest at your back. I'm coming."

Their gazes were locked for several moments before her expression softened just a bit and she looked away with a nod.

"Fine. Now leave me alone."

He was only too happy to leave the stuffy confines of the cabin.

Now he had something to focus on; something to think about as the ship made its way westward.

And he'd just have to get a woman through the doors of One-Eyed Jack's alive to do it.

Chapter 21
1675 - Port Royal, Jamaica

As the *Laughing Jacques* came up into the wind, her sails luffing overhead and her speed dropping down to a manageable approach, the sailors all around her scrambled to bring the sailcloth in, heave lines ashore, and prepare to make the ship fast against the solid sandstone quay.

The rush of jealousy Shanae felt at the condition of the Port Royal waterfront was understandable, she felt, but not entirely valid. The wide stretch of smoothly cobbled thoroughfare, the solid brick construction of the buildings lining the docks, and the bustle of a busy commercial center gave the appearance of a vibrant, powerful community, in sharp contrast to the ramshackle, frontier-like façade of Tortuga.

But there were red-uniformed marines scattered throughout the crowds; the damned white and red of the British ensign flew from too many flagstaffs for her liking. Were the people who walked back and forth, perusing the vendor stalls, moving in and out of the shops, and just walking up and down the extensive docks a little too furtive in their movements? Were the looks they exchanged just a tad more hooded than the situation would seem to call for?

Where was the vibrant energy she had expected of the premier pirate city in the New World? She was willing to admit it might be her own mood coloring her observations, but this busy town hardly seemed like the promised land to her.

Why would Maguire ever want to shift their flag to this sad little prison?

The crew of the *Laughing Jacques* had been subdued as they slid past the heavy guns of the forts guarding the various approaches to Port Royal, and the small flotilla of Navy ships, shepherded by the frigate *Venator*. There had easily been enough weight of metal represented in those tawny castles and pristine ships to make swift work of the *Ultimo Arbiter*, if ever she could sail into that harbor; never mind the mincemeat they would make of the little sloop.

But the men and women of Houdin's ship seemed happy enough now that they were tying her up to the docks, the many attractions of a bustling port city visible all around.

She sighed. Given a choice between the squalid freedom of Tortuga and the regimented comfort of Port Royal she thought she knew which she would choose. But she also knew there were many of her Brethren who would choose differently.

Many aboard this very ship, in fact.

And what if Tortuga ceased to be an option at all?

She picked up the crutch she had asked the ship's young carpenter, Luc Masse, to make for her during the voyage. A stout length of heavy oak with a cross brace affixed to the top wrapped in sailcloth, it was just the thing for an invalid recovering from battle injuries and given to dizzy spells from a head wound still wrapped in pristine white gauze.

The pretty blonde boy had been quick to comply, eager to work for the promise of a quick smile and willing ear.

She looked around for Hunt and rolled her eyes as she saw him lurking in the shade of the hold below.

She didn't know why Maguire had wanted the madman to accompany her. She would rather have had Aidan, or any of the other more capable sailors or mates.

She didn't mind Aston Hunt's company, although it could be a bit much when meeting new folk. But he wasn't of much use in a tight spot, and his attitude toward Port Royal was particularly odd, even given the range of his own odd attitudes.

He had cowered in the orlop, almost hugging the decking above the bilge, for most of the voyage, muttering something about the waters from Cayona Harbor and the impermanence of 'that gods-forsaken place'. She could only assume he meant Port Royal, although he never said the name aloud.

"Hunt, we have to go. We're losing daylight."

The men and women of the *Jacques* made room for her as they went about their tasks, securing the ship from her journey and preparing her for a short stay. They had been respectful for the entire trip, if a bit standoffish. She attributed that to having an outsider aboard who appeared to be their primary purpose in taking the unaccustomed late-winter journey into the west.

"We're going ashore?" Boothe stepped up behind her and she made a concerted effort not to jump.

He had been doing that a lot, lately; haunting isolated areas of the ship only to step out of the shadows without warning.

She felt for the man; she really did.

That didn't mean, however, that she was eager to share her strange mission with him. For as long as she could remember, anyone associated with the *Arbiter* had been, if not an enemy, then certainly not a friend. She was less than eager having him accompany her ashore, especially considering how vague her own understanding of her mission was.

"*I'm* going ashore. I'm not at all certain what you are doing." She gave him an arch look. "That is far more your affair than mine, I'm sure."

The words didn't seem to have any appreciable effect, however, as he just smiled his sad, damaged smile.

It stirred some small amount of pity in her heart that was immediately drowned out by the contempt it churned up in equal measure.

"But you're going to take the lunatic with you."

She smiled at that. Jealousy hardly became him, but it was more emotion than he had shown since punching her doorframe a week or more ago.

"Having an anointed of Poseidon along can never go amiss, no?"

He made a face as if he'd bitten into a rotten fruit. "Anointed." He spat. "Anointed by whom?"

"By the Lord of the Waves, unbeliever."

It appeared as if Boothe's disdain had been enough to drive Hunt from communing with the rancid waters of Cayona.

"The Master of the Seas has no need of your belief, sir." Hunt's green eyes were once again alight with fever, the glaze of his strange fear of Port Royal having given way to the furor of his mis-placed belief in ancient superstition. "I shall walk upon this ephemeral shore by the lady's side, and together we will be the equal of whatever this doomed land might throw against us. We have no need of you."

It might be that Boothe was recovering from his malaise, judging by the rising annoyance in his dark eyes. "Well, I'll come along anyway, if you don't mind. It might just be that I can offer some assistance as well, if difficulties arise."

She shrugged. She'd already given him permission to join them if he wished. She wasn't about to get into a snitty little fight here in front of the entire complement of the *Laughing Jacques*.

They said their farewells to a strangely subdued Bastian Houdin, who bid them good luck before quickly turning back to his sailing master and the flamboyantly Spanish quartermaster.

She hobbled down the loading ramp, ignoring Boothe's strange gaze as she maneuvered down the narrow plank with her crutch clutched beneath her arm.

As they stepped onto the cobbles of the waterfront plaza, she was annoyed again to note how even and well-laid they were. The men who had built Port Royal had built her for the ages. This was no quick-and-dirty town on the border of the known world. This was an up-and-coming city meant to rule the seas all around.

Behind her, Hunt stepped onto the stones with the ginger step of a man stepping onto rotten ice. Boothe grunted with disgust and slipped past the priest, coming to stand beside her as she surveyed the nearby market stalls and store fronts, with the tall, blind walls of warehouses rising up just behind.

"We've only got an hour or so left before sunset." Boothe's voice was gruff, indifferent.

She gazed at him out of the corner of her eyes, wondering what that effort cost the man.

"If we're going to get to One-Eyed Jack's before the usual evening crowd, we should keep moving."

She nodded. She was watching the men and women walking past for any kind of reaction they might have toward her. She had heard terrible stories from several members of *Chainbreaker's* crew who had ventured into this den of hypocrisy. She had half-expected to be excoriated for the color of her skin before she moved a hundred paces into the town.

Instead, although she did receive a passing glance here or there, it seemed little different from the streets of Cayona, if a little more crowded.

Boothe led them out from the waterfront area, through some smaller avenues, and then into a twisted warren of alleys and side streets that felt much more like home.

Here, the smells of the waterfront were more familiar, a little danker than the warm, sun-bleached pale stones along the harbor.

Boothe led them unerringly past several disreputable-looking grog shops and thieves' dens of various types. She had no doubt she would be able to procure anything she could imagine behind those heavy, nondescript doors.

Hunt fell further and further behind them, his hesitant steps unable to keep pace. She gave one last look back and then went on with a shrug. He'd catch up in due time.

One-Eyed Jack's was at the end of a dark, stinking alley, and at first glance, she knew she was home. The half-timbered construction was not the stucco and red tile she was familiar with from Cayona, of course, but the spirit of the place could never have been hidden by mere physical traits.

The windows were small and clouded, cheap glass further occluded by years of smoke, humidity, and worse. The finish of the outer walls had been painted, once, but that had been long ago in a forgotten age. The pale bone between the dark wood supports was all but lost beneath a layer of grime and soil so thick as to almost blend in with the stained wood.

The door was small, much smaller than she would have expected from a place with such a reputation. But then she realized that if a large group of people were trying to force their way in, they would have to come in one at a time, making a full, frontal assault almost impossible.

A moment later she realized it would make it equally difficult for a large group to leave.

The small sign above the door showed a gruesomely detailed skull with only a single remaining eye glaring balefully down at them as they approached.

"It might be early enough, yet, we can talk to Billy Smyth, the owner. If Porter's still around, this is where he'll be."

While they talked, speaking in hushed tones that felt odd given the still-bright strip of sky overhead, Aston Hunt rejoined them. His moves were still furtive, he still held himself nervously, his gaze never resting on one place for long, glaring about him at the buildings as if half-expecting them to collapse upon him.

She shrugged. "We're not going to solve any of this nonsense standing here in this stinking alley."

She reached out to push the door open with her free hand and Boothe stepped in front of her, putting one hand on her arm.

The crutch whistled around her head and cracked into his forearm.

Boothe stepped back, holding his arm, glaring at her. "What the hell did you do that for?"

"Don't touch me, Boothe. Your guidance was helpful, and I thank you for that. But don't lose sight of the fact that this is my task."

He snarled but said no more.

"I could have gotten us here without trouble." Hunt's petulant voice was underscored by the fact that his eyes continued darting all around them.

The scruffy, dark-haired former first mate looked at them both through narrowed eyes, then sighed, gesturing her to the door with a sweeping movement of his uninjured arm.

She looked at him a moment more, then nodded, swinging the crutch back under her arm, and went in.

It took a moment for her eyes to adjust to the gloom, but the scene that resolved itself around her would have been familiar in any port. They were in a narrow chamber, the front door about half-way along one long wall. A bar was before them against the opposite wall, just a few paces away. To the right the room opened into a much larger hall, dimly lit with wall sconces filled with cheap oil, if the smoke was any indication.

What light was making it through the small windows barely lent any illumination to the scene at all.

Behind the bar two weary barmaids seemed to be making a perfunctory attempt at cleaning a row of metal tankards, looking up from their tasks as if eager for the distraction.

When they saw Shanae, their eyes narrowed, their mouths hardening.

She recognized the look. She had seen it many times before, and it drove her to distraction each and every time.

As if she was here to compete with these two trollops for the dregs they built their lives around.

She moved to the bar with two long steps, crutch tapping hollowly on the wooden floor.

"I'm looking for Captain Porter." She let her voice convey the command, her chin lifting, anticipating the confrontation she knew was coming.

It came from a completely unexpected quarter.

"What's this, then?"

The voice was greasy, if that was possible, while gruff at the same time.

She turned to see that there were several makeshift tables along the wall behind her and to the left. At one of them sat two large men wearing heavy frockcoats, fancy hats on the dirty table between them.

She looked them up and down and dismissed them as unimportant. Mates or masters of ships in dock, perhaps, but they lacked the edge of dangerous men and the polish of powerful ones.

She sniffed and turned back to the women. "Captain Porter. Does he frequent this...place?"

She saw the resentment and suspicion harden in their eyes and hid a small smile.

She had always enjoyed baiting petty women.

"Maybe you didn't hear me, missy." One of the men behind her rose, chair scraping against the worn wood of the floor. "You got business here? You leave off bothering Liz and Lucy. You can talk with me."

She turned slowly to give the man a second glance; scraggly blond beard, thinning hair, a squint to his watery eyes.

He fared no better in her second assessment, and she turned away again.

"If I may—"

Boothe stepped between her and the two men; she wanted to scream. Why couldn't the man just mind his own business? Did she have to worry about herself, the madman, and *him* as well?

"No need for unpleasantness, mates."

"We're no mates of yours, whoreson." A second voice. So Boothe had succeeded in getting both of the Port Royal gawks into the mix.

She looked down, shaking her head.

The two bar women — they were far too old and hard-used to be maids — were grinning at her when she raised her eyes.

"Come on, now." Boothe's attempts at diplomacy were wearing thin, she could tell from his voice.

"Only reason for you to be cutting into our wind here, *mate*, is if you're selling this sweet morsel?"

The women's smiles widened, there was a gasp by the door; probably Hunt. And stunned silence from Boothe.

"Yeah," the second voice again. "This mulatto princess your chattel, fancy-man? I'll give you five sovereigns for her, if you've got some silver to make change."

Something bubbled up from deep within her. She had been spoken to like this before, once or twice, on Tortuga; men new to the island who had not known who she was. But then she was surrounded by friends and mates. She was in familiar waters.

There had been no danger.

This new situation filled her with a growing, glowing rage.

The door opened to admit several more men and a woman as she turned around, but she had eyes only for the big balding blonde and his companion.

"You want to buy me?" Her voice was steady, her eyes cold. "You couldn't afford me."

The blonde leaned forward. "I could buy you twice over with the change in my purse, bitch, the price you're going to fetch when we're done with you."

Boothe gasped. Hunt growled. The faces at the door, glimpsed from the corner of her vision, seemed to be taking the situation in with neutral curiosity.

She knew what was happening, and she was more than willing to play by the local rules.

The handle of the crutch, solid oak specifically built to take the strain of such a blow, caught the blonde man in the ear and sent him careening into the wall, eyes wide, blood splattering the side of his face, mouth open in an eerie, silent scream.

Before the man's companion could adjust to the new situation, the crutch swept back and up, crashing down on the crown of his head.

The man's eyes crossed at the hollow, echoing sound and he dropped straight down to the foul floor, sliding beneath the table without a noise.

She sent the crutch whistling in a wheel around her arm and then into her armpit in a ready position to continue the fight if any of the newcomers wished. She glared at them over her shoulder, but relaxed as she saw nothing but wry amusement and a note of satisfaction in their faces.

The man leading the group nodded to her and tipped his silver-edged hat. "Ma'am." And he led them past her into the larger common room beyond.

She wasn't even breathing heavily as she turned back to the bar, where Liz and Lucy were staring at the men, dead or unconscious, on the floor.

"Captain Porter?"

Their eyes shifted to her, but they made no move to speak.

She sighed again. If she was going to have to beat them, too, she was more than willing, but she'd rather not expend the effort.

"What the hell is going on up here?" This new voice belonged to a gruff bald man with iron gray side whiskers and a red complexion. He came up behind the bar from a small set of stairs in the corner and looked over it at the two still forms on the ground.

"Damnit. Are they dead?" He was asking the women, but it was Boothe who answered, kneeling down between her victims.

"They are not." He tapped the first man. "He's not doing so well. Bleeding from the left eye, it seems. But this other one should wake up fit as a fiddle, save for the headache, in an hour or two."

The bald man looked owlishly at Boothe. "And who are you? This your handywork?"

Boothe rose, his hands in the air. "No, sir." He smiled and nodded toward Shanae. "I'm with the lady. Seems the men took exception to her entering, wanted a bit of a discussion before they were willing to accept her presence."

She looked at Boothe through narrowed eyes, then turned back to this new man. "I'm looking for Lachlan Porter."

The man took her in, but there was nothing venal or offensive in the look. He was sizing her up as a potential threat to the peace and stability of his establishment rather than anything less savory.

"What would you want with him, if I knew where to find him?"

She was in no mood for further games. "I need to speak with him. I was told he would be here, eventually. Is he here or not?"

His gaze hardened. "I'm not in the habit of speaking about such things to strangers, miss. To be blunt, I wouldn't tell you I knew the gentlemen whether I did or not. Now, you're more than welcome to stay if you'd like to buy a drink or some food. But that's all I can offer you."

She felt the anger again. Why were things always so hard?

"Could we speak with Billy Smyth, maybe?" Boothe stepped out from behind her, leaning an elbow against the bar. "He'll know me. Myles Boothe? We sailed together, in another life."

The bald man looked from Shanae to Boothe from beneath lowered brows. "Smyth passed years ago, mister. You're not too good a friend, if you don't know that."

"It's alright, Mr. Hall. We've come from Eamon Maguire. You'll know me? Aston Hunt?"

The madman was now beside her, a sheepish grin on his face.

Boothe glared at him. "You bastard, you knew all along? Why—"

Hunt smiled directly at him. "I'm just a madman, Myles. Why do I do anything?" He turned back to the bald man. "Captain Maguire has messages for Captain Porter. It's urgent."

Hall now looked completely baffled, eyes shifting from one of them to the next before settling back on Hunt. "You're the one thinks he's a priest of Poseidon."

Hunt waved the comment away. "I am a priest, sir, but that's neither here nor there. Is Captain Porter's ship in, do you know?"

The man looked at him a moment more, then shifted his gaze back to Shanae. "You've got to be that elusive first mate of his, then." His eyes twinkled as a sudden smile shifted the muscles of his face. He looked down at the two unconscious men, smile widening. "You're everything I've heard and more."

She didn't know what to make of that so decided to ignore it altogether. "Captain Porter?"

The bald man nodded. "Of course. He usually comes in around the end of the first dog's watch; shouldn't be too long now. If you'd like to have a seat, I'll have the girls clean up your mess before they bring you some drink?"

They ended up waiting for over three bells. One-Eyed Jack's had begun to fill. There had been several brawls and at least two stabbings that she had counted. It looked as if Boothe had not been exaggerating the place's reputation. Word of her own unpleasantness seemed to have made the rounds. No one had shown them more than passing curiosity or a grudging respect, for which she was duly grateful.

She was amused to hear several men from a nearby table complaining of a recent action that hadn't gone entirely their way. A French cog named *Amelie Carre* had been taken, but with the ever-shifting situation in Europe, it was politically inadvisable for them to bring her into Port Royal.

She smiled. It reminded her of Tortuga and the fluyts. Except these poor lads hadn't had someone like captain Maguire to finesse the situation.

Things were tough all over, it seemed.

The little pub continued to fill. There were only a few empty tables by the time Hunt tapped her arm and nodded to the door.

The man who entered was much older than Captain Maguire. A mane of white hair swept down from a dramatic widow's peak, flowing smoothly into a heavy beard. His gray eyes were surrounded by laugh lines, and as he swept into the room he looked around with a warm glow, hailing several friends in the crowd.

"That's him?" She leaned in close to be heard without shouting, and Hunt nodded.

She stood, moving into the tall man's path as he made to slide past their table. He looked startled for a moment, the smile still in place, then focused on her more closely.

Something happened in those pale gray eyes. It wasn't recognition. They had never met; she was sure of it. But it was as if he knew her the moment he looked into her eyes.

"You must be Shanae."

*****

The four of them moved to a corner table where the shadows were a little thicker, the noise not quite so intrusive.

"We've met several times, but you were only a small child." Porter was nursing a pewter tankard of ale. Boothe was on his third or fourth, but she had stopped after her first, keeping the empty cup nearby to allay suspicions.

"I figured, if things on Tortuga went south, he would have to send you eventually." He leaned back to regard her. "Must have been you who did for Sulley and Tannen, then?"

"If those were the two oafs hanging off a table when we arrived, yes."

The man's smile broadened as he nodded. "Would have loved to see that."

She shook that away. "Sir, Captain Maguire did send me, and I'm not entirely certain why. I doubt it was to talk about my spat with some uncouth locals."

He nodded. "No, you're quite right. If Eamon sent you here instead of coming himself, things must be moving quickly?"

She sighed. "I don't know what you're talking about, but things aren't well."

"Commodore Hart is dead." Boothe's voice shook a little as he said it. Had he even said those words aloud since they had heard?

"Commodore." Porter shook his head, smile fading just slightly. "The bastard always did have delusions of grandeur. Still, I'm sorry to hear it. He wasn't a half-bad buccaneer, back when we were all younger."

"You sailed with the squadron?" She leaned forward. "Is that how you know Captain Maguire?"

Porter nodded. "I did. It wasn't a squadron, then, of course. Just a band of Brethren sharing the most chaotic, free, and open port in the New World."

"When did you leave?" Boothe was staring at the old man. "*Why* did you leave?"

Porter didn't look like the question amused him. "Why did I leave? Why did everyone leave? Why did the poor bastards who stayed stay?" He shrugged. "Politics, of course. As the great and powerful back home continued their old feuds, they needed ships and men." He tilted his head toward Shanae in apology. "Sorry, lass. No women in the King's Navy, as you know."

"Just one of many reasons they're worse off." She said in a low voice.

He laughed. "I can't argue. I truly cannot." He took a sip before continuing. "Anyway, with the Spanish and the English making offers, amnesty, gold, even chances for booty and prizes? And all we had to do was shift our targets a little bit? Raise the right color cloth from time to time? Of course, there were plenty of us didn't want to sail with *any* navy. Old habits die hard." He shrugged, looking sad.

"There were those, wouldn't have been welcome hereabouts, back then. Hamidi still with you all? What about Maguire's right hand gal, Sasha Semprun? Double marks against her, of course. A woman and French to boot?"

"Captain Maguire seems to think there might be a chance for some of us to shift back to Port Royal." Hunt was looking into an empty cup, hunched in the corner, still shooting suspicious looks at the floor from time to time. "Commodore wanted to make Tortuga a pirate's paradise, but the captain never agreed."

Porter nodded. "No, that wasn't going to happen, I'm afraid."

Boothe looked up angrily, but the old man waved the glare away.

"Port Royal has successfully wed the energy and the fury of the buccaneers with the power and the resources of the British Empire. The Spanish have half a dozen ports strung across nearly as many islands, each of them doing the same, near enough." He looked sadly into his tankard, but his voice did not waver. "There is no way an independent port can withstand the attention of the continental powers, should they ever turn their gaze your way."

Shanae knew the words were true even as each registered like a blow to her stomach.

She had always known the Commodore's plan wasn't realistic. Captain Maguire had never had faith in Tortuga, although he had never voiced his reasons so plainly.

But if there was no hope for Tortuga, and no place for so many of the squadron here...

Porter was looking at her, his old eyes soft. "It's not all bad, lass."

She shook herself, trying to reign her bitterness in. "No? Would a ship of women be welcomed in Port Royal? Would a ship of Africans? Must we be left behind, to give any hope to the others?"

The man's gray eyes hardened, and he leaned forward. "No, you need not be left behind. And the difficulties ahead have very little do to with the color of your skin or the body you were born in. That sloop you arrived in would have a hard course to chart, as well. As would the *Bonnie Kate* and the others."

"We missed our chance." Hunt's voice was soft as he slumped back in his chair.

Even Boothe looked despondent.

But Porter wasn't done. "No. You've missed *a* chance. Should you all arrive right now, you would find no welcome here, that's true. But Maguire has spent years working towards giving you another chance. And the fact that you've come here, to sit with me in this nest of harlots and serpents, tells me that chance might well be near."

Boothe looked angry, and she couldn't see why. Hunt looked as if he had been granted a last-minute reprieve. She found herself somewhere between the two, and as confused as both.

"I don't understand."

"Greene." The single sound only confused her more, before her mind caught up and connected it to the bastard who had taken the squadron away from them.

She could see that Boothe hadn't taken nearly that much time.

"What about him?" His voice was rough with emotion.

Porter looked at each of them in turn, then back to her. "What do you know of him and his family?"

She shook her head. "Not much. The captain doesn't seem to have much use for him. I believe he knew him, or his family at least, from his visits here."

Porter took another sip before continuing. "The Greene's own a counting house here in Port Royal, but their primary source of incomes is trade."

"Forced trade." Hunt nearly spat the words, and Shanae looked at him, then back to Porter, who was nodding.

"Forced trade."

Boothe shook his head. "That's illegal. I thought you lot were all about law and order? The Greenes are powerful, but could they have risen that high on the forced trade alone?"

She shook her head, looking to Porter for confirmation, but the man was staring at Boothe with a look equal parts pity and exasperation.

"Like most things, it's only illegal if you get caught. Entering into an illegal contract with a shipping concern from a foreign power to deliver trade goods, then entering into another illegal contract with a privateer to hit that shipping, thereby keeping the initial payment and then splitting the goods, is a very good cycle to be in, if you can get there. If your credit is good back home, and they managed to spread their debts widely enough, and have just a little bit of luck..."

"And that's what they've done?" Boothe was obviously disgusted.

Buccaneering was a dangerous life, but few turned to the forced trade.

To go from a free, sea-roving warrior to a tame lapdog was surely to be a fate worse than death.

She understood Boothe's rising fury, now. Even Hunt was sitting stock-still, staring at Porter.

But Porter was staring at her.

As if he was waiting for her to say something.

She felt her annoyance rising. What was he waiting for? What was he expecting her to take from all of this?

She felt like she was back aboard the *Kate* in her youth, undergoing one of Captain Maguire's many lessons.

The forced trade was foul, but many of the families and consortiums in English territory undertook it at one level or another.

Their ability to truly make a profit, however, was always limited by the number of buccaneering crews they could call upon.

She sat back.

If they could command more crews...

If they could command an entire squadron of privateers...

The squadron...

If they could transform them from free buccaneers to a tame naval force of no national loyalty...

She felt her gorge rising up in her throat.

Porter nodded. "This was what Maguire was afraid of. That you are here now tells me he was right, and that Sidney Greene is making his move."

"I don't understand." Boothe looked from her to the old captain and back. "What is Greene trying to... Oh—"

"That rat bastard." Hunt's voice was raw with hatred.

"Wait, you said Captain Maguire thought he was doing this. How? Why am I here? What can we do?"

She had never felt so isolated from everything that mattered to her.

She had abandoned Captain Maguire in the heart of the enemy's growing power. Never mind that it was at his orders. She was here, hundreds of leagues away, and Greene, that snake, was making his move.

She knew it.

Porter turned in his chair to look back at the bar where the brawny bald man was standing, talking with one of the women.

Jamie Hall, the owner of One-Eyed Jack's, had looked like he wasn't paying attention, but at a gesture from Porter he straightened with a nod, and disappeared down the rickety stairs.

"Maguire knew your squadron would have to offer the authorities at Port Royal something spectacular to earn their place here." He turned back to the table, taking the tankard into both hands. "But that wasn't all that would be required. The Brethren still operating here would require some show of force, as well. Some proof of your power." He took a sip. "Now, I know there was some talk about Bonaire, but that didn't go well?"

She looked away and Boothe shook his head.

Porter nodded. "And then there were whispers of the *Oscuridad*, but nothing but rumors. I'm guessing that didn't go so well either, then?"

She felt her chin rising. "The squadron took the ship."

"And Greene sent her to the bottom, along with Hart's body." Boothe spat the words.

"And passed most of the gold along to d'Ogeron and his cronies." Hunt was leaning forward now, the fever in his eyes not in the least connected to his madness.

Porter nodded thoughtfully. "Well, then it would appear that Eamon's last option would now be on the table."

Jamie Hall lumbered over to their table and rested a small leather book between her and Porter. With a nod to the old captain, he turned and went back to the bar.

Porter looked at the book for a moment, then slid it across the table toward her.

"What's this?" She picked it up. There was a leather cord wrapped around the soft covers, keeping the entire thing in a tight bundle.

She opened it but could make very little from it. Columns of numbers, random-seeming words. Some were names, others were obviously locations: ports, cities, and such.

It looked a lot like the ledger he had shown her after the commodore's death, she realized.

"Could I see?" Hunt took the book from her before she could reply.

The crazed priest flipped through the rough pages for several moments, his eyebrows slowly rising.

"I've never opened it," Porter admitted. "Hall is another old shipmate. We've kept it safe for Eamon, for the day he needed it." He looked at her. "For today, it would appear."

Hunt whistled. "Incredible." He breathed the word softly, almost reverently.

"What is it, mooncalf?" Boothe growled.

She gave him a glare, then leaned forward. "What is it, Hunt?"

He looked up at her with a beatific smile. "The Captain and the Chartiers have been hiding this for years. Captain's been moving his treasure to a number of counting houses here in Port Royal for over a decade." He flipped the pages at the beginning of the book. "Invested wisely, too. In shipping firms, insurers, victualers, and the like." He then flipped toward the end of the journal. "And here, he started to spend it all."

She took the book and tried to make sense of the numbers.

"How do you know any of this?"

He looked sheepish, taking the book back. "I used to keep the ledgers for my vicarage...or, rather...for the temple..."

Boothe looked like he was about to reach across and slap Hunt, and she gave him another glare before turning back to the sailor.

"What happened to the treasure, Hunt? What did he spend it on?"

Hunt was pouring over the entries again, looking at them first from one angle, then from another, as if that might change their values. When he looked up, his eyes were wide.

"Debt."

Chapter 22
1675 – Cayona, Tortuga

"There, by the wall." Aidan Allen directed the sailors shifting a small two-pounder against the wall bordering the far side of the compound. Beyond the wall was a long, open street; the only approach to the run-down villa that would allow a concerted attack.

The first shot would blow a hole in the thin wall. The second, God willing, would blow a hole in the attackers.

He watched as his loyal master gunner rested his head against the cool stucco surface of the wall with a sigh. The man had always feared shore-bound actions. And Bonaire had done nothing to alleviate that dread, it would seem.

And now here they were, trapped in a ramshackle old Spanish villa near the top of Cayona's hill, surrounded by enemies, waiting for an attack that might kill them all.

How had Mrs. Maguire's little boy ever let it come to this?

He blamed bad company. He thought this with a smile. For the first time in a long time, he felt like he was right where he was supposed to be.

"The gun in place?" He pushed himself away from the wall and stepped up beside Aidan, watching the sailors complete the nest of bracing cords that would hold the little weapon in place when it fired.

He could see for himself that the men were ably finishing the preparation.

The waiting must be getting to him as well.

"They are, sir. I wish we had more."

Maguire laughed. "Not if you'd have been the one who needed to fetch them, Aidan. Even getting that little beast up the hill wasn't easy."

Aidan shook his head but stood his ground. "No, sir, I'm sure it wasn't. But when we need them, I'll be wishing we'd shed the blood and sweat needed to get more up here. There's not much I wouldn't give, including my own sainted mother, for a six, or maybe even a nine-pounder loaded with grape, when all is done."

Maguire sighed. "I can't disagree with you, Aidan. Fortunately, or unfortunately, depending on how you're looking at things, this is all Filip had lying about."

Filip Chartier had been a good friend for a long time, but he couldn't expect the man to put everything on the line for him now that things had gone so badly wrong. With the shift in power on the island, Filip had to watch out for his own.

As it was, without the man's help, Maguire would never have been able to secure even the relative strength of this little manse.

He had maintained the illusion of a wealthy buccaneer captain for years while sending most of his gold west to Port Royal, where he believed the future had to rest. It was ironic that now, when he had decided to make a principled stand at last, he had to borrow the money to make what could very well be his valiant last stand.

"We've got the swivel guns, anyway. See that they're placed in the upper windows, if you would be so kind?"

Firing the large scatter guns from those vantage points would multiply their effect, should Greene feel moved to take this to the next level.

And Maguire had left the bastard little choice, if he wanted to complete his conquest of the squadron and Tortuga.

"Sir, what happens when she comes back?" Aidan stood nearby, his arms crossed, looking out over the courtyard where three other sailors from the *Bonnie Kate* stood, heads close together, speaking quietly. "*Laughing Jacques* could return any day now."

Maguire bit his lip. He had been thinking the same thing for days. When he had thrown down the gauntlet, working on an impulse he had never accounted for in all his varied plans, he had not allowed for Bastian Houdin's ship, nor the absence of his own first mate.

Well, he sighed. That was not quite true. Had Shanae been with him, he probably would not have had the courage to do what he did.

"Greene won't attack without provocation, Aidan." He wished he felt as much conviction as he was forcing into his voice. "There's no reason for him to suspect Bastian is disloyal. He might not even know Shanae is aboard."

Aidan nodded, but he didn't seem convinced. "If you say so, Captain."

Maguire forced himself to reach out and take the boy by the shoulders. He thought he knew how the young gunner felt about Shanae, even if Aidan himself was not. But he needed the best from everyone who had followed him ashore for his gambit to have any chance of success.

"We need to worry about ourselves for a little while, Aidan. Shanae is more than capable of taking care of herself. And besides, she's not alone. I sent Hunt with her." He smiled at the young man's reaction to that. "And I'm pretty sure Myles Boothe slipped aboard the *Laughing Jacques* as well, before she set sail."

Aidan's look of confused ambivalence for the addled priest turned to sharp disdain at the mention of the *Arbiter's* former first mate. "That bastard. What possible good could he be, wherever they went and whatever they're doing?"

Maguire looked away. He hoped the three of them had puzzled out why he had sent them and set in motion the last pieces of his plan regarding the Greenes and their holdings in Port Royal.

Truth be told, he hadn't thought about their return when he had, in the end, refused Greene's offer of the captaincy of the *Arbiter*.

Nothing he had said to the other captains had shifted their positions on the new Commodore. He needed to do something drastic, to set an example for the others; to wake them to the dangers ahead.

There was no way Thomas, Bastian, and especially Sasha could misunderstand the gravity of the situation now that he had beached himself. If they followed, it wouldn't even matter which way Fowler and the *Jaguar* leapt. Two brigantines and two sloops, working in concert, would be more than a match for the others.

Especially when you took into account the worth of the captains involved.

And if they came to their senses, if they awoke from the nightmare Greene's ascension meant for all of them, there would still be time to make things right.

Between the fortune they might take away from the *Chasseur*, the one he had spent on Port Royal, and the defeat of one of the darkest, most powerful families in Jamaica, maybe, just maybe, there would be a place for all of them in the new order.

But a lot was riding on his fellow captains coming to their senses before Greene was able to consolidate his hold on the island.

And the only thing standing between him and that last step to power, currently, was Eamon Maguire and a handful of loyal buccaneers holding a small villa just below the governor's manse.

The manse that had stood empty for nearly two weeks since d'Ogeron and his amadan entourage had left for France.

Aidan cleared his throat, obviously seeing that his captain's mind had wandered. "Sir, what if this doesn't work? What if the others don't follow us? How do we going to get to her then?"

It did the boy some credit, he realized, that he was more concerned for his first mate than for his ship.

He took the boy by the shoulder again and gave him another smile. "Enough time to cross that rip-current when we come to it, Aidan. For now, we need to make this little hovel as strong as we can. If you can get those swivel guns up to the windows and make sure we have enough powder and shot to stand a small siege, that will be more helpful than all this senseless whinging."

It was a little sharp, perhaps, but it reached the lad.

With a nod, Aidan turned back toward the old house. "Costa, Carpentier, with me. You others, start moving charges out to the gun. We don't have a ship of our own to worry about sinking, might as well make the most of it."

They went about their tasks, and Maguire smiled at the sense of honest work being done, even in a hopeless cause.

Shanae would be back soon, no matter how things had gone at Port Royal. He couldn't let her sail into the teeth of that covetous madman. There was no telling what Greene might do just out of spite, if he felt the squadron was strong enough without one more sloop in the lists.

He moved to the rusty gate out onto the rutted street. It was almost deserted. Since the governor had left and Sidney Greene had declared himself the ruler of Tortuga, the townsfolk had apparently decided to lay low until things shook out.

When Maguire and his ragtag little shore party had taken up residence in the empty villa on the outskirts of town, the neighborhood had gotten even quieter.

But now there was a change in the air. He was no land-bound commander; the few times he had ventured off his ship, from the first time, after the massacre at Wexford where he had lost everything, things had never gone his way with dirt beneath his boots.

He couldn't help but feel that he had turned some corner, spitting in that damned English puppy's face and throwing his offer at his feet.

He might be trapped up here on this muddy hill, in this hovel of an estate, with only a few loyal men cleaving to his cause.

But he had taken a stand for the life he had come to love, and the men and women who depended on him. And, with God's help, the others would see their options more clearly, now.

Greene meant nothing good for any of them, and the only way clear was to abandon him and this enslaving hell he was building.

Tortuga was not their home, now. It would never be a home to the Brethren again.

It would be home to whatever twisted vision Greene and his family held to, or it would fade away into the fog of history altogether.

Either way, no self-respecting buccaneer would call this port their home again.

He could only hope his friends came to their senses before it was too late.

*****

His wife looked down at him with nothing but love in her eyes. Behind her, hiding behind her skirts, his daughter Kate looked on with wide eyes and a gorgeous smile.

His daughter, Kate.

Eamon Maguire lurched out of sleep with a pained gasp.

The dream. The old dream.

Except that it hadn't been. In the old dream, Shannon and Kate were dying in Wexford. He had arrived too late; the damned Parliamentarian forces were sacking the city by the time he leapt off the *Bonnie Kate's* deck onto the quay, running for the burning center of town.

They had had to drag him back to the ship when they had realized it was hopeless. He had screamed his voice raw, clawing at them, begging that they let him go die with his wife and daughter.

They had locked him in his cabin as they sailed south, trying to link up with the remnants of the Royalist fleet. But after what Cromwell had done to first Drogheda and then Wexford, the other eastern ports had fallen, one by one, at the mere sight of the Defender's flags.

While he was still incapacitated, the crew had decided to strike out from Waterford before that city fell and make for the new world.

He had come to realize how lucky he had been that, beyond their decision to flee without his order, discipline had held. As he regained himself, they had reinstated him as captain.

Had they been true buccaneers back then, he never would have retained command.

But ever since that lapse into madness, his dreams had been haunted with images of Shannon and Kate burning; burning alive, their beloved features melting as they held flame-wreathed arms out to him in mute supplication.

He settled back onto the sweat-damp pillow, heart hammering.

But not in fear or torturous sadness.

For the first time in decades, he awoke with the beautiful, healthy, happy faces of his wife and daughter fresh in his mind.

He smiled as tears coursed from the corners of his eyes.

When the pounding on his door began, his heart nearly stopped.

"What?" He shouted, in a voice that could be heard across the deck of a brigantine in a high gale.

Judging from the light through the windows, it wasn't quite eight bells in the middle watch. At least two more hours before the sky even contemplated brightening into dawn.

The muffled response from outside his door was unintelligible.

He rolled out of the musty, too-soft bed and whipped a robe around himself before stalking to the door and ripping it open.

"What, for the love of Jesus, Mary and Joseph?" He glared out at Alonso Costa, the card-shark of the port watch. The man's eyes were wild with fear.

"They're here, sir! They're coming!" His voice shook, although the cutlass in his hand was as steady as stone.

After just a moment, Maguire wheeled away from the door and moved toward the wide doors out onto the balcony overlooking the courtyard and the street beyond.

The ever-present stench of mildew, one of the near constants of life ashore in this grand new world, almost had him gagging as he pushed open the doors.

Peering out into the gloom he could just make out forms moving along the street.

Greene would never trust members of the squadron for this, and he wouldn't weaken his own ship by taking too many of his men away.

This attack, if attack it was, made no sense. Why now? Over a week had gone by, and the new commodore had seemed quite content to let him rot up here on his newly-acquired hill.

Something must have changed down in the harbor. Either the others had come to their senses, or someone else had rebelled against their new master, or—

Or the *Laughing Jacques* had been spotted.

They would want him dead before Houdin returned with Shanae.

Or maybe they were just coming to talk?

An echoing shot rang out and the street lit with a muzzle flash as someone below fired too soon.

There was no way Greene would have wanted them to announce their presence so soon. Maguire crouched down behind the balustrade of the balcony, peering one last time down at the milling forms and seeing his own men rushing into the courtyard, making for the cannon.

That little cannon seemed like a pathetic defense, now that the attack was at hand.

Maguire rushed back inside and got dressed, stuffing loaded pistols into the various straps and belts he used for boarding actions.

He took the stairs two at a time, the four pistols bouncing, a heavy cutlass in one hand, a grenado in the other.

He had had Aidan make several of the little bombs during his free time over the last week or more.

Grenadoes were dangerous things, as likely to blow a man's hand off as to savage the enemy. But when they worked, there was little a single man could do to equal them.

Out in the courtyard, Aidan Allen was marshalling the men, overseeing two of them working the little gun as they prepared to blow a hole through their own defenses.

He wished, once again, that the gate gave anything resembling a clear shot of the street.

The little manse was surrounded by jungle on three sides. If Greene had sent men infiltrating through the trees, they would have little warning. Aidan had set a man to watch each of those approaches, but the tangled undergrowth meant visibility was laughable. Their only saving grace was that the same tangle would hardly allow a forceful charge against the walls.

At least, that's what he was hoping.

There were ten of them in all, behind the thin walls of the villa. They were fighting from prepared positions with plenty of powder and shot at the ready, with loaded pistols and rifles and scatter guns as well.

But Greene could bring several times their number to bear if he thought it was important enough.

And, as they were attacking now, after so many days of idleness, the bastard obviously felt it was important enough now.

Maguire grabbed Aidan and pulled him close. "Shanae must be here! It's the only thing that makes any sense!"

He saw the light dawn in the young man's eyes.

If Greene was willing to openly attack them here, what would stop him from attacking the *Laughing Jacques* as she came into the harbor?

There was no way Greene was going to be able to hide this from the other captains. He either believed his position was strong enough to withstand their anger, or it was tenuous enough to demand a bold, unequivocal action.

"We need to get down to the waterfront!" Maguire snarled the words out. He had been prepared to sell himself as dearly as he could here at the end of all his poor decisions and the bad cards he had been dealt.

But now, with Shanae so close and in such danger, a renewed sense of purpose filled him.

And he could see his daughter's eyes shining brightly in his mind.

"Fire!" he ordered the young man at the cannon. Young Axel Perry, he saw. What did a boatswain know about laying a gun?

He laughed out loud.

What did anyone need to know about laying a gun when it was pointed at a wall?

Aidan was peering around the gate, and his hand flashed down as the attackers surged from cover.

The little cannon bucked, filling the courtyard with thick smoke and thunderous noise.

Dust and bits of plaster cascaded down around them.

"It worked! Again!" Aidan roared over the ringing in all their ears, as beyond the walls, men screamed, probably more in shock than pain.

Then, from over his shoulder, another deafening detonation as one of the swivel guns was fired. The top edge of the wall in front of them seemed to jump and jitter as countless holes appeared along its length, the lower edge of the spread of shot chewing at it as it flew past and into the men beyond.

Now the screams outside contained real pain.

"Fire!" Aidan shouted again, and again the little cannon fired.

This time they had filled it with a cannister of grape, and the horrific insectile whistle of the shot flying through the ragged hole in the wall and into the men beyond was enough to send a chill down his spine.

The other swivel gun barked out its own defiance, pointed off to port … or left, as the case surely was here. This time the gunner's aim was a little worse, and more of the shot was wasted against the wall, giving it an ancient, weather-beaten affect in a moment's time. The rest of the shot, however, rained down on a cluster of attackers outside the walls. Again, screams rose into the night.

Maguire took just a moment to wonder what the neighbors would think.

A manic laugh escaped his lips before he clamped them shut. He felt madness gnawing at the edges of his vision.

The higher-pitched reports of small arms began to echo off the surrounding walls. The attackers striking back, as return fire poured into them from the upper level of the manse.

He looked around and found Aidan recoiling from taking a rifle shot out the front gate, throwing the long gun behind him and grasping for another.

"Aidan, we need to head for the waterfront!" He shook the man. "We can't stay here. They're stunned! They'll fall back. While they do, we need to get around them, make for the port!"

Aidan's wild, battle-frenzied eyes stared at him for a moment, then he shook his head and nodded.

"Right." The gunner stood straighter, checked the powder in his new rifle and nodded again. "I'll gather the lads, sir. You wait here."

Maguire crouched by the gate, peering out through the drifting smoke and fog. When he thought he saw a group making another cautious advance, he put his slow match to the wick of his grenado and tossed it down the street into their midst.

He whipped himself back behind the wall as the crack of the explosive's detonation shook the ground beneath his feet, and again English screams rose into the night.

He did not fight down the grin.

And then he was surrounded. Aidan was returning that maddening smirk, along with young Perry, Costa, and Carpentier the topman. He tried to fix each man's features and name in his mind, but he was already too jittery with battle-rage. He tried to count and came up with seven. He panicked, counted again, and came up with eight.

He had lost two men already?

Then, looming out of the darkness, the huge Frenchman, Fabien Astier, who had joined the crew from the fluyt *Marie Lajoie*. At Shanae's invitation.

The man's eyes flashed green like some crazed jungle cat, and his smile was feral.

Maguire smiled back.

"Alright, this should be easy." He nodded at the gate behind him. "Nothing you lot haven't done a hundred times before, and three sheets to the wind, too. We're going back down to the waterfront. It's nearly a straight shot from here. This bunch is just about done; I think. They didn't know what they were getting into, and you made it plain to them, sure enough."

They smiled at that, and he tried to forget that they had already lost one man, and could all be dead before dawn.

"*Laughing Jacques* is making for the harbor. She must be. And aboard her, as you know, is our first mate. We can't let them sail into Greene's guns all unknowing. We owe them more than that."

Even as the words left his lips, he knew what he really meant was that *he* owed *her* more than that. But perhaps Greene's attack meant the man was feeling the pressure.

The dawn might rise on their dead bodies, for a certainty.

But it might just dawn on Greene's demise, as well.

"All together now!" Maguire turned back to the gate as Aidan handed out grenadoes. They would lob those first, then make a break for the jungle paths that would lead them down and around any cordon Greene might have laid, and then straight for the harbor.

If the fighting wasn't too intense, they should get there long before the sun stained the eastern sky.

He could only hope that would be soon enough.

Chapter 23
1675 ~ Cayona, Tortuga

"Thank you, Lord! Thank you for delivering us once more to solid land!" Hunt fell out of the jolly boat and into the surf on his knees.

Shanae leapt out after him, hauling the boat's cable with her. She shook her head as she pushed through the surf past him. This was hard enough already, in the pre-dawn darkness, without him carrying on.

"What the hell are you on about?" Boothe passed the kneeling madman on the other side, taking up the rope and helping her pull the boat to shore.

"You'd think Poseidon would want you to stay on the water, no?" The *Arbiter's* former first mate had made a speedy recovery from the doldrums that had darkened his mood for weeks now. She smiled, figuring it had something to do with a sudden, dark turn in the Greene family fortunes.

"The lord would prefer we stay on the waves, of course. But he also prefers the land leave ephemeral insolidity to the waters."

She shook her head as she made the cord fast around a heavy tangle of ancient driftwood. Hunt made little enough sense most of the time; when he spoke of Port Royal, he was downright incomprehensible.

"Captain Houdin should be bringing the *Jacques* in toward the harbor soon." She looked out to the east, past La Montagne rising in the darkness, but could make out no change in the distant skyline.

"There's no reason they should be suspicious." Boothe came back from the boat loaded with gear and dropped it unceremoniously onto the sand. "The sloops are in and out all the time. They won't be in any danger, don't worry."

"Worry." Hunt was still kneeling in the surf, filling up various bottles with foaming seawater. "This is an ill-omened night, I fear." He looked up into the dark sky, tracking the sparkling trail of stars that bisected it. "We have struck our foe a grievous blow, true. But he knows it not. And here, on Tortuga, his power is still strong."

She felt a slight shiver run up her spine at his words but shook her head. "We've only been gone three weeks. How much could have changed in three weeks? No. It is only prudence, approaching Cayona from the landward side. We'll see how things stand, stop by the Dog, maybe Chartier's, and then head down to the waterfront." She slid her weapons into their various holders and hangers.

It gave her a sick feeling, thinking of Tortuga as enemy-held territory. But now, so close to actual victory, she wasn't going to take any chances.

"Captain Houdin will take his time getting the *Jacques* to the quay. If Greene or any of the other captains hails him along the way, he's going to say we stayed in Port Royal. No one will think twice about that."

"Greene'll probably be relieved." Boothe heaved a heavy scatter gun onto his shoulder with a grunt. "Fewer recalcitrants to cause him problems."

She gave him a glance by the waning moonlight. "You look ridiculous with that cannon, you know."

"Let's see how ridiculous I look when some *Chasseur* tries to ambush us and I blow them away." He grinned. He hadn't grinned like that in a long time.

She cocked her head as she pushed off into the undergrowth.

She couldn't recall him ever grinning like that, she realized.

"You'd still look pretty ridiculous, dumped on your arse by the recoil."

Hunt, at the back of their little column of three, gave a single, startled yip of laughter, and even Boothe chuckled.

"It'll be worth it, to take some of those bastards down."

*****

The walk through the jungle was exhausting. The trees kept the temperature lower during the day, but retained the heat long into the night, and the steamy air clung to her lungs as she drove one foot before the other, pressing on despite her fatigue.

She had no idea what to expect when they reached Cayona, but she repeated in the silence of her mind what she'd told the men: it couldn't be that bad.

Had Captain Maguire taken the *Arbiter*? Would they be able to reach him without Greene or his bastards seeing them?

She wiped sweat from her brow as she took a moment to sip from a waterskin. She looked back and held it up to the others, signaling that they should do the same.

Boothe shook his head. He was a stubborn fool, even if when she was merely speaking sense.

Hunt took a sip, but in the dark, he had mistaken one of his sacred vessels for his waterskin and dashed a mouthful of seawater down his throat.

When he was done coughing and choking, he gave an apologetic little smile and gestured for her to continue on.

With a sigh and a shake of her head, she did.

The jungle was full of noises. Birds, chattering monkeys, and other wildlife hooted and howled all around them, falling silent as they approached and then roaring back to life as they passed.

There was no way they would ever be able to hear anyone approaching through the undergrowth, but then, no one was going to be able to hear them either, so she decided to ignore the creeping sensation the entire situation was sending down her back. There was nothing they could do about it either way, so she may as well focus on matters that were under her control.

In a clearing about two bells after they had left the boat behind, she checked the sky again. There was a rough, textured light just starting to glow along the eastern sky, outlining the mountain. Thin trails of smoke rose into that lightening sky, marking the location of Cayona just over a small rise.

She couldn't see the waterfront from where they were, but she knew that Houdin would be sliding his ship into the harbor soon. She had wanted to be on the streets by then.

She hadn't wanted to mention it to the others, but if they found the situation untenable, she wanted to be able to somehow signal to the *Jacques* to flee before they were trapped against the tide and the prevailing wind.

She had a rocket in her pack, and Bastian Houdin would be watching for it as he made his approach. But for any of this to matter, they had to make it to the town before first full light.

She picked up her pace and the men followed. None of them had the breath to argue at this point, and she smiled slightly at the thought. Was this, then, the secret to effective leadership? Keep the men so tired they can't complain, even if they wanted to?

She doubted Captain Maguire would agree, but then, she figured he still had some tricks to teach her. Maybe this was one.

From out of the gloom before them they could see the dilapidated buildings marking the outskirts of Cayona looming up before them. As the town had grown, it had pushed up the hill rather than spreading outward to either side. Some intrepid settlers had tried, but the jungle, or circumstance, had eventually pushed them back, and those buildings had been abandoned. They had mostly returned to the jungle at this point, marking a soft border between what passed for civilization on Tortuga and the forces of Mother Nature.

She moved to one leaning wall and knelt. The men settled down to either side, all of them peering around the broken masonry into the shifting, gray shadows.

"Let's first head up to the Dog." She tilted her head up the hill. "We'll have a clear view of the harbor from there, and Serre or the others will know the lay of the land. We'll keep to these old roads for a bit before moving out to the main street. This time of morning, most folks will still be sleeping. Let's not wake anybody up we don't have to."

Boothe nodded distractedly, still looking out toward the town, while Hunt's bright green eyes shifted to hers. There was a touch of sadness there she didn't understand, but now wasn't the time to indulge their pet madman.

She rose, shifted the straps of her pack on her shoulders, and slipped around the ruin, stepping carefully over snake-like creepers and tree roots. She was just coming to the edge of this first wrecked plot when a distant pop brought them all up short.

A gunshot. She was certain of it. They crouched in place, listening for more. There were no angry shouts, no cries for help. Just that one report. Around them, the jungle life was growing louder again.

And then the morning exploded.

It was the sharp detonation of a small gun. Maybe a two or three pounder, if the echoes weren't throwing her off. It was distant, somewhere higher up the hill, but it was unmistakable.

Before the echoes of that first shot faded into nothing, another blast followed, this time accompanied by the distant wailing of screams.

The rippling detonation of small arms crackled out, like grease on a hot skittle. A louder, sharper snap echoed through the jungle, then another. The cries were rising and falling.

Somewhere up the hill a full-on battle was unfolding.

"Come on!" She dropped her pack, pulled her cutlass and a pistol, and shouldered through a veil of palm fronds onto the pitted, rutted track of a forgotten street. Behind her she could hear the men following wordlessly. Boothe was grunting beneath the weight of his little cannon, but she suddenly realized they were probably going to be gladder to have it than any of them had thought.

Ahead and above them the gunfire died down to a sporadic grating sound. Either one side or the other had won the day, or the two forces, whoever they were, were regrouping for another go.

She stopped beside a taller ruin, resting her shoulder against it and peering around the corner again. It was brighter. She could make out swaths of shadow ahead that had to be the space between more intact buildings. They were probably just a hundred paces or so from the more viable parts of town.

They needn't worry about waking anyone up now, of course. The battle up the hill would have ensured that anyone from the governor's manse to the ships in the harbor would be awake.

What they *did* need to worry about was who was fighting, and who might need their help.

Boothe's little cannon could be just the thing to turn the tide, applied from an unexpected quarter at just the right moment.

The three of them moved up another row of collapsing structures, then another.

Now the walls of intact houses rose up on either side, and they found themselves in an alleyway good and proper. There were no sounds from up the hill. There hadn't been a shot fired in several minutes, and even the shouts and cries had died away.

Either they were too late, one way or the other, or it had become a game of cat and mouse up there.

The question was, who was the cat and who was the mouse?

She looked back, a little surprised that she could see Boothe and Hunt plainly now.

But that's how it always was, with dawn actions. One moment you were struggling through the dark, the next it was full light and you couldn't remember when it happened.

Full light.

Somewhere far below, the *Laughing Jacques* was navigating its way through the approaching channel toward the harbor.

She needed to know who was fighting, and how they fared, in case she needed to fire the rocket.

She pushed off from the wall, waving her pistol low without looking back, and walked awkwardly toward the far wall. There was a street beyond. This one even had a few cobbles left, peeking out from the dark mud.

And somewhere off to the left, up the hill, she heard someone slip in that mud with a sharp, low curse.

She dropped to one knee, signaling again with her pistol for Boothe and Hunt to do the same.

They waited at the mouth of the alley, aiming pistols and the small swivel gun up the hill, waiting to see what they might see.

Another curse, and then a lower voice berated the first. There was a sheepish, muttered apology.

And Shanae almost laughed.

She knew that voice.

She should have recognized the curse, but she sure as hell knew that hangdog apology.

She stood, looking over her shoulder as she gestured for Boothe to lower his weapon.

He shook his head, face angry.

She almost turned to him, then, to order him to drop the gun. She noticed that behind the tall man Hunt had already lowered his pistol.

"It's Captain Maguire." She didn't even try to lower her voice.

"Captain, it's Shanae." She stepped out from her position beside the old building, both hands in the air.

She smiled at the strange, bird-like sound Aidan made as she appeared out of the shadows.

They were a sorry bunch, spending more time looking over their shoulders than in the direction they had been running.

Captain Maguire looked haggard and pale, but he smiled when he saw her. Aidan, a ghostly pallor turning his usual bronzed skin gray, smiled as well, but his was a bit more sheepish.

Behind them were a handful of sailors from the *Kate*, including the tall Frenchman from the *Marie Lajoie*, Astier, looming behind the more familiar faces.

"Jesus, Marie, and Joseph, girl, you're a sight for sore eyes, but what're you trying to do, stop my heart before her time?" Maguire shouldered his way past Aidan and gave her a quick, tight embrace.

She was stock still as he held her. She couldn't remember the last time he had shown her such affection in front of the crew.

He pulled away seemingly unaware of the impact the contact had had on her. He looked behind her, eyes widening just a bit as he saw Boothe, then his grin returning in full force when he recognized Hunt, smiling openly, behind him.

"Goodness, girl. You're a sight for sore eyes." Then his smiled dimmed. "Where's the *Jacques*?"

Before she could reply, there was a deep, thunderous boom from far down the mountain.

From the harbor.

She turned in that direction as the others did the same. She was opening her mouth to respond when the first cannon shot was followed by a shattering barrage. The entire harbor echoed with the fury of the big guns.

She looked from Boothe to Maguire, her eyes desperate. "They were going to head into the harbor at first light." She looked up, cursing the brightening sky. "That has to be them."

It seemed like the cannon fire went on forever. It had to be more than just the *Chasseur*, too. Punctuating the higher blasts were occasional detonations as deep as the oceans; the guns of the *Arbiter*. She glanced at Boothe and saw the same realization in his own eyes.

Below them, far out of sight, his own ship was firing on a member of the squadron.

She wondered if the lesser guns were coming from the other ships.

Was *Syren* even now doing her best to kill Houdin and his crew?

Was *Chainbreaker* trying to destroy her sister as they stood there, helpless?

The pain and horror she felt churning through her stomach were plainly visible on her captain's face as well.

"Captain, what do we do?"

He shook himself out of his paralysis. "How did you get here? Did you take a boat?"

She nodded. "The *Jacques's* jollyboat is a few hours back west."

Maguire paused for thought. "Not supplied for a run, though."

It wasn't a question. He would know they hadn't stocked the small boat for any kind of desperate sea voyage.

"We could get supplies from Chartiers, sir?" Aidan was breathing heavily, but he seemed to have come back to himself.

Maguire nodded. "We could, at that." He turned back to her. "Do you have the mast and material for a jury rig?"

She shook her head. They hadn't expected to have to sail the boat. "There's some cordage, but no sail, no mast."

He swore under his breath. "We could get that, too, from Chartiers', I suspect. But we'll want to travel light."

"Sir, where are we going to go?" She realized suddenly, the strangeness of finding him here on the outskirts of Cayona, obviously running from someone. "Sir, what's happening?"

Before he could respond, there was a shout further up the hill, and the sharp report of a pistol or rifle.

"Here they come!" The high-pitched voice could only be Axel Perry, the boatswain.

"You brought Perry?" She shot Maguire an accusatory look. The boy was too young to be caught up in a mutiny, no matter how justifiable.

The captain grinned at her. "You think *you'd* have been able to keep him away?"

The sailors from the captain's party were taking cover around them, all looking back up the hill.

Another shot rang out beneath the looming trees, and the sharp whine of a near miss hissed by her shoulder.

She ducked, bringing her pistol back up.

"Who *is* it?" She knew, of course, but she might have been wrong.

"*Chasseurs*." Aidan spat. "At least the others aren't that far fallen, yet."

Maguire nodded, peering into the green gloom. "Greene made his offer, and I turned him down. Looks like he wasn't happy with my response."

She started, turning to stare at him. "You turned him down?"

Maguire's answering smile was tight. "Someone put a bug in my ear, it would seem. Decided beaching myself made a stronger statement to the others." He spat into the undergrowth. "Not that they seem to have taken the signal."

"We've been holed up in a manse Chartier let him borrow the rent for." Aidan was crouched beside her.

At the word borrow, she turned back again to the captain. "Ah, yes. Borrow. Seems you haven't been above-board concerning your finances, sir."

He barked a laugh, lowering his head. "Found the book then. Good." He looked over his shoulder. "And the factors in Port Royal?"

She wanted to push him into the loam. "Your instructions were being put into effect before we returned. The debts should have all been called in by now. You are the proud owner of nearly everything the Greene family claims on the island of Jamaica and its other Caribbean holdings."

This time the captain's grin was downright feral. "Well, that's a pleasant prospect."

Another shot from up the hill sent them all ducking. "Not that it would stop a ball, mind you."

Boothe was breathing heavily behind her. The tension of the morning had hit a milestone for him at the sound of his old ship's guns, and he had been almost vibrating with strain since.

She realized, at the thought, that the cannons down the hill had stopped.

A sloop wasn't a strong ship, when receiving the attention of several warships at once.

"Boothe, you need to calm—"

She began, but he pushed off her hand and lurched upright.

"Bullocks." He spat, moving forward like a man in a nightmare, the swivel gun presented like the polished weapon of an honor guard.

"Boothe, get down." Maguire snapped, but even the command voice of a born captain couldn't reach the man now.

"Boothe, what are you doing, you fool." Aidan reached out for the older mate as he passed, but he too was brushed away.

Ahead, several shadows burst from the undergrowth and skidded to a stop among the debris of the jungle floor. Their eyes narrowed, teeth gleaming in vicious grins.

And then they saw what the figure before them was holding.

And their narrowed eyes widened.

And with a roar, Boothe touched his slow match to the gun's powder.

Booth was thrown back as if he had been kicked by a mule.

The little clearing filled with thick, acrid smoke that billowed out through the looming trees and swirled into the air over their heads. The light spilling through the green canopy sliced through the cloud in solid-seeming bars.

Up the trail, from the direction of Greene's party, men screamed in agony.

Only Captain Maguire maintained the presence of mind to take advantage of the situation.

"Pull back! Now!" He was dragging his own sailors and pushing them down the hill, through the alley she had passed through only moments ago. "Go!"

The others moved swiftly. She hesitated, wondering if maybe a frontal assault through the gun smoke might be able to defeat this band and give them the breathing room they would need to regroup, but if the captain was ordering them to retreat, there must be more *Chasseurs* above them than they could handle.

She looked back up the hill and watched as Maguire dragged Boothe up by one shoulder.

The former first mate of the *Arbiter* was bloody and stained with soot, but he was grinning with a vacant, dreamy expression that would have looked more appropriate on Hunt's face at full tide.

She turned, sliding her cutlass home to free up her hand for the mad scramble down the hill.

It occurred to her, even as she was pumping for the full jungle beyond the ruins, that they were moving farther from Chartier's and the supplies they would need to make a boat journey back to Jamaica even possible.

They were all running through the jungle, now. The sun was pounding on the canopy high overhead, the green all around them growing hot and steamy.

Up the hill the crack of pistol shots resumed. She chanced a quick glance over her shoulder and watched the captain hand Boothe off to the giant carpenter, Astier.

He looked up and saw her, giving her a reassuring smile and a nod.

Then his eyes widened in surprise.

She turned back front, fearing another party of *Chasseurs* had set an ambush for them, but the jungle was clear ahead save for her friends and allies making their headlong tumble.

She looked back to the captain for an explanation, but he was nowhere to be seen.

Captain Maguire had disappeared.

She stopped, letting the others pass her. She began to move back up toward the sound of the approaching hunters.

Astier ran past, supporting Boothe, and growled at her to keep moving.

But Captain Maguire was till nowhere to be seen. She looked from side to side, thinking maybe he had changed course in an attempt to lead their pursuers away.

Then she saw the splash of blue among the green.

"Shanae! What are you doing!?!" Aidan's voice, but it sounded hollow and far away, as if they were all in a deep cavern.

She slowed as she approached the blue.

It was a coat, nearly hidden by a spray of fronds and ferns swinging wildly.

It was Maguire's coat.

And it was wet with blood.

She fell to her knees by his side. He was face down in the wet earth of the jungle floor.

She flipped him with strength augmented by sheer terror, heedless of his injuries. His pale face came around, his eyes fixed on the trees overhead.

She could see, without even thinking about it, that he was dead.

He was dead.

He was gone.

Captain Maguire was dead.

She rose without thought. Her mind was cold. Everything was sharp. It hurt to think, so she did not think.

She looked up. Figures moved through the green shadows. She raised her pistol and pulled the trigger, but nothing happened.

She had already fired it.

She was robbed of even that unsatisfying revenge before the end.

Sound faded away. She heard noises, but could not identify what they might be, or what they might mean.

She did not care.

There were flashes of light up the hill as small shadows sailed overhead in that direction.

Grenadoes, a small voice said.

But she didn't care.

She was pulled backwards; dragged through the undergrowth, but it felt as if this was happening to another person.

At her core, in her heart, there was nothing but a heavy numbness as the jungle flashed past.

More shouting, she thought, but didn't care to translate into meaningful speech.

She was forced at speed through the jungle, pushed, prodded, and dragged, but her mind had ceased to work through any of it with logic or sense.

The jungle gave way to a blindingly bright swath of white. There was a sparkling blue expanse.

She was tossed unceremoniously onto a rough wooden surface where she lay still, staring up at a clear sky a beautiful deep blue.

Tears coursed down her cheeks at that. It was such a pure sapphire blue. Why did that make her sad?

The sky was eclipsed with bodies crushing in all around. There were sharp noises, smoke.

Someone nearby cried out in pain, and this almost reached her. She was in pain herself, although she couldn't remember why that might be. Someone else was hurt.

Someone important was hurt.

The wood beneath her heaved and pitched.

A boat.

They were on a boat.

Why were they on a boat?

Where did they think they were going?

But all she could do was stare upward, catching glimpses of that beautiful sky beyond the harsh, cruel shadows of the figures laboring above her.

Saltwater coursed down her cheeks.

It was such a beautiful shade of blue.

Chapter 24
1675 - Port Royal, Jamaica

No matter how many evenings he took his leisure in One-Eyed Jack's, no matter how familiar so much of the place came to be, it would always seem alien to him.

Or maybe no new place would ever seem to fit, in this new world without Captain Maguire in it.

He bowed his head over his tankard.

That thought struck him about a hundred times a day, and it always surprised him, like a cowardly punch to the gut before a brawl got good and started.

They had been in Port Royal for over two weeks, but nothing had settled down in his mind.

He could barely remember that terrifying flight down the mountain. He remembered thinking, as they all leapt into the *Jacques's* jollyboat, that they were going to either die on that beach like the captain in the jungle or they were going to starve on the waves.

But then there was a distant crack, a horrifying tearing sound from overhead, and the tree line behind them had exploded, sending dark dirt, burning palm fronds, and twisted tree trunks high into the air.

How the *Laughing Jacques* had escaped Cayona Harbor they had not known, then, but they had all cried out with disbelieving relief.

The little sloop had kept their pursuers back long enough for them to get the boat out of the surf and back to the ship. Captain Houdin was horrified at the news they carried but maintained his composure and ordered their return to Jamaica without hesitation.

Their relief at the unexpected rescue was only overshadowed by the horrible, mind-numbing loss of the captain.

That was almost enough to blot their survival away completely.

For Shanae, it appeared as if it had been more than enough.

She had been catatonic the entire way down the mountain, insensate as they dragged her through the jungle and threw her into the boat.

She had lost consciousness at some point during their harrowing rush back to the *Jacques*, and she hadn't recovered since.

Aidan realized with mild surprise that his tankard was empty. He couldn't remember taking a single sip.

They were currently living under the benevolent kindness of captain Houdin and the Jack's owner, a brawny bald man named Jamie Hall. The remnants of the *Kate's* crew stranded in Port Royal had no funds of their own, and it galled him to depend on anyone's charity even as he forced himself to remember how lucky they must count themselves to have any help in this foreign port at all.

He sighed, looking around the gloomy interior of the tavern. None of the others were in yet. Most of them were haunting the waterfront for news from Tortuga or up in the rooms watching over Shanae.

Hunt was upstairs, he knew. The madman would not leave their first mate's side.

Strangely enough, the self-proclaimed priest of Poseidon did not seem to be nearly as despondent as the rest of them, almost as if he were waiting for something that could well be glorious, sitting just over the horizon.

Aidan found no more comfort in the ramblings of a madman than he found discomfort in the man's rants.

He pushed himself heavily away from the table, nodded to the dark barkeep, Liz, behind the long counter.

She wouldn't normally let a patron wander off without paying, he knew. But the bald man had given the word, and so with no more than a strange look, she nodded back and went back to talking with two shady-looking patrons at the bar.

He pushed his way out into the alley and took a deep breath before remembering he wasn't in Cayona anymore.

He coughed on the noisome effluvium of the Port Royal night.

It wasn't that Tortuga's city smelled any sweeter, but at least, being far less built up than the English town, the smells dispersed more quickly. They didn't fester in pockets of breath-stealing foulness as they seemed to in Jamaica.

Pulling a kerchief up over his nose, Aidan quick-stepped toward the harbor. Maybe he'd run into one or two of the other *Kates* out there, or at the very least be able to clear his mind, and his nostrils, with the more familiar scents of the harbor.

The maze of alleys and winding streets was familiar now, no longer the confusing tangle they had been upon his most recent arrival. He had been here many times with the captain, of course, but not often enough to learn the dizzying patterns of the city.

Now, however, after being stranded here for weeks, he knew, by practical experimentation, that he could navigate the labyrinth with his head half-lost in a rum fog, to any of a number of establishments willing to offer credit to a reasonable-looking man.

The streets opened out onto the waterfront and he paused to take in the sharp, salt-smell of the water. It was low tide, and he felt a twinge of guilt that he had lost track of the tides; he had been trapped ashore too long with his own misery.

He walked to the edge of the stone quay and looked up and down the harbor. Even this late at night the place was bustling with the business of cargo ships loading and unloading. Many, including several that had the unmistakable look of buccaneering ships, made preparations for morning departures, despite the little Navy squadron floating so close by, beneath the guns of the fort. The *Venator*, a navy frigate bigger even than *Jaguar*, looked fierce, watching over the harbor.

He sighed again, lowering himself to the warm stony surface. Sitting on the edge, He let his legs dangle out over the water.

There was some confusion among the *Kates* as to what they should do next.

With no money, no ship, and no prospects other than the tiny sloop for support, he didn't see that they had many options.

Captain Porter, captain Maguire's old friend, had been trying to buck up their spirits, claiming that a solicitor farther into the city proper would be able to help them once Shanae was up and functioning.

That was all well and good, but what kind of self-respecting buccaneer would trust to a solicitor, when their heart cried out for revenge?

That sort of thing didn't sit well with him, and he knew it didn't sit well with the rest of his shipmates either, except maybe for the giant Frenchman, Astier. But Fabien hadn't been a pirate long; it seemed like only yesterday the man had nearly brained Shanae defending the *Marie Lajoie*.

He wanted to shout to the heavens, to scream his defiance and his anger.

He'd done that already, and it earned him nothing more than a few strange, dark looks from passersby.

Looks that reminded him of the looks Hunt received on a regular basis.

And that just rankled all the more.

How could this all have happened? His head fell, his chin hitting his chest. He let the despair that was never far from the surface well up once more.

He spat into the water, thinking of the captain's friends, especially captain Semprun. How had the mistress of the *Syren* let this happen?

Did Semprun, Hamidi, and Fowler know captain Maguire was dead?

What would Greene have done with the captain's body?

His stomach tightened around the renewed grief, but he forced his mind to continue down its current, dark path.

He thought it was even odds that Greene might parade the captain's body before all of Tortuga to prove the error of crossing the new commodore and de facto governor of the island, or quietly disposing of the body in the jungle and pretending he knew nothing of what had gone on that morning.

He wanted to think that Semprun and Hamidi, at least, would not have stood for the slaughter of their friend.

But then, they had allowed the captain to beach himself, had they not? They had sat idly by while one of the most effective of their number had left the squadron rather than working with the poisonous trader from Port Royal.

Captain Maguire had hoped that, when the others realized how serious he was, they would take up his cause and remove Greene, or at least declare their three ships independent.

He had even hoped, although he gave the chance no real merit, that captain Fowler might join them if he saw that all the other captains were unwilling to stick with the English swine.

The captain had had some plan regarding Port Royal, as well, although Aidan had no idea what that might have been.

Aidan wiped the back of one hand across his eyes. His sorrow at the captain's loss was matched only by his anger at the man who had occasioned his death. There was no way Greene was going to survive this coup, even if Aidan Allen had to swim back to Tortuga and kill the man himself, and damned be the consequences.

But revenge, as the captain had always said, was best served cold, and from a distance.

And better still, if one survived to enjoy it.

But he was only one man, and no match for the powers that had set themselves against everything he had felt real and solid in life.

Captain Houdin was a good man, but he was no hero from the old stories, and *Laughing Jacques* was no fit steed for such work.

Shanae would lead them, he knew. If only she would shake off the fugue of the captain's death.

But lead them where? And why? And with what?

And that's why she needed to wake up. He was frozen in place. He would rush the deck of the *Chasseur* in a heartbeat, teeth bared and guns blazing.

But for a more realistic solution?

He sighed again, curled up even more, hanging his torso out over the whispering waves.

"Ah, good!"

The high-pitched voice almost saw him tossed over into the water, and Aidan shot up, hands balled tight, ready for a fight.

It was Hunt, of course.

And the man's open, smiling face, as gormless and devoid of thought as ever, was the only thing that stayed Aidan's fist.

"What in the name of all the saints are you going on about?" He couldn't think of anyone he wanted to see less at the moment than Shanae's tame madman.

Hunt was looking out over the water, at the ships and their bobbing working lights, at the distant stands of mangrove rising from the waters beyond the harbor, outlined against the dazzling stars of the Caribbean night.

The man shivered despite the humid warmth.

"What's wrong?" Aidan felt a sudden, cold dread sweep down his spine. "Is it Shanae?"

His body jerked with the need to rush back to Jack's to check on her.

"Wha?" Hunt's voice was distant, and when Aidan turned back to look at him again by the dim light of distant streetlamps, he saw that the man looked terrified.

"Hunt, what is it?"

It was Shanae. It had to be Shanae. The man hadn't left her side. She was all he was concerned about.

And now he looked like he thought the world was going to end.

And the only thing Aidan could think might feel like that, more than the captain's death, was Shanae's.

The lunatic looked down as if to reassure himself the well-set cobbles were still there. His legs were partially bent, as if he thought the ground beneath him was going to shift away without warning.

Hunt's fevered green eyes flashed at him from beneath his wild eyebrows. "Huh?"

"What's wrong?" He pushed down the nearly overwhelming urge to push the man into the harbor.

"Oh," Hunt shook his head. "Nothing. The impermanence of this place plagues my mind, is all."

Aidan felt his brow furrow as he looked back at the tall brick buildings fronting the harbor, at the level stretch of cobbled plaza, and the well-laid stones of the quay and walls all around.

When compared to the slapdash Spanish mess of Cayona, Port Royal seemed like a metropolis that might be expected to stand until Judgement Day.

"Oh, and the first mate wishes to speak with you."

This time he gave in to the violent urge that surged up into his throat. He took the crazed loon by the lapels of his jacket and nearly hoisted him off his feet.

"What?" He shook the man. "What?" He sputtered, trying to make sense of the emotions churning through his mind. "Why wouldn't you tell me that immediately?"

He pushed Hunt away and spun, running for the close streets of Port Royal, and One-Eyed Jack's, buried somewhere in their midst.

*****

The tavern was doing a brisk business, as it was every night, when he crashed through the door, coming to a skidding stop in the tight confines of the front room. All conversation ceased as he looked around, but none of the blank faces communicated anything like the information he sought.

Then he saw Liz's face lighting up behind the bar. The woman nodded, tilting her head toward the back stairs with a broad smile, and without responding, he was off again.

He pushed his way through the crowd, but the *Kates* had been staying in the little rooms overhead long enough now that the regulars knew him, and they must have realized what his rush meant. Soon, his path was lined with rough, smiling faces, and he felt resounding thumps on his back as if they were happening through a thick winter coat, or to another person altogether.

He rushed up the narrow stair and slammed open the door to the little room without bothering to knock.

He had expected to see Shanae sitting up in bed, maybe with a cup of broth in her hands, maybe a tankard of small beer if she was feeling better than he would have anticipated.

She was fully-clothed, standing over the small table in the corner with Captain Porter. Scattered across the table were several books and charts he didn't recognize.

"You're up!" He knew, as far as declarations of support were concerned, that would never make the history books. But it was all he could think about.

She turned, and he expected her to smile broadly at the sight of him. Or maybe she would respond with a caustic quip at his absence, or his unartful statement.

Instead, her eyes burned with an intense anger he had never seen in them before.

And he had seen Shanae Bure angry on many, many occasions.

He had even been the subject of that anger more than once.

But her eyes flashed now with a fire that reminded him of some of the more colorful sermons he had sat through in his youth. The kind that featured sulfur and brimstone prominently.

"Where have you been?" Those eyes flickered over him and then dismissively away, back to the papers before her. "We've got work to do."

He wanted to object, but instead nodded and approached the table.

The corner was cramped with the two of them already in it, and he stopped before he got too close, peering down, trying to make sense of the papers.

It looked to be ledgers and charts, for the most part. With two very official-looking papers off to the side, adorned with several impressive seals and multiple signatures.

There was nothing there he could have helped her with.

"What do you want me to do?"

She looked over her shoulder at him, then back down. "Someone's already gone to fetch Houdin. We need *Laughing Jacques* to be ready to leave on the morning tide. I'll need you to gather up the remaining *Kates*. Is Hunt with you?"

Aidan looked around in time to see the madman enter the room. He was looking about him with a sense of vague, formless trepidation that made the master gunner found oddly contagious, but when the crazed former curate saw Shanae up and moving, all that fell away.

The gleaming eyes flashed like emeralds, and the man's smile had a vicious edge.

"I'm here, Captain."

At the title all activity in the room ceased, and Aidan looked back at him in confusion.

Shanae looked up, nonplussed, as well. But then her eyes tightened, she gave a quick, sharp nod, and bent back to her work.

"Help Aidan. We're leaving in the morning. Make sure the *Jacques* has everything aboard we might require. I've already sent Perry down to the harbor with a list."

"What are you doing?" Aidan took another step into the corner but stopped when Porter shook his white-maned head. "Can't I help you here?"

He pushed forward despite Porter's silent warning. He wedged himself in between the two and looked down at the charts and papers.

His brow furrowed. "Who's Amelie Carre?"

She shot him a look that mixed contempt and pity in equal, insulting measure, and he stepped back.

"We've got to secure everything here before we make for Tortuga. The captain put a great many things in motion, and I have to make sure they're set in case Greene makes it back here after we hit him."

Aidan shook his head. He was a simple man. He understood sailing, he understood his guns, and he understood women. He *thought* he understood women.

He didn't understand *this* woman.

He never had.

But sometimes he was smarter than others.

"I don't understand."

Porter picked up the fanciest-looking piece of paper. "Captain Maguire's last will and testament. Leaving off his holdings, in Jamaica and beyond, to Shanae Bure."

Aidan's eyes flicked to her in time to see a slight shiver run over her features before they almost immediately returned to stony impassivity.

"Captain Maguire's factors in Jamaica have been working diligently for weeks, and have, tonight, put his final plans here into motion. When Sidney Greene returns home, he will find no welcome here."

"But first we have to drive him from Tortuga." Shanae's voice was a growl.

Aidan shook his head. "How?" He knew he should be off, following orders and leaving this higher-level planning to those better suited to it. He wanted to leave it to them. He wanted to trust that it would work out.

But Shanae had not been with the squadron when Greene made his move against the captain. She hadn't seen Semprun and Hamidi turn their backs on Captain Maguire, shame on their faces.

"How are you going to force Greene out of Cayona? Did the captain have a fleet we didn't know about?" He needed her to understand.

He couldn't lose her too.

"We won't have a prayer if all we have is one Frenchman's sloop. *Jacques* won't have a prayer against the entire squadron."

Her look was predatory, her teeth flashing in a hungry grin. "We won't need a fleet. We already have a squadron. And we won't be fighting that squadron. That squadron will be fighting for us."

He shook his head. "You don't understand, Shanae. They didn't stand with the captain. They could have. Nothing was stopping them, and their situation was considerably stronger than ours is today. Even then, they opted to stay with Greene."

He felt his shoulders slump. He didn't understand the choice the captains had made, but that they had made it could not be denied. "They chose Greene and Tortuga over captain Maguire and Port Royal. They're not going to go back on that choice just because we say so."

It was Porter's turn to snarl, catching Aidan off guard. "Greene's a little pissant. And the Greene family fortunes are now yours. If you can defeat Greene and stave off this attempt to steal the squadron; well, with that fortune, Port Royal would welcome you. The forced trade is still frowned upon by many here, buccaneers and British both. Having exposed the Greenes and freed your friends, both sides of the equation here would be well-disposed toward you."

What Porter had riding on these events he didn't know, but the man's words had not made him feel any better.

He turned back to Shanae.

"How do you intend to convince them of all this during a battle? It's a little complicated to be shouted rail to rail as we launch broadsides into each other."

Shanae's grin hadn't faded. "Don't worry about that." But there was a shade of doubt in her own eyes that he couldn't ignore. He saw an avenue there, even if it wasn't one he would have chosen.

"They won't listen to you, Shanae." He hated even saying the words. He knew them to be false, but there would be time to clear the air after everyone had calmed down, and a more realistic plan could be formulated.

Her eyes flicked toward him, then away.

"They won't listen to a woman—"

He never saw it coming.

One moment he was pleading for her not to throw her life away, the next he was grasping the rough wood of the floor, the room spinning above him, his left cheek aflame.

He rolled onto his back, flailing with his arms, trying to get the floor to stop moving, when she swam into his vision above him, glowering down, her hands on her hips.

He became painfully aware of the two pistols riding there, just in front of her thumbs.

"Was that any less effective for what I've in my trousers, you bastard?"

To his immense surprise, her voice was devoid of anger.

Was she laughing at him?

He tried to shake his head, but the pain came roaring back and he winced, lowering himself again to the floor.

"No. And it won't matter when I hit Greene, either. That was a sad, pathetic trick, Aidan."

She moved back to the table, and he watched as the others turned away as well, ignoring his attempts to stand, nearly thwarted by the still-shifting floor.

Maybe Hunt was on to something after all.

Over her shoulder, without looking at him, she growled.

"I've got a plan, Aidan Allen. Let's hope Greene has no more faith in me than you."

Chapter 25
1675 ~ Port Royal, Jamaica

Boothe could not shake his silly grin after Hunt told him about Allen's encounter with Shanae the next morning.

The insufferable little weasel was always mucking about with his superiors, nosing his way into places he never should have been.

It was only justice it be pushed in.

Scuttlebutt had it he had insulted her resolve and ability, as well. As if he didn't even know the woman!

He sneered, then, shaking his head. Of course, if Allen had been able to control his mouth, Boothe would probably be having an easier time now. It had been a long time since he was last called on to recruit crew.

He rested against a cast iron bollard and took his hat off, wiping his forearm across his brow.

He was glad to have a purpose again, but it wasn't easy, even in a bustling town like Port Royal, to find men and women willing to sign on for work he couldn't even begin to describe.

Captain Porter had been pulling strings as well, he knew, and had quite a group forming up in the warehouse Shanae had secured with some of her newfound wealth.

But Porter had been no more forthcoming than Shanae, and so, aside from knowing they would be crossing the harbor and heading inland across Jamaica, he knew nothing.

Jacques had been gone with Shanae and most of the other *Kate*s for two days, and no one left was saying where they were headed.

He wanted to strike something, but since the only object to hand was the squat metal post he was sitting on, he refrained.

How was he supposed to entice sailors and fighters to join him if he had no idea what they were being asked to do?

He settled for slapping the hot metal hard enough to set his palm stinging, then stood up. Anyone who might possibly be open to taking on such a contract would hardly be awake yet, it being just past three bells in the forenoon watch. With noon almost two and a half hours away, idlers without a ready place on a ship would have been up into the wee hours making merry and might be expected to sleep well into the afternoon watch.

He paused. He had spent two days trying to gather men and women stuck ashore, detached from a ship or crew, and had had very little success.

What if he tried to hire an entire crew?

All they had told him, before leaving for whatever destination had called them away, was that he would need a skeleton crew big enough for a large ship to make a single journey of a week or more. The number he had been given had been 'about thirty', with no need of gunners, powder monkeys, or the like.

It was through such instruction that he was able to glean what little knowledge he had of this action.

He had thought he might lure some merchantmen to dance along the buccaneer's path for a little extra coin and no real danger, but then Shanae had told him the crew he gathered might have to fight over a bit of deck space before their cruise.

So, he needed men and women who could sail a large ship but wouldn't need to fight it.

But might have to fight their way aboard.

All before they mounted whatever attack on Tortuga Shanae had in mind.

So, he had abandoned his plan to recruit merchantmen. Instead, he had gone back to looking for the dregs and drippings from the local buccaneer community, many of whom frequented Jack's at one time or another over the course of their idler's day.

And he had had precious little luck with that, either.

But now, if he were to focus on an entire ship? If he focused on, say, a sloop that might be down and out?

There were plenty of Brethren in and about Port Royal. It was the density of the local population that had convinced so many in the squadron that there wouldn't be a place for them here.

And many of the locals looked to be having just as much trouble finding ripe targets out of Jamaica as the squadron had working out of Tortuga.

He went north along the waterfront, the brick and timber buildings on his right, the busy, noisy harbor on his left, and moved toward the smaller docks where most of the Brethren down on their luck were pushed.

At the very end of the farthest dock was a ship that most of the regulars at Jack's said hadn't left Port Royal in almost a year. It was spoken of in whispers, with a little vicious gleam of humor in the eye.

Chaucer's Pride had been black, once. But that was a long time ago, and sun and weather had beaten most of the color out of the old wood, leaving it with a gray, sickly pallor.

As Boothe walked up to the boarding plank, he noticed that not a soul seemed to be stirring aboard.

The captain of the Pride had stopped into One-Eyed Jack's once, but bald Jamie Hall had seen him out right quick.

It seemed like the fat man's credit had run out in most of the more reputable dives some time ago.

Boothe didn't know if any of the sailors of the old ship had been in, because he doubted any of them would have claimed the ship as their own voluntarily.

"Ahoy!" He called out, wanting to follow the forms.

One did not board a ship of the Brethren without invitation.

"Is anyone about?"

"Wha?" He heard the muffled call from on high and shielded his eyes with an upraised hand to peer up into the tangled rigging. In the distant platform of a dilapidated crow's nest, a head could just be made out against the dazzle of the sun. "Wha'you wan'?"

Well, the ship's reputation for discipline seemed to be spot on, anyway.

Boothe looked back down the dock, at the other sloops and small ships. But there didn't seem to be any better candidates for what he could offer, and he was sick to death of wandering the town hoping to stumble upon a crew.

"I'd like to speak to your captain, if he's aboard?" He wracked his brain for the man's name. "Captain Kay, isn't it? I have a job."

That seemed to stump the figure in the crow's nest, given the sudden stretch of silence from on high. But another voice, just as ragged, called out nearer to hand, and Boothe lowered his eyes to a hatch just aft of the mast, where a jowly face, covered in a patchy black beard, had emerged like a monster from the deep.

"I'm Captain Kay." He struggled against something, it might have been tangled rigging or perhaps the limbs of some dockside whore and stepped up onto the deck.

Boothe had had no luck explaining this ridiculous idea to men one at a time. Would it be harder or easier, speaking to a representative of many?

"I've a proposition for you, if you'd care to entertain one?"

He was still on the dock, not wanting to step onto the flimsy-looking plank too soon.

Kay came up to the railing amidships, apparently trying to compose his face into a receptive smile. "Of course, of course! Come aboard. What can the *Chaucer's Pride* do for you, master?"

It was only a few minutes later when the man's good will evaporated.

"I don't understand. If you don't want my ship, what do you want, then? My men? All of them? For what? A trek overland? Where to?"

Boothe sighed. He had known it was going to come to this, of course. Kay was asking all the right questions, and he had every right to demand answers.

It was just that Boothe didn't have any of them.

"You will be well-compensated. We will be going overland, taking possession of a ship, and then sailing it a short distance. Easy as a dream; no risk at all, aside from those risks we all face every day at sea, am I right?"

He had tried already to butter the man up, to play comrade to his breezy buccaneer's persona. But all of that foundation had vanished when Kay realized his ship was being spurned for some mysterious craft half an island away.

And that he'd have to walk there.

The man's greed battled with his obvious distaste for labor, and Boothe again had to question himself, whether or not this would even be worth it.

"If you need to get to whichever place you need to get to, why don't you sail aboard my fine vessel? Or, if she's not big enough, but my crew is, why don't we sail to wherever this other ship is?" His voice returned to its whiny tone. "I don't understand why we would have to walk across Jamaica for a ship!"

Boothe was losing his patience. "Captain, I promise you; you and your men will be richly rewarded for a very simple service. And if more is required, more will be provided, I assure you."

He hadn't wanted to do it, but he knew it had come to this. He took out one of the gold coins Shanae had left with him. It gleamed in the morning sun, sending sparks of light flashing across the old ship all around them.

"This is the merest trinket of the promised treasure." He handed the captain the coin. "There will be many more coming your way, and the same again to share out among your crew. You wouldn't bring so much home after the most successful action you've undertaken in a decade, I promise you."

Boothe knew no captain worthy of the name would have undertaken anything like this proposition without knowing exactly what they would gain at the other end.

But he was counting on the fact that, since he was getting less than the best Port Royal had to offer, there must be some compensation. And that was most likely going to come in the form of a lack of sophistication in the man conducting the negotiations.

He thought for sure gold in the hand would convince Kay. The man's mud-colored eyes took on an avaricious shine.

And then they dulled with fear, and he handed the coin back. "No. We're not deck-hands for hire, sir. We have a ship. She's a good ship. And we won't be leaving her behind for some Johnny-come-lately flashing a bit of gold."

Boothe couldn't believe his ears. Had Kay just turned him down? He looked at the coin in his hand, closing his fingers over it, and shook his head.

He didn't want to go back to Jack's empty handed, but his pride was already stung, and this latest rebuke hurt even more. He wasn't going to march up and down these derelict ships and be spurned by every failed riverboatman with delusions of captaincy.

He nodded, shrugging at the fat oaf, doing his utmost to maintain his composure, and stepped back out onto the boarding ramp, tipping his hat to the man for the form of the thing as he turned away.

"I'll take your gold!" The voice from the crow's nest shouted down to him, and he looked up to see a spidery bald man scrambling down the rigging.

"I'll take it as well!" Another man emerged from the hatch, kicking a bundle of rigging out of his way.

Soon enough, there was a crowd of disreputable men surrounding him, each of them with hat in hand, and captain Kay standing behind the lot, hopping from one foot to the next in agitation.

"No! You are *my* crew! You are *not* going with this man!"

The spidery bald topman was twisting a knit cap in his hand. "I'm Alvin Simms, m'lord. Quartermaster of the Pride. If Kay's too much of a coward to cross the island, you can count on the rest of us, sir."

"No!" Kay pushed through the mob. "That's not what I meant!" The man was sweating, and Boothe didn't know if it was because of the rising heat of the day, the man's insulating fat, or the pressure of the moment. "We'll vote on the issue! Of course, we will!"

Ah, that was it. Boothe realized what was happening. If this lot took up with him and returned to Port Royal with anything close to the amount of treasure he was hinting at, this Simms would be elected captain in one shake of a lamb's tail, as Maguire used to say.

Boothe grinned. "Now, don't get me wrong. It won't be all your way. We'll be walking, and there might be a bit of a disagreement along the way. But we'll have others with us to do most of the fighting. You lot will be doing the sailing, for the most part."

That gave Kay yet another pause, but the rest of the Pride's men merely nodded, accepting the possibility of violence as a matter of course.

"Alright then." He smiled, feeling the pressure on his shoulders relax for the first time since the *Jacques* had left Port Royal. "We'll be gathering at the small green warehouse right here at the north end of the waterfront tomorrow morning. Bring with you anything you'll need for the journey. We'll have provisions and all the material for working the ship, so don't burden yourself with anything more than the food and water you'll require to cross the island.

One of the men, a squat little dwarf with a mop of copper hair and an unsteady eye burped a sick-sounding laugh. "Water. Right."

This was going to be harder than even he thought it would be.

He had been a buccaneer for years, his own navy days long behind him. But the Commodore had cultivated an atmosphere of discipline and purpose among the squadron, especially on his hulk of a flagship.

If the Brethren were a spectrum of personalities, techniques, and approaches, this lot were at the far end.

He only nodded, tipped his hat again to the mob, giving Kay a tightened glare to keep him in line, and then made his way back onto the quay.

Now he just had to find himself a cadre of coopers and carpenters eager for a little adventure.

Whatever Shanae needed *them* for, he couldn't even begin to guess.

Chapter 26
1675 ~ Port Royal and the Interior, Jamaica

Aidan leapt off the boat, waved his thanks to the two sailors manning the oars, and made his way toward One-Eyed Jack's.

He was trying to be sanguine with his current role. The *Laughing Jacques* had a full complement and then some, with Shanae still on board with the majority of the displaced *Kates*.

He tried to tell himself it was an honor that he'd been trusted to meet up with Boothe and his little band of cutthroats and lead them across the island.

If Boothe was still here.

If Boothe had managed to gather together a band of cutthroats at all.

At Jack's Porter directed him to a small green warehouse on the northern verge of the waterfront. The old captain was staying behind to watch over the financial side of things in Port Royal and assure that, should Greene beat them back after Shanae's attack, there would be a warm welcome.

They had also put quite a bit of captain Maguire's newly discovered wealth behind ensuring that no word could escape the collapsing Greene empire on Jamaica and reach the prodigal son on Tortuga.

At least, they thought they had managed that. A score of ships left or arrived in Port Royal every day. Any one of them could have taken the current gossip of the Greene family's turn in fortune to Cayona.

Hopefully, however, even if such a tale *did* reach the bastard, he would stay put for now, consolidating his hold over the others long enough to lose it all.

He found the warehouse easy enough and found that Boothe had moved a tidy little cohort across the harbor earlier that day.

The paper in his pocket with Shanae's mark on it was enough to secure him the short boat ride across the choppy water and a horse and supplies from a provisioner on the mainland.

He told no one, especially Shanae, that he had only the vaguest of ideas concerning how to ride a horse.

He fought with the beast for nearly two bells, riding through sugarcane and past sprawling plantations, then driving it relentlessly deeper into the jungle, leaving the fields and manor houses behind faster than he would have liked. He had been told by countless men and women who claimed to know, that the Tainos on Jamaica were far fewer than those who haunted the hidden valleys and green depths of Tortuga.

Of course, that didn't address the Maroons. The escaped slaves of Jamaica, free since the fall of the Spanish over a decade ago, were said to be quite short with uninvited guests to the interior. He took little comfort in the knowledge that they usually kept to the mountains.

There was a distinct difference, however, between the drunken reassurances of an acquaintance and the echoing verdant emptiness swallowing you up, where every shadow and fern threatened to hold a war party that might wish to take decades of maltreatment and unfair dealing out of your own precious hide.

Eventually, the road became a path, the path a track, and then, just as he was getting nervous that the scrawled map he had been given might have led him astray, the track widened out into a clearing, thick jungle all around.

In the center of the clearing, standing breast to breast with a fat, balding man in the faded finery of a captain whose luck had run out two or three storms ago, was the once grandiose former first mate of the greatest stationary floating beehive the Caribbean had ever seen.

Boothe looked like he was ready to pull his hair out in frustration. His hat was already off, and Aidan would have given even odds that he was about to cold-cock the portly man opposite him, regardless of what the small crowd around them might do next.

And it was quite a little group that circled the two, at that.

All of Aidan's adult life had been spent among the Brethren of the Coast. He was not one for stilted social niceties or a slavish adherence to fashion.

Still, however, he had come to appreciate the finer points of basic hygiene and a good scrubbing every fortnight or so, whether one needed it or not.

This lot was filthy, threadbare, and none-too-pleased with their current situation, if the looks on their gaunt faces were any indication.

Behind the cluster of buccaneers stood another group, mostly dressed in the rough, serviceable garb of tradesmen. There were two carts with them, their loads covered in canvas tarps, two placid-looking mules hitched to each.

Aidan pulled his mount up and slid from the saddle, not even trying to hide his relief.

He did, however, try to hide his discomfort as he approached the group, although he knew he could have only met with minimum success. His arse hurt as it hadn't since the beating that had seen him flee his home when he was ten.

"We ready to proceed?"

He didn't have the patience to deal with the dregs Boothe had dredged up for this caper. Not with most of the island still ahead of them. "We'll need to be making better time than this if we're to be in place for Captain Bure."

That still felt odd to say, and in the silence of his own mind, she was still Shanae.

Not 'just' Shanae. She had never been 'just' Shanae; and he was only recently realizing this.

He gave his most ingratiating smile to the man with the tarnished golden braid on his frockcoat. "Do you mind if I speak with Mr. Boothe for a moment, sir?"

That kind almost always responded to being called 'sir'.

The man looked confused, the anger in his face only relaxing a touch, but he nodded, taking a step back and gesturing toward an empty part of the clearing.

"By all means, of course." He shot a glance back at Boothe. "But if we don't hear more, we'll be turning around. We're not fools, to be led on some lark through the jungle."

Boothe looked like he was going to lunge for the man, so Aidan quickly stepped in and took him by the elbow, leading him some few feet away.

"We need to talk. Whatever this is can wait." He hissed at the other man.

Boothe relented, pulling his arm free but following all the same.

"You have word from Shanae?"

Obviously, Aidan was not the only one having a hard time with the new realities.

He nodded. "Looks like it's going to be a fight." He said this through his teeth, throwing a disarming grin back at the band of cutthroats that stood in the green shadows watching them.

"We knew it was going to be a fight." Boothe would not smile, but he had schooled his face to stillness, and his expression gave nothing of his frustration away.

"Is this lot going to be up for it, do you think?" He looked them up and down, trying to appear nonchalant. "They look a little hard up, to be honest."

Boothe nodded, looking back out into the jungle. "They'll fight when it's the only way to get a ride back to civilization. Most of them have forgotten they were ever of the Brethren, but enough of them will remember, soon enough." He sighed, giving Aidan a sly, sideways grin. "Hell, if this all goes well, the squadron might grow by a sloop, if we can just get rid of Captain bloody Kay, over there."

Aidan wasn't sure the squadron needed another sloop, but he would take one if it meant he got this group where they needed to be when Shanae needed them to be there.

He had been given a small pouch of gold for just such an eventuality, and with some fast talking and the shining coins he was able to smooth over whatever disagreement Boothe and the inestimable Captain Kay had been embroiled in when he arrived. Soon enough, he had the party moving again, the tradesmen in the middle with Kay and a few of his more timid shipmates, while he moved forward with the vanguard, and Boothe led a small band behind all the rest.

He found occasion, soon enough, to be thankful for the foresight that had led someone to load several casks of water onto one of the mule carts. The tropical jungle had a way of leeching the moisture from a man, even as it soaked him in his own sweat.

The majority of the men from the *Chaucer's Pride*, as their little sloop appeared to be named, looked like they hadn't exerted themselves in a very long time. More than one man fell by the wayside, splashing his lunch across the tangled undergrowth. Boothe's party swept them all up as they moved, and for a while it looked as if the entire complement was going to arrive at their rendezvous with Shanae.

But a dark, heavy whispering began in the core group as the sun, unseen overhead through the thick foliage, began to dip toward the west.

He heard several words he hadn't wanted to hear. They were speaking of savages and escaped slaves and fearing for their lives as the darkness of night began to seep into the shadows all around.

Aidan laughed off their concerns, but he wasn't at all certain he was correct.

He called a halt to their march as the light continued to dim, and was more than generous with the cheap rum that had been tucked in behind the water casks, once the animals had been looked after and he had seen the men and women fed.

It was an uncomfortable night and seeing as he and Boothe needed to keep their newfound companions honest, they had to divide the first and middle watches between themselves.

When the light began to return, his head was full of wool, his eyes scratchy, and his skin crawling with the sensation he always got after sleeping ashore, out in the open.

He hated being out in the open, away from the sea.

There was some grumbling, of course, from the men of the *Pride* and even a few of the coopers and carpenters Boothe had gathered. But he was able to jolly them along, and soon enough, they were moving.

And that was the pattern for several days. The men of the *Pride* would grumble, Boothe would growl, the tradesmen would whine, and Aidan would force a smile through it all.

The exertion of the journey grew with each passing mile, distracting them from their fear of attack.

It was a tradeoff he was more than willing to make, as the emotional toll of that fear was something even extra grog couldn't address.

As it was, the men were so tired as darkness fell, it took less and less of the liquor to quiet them at night.

As habit and momentum asserted themselves and the little column made its slow progress through the interior jungles, Aidan found his mind wandering. What if they took too long? What if Shanae decided not to wait for them, and moved without the support of the reinforcements he was driving toward her?

And, having said that much, would these men be any use in a fight by the time they emerged onto the far beach?

They were breaking camp on the sixth night – or maybe the seventh, he was losing track of time – when he realized there were fewer men than there should have been.

A quick, cursory glance along the group revealed that Captain Kay was no longer among them.

But when he questioned the men, they averted their eyes, shrugged their shoulders, and told him they had no idea where he had gotten off to.

There were three or four other *Prides* gone as well, and he knew they must have decided the fool's errand wasn't worth it. They had probably hounded the gold from the others in the night and made their escape while either he or Boothe had been distracted, whoever had had that watch.

He made a point of seeming angry, but secretly, Aidan was happy with the result.

The only thing worse than going into action with an untrained amateur was facing the enemy with a coward at your side.

The coward was certain to run at the worst possible moment. At least the amateur might get lucky and hit someone as he flailed about.

He had been worried what kind of effect that Captain Kay might have on these men in battle since first meeting up with them, and the fact that the man had removed himself from the equation was quite satisfying, if he was being honest with himself.

That comfort dissolved when an enraged Boothe reminded him of the need for utmost secrecy in their venture.

What was the chance that Kay, newly flush with gold, was going to keep his mouth shut about the strangers who had foolishly given it to him, and robbed him of his crew?

Aidan's stomach sank at the realization, but before he could ask Boothe what they should do, the man had leapt upon Aidan's own horse, yanked the poor, whickering animal around with a savage sawing at the reins, and kicked the beast into a furious gallop back down the trail the way they had come.

He thought for a moment about following, but without a horse, there was no chance at all that he could catch up. Maybe one of the mules hitched to the carts...

Then, looking back at the Prides around him, he realized that if he left them now, he and Boothe might just return to find them gone as well.

So, deflecting the grousing buccaneers' questions with vague fripperies and wide smiles, he led them onwards, toward the distant northern shore, beneath the thick canopy of jungle trees and through the rising humidity of yet another day in the steaming interior of Jamaica.

It was just about noon when Boothe pounded up on them again without a word.

The man's eyes were grim and hard, and Aidan decided he'd rather not ask after what had happened.

Boothe rode for a while, reloading pistols and lost in his grim silence, before dismounting to give the horse a rest, and taking up his accustomed place at the rear of the short column.

It appeared that the men who remained soon realized they were better off without their captain, no matter what might have happened. The overall tenor of conversations improved, and even the tradesmen seemed to be in better spirits after each day's march.

The first leg of the journey had seemed interminable, but soon enough, as the trail dipped down toward the unseen shore, he knew the end was near.

It was just about midday when they came to another clearing, and found Shanae, Hunt, and the other *Kate*s waiting for them. They had a small cache of supplies including water, rum, and enough food for a grand feast.

The men were pleased, falling upon the food and drink as if they had just fought their way clear of hell. He and Boothe, however, skirted the mob and came toward Shanae.

"You're late." She greeted them both with a flat stare. "I needed your best speed."

Aidan was about to respond, trying to ease the tension rising between the three of them, but Boothe beat him to it.

"And you got it." He spat into ferns along the clearing's verge. "These aren't Britain's finest. They're a sorry lot of buccaneers and townsfolk. You're lucky you got us at all, and this early."

Aidan cringed, waiting for the detonation he knew would come, and Shanae's glare seemed to promise just that. But then she paused, her anger still very much in evidence, and clearly made the choice not to respond at all.

"We're going to take them at the turning of the middle watch." She turned to look at the men eating as if it was their first meal in a week. "Your lot should eat their fill, then get some rest. There's not even enough left aboard to make up a skeleton crew, but they won't be giving up their prize without a fight."

She turned and walked out of the clearing without another word.

Aidan watched her, wishing she had told him a little more of what to expect.

The emerald twilight was fading all around them. There would barely be ten bells before they would have to rouse their erstwhile new companions to action.

"Excuse me." A short, copper-haired old man stumped up to him, a bottle clutched it one white-knuckled hand. "Yon lass mentioned a fight?"

"Told you there might be some heat, Suther." Boothe came up, then, and Aidan was thankful for the reminder. He had met Ben Suther a time or two during the crossing and had decided the man drank more than was good for him, but always seemed game for whatever needed doing, no matter how much rum he took aboard.

Suther nodded, a wry smile playing among the tangled gray and copper wires of his beard. "No doubt, master. No doubt. Just wanted to be sure." He looked over his shoulder to where his shipmates were feasting. "Might want to keep it from the others, though, until you can't anymore."

The man's green eyes were clear enough, despite the fog of drink. "They're good lads, sir. They'll remember how to fight when the time comes. But best not let them have the time to brood aforehand, if you get my meaning." He cast a furtive glance between his companions and Boothe. "Wouldn't want to lose anymore boon companions."

He didn't wait to see their reaction before turning on one loose heel and moving back to the feast.

Aidan and Boothe exchanged a curious look, and then shrugged in unison.

Aidan made a point to remember Suther's name for the future.

There would be a place on the *Bonnie Kate* for such a man.

If they ever made it back aboard the *Bonnie Kate*.

*****

Two small boats had been dragged ashore, hidden beneath a thick canopy of overhanging palm fronds. As Boothe's little group of would-be Brethren made their slow, methodical way through the stretch of thick jungle, Aidan took the time to curse the whole venture once again.

He still didn't understand why the *Laughing Jacques*, theoretically just up the coast waiting for their signal, couldn't have come sailing right into the harbor, put a shot or two over the fat cog's bow, and been done with it.

There was no need of a risky boarding action; and given the dangers that still lay ahead, including an entire squadron of buccaneers who might well be gunning for them soon enough, didn't it make the most sense to limit the risks at this end as much as they could?

But Shanae wasn't listening to reason. Apparently, there were only ten or so Port Royal privateers aboard the *Amelie Carre*, a French cog that had been languishing in a little cove on the north of the island for weeks. The ship was the target of this first stretch of her plan, and Shanae had decided to brace them all aboard their stolen vessel, face to face.

As he slid down a muddy embankment toward the surf, he saw dark figures huddled together by the boats, leaning toward each other, muttering words he could not decipher.

Shanae's laugh, stifled before it even really began, sounded thin and hard. The hulking shadow next to her had to be the Frenchmen, Astier.

Aidan tried to suppress the surge of jealous bile that filled his mouth at seeing them sharing this moment, as he shepherded their wayward herd onto the beach.

"So, is the *Jacques* going to come in guns blazing? I think I've heard this tale before." He tried to make light of the question, but he was curious.

Shanae had been ridiculously tight-lipped about each aspect of her plan. He had no idea what they were going to do after taking the cog.

He still had no real clue why he had been playing nursemaid to the huddled, unhappy group of coopers and carpenters he had left back in the last clearing with the carts and his own mount.

There was always a danger, when clever people were in charge, that a plan would be *too* clever by half. Clever plans had a way of coming apart when they hit the rough surf of reality.

And he knew, better than anyone, how clever Shanae truly was.

She gathered them all up, then, around the beached boats. He could tell by the shifting silvery moonlight that they were dark red with white trim.

Laughing Jacques's, then. He hoped Houdin had no need of them before this was all through.

"They haven't been mounting any kind of deep night watch the entire time we've watched them."

Shanae's words were soft, but the tone still carried that strange edge.

Aidan had to remind himself, yet again, that between the wound she had taken on Bonaire, and then the blow of the captain's death, the woman was still half an invalid herself.

"There won't be any need of a distraction." She shot him a smile, and he could almost pretend, in the near-total darkness, that he missed the hint of sardonic amusement at its edges.

"The oarlocks have been muffled, there's none of you lily-white enough to draw undue attention, and so, with even a little luck, we should be feasting aboard the *Amelie Carre* before the last bell of the middle watch is rung."

Aidan hoped she was right. If they couldn't take the big ship in four hours' time, something had certainly gone terribly wrong.

"Our Lord is with us, this night." Hunt's voice emerged from the shadows, and Aidan turned to see the madman walk out of the surf, slipping through the curtain of palm fronds as an actor on a stage. "There is no doubt that all the gods smile down upon our endeavor, for they each of them abhor betrayal." He stood tall, as if he took strength from the water lapping at his ankles. "With all of Olympus with us, who can stand against us?"

Aidan wanted to push him back into the water, but something in the man's voice did, in fact, stir something in his own chest.

Not that he would have admitted that to anyone.

"Right. Thank you, Aston. As always, we appreciate your intercession on our behalf." Shanae dipped her head toward the lunatic, then turned back toward the raiding party.

"I will be in the first boat with Hunt, Astier, Perry, Allen, and six of you new men. Boothe will take the second boat with the rest of you."

She turned toward the former first mate. "Push off about half a bell after us. If something goes wrong, you'll be in position to hit as a second wave."

Boothe shook his head. "That makes no sense. If they're not keeping a watch, why not hit them together? We could come over the sides, port and starboard both, at the same time—"

"Follow." The word was like the crack of a pistol on the quiet beach, and Aidan was thankful he hadn't asked the question himself.

Shanae was done explaining herself, no matter how little she had already said.

He just had to hope she had thought this all through.

They all had to hope that.

He decided to content himself with being in her boat.

They boarded, with Astier staying back to push them from beneath the green curtain and into the gently rolling surf. Four men sat easily at the oars and began to propel them across the moon-sparkled water toward the moored transport in the distance.

He had thought to speak with Shanae in the bows as they traversed the little bay but thought better of it at her last retort. Instead, he settled into the stern, near young Perry manning the tiller, and scanned the distant ship as they made their approach.

It was a fat, ungainly-looking vessel. No one would ever mistake a cog for a fighting ship, with its rounded features and complete lack of gunports, forecastle, or the afterdeck of a warship of this size.

Years at sea made him wince to think about taking the Windward Passage in any kind of heavy weather in the thing. It must toss and pitch like a cork.

There weren't any lights, which was odd, even for a lazy group of second raters like the Port Royal crew.

Could they all really be asleep?

Or were they lying in wait even now, watching the little boat approach down the barrels of rifles and swivel guns?

But as the *Jacques's* boat slid up alongside the *Amelie Carre,* there was no sign they had been seen. Nothing was shot at them, nothing was dropped down on their heads, and soon enough, Shanae was carefully scaling the ship's hull, moving slowly from handhold to handhold, weapons stowed for the climb.

She disappeared over the railing high overhead, and a moment later dropped the rope she'd had wound around her shoulder.

Aidan began to push his way across the pitching boat, but the other *Kate*s, the men who had been with Shanae during his own trek across the island, stood first, glaring at him in the moonlight and refusing to give ground.

Astier was the next up, and then Hunt.

Perry would stay with the boat, but Aidan made sure he was climbing the rope before any of the Port Royal lot got their chance. He'd be damned if the new meat was going to beat him to the strange prize's deck.

He was only halfway up, though, when all hell broke loose above.

He recognized the first voice and tried to figure out why Shanae would have charged the prize crew if they were really asleep.

Several distant pops echoed out over the water from the ship. Pistol shots, and he redoubled his efforts, scrambling over the railing as he drew one of his own guns, rolling down into the shadows, pressing his back to the ship's bulwark and searching for a threat.

There was no movement on the broad, open deck. He saw two still forms splayed out just forward of the mainmast, but most of the action seemed to be happening at the aft of the ship.

Two more gunshots cracked out, and he began to run.

The first had been accompanied by a high-pitched cry. Whether it had been of pain or surprise he couldn't have said. He only knew one thing.

It had been Shanae.

Two more reports echoed up into the surrounding hills, and then a series of vicious-sounding, heavy slaps.

The low wall of the quarterdeck bulkhead had a small, sunken door, and he took the three low steps in one leap, shouldering aside the already-broken door, and drew himself up in the short companionway beyond. There were tight, confined cabin cells to either side, but at the end another door swinging wildly on broken hinges, was the captain's cabin.

And standing in that doorway, breathing heavily, was Shanae. She was leaning against the doorframe, holding a kerchief to her left shoulder, watching as several figures worked in the room beyond.

She turned as he stopped, and gave him a dreadful smile, made all the worse by the blood-flecked pallor of her face.

"Told you, Aidan. It was nothing."

He approached her warily, looking around her into the cabin that had belonged to the *Amelie Carre's* captain.

It looked like an abattoir. Six bodies were sprawled around the little room, pools of blood spreading beneath each of them.

There were weapons scattered around as well, but other than one or two pistols, he doubted any had seen use that night.

He looked at Shanae again.

She was staring into the cabin, not really watching Astir and Hunt moving about in the dark.

She was staring at the bodies.

And her smile had not shifted.

Aidan shook his head, not sure if the scene, the smell, or something else was getting to him. He turned and made his way back out onto the deck.

He had a sudden, flashing memory of the captain's cabin aboard the *Bonnie Kate*, on their way home from the raid on Kralendijk.

Captain Maguire had muttered that Shanae was the last, best hope they had.

He threw a hooded glance back at the bloody darkness beneath the quarterdeck.

Best hope for what?

Chapter 27

1675 ~ The Windward Passage, In Route to Tortuga

Shanae sat in the plain wooden chair and brooded, staring at the dark stains on the floor. Around her, the plain cabin of the cog's former captain seemed to loom, demanding something she could not name.

The blood stains didn't bother her in the slightest. Try as she might, knowing full well those men and been Brethren just as surely as any man or woman aboard the *Bonnie Kate*, she could not conjure up a jot of sympathy for their deaths.

She had come to accept that she viewed the thin-blooded, cowardly creatures of Jamaica as inferior in the past few weeks. They had bred the creature that had destroyed her world, and aside from the vague sense of a job well done, she cared nothing for their bloody ends.

That said something alarming about her continuing the captain's plan to shift the squadron to the God-forsaken place, but that was another dark place in her mind she had decided not to examine for the time being.

Outside, she could hear the shouts, the snap of taut canvas, and the singing of the ropes of a ship being worked before the wind. They were making excellent time and would be reaching Tortuga ahead of schedule. She had been keeping a close eye on her tradesmen, who had assured her they could complete their tasks in the time remaining.

She hoped they would. Her plan had little hope of success if they were wrong.

The constant cacophony of construction had been unrelenting since leaving the quiet little cove days ago. Sawing, hammering, shouting, cursing. All the sounds of an active work sight had drowned out the quiet efficiency of a ship at sea.

The *Amelie Carre* had been a nice enough boat when they had taken her from the prize crew. Well-maintained, with solid bones, she would fetch a tidy profit from any broker than might be convinced to ignore her French provenance or be fooled into a similar misunderstanding.

The work continuing around the clock all around her would go a long way toward seeing that come to pass, if she survived to return to Port Royal.

But that would be a happy coincidence. Shanae's plans did not require the *Amelie Carre* to survive.

There was a sharp knock on the door, and she grunted, still lost in her own dark thoughts.

She knew who it would be. Just about this time every day Aidan came to her seeking to assuage his own guilt; his doubts and fears were nearly his masters, and she had come to realize he lacked her own resolve in this.

Still, he was a friend, and deserved her best efforts while she could afford to provide them.

It was Aidan, of course. And of course, he looked as nervous as he always seemed to, now.

"Yes?"

She would offer him comfort where she could, but Shanae was finding that her patience was waning with each mile that churned beneath the cog's keel.

Aidan looked ashen. The nighttime crossing of Jamaica had taken a toll on the gunner.

Truth to tell, she thought it might be the abrupt ending of that journey for the Port Royal captain and his lackeys that weighed more heavily upon her friend than the rest of the journey.

Boothe had done what he had to do, of course. If that Captain Kay had made it back to Port Royal with word of their intentions, everything would have been for nothing. Even if they *had* succeeded at Tortuga, the rest of Captain Maguire's plan would have failed.

Port Royal was not going to entertain buccaneers who attacked one another in the light of day. There were certain conventions that were expected, of course.

Blatantly stealing a crew's prize, slaughtering the prize crew, and then claiming it as one's own fit squarely outside of those conventions, in the absence of at least a modicum of artifice.

But still, the fate of the big bellied old captain and his followers haunted Aidan, she knew.

She could even understand his feelings, at least a little.

But she could not allow such sensitivities to get between her and the captain's final plans for the squadron.

He slumped down into another seat at the small table with a grunt.

The crew of the *Chaucer's Pride* was not large. They provided the manpower to sail a big cog like the *Amelie Carre*, but just barely. She was working everyone to exhaustion. If they were to outrun any rumor from Jamaica, she had to push every last knot of speed from the clumsy whale.

"Have you been sleeping?"

The question caught her off guard, as she had been thinking to ask the same of him.

She paused for a moment, eyes narrowing as she regarded him.

He looked concerned, and that was even more confusing. Why would *he* be concerned for *her*?

"I sleep when I can. There'll be plenty of time for rest when this is all done."

She had made it a point not to rest any more than she was allowing the others to rest. She knew a captain could quickly lose the allegiance of her crew once she earned the reputation of a taskmaster.

Aidan shook his head, clearly not satisfied with the response. "You're working yourself ragged. You need to rest."

That was nonsense. *Everyone* was working hard. If the alterations on the cog were not completed before they arrived, there was no way the plan was going to work.

"We're all working hard, Aidan. I'm not working any harder than any of the others."

He knew all this. Why did he need so much careful handling, lately?

Aidan looked doubtful, shaking his head, searching her eyes for something she could hardly guess at.

"You fought like a demon taking this ship."

She snorted. He had always found her fighting style intimidating. She waved the comment away. "Everyone fought well." She worked her shoulder, wincing at the twinge on her left side. "The Port Royal boys fought well, also. She wasn't an easy prize."

He shook his head again, and she felt something hot twist in her gut. "She could have been an easy prize, Shanae. None of those Port Royal buffoons were ready for anything, never mind what we unleashed on them."

That wasn't what he meant, and she could see that in his eyes.

"Speak plainly, Aidan. I have a lot to go over before we arrive."

He stood, obviously steeling his resolve. "Those men didn't need to die, Shanae. A month ago, you would have seen that too. We don't shy from what must be done, but we don't wantonly slay Brethren, either."

She scoffed at that, turning away. "These tame puppies hardly merit the term." She made no effort to hide the contempt she felt for the buccaneers of Port Royal.

She could hear him rise, the chair scrapping against the well-scrubbed floor. "Well, that makes all efforts to join them rather strange, to be honest."

There was something in his tone she didn't like, but she couldn't quite place it.

She bent down over the charts scattered across the table. If they made their approach along the usual routes, there was a chance a faster ship would see them making for Tortuga and pass that along to Greene. He wouldn't know the significance of that, but she needed the first appearance of the altered *Amelie Carre* to be when she rounded the point into Cayona Harbor.

The door to the cabin opened, and she heard a muttered comment.

Aidan, trying to elicit further comment, she knew.

She felt her lip curl in disdain and refused to turn around.

He spoke, then, of course. As he always did when she refused to rise to his bait.

But the words were strange.

"Good luck. She's not hearing me."

The door closed, and she sighed with a relief she didn't really understand.

Then she stopped.

She wasn't alone.

She turned in her chair to find Aston Hunt standing before the closed door, staring at her with undecipherable green eyes.

She blinked. His eyes were always burning, fever bright, with his strange faith.

Now, they looked diminished. Sad. Worried.

Worried for what?

"What is it, Hunt? I need to have a plot laid in for Tortuga before our next course change."

The man approached the table without taking his eyes from hers, and she felt something stir between them that she couldn't have named.

The madman did not speak, did not look away, but moved toward her as if in a dream.

"Hunt, if you've words, I'd hear them, and then you can be on your way. I've no time for foolishness right now."

He glided forward, sliding, without an invitation, into the seat Aidan had just left.

"The course." He spoke in a soft mumble, devoid of meaning.

She nodded, slapping the charts on the table. "Yes, a course. We need to approach the island obliquely, lest we are seen before we desire."

"You're off course." He said this without judgment, but with something almost like concern.

She shook her head. "No, we're right where we're meant to be."

She almost turned to indicate the charts, to show him where they were sliding between Cuba and Hispaniola, making directly for Tortuga.

The Windward Passage was narrow and did not allow for much deviation. She had them hewing closer to Cuba, for now, trying to avoid the more populated western coast of Hispaniola, lest the Spanish take an interest in their movements. But soon they would need to shift course again as they emerged into the sea north of the big islands.

What they did then might well spell success or failure for the entire endeavor, and the last thing she needed now was coddling master gunners or lunatics mumbling nonsense in her ear.

"No." He shook his head, and again she was struck by the lack of frenetic energy about him. He was completely still, which was uncharacteristic of him. "You are off course, Captain. There are rocks ahead, and if you do not keep a weather eye on the horizon, we will all surely founder and die."

The skies had been clear since leaving Jamaica, and she wasn't about to spend another moment trying to puzzle out any deeper meaning to the crazed priest's words.

Aston Hunt had proven a valuable companion through the years, and an invaluable asset in their efforts in Port Royal, with his surprising knowledge of finance.

But she wasn't about to let anyone distract her from what needed to be done now.

Greene needed to be stopped. Everything he had seized from the squadron needed to be wrested back from him, and the man and all who followed him needed to pay for what they had done.

Nothing else mattered.

She glared at Hunt, shaking her head. "The course is sound, Aston. I need you to leave now, before I lose my temper."

Something in his face shifted from concern to pity. She suppressed the sudden, nearly undeniable urge to strike the man.

That surge of violence scared her, and she sat back in her chair.

He seemed to sense what had happened and nodded.

What that nod might mean, she couldn't have said. Who knew what significance to read into any action of a madman?

He rose without a word, turned smoothly, and left without a sound.

She stared at the closed door for a long time afterward, refusing to wonder what the man might have been about.

*****

The course plotted and passed along to Vallance, the sailing master from the *Pride*, Shanae decided to take the air up on deck and see what there was to see of all the efforts that had been making so much noise for the duration of their journey.

The deck had been cleared, and only those sailors who needed to move about for the working of the ship were there while the coopers plied their trade in the vast, empty space.

Strange barrels were stacked up against the gunwales along the ship's flanks. Long, thin containers whose staves had been polished smooth by the hands of idle crew, there was almost no taper to them at all, further adding to their odd appearance.

Fore and aft, carpenters worked with a steady, grinding pace, off-watch crew providing assistance where they could, as the forecastle and the stern were slowly transformed, built upon, expanded, and reinforced.

By the time her crews were done, if they were allowed to complete their efforts, the *Amelie Carre's* lines would be completely different. Not only would she appear to be a different ship; she would appear to be an entirely different *breed* of ship.

Normally, she would have repaired to the quarterdeck to survey the efforts being employed on her behalf. As it was, however, there was barely enough room up there, amidst the scaffolding, the workers, and the piles of lumber for Derrick Vallance and the copper-haired boatswain, Suther, to man the wheel.

It still felt strange, being aboard a ship so markedly lacking in *Kates*. Each time she turned around, expecting to see Martin Ruiz and his impeccably trimmed goatee, black eyes flashing from behind the ship's wheel, or Hector Fraga, the irascible old ship's carpenter, she was struck again by how much her life had changed, and how much she had lost.

Were those old shipmates still loyal to their fallen captain's dream? Did they know Maguire was dead, struck down by Greene's minions in the jungles outside Cayona?

Did it matter if they knew?

She felt that twisting heat in her gut again. She was growing accustomed to that warmth; had found herself clinging to it in the relative quiet of the night as the hammers and saws continued their rumbling work by lamplight.

Something about that familiarity worried her, but again, she fixed her eyes on the horizon and refused to dwell on such thoughts. There would be plenty of time to square her actions with her unquiet mind when Greene was gone, and Captain Maguire's people safe.

"Do you think this will work?"

She was standing beneath the main mast, resting against the warm wood and watching a reinforced bulkhead rise aft, finishing up the rough box that would be the new stern castle.

Boothe.

She looked over at the man who had once been the first mate of the only Brethren-held galleon in that part of the world.

He looked like a gaunt wolf.

Whatever the intervening time between Greene's move on the squadron and the present moment might have done to Aidan Allen or Aston Hunt or even Shanae herself, it had been most cruel to Myles Boothe.

Even in her darkest moments, Shanae knew she had friends. Aidan, Hunt, young Perry and the others had followed her off Tortuga on that horri-

- 274 -

ble day and had followed her since. They carried enough of the spirit of the *Bonnie Kate* with them, that she had never felt completely dispossessed.

Boothe had no such comfort. There were no friendly faces among those he now moved. The *Kates* had felt very little warmth for anyone from the *Arbiter*, especially the Commodore's first mate. There was too much bad blood between that old fool, Hart, and their beloved captain for Boothe to find real welcome among them, even after all that had passed.

Boothe was a man with no ship, no crew, and no home. Everything had been taken from him.

He had as much to hate Greene for as she herself; more, perhaps, if she was going to be honest.

And yet he continued moving. He slid forward through the dark twilight, refusing to succumb to despair or the fury that must have burned deep in his gut.

He had embraced Shanae's plan wholeheartedly despite what it was going to cost him, personally.

He was a man whose loses had already been calculated into his revised world view. All that mattered now was that the scales be returned to even. Whatever else might be made of the world, that could come after.

For now, there was only the usurper, and the man's removal.

"Do you?" He repeated, and she had to shake herself out of the looping track of her dark thoughts.

"Do I?"

He smiled, but there was no humor in his eyes. "Do you think this will work?"

She turned to look down the deck at the swarm of men fixing the new bulkhead in place, then forward, at the work being done there. She took in the stacks of strange barrels, and then she shrugged. "I don't know, Boothe." She smiled back at him, the expression containing just as much mirth as his own. "Do you perhaps have a better idea?"

He shrugged. "I don't, or I would have suggested it. There's no way to know how deeply that bastard has sunk his claws into our former compatriots—"

"They're loyal." She nearly cursed at the plaintive note she detected in her own voice.

Boothe shrugged. "They might be. They could each of them be merely biding their time, waiting for their chance to strike a blow for the Commodore and your captain. Greene could have also placed his own people on each of their ships, boots firmly on the necks of those who might turn on him. Or maybe the tried and true buccaneer tendency toward self-preservation and ambition has led them to shift their own allegiance, and we are even now sailing into the teeth of our own destruction at the hands of those we would call our friends." He shrugged, and she truly believed he didn't care which of those it might be. "This plan of yours, I believe, offers us the best chance to make the most of the situation. Bold enough to seize what should be ours and free our friends, if friends they are, and cautious enough to provide the chance, at least, for revenge before we join those have gone before, in the bellies of the tiny fishes."

That was not the comfort she might have liked, but who was Boothe, that she should be looking to him for comfort, anyway?

"There are those who say we have lost our path in this, you know." He wasn't looking at her, then, but out over the side, at the wide expanse of the sea. Somewhere off in the distance, lost to sight and sensibility, was Hispaniola, the island where she had been found all those years ago.

"They do." She agreed, looking off the starboard quarter as well. "And you?"

"Your path has been burned from beneath you, Shanae. There is no path now." He shrugged, showing all signs of nonchalance.

But she thought she could detect more than a hint of anger there.

He wasn't as dispassionate as he might pretend.

"We have both lost our way, but that was no doing of ours. And when your path is gone, you have no choice but to forge a new one."

She nodded but was alarmed to realize she had derived no comfort from those words.

Just because she had been forced to choose a new path was no guarantee that she had made the right choice.

She could be driving them all to exhaustion for no good purpose at all, if Greene had outsmarted them all yet again, or if she had sorely misjudged those she had considered friends all her life.

There were countless ways this path might twist before she found its ending.

And now, thanks to Boothe, she had one more thing to worry about, as she tried to steal what moments of peace were left her, before the end.

Chapter 28
1675 – Off Tortuga

In the bow the *Kate's* boatswain, Perry, called the beat as the hard-scrabble men of the *Pride* pulled the oars. Behind Perry, the dark green of the jungle lurched larger with each pull. The strip of golden sand expanded as well, and Boothe shook himself, forcing himself to look away.

Captain Maguire had died somewhere beyond that beach, some-where in the green shadows rising on the other side.

He knew enough about human nature to realize that this opportunity would probably never have come his way had the captain of the *Bonnie Kate* did not meet his doom beneath the looming trees.

Shanae was a strong captain, an exemplary officer and an intuitive commander. She would never have conceived such a foolhardy mission as this, let alone allowed it to move forward, without the pressures of grief and rage fueling her mind and her resolve.

He glanced behind them at the *Amelie Carre*, a cog no more.

The big ship looked like nothing so much as a galleon now, her lines and bulk altered beyond recognition by the carpenters and other tradesmen now crowding the other boats pulling for shore.

There was no need for them to face what that poor ship was about to face on the other side of Tortuga, if even their best estimates of the action's resolution bore out.

The hull of the ship had been altered as well, with elaborate changes wrought upon her sides further hiding her origins and helping her to assume the role they needed her to play.

He sighed. It was only too bad there were no cannons behind her lovely new gun ports. She could look as fierce as they wished, but when the flame touched the powder in Cayona Harbor, the *Amelie Carre* would be on her own against the full fury of an unknown enemy.

He turned back to the bow of the boat and hunched his shoulders against the doubts rising up in his mind. They set a chill growing in his bones that even the blazing tropical sun could not dispel.

A small but substantial portion of the late Captain Maguire's Port Royal treasure was weighing down the two boats containing Shanae's craftsmen. It should be enough and more to keep the fort's garrisons fat and happy, and away from their guns, while the squadron sorted its own business out.

At least, that was what Shanae thought, anyway.

And who was he to doubt her? It wasn't as if his own record, lately, was anything to rest a laurel on.

His own boat, in company with the fourth and final jollyboat they had brought with them, was carrying the last *Kate*s among their company, barring Shanae herself, of course, as well as a small number of the men from the *Chaucer's Pride* who had managed to convince Shanae of their loyalty during the brief journey north.

That was another thing he had argued against. And again, he had been ignored.

But this, at least, was something he could do something about. He checked the pistols hung about his person with grim purpose. He might not be able to force the carpenters to give up their gold, but he could sure as hell bring down any traitorous Port Royal drudge who thought to turn his cloak in the coming action.

He wasn't looking forward to another trek over land but knew there was no better way to infiltrate Cayona Harbor without Greene, or anyone else, being the wiser.

At least he could hope he wouldn't be called upon to shoot anyone in the back this time around. His luck with work ashore seemed to have abandoned him lately as surely as all his other luck. He hadn't hesitated when it became clear he would need to drop that weasel, Captain Kay and his little cohort of traitors back on Jamaica. But neither had he relished it. And he'd just as soon get back aboard a ship without further fuss than be forced to make such a move again so soon.

He glanced at the little drunk, Ben Suther, the red-headed old Boatswain from the Port Royal crew and hitched one of his pistols higher.

He didn't want to, but he'd do it if he had to.

He wanted to look forward to his own part in that night's work. It seemed like it had been several lifetimes since he had last been aboard the *Arbiter*. But there were too many unknowns for him to indulge in such sentiments now. He needed to focus on Shanae's plan, and his part in it, rather than in the sentimentality of returning to the ship that had, if he was going to be honest with himself, been half a home and half a prison for most of his adult life.

The damned ship hadn't left its mooring in years; and hadn't left the harbor in over a decade. Being the first mate of such a vessel, no matter her relative position in their ad hoc little squadron, had always been a mixed blessing.

But it had given him the opportunity to learn everything he was going to need to know tonight.

The *Amelie Carre* might not have teeth, but the teeth of Shanae's trap had never been intended to come from the butchered cog.

No, the teeth would be provided by the squadron itself if everything went according to the girl's plan.

And if it went according to his *own* version of that plan, the full weight of the trap would be borne up by the *Arbiter* herself, finally living up to the old dowager hag's name.

He knew the men around him must have all been sharing similar thoughts. Would their work on the *Amelie Carre* be enough to convince the squadron they were in danger? If the lookouts aboard their former companions' ships were not convinced the true threat was coming in from the open sea, there would be little to distract them from the commandeered boats sliding out from the docks, attempting to take them unawares.

And if they were spotted making such a move, there would be precious little time for the returned buccaneers to convince anyone of their benign intentions.

Pulling their boats ashore, the *Kates* and *Prides* bid farewell to the gun-shy tradesmen, who began almost immediately to make camp on the sandy strand. The buccaneers needed to push into the jungle without delay if they wanted to get the gold to the forts and be in position by the time the former cog made her big appearance in the harbor.

Boothe felt no need to lead the party into the green darkness. He allowed Aidan Allen to push through the ferns and bushes first, the madman, Hunt, at his side. The hulking Frenchmen, Astier, with the gold over his broad shoulders, was right behind.

He wondered, as he fell in with the others, if the man was entertaining second thoughts about joining the Brethren after their raid on his old fluyt.

The man had seemed solidly loyal to Shanae, and maybe he was. But in Boothe's experience, it took a singular type of man to shift from a merchantman to a buccaneer in the first place, never mind all the trials and tribulations they had suffered since.

As they trudged through the steaming heat of the jungle, swatting at the swarming mosquitos that seemed to have sensed their arrival from miles around, he bent his thoughts back to the *Ultimo Arbiter*. He understood his role in this as well as any other man in the column. And no one was better suited to what needed to be done aboard the old galleon.

He wiled away the time of their trek factoring sums in his head, of powder loads, the strength and durability of the ship, and the concussive force of multiple guns firing at once.

He and Shanae, with Allen's help, had come up with a ceiling on the number of guns he should be able to fire at a single volley without endangering the ship, but he had been running those numbers in his head ever since, wondering if there was a way to squeeze maybe a few more pounds of metal downrange on that bastard's head in the opening moment of the engagement.

He had no doubt in his ability to lay the guns for a true shot, but even with the galleon's twenty-four pounders, there was only so much damage they could hope to inflict with the six gun volley their most generous estimates had suggested.

Hell, even the full 20-gun broadside, should he unleash the galleon's full fury on the *Chasseur*, might not be enough if luck was with the Jamaican.

But no matter how he shifted the numbers in his mind, he couldn't see his way clear to adding so much as a single nine pounder to the mix without endangering the *Arbiter* and every soul aboard her.

Shanae believed repeated volleys with the limited number of big guns could be effective, but he wasn't sure.

His foot came down on the heel of the man before him, and he pulled up short before driving into his back.

Their little column had halted, and the confining corridor of greenery pressing in from all sides meant he couldn't really see what had caused the pause.

With a gruff curse under his breath, he pushed the milling *Prides* out of his way, eyes fixed on Astier's towering bulk.

If Allen had gotten them lost amidst the twisting jungle paths, he swore, he would end the little jackanapes no matter how his death might impact their schemes.

He pulled up short when he saw the wall of bronzed bodies standing athwart their course.

He took in the clubs, the spears, the fierce black-eyed glares, the swathes of red paint.

A Taino war party.

The natives and the European inhabitants of the Caribbean islands seldom crossed paths unless one side or the other was looking for trouble. He knew more than one shore party that had run afoul of the brutal locals, and he wondered how many there might be surrounding them at the moment, aside from those blocking their advance in plain sight.

He loosened one pistol, looking around as if he could penetrate the jungle with his will alone.

If a Taino warrior did not wish to be seen, you wouldn't see him until he planted his spear in your back.

But while Boothe was trying to calculate the odds of their fighting clear of the ambush, he realized that it might not be necessary after all.

The leader of the war party, an older warrior with graying hair and a seamed, weathered face, was not glaring at Allen, but rather looking at him with some strange level of recognition that made no sense to Boothe himself.

If he hadn't known better, he would have said the man was looking at the gunner with recognition and respect.

What was there to respect Allen for? Especially this strange little party in the middle of this hot, green hell?

Without a word, and with a silent nod the only sign of acknowledgment between them, the war leader faded away into the jungle, his warriors following suit, their own glares, at least, not mitigated by the odd emotion that had somehow infected their leader.

Once the war party was gone, the buccaneers stood in silence for several minutes, as if none of them wanted to be the first to move.

It was almost as if they feared attracting the attention of the Taino all over again, afraid that another visit would not end so well.

The men at the front of the column were exchanging wondering glances, even the madman, Hunt, seeming at a loss for words.

Boothe glanced down at his time piece. They were losing daylight and needed to be in position on the waterfront by the time Shanae brought the *Amelie Carre* around or this was all going to be for nothing, strange natives or not.

He cursed again, pushed his way to the front, and drew a cutlass to cut back the encroaching plants pressing in from either side.

"For the love of God, Allen." He shot over his shoulder before turning back to the business of hacking a wider path. "We've places to be, man."

He heard the *Kates* muttering behind him as they followed moments later and smiled a grim smile.

Strange natives notwithstanding, he had an appointment with a row of cannons, and he wasn't about to miss it due to the timidity of a child afraid of his own shadow.

Somewhere ahead of them waited his ship, and he wasn't about to put off their reunion any longer.

Chapter 29
1675 ~ Cayona Harbor, Tortuga

Holding the gold pocket watch up to the moonlight, Aidan could just make out the face. It was almost time.

In boats all around the quays, similar newly purchased timepieces were passing along similar messages to their new owners.

Hunkered down in the little skiff beneath the battered pier at the very edge of the Cayona waterfront, he squinted out into the moonlight, looking for a glimpse of movement that would tell him the others had left for their own destinations.

In the distance, he could clearly see the *Bonnie Kate* lying at anchor. Her watch lights were out, and he could see figures moving along her decks.

From this distance, not knowing what he knew, he might almost think everything was well with his old ship. Captain Maguire could be asleep in his cabin. Shanae could be strolling the decks, making sure everything was ship-shape and trim. The other *Kates* might be dicing, or playing at cards, or drinking and reminiscing about their last big caper or their next grand triumph.

But he knew better. Captain Maguire was dead. Shanae was standing by the *Amelie Carre's* big wheel right now, staring into the shadows of Cayona Harbor as Derrick Vallance, a man he hadn't even known a few weeks ago, steered her toward the guns of her bitter enemies.

And he didn't even know if he could count the other *Kates* as companions anymore, nor how they might now spend the dark watches of the night.

He could see the other ships of the squadron resting at anchor as well. The massive bulk of the *Arbiter* sat at the mouth of the harbor where she had been for as long as he could remember. She seemed strangely dark and still, with few watch lanterns and no movement he could see. Across from her lay *Jaguar*, the frigate rocking gently to the waves that made it in at the harbor mouth. Forward of the *Kate* by about two hundred paces was her sister, *Syren*. And across the harbor, aft of the *Jaguar*, was the sloop *Chainbreaker*.

And over them all, in the shadows of the island's bulk, the two forts that could put an end to all their plans if the Frenchmen behind the guns there didn't stay bought like honest men.

At first, he couldn't find *Laughing Jacques* anywhere. That would have been just as well, Aidan knew. The sloop would provide little by way of support, and Captain Houdin wasn't much of a battle commander, truth be told.

Then, behind a line of fishing ketches, he saw the lights. The little Frenchmen had made it back safely, had convinced Greene of his good intentions, and had placed his ship off the aft port quarter of *Chasseur*, anchored in the very center of the harbor.

The bastard that had cast a curse over his entire existence, and caused the death of so many, and so much, that he cared about.

He felt his eyes tighten as he focused on that distant shape. A brigantine like the *Kate* and the *Syren*, *Chasseur* was a far newer ship, bigger, with sleek lines and a similar paint scheme to his own *Kate*, but with green and gold much darker, more prone to fade into the shadows of night.

And aboard that sleek, beautiful craft must be the bitch's whelp that had brought hell down on them all.

Glaring over the sparkling harbor, he almost missed the dart of movement off to his left. A longboat slid out from the docks at the eastern end of the harbor, making for the *Arbiter*.

That must have been Boothe, returning home at last.

A soft splash to his right marked where Hunt's boat was pushing off, making for the *Syren*.

And farther west would be Perry and the big Frenchman, heading for *Chainbreaker*.

Houdin would be ready, knowing what was to happen next. Noboa, the *Jacques'* scar-faced gunner, knew his business well. His guns would be double-charged and laid for *Chasseur*, waiting for the excitement to begin.

Aidan doubted what good three six-pounders were going to contribute, but better they be throwing steel at *Chasseur* and not at him.

If everything worked the way it was supposed to, there would be so much powder being burned, there would be no way Greene could escape.

They had decided not to send emissaries to *Jaguar*. Fowler was a good enough captain when he had someone to follow, but he was no tiger in battle, and Shanae had doubted he would have any powder ready at all while *Jaguar* sat in its home port, surrounded by friends.

Boothe had been against leaving *Jaguar* out of the fray, afraid what kind of damage the twelve pounders the frigate bore could inflict if things lasted long enough for Fowler to make his mind up. But Shanae had had the final say, and the others, Aidan included, had all agreed.

Certainly, Fowler might have agreed to join them. There was really no telling what might have transpired within the squadron while they had been away. And Fowler had always been a loyal follower of Commodore Hart. It was possible the man's murder might spur Fowler to action.

But there was an equal chance that the man was still an errant coward, and would sit tight, waiting for the smoke to clear, not wanting to choose a side until there was an obvious winner either way. If that winner was them, all the better.

And there was also the possibility, no matter how small, that Fowler had developed some intestinal fortitude while they were gone, and would seize their messenger on sight, alerting Greene of the danger.

Aidan had felt that last scenario by far the most likely, but all of them argued against sending someone to sound out the *Jaguar* before the action.

And so here they were, with boats heading toward *Arbiter*, *Syren*, and *Chainbreaker*.

He shook himself.

And *Bonnie Kate*!

He shoved the oarsmen before him, and someone behind him cast off the line holding them to the quay and their boat slid out into the moonlight.

"Pull hard, damn your eyes!" He whispered the words, but they were no less violent for their hissing lack of volume.

Everyone knew the timetable. The boat's crew must have seen the others leaving as clearly as he had. They should have said something.

But then, they must have assumed he knew what he was about.

And now, they had caught his own urgency like an ague among a crew of lubbers and were pulling for all they were worth.

They needed to be in the shadow of the *Bonnie Kate* before Greene knew what was happening. But under the bright moon, there was almost nothing stopping any of the well-placed lookouts from seeing the boats.

One boat could easily be explained away. There were always crew ashore for a variety of reasons, good and bad. And they would make their way home via boat, either the ship's own or some enterprising dockworker or fisherman out to make an extra penny or two.

Maybe even two boats, returning to their various ships at the same time, wouldn't raise an eyebrow.

But there were currently four boats, all making for a different ship of the squadron. Each had left shore at nearly the same time.

Well, three of them left at the same time. The one boat, the laggard, him, broke that pattern ever so slightly.

Either way, there wasn't anything protecting him from the probing eyes of his enemies now.

If they *were* his enemies.

It was hard to think of the squadron in any other way, at the moment.

He remembered the squadron's attack on the fluyts in another lifetime.

He remembered when they had taken the *Amelie Carre* away from the Port Royal Brethren, just a few short days ago.

They said third time pays for all. But this time, the ruse was being employed for grand stakes indeed. They might win and sail off with the squadron intact, Greene sucking seawater and the Commodore and the Captain avenged.

Or they could be dead, feeding the fish of Cayona Harbor, no longer concerned after Sidney Greene's business.

Aidan couldn't see much daylight between those two outcomes.

And all it would take was the wrong person to remember the *Marie Lajoie* and the *Courageaux* at the wrong moment and everything would be over.

Or maybe Shanae's modifications to the *Amelie Carre* would be insufficient. Maybe no one in the harbor would be fooled, or Shanae's messengers would be rebuffed and taken, the fat little cog burned down to the waterline.

There were so many ways this could go wrong.

Aidan swallowed, glaring forward at the *Bonnie Kate* growing larger with each passing moment.

He had to trust Shanae. It all came down to that: trust. And he had trusted her this far. He had no choice but to continue, or to slink away and try to make his living in the jungles somewhere. Perhaps the woodcutters would accept him.

What kind of life would *that* be?

The cry, thin and reedy over the fitful offshore wind, came from off to the right. Somewhere up in the rigging of the *Syren*, someone had seen something. That falsetto voice could only be a crewwoman, and although there were women serving on every ship of the squadron, the odds, and the direction of the cry, argued that Captain Semprun would be the first to hear about the night's activities.

They might have seen Hunt's boat. He found the lunatic maddening at times, to be sure, but he found himself praying, for all he was worth, that the fallen priest might make it to *Syren* safely.

Beyond *Syren* another cry, this was more sonorous, carrying more easily over wind and wave.

It might have been the *Chasseur* or it might have been *Jaguar*. It didn't matter.

Because there were no boats making for either the new-come brigantine or the frigate.

And that could only mean—

Cries rose up all around the squadron now, and as his own boat cleared the obscuring shadow of the *Bonnie Kate*, he could see why.

The *Amelie Carre* made a brave sight, sliding out from around the headlands, gilt in the silver of the moon that danced upon the water, every inch of her the brooding image of a savage galleon.

And as she moved into the harbor, making straight for the squadron, the moonlight along her hull limned the brave red and white of her fresh paint. A broad white line swept down the big ship's flank, and one by one, dark mouths gaped in that gleaming white.

Gun ports opened all along the *Amelie Carre's* sides, threatening every ship in the harbor.

High above, the shouts of the sentries took on a terrified, desperate note.

Chapter 30
1675 ~ Cayona Harbor, Tortuga

Boothe expected to be hailed as his boat approached the dark hulk of the *Arbiter*, but no call came.

He expected to be challenged as the bow of the little craft butted up against the galleon's massive flank, but still, nothing but silence above.

As he began to climb up the elaborate woodwork in the absence of ropes or nets, he began to wonder what he would find when he reached the main deck. There had only been a few lamps hung along the rails, and the silence from throughout the ship was alarming to the man who had been charged with her security for so long.

He climbed through one of the gun deck's massive ports, careful to make no sound. By the light of the moon pouring in, he expected to see the floor packed with *Arbiters* sleeping off their latest excesses, but there was no one.

A cold wind seemed to draw claws of ice across his back.

He crept through the silver-gilt shadows toward the ship's ladder aft of the huge column of the mainmast. Here, behind the bulkheads that sectioned off the capstan and the mast, he found a few bodies scattered across the floor, their soft snores setting his jangling nerves at ease.

He didn't recognize any of the sleepers here, but the conditions were less than ideal for such identification.

Rather than chance waking someone ill-disposed toward him, he decided to continue moving through the ship until he had a better idea of what to expect. With a last glance down at the slumbering forms, he moved up the ship's ladder and pushed the hatch open, slowly so as to avoid the telltale creak it always let out and pulled himself up onto the main deck.

He had found the crew.

He had never let the crew sleep on the main deck, for fear they would get in the way should something arise requiring fast action. Such precautions were remnants of his near-forgotten navy days, he knew. No other buccaneer ship he was aware of held to such discipline, and especially not a ship that would have been incapable of stirring even in her own defense.

In his absence, it seemed like even this remnant discipline had gone over the side; the crew sprawled over every available space.

He made his way across the crowded deck toward the stern castle. Whoever had come to command here, they would most likely be in the Commodore's grand cabin. He would start there, and then go looking for friendly faces among the crowd.

When they had concocted this scheme in the first place aboard the *Amelie Carre* crossing the Windward Passage, he hadn't taken into account how onerous it might be, trying to find the right allies on a dark and sleeping ship the size of the *Ultimo Arbiter*.

The door to the long companionway creaked, as it always had, and for some reason, that, more than anything else, made Boothe feel like he was home.

He shook that off and continued to pad down the hall, eyes fixed on the ornate door at the end.

One of the side doors opened as he passed, and a pale face loomed up out of the shadows.

Boothe's knife flashed from its sheath with a hiss of steel on leather.

Cold blue eyes widened in that pale face, then hardened. A boney forearm shot out of the darkness and took him in the throat while a spidery hand, strong and wiry, caught his knife hand with a twist, pulling the weapon away even as the other hand closed on his wrist, yanking him into the cabin.

Boothe growled, pulling his arm free and going for another knife.

"Oh, God damnit." The muttered oath seemed more annoyed than anything, and a businesslike knee was driven into his groin with a quick jerk.

Boothe gasped, dropping to the deck, knife forgotten.

Fingers tangled in his hair and yanked his head back. Through the gut-roiling agony burning around his manhood, he could feel the blade of a knife, probably his knife, against his throat.

"Ready to talk?" His breath came in ragged gasps, his struggles having stopped at the first caress of the steel but nodded as best he could with his captor holding his head at such a brutal angle.

The man released him and pushed him against the door with a gentle shove.

Boothe drew a shuddering breath, pressing his hand over his throat to ensure himself there was no blood, while a lamp brightened before him, his captor winding up the wick.

Despite the world-encompassing agony, he didn't try to hide the rueful smile that rose to his lips.

"Rees."

The man shook his head, sending his mane of pale blonde hair waving. "Boothe, I always knew you lacked intelligence, but I gave you some credit for native cunning, at least."

Boothe braced himself against the wall of the cabin and rose, tears of pain dancing in his eyes. The quartermaster reached out and they clasped forearms like long-lost brothers. "What brings you back to our special little corner of hell? The ship's developed an entire economy based on wagers concerning whether or not we'd ever see you again."

Boothe smiled, one hand rubbing at his hip. "Where'd you put your money?"

Zachariah Rees grinned. "I never gave you much credit where self-preservation was concerned. Teddy's going to rue the day he accepted my marker on this one. He thought you'd be halfway back to England by now."

Boothe shook his head. "Nothing for me in England."

Rees's cold eyes narrowed. "Nothing much for you on Tortuga, either, my friend. The truth, now. Why have you returned in the dead of night, creeping through the darkness toward our lord and master's demesnes?"

Boothe looked toward the door, then back to his friend. He and Rees had been through a lot together, but a lot had happened since he had left the *Arbiter*. He had no idea who he could trust at this point. How much did he dare to tell the other man?

"Why don't you give me my knife back, as a point of honor, and then we can sit and have a nice little chat on that score, shall we?"

Rees scoffed, then gestured behind him to the small cabin. "Firstly, I'll keep the steel for now, thank you. And secondly, where would you suggest we sit? You must have mistaken my little cell for your grandiose old chambers, my friend." Those long fingers writhed, and the knife danced among them as if it had a mind of its own.

"Now, why don't you tell me what you're about, and together we can come to some kind of understanding before you interrupt his high and mightiness's sleep?"

Boothe paused, but he saw little choice in the matter. Rees had him at a severe disadvantage, and if he had to fight, he didn't like his chances at all.

He was going to have to trust one of his old shipmates eventually if their plan was going to work.

It might has well be Rees.

It only took a few minutes to lay out his part of Shanae's plan. He didn't mention the rest, not willing to push his trust in his old friend too far.

But time was surging forward, and if he was going to be able to support the others, he needed to bring Rees aboard or find a way around him.

But judging by the way the man's eyes were lighting up, he wouldn't have to worry about that, at least.

"When you left, Greene put one of his Port Royal bastards in charge. The fool even moved right into the commodore's cabin. He's got two brutes from the *Chasseur* with him, day and night, to keep him nice and safe." The man's pale blue eyes turned cruel as his teeth gleamed in the lamplight. "It's almost like he doesn't trust us. What have the Brethren come to, I ask, when a lowly usurper can't trust the crew of the ship he stole?"

"Who is it?" Boothe hadn't met many of the *Chasseur's* crew, but it might help to at least know the man's name.

"Barnes. Quartermaster of the *Chasseur*, now risen to captain the biggest, baddest buccaneer ship in the New World."

Boothe smiled to hear the bitterness in the other man's voice. "Seems he's come up in the world, indeed."

The knife in Rees's hand flipped, and he presented it, hilt first, to Boothe. "Maybe tonight it's time he came back down?"

*****

Boothe wiped blood from the blade as he strode down the companionway, Rees not bothering to clean his own cutlass as he followed.

Behind them, in the cabin that had once belonged to Solomon Hart, Commodore of the Buccaneer Squadron of Tortuga, three bodies lay cooling in the night air.

Someone was going to have to clean up the mess, but that wasn't going to be Boothe's problem. He had no interest in staying aboard after his work here was done.

Seeing those slimy bilge rats in Commodore Hart's cabin had been a blow he hadn't anticipated. His vision had gone red, and the crimson stain still colored the edges of everything he saw.

"I'll fetch Teddy." Rees muttered, skipping past him down the narrow hall and out onto the main deck.

As he emerged himself into the cool night air, Boothe took a massive breath through his nose, resting his fists on his hips and surveying the ship that had been his home for so many years.

Greene didn't think much of the *Arbiter*. That was obvious. Had he made a survey of the ship's interior? Did he know why she hadn't moved?

He had a hard time thinking the man would have been so dismissive of a healthy galleon. He had to know.

The bastard's lack of respect for the old girl only stoked the flames of his anger even higher. Respect among the Brethren was something one earned, it was not bought or inherited. And the squadron had respected the *Arbiter*, if not for what she was, then at least for what she had once been.

Greene, clearly, had no such esteem to offer.

That was going to cost the man.

"Boothe, well I'll be damned." Teddy was rubbing sleep from his eyes as Rees brought him forward. The *Arbiter's* master gunner looked like he hadn't been skipping any meals. His broad chest was now nearly matched by the belly pushing against his shirt.

Greene's neglect seemed to have infected the entire ship and her crew.

"Rees tells me we've had another change of masters? Some heat in the offing?"

Boothe shook his head. "No new master, Teddy. You lot can do whatever you like with the ship when we're done here tonight. But I would like to let the old girl maybe get little of her own back, from the lubbers who laid her low."

And who killed her commodore. He left those words unsaid. The other members of the squadron might have had mixed feelings about Hart, but aboard his ship, the men and women of the *Arbiter's* crew had had nothing but affection and warm regard for the man.

"I've got the monkeys running charges up. Rees is telling me full loads? We going into battle?"

The great guns of the *Arbiter* were seldom fired, and never more than one at a time. Boothe could see the gleam of moonlight in Teddy DeVillepin's eyes at the thought of what the next hour might bring.

Boothe nodded. "Let's see how well you've drilled these crews, shall we? Why don't we give a double charge to each crew, first? Let's see what good we can't do with a little surprise?"

Teddy's grin widened and he spun around, dropping down through the hatch into the gundeck.

He turned to find Rees regarding him with icy eyes.

"What?"

The face tightened. "I'm for striking a blow in the old man's honor as much as the next, Myles. But you know as well as I do what might happen if we strain the hull."

Boothe shook his head. "Shanae's got it all figured out down to the last grain of powder. We'll be the thumb on the shopkeeper's scale, not the pistol to the back of his head."

Rees's eyes didn't waver. "You've been gone a long time, and that time has changed you. We're all angry, Boothe, but you can't let your anger blind you to your own self-preservation and the good of the ship and her crew."

Boothe shook his head, moving to the hatch. He didn't speak, hoping the quartermaster would take his silence for agreement.

Boothe's real problem, bubbling up through the gelid sediment of resentment that had formed over his emotions since leaving the *Arbiter*, was the fury, now unchecked, blossoming just behind his breastbone.

The gundeck was a flurry of activity as he dropped down to the solid-seeming deck. Boys and girls were running back and forth, scurrying down into the holds below to fetch charges up from the magazine. Crews were scrambling around the big guns, dragging chests of balls into position, checking the restraining harnesses, and setting their slow matches, preparing to fire their guns in anger for the first time in living memory.

Boothe leaned down beside the first gun and sighted down its dark, cold length at the sleek green and gold shape of the *Chasseur* as she rocked gently at anchor. A proper watch was set across the water; he could tell by the placement of the lanterns and the movement of shadows on deck.

Greene might have put a moron in charge of the *Arbiter*, but he was no fool himself when it came to the security of his own ship.

For all the good that would do him.

He glared at the distant brigantine, and all the rage and resentment, the fear and the fury, surged up in him again.

That bastard.

That utter and complete bastard.

Boothe pulled himself up short, looking down in confusion as he felt his hand, still clutching the small fighting knife, begin to tremble.

After all the transgressions that Port Royal merchant's son had committed.

After all the deaths and the betrayals.

Boothe glared at the offending hand.

He had always prided himself on his ability to remain calm under the pressures of battle and the buccaneer's life.

He squeezed the hilt of his knife with all his strength. Slowly, the tremors subsided.

His hand stilled.

But the anger remained. And now there was another crime for Greene to answer for.

Boothe's heart began to race, sweat trickled down his face into his wild beard.

He would reestablish his own sense of wellbeing on the blood of Sidney Greene and the fools that followed him.

He would reestablish the natural order of the world with fire.

Boothe stood, glaring down the length of the gundeck. He felt a shared sense of purpose among the men and women toiling all around him in the dark.

They wanted what he wanted. They wanted to be the ones to blot Greene from the waves once and for all.

They didn't know what he knew; what Rees knew.

What Dante Poza, the ship's carpenter, knew better than any of them.

The gun crews wouldn't hesitate.

They would answer the call.

Rees and Poza wouldn't know what he intended until it was too late.

The expression that twisted Boothe's face then could not have been called a smile. It was, if anything human at all, a sardonic sneer.

It would have been more at home on a wolf, closing in for the kill.

He leaned back to the number one gun, muttering for the crew to assist him, and began to lay it toward the silent brigantine in the distance.

Chapter 31
1675 ~ Cayona Harbor, Tortuga

Shanae watched as the *Chasseur* grew larger within the field of her spyglass. The quarterdeck of the *Amelie Carre* felt nearly empty with only Vallance, the Port Royal sailing master, sharing the space. The other former *Prides* were scattered across the old cog, waiting for orders they knew must come soon.

The *Amelie Carre* was plowing into the harbor at an oblique angle, bringing her broadside to bear upon the *Chasseur* in the center of the bay. She felt her palms itching and rubbed first one, then the other, against her hips, never taking the spyglass from her eye.

She scanned the other ships of the squadron, hoping to see some sign of shared purpose.

With an angry snarl, she snapped out several orders, and the few sailors waiting in the waist relayed them down into the hold. She could hear the rumble of hawsers and lines as her makeshift gun ports opened.

Another command, another rumble, and 20 muzzles emerged to gleam in the moonlight.

From the ships ahead they would appear to be 24-pounders, at least. And their fresh paint would give them a metallic sheen that would fool even the keenest sentinels.

At least, that was the plan.

The harbor remained silent for a moment that seemed to drag ever closer to forever. If her messengers had failed, if she had misjudged the loyalties of the squadron, or if Greene had somehow forestalled her plans before she had even conceived them, this would all end badly.

Such a weight of metal as the *Amelie Carre* appeared to carry would be a dire threat to the entire squadron. Sadly, in reality, her ship had no teeth at all.

If none of her old companions rose in her defense, or if the men in the forts decided to take a hand, she would be helpless before their guns.

Her triumphant return to the squadron would be over before it even began.

Captain Maguire's dreams would die here, with her.

There would be nothing left of the ambition that had guided him for longer than she had been alive.

She would have failed him utterly.

The moment continued to stretch, and she prayed.

She prayed to the God and saints of her people on Hispaniola.

She prayed to Maguire's God, who had seemingly forsaken him all those years ago in his distant homeland.

With a bitter twist to her lip, she prayed to Hunt's Poseidon.

What god of the sea would deny such a feast as she proposed to provide that night?

A cry rose up from ahead.

It seemed to be coming from the *Syren*.

Syren; the ship she had assigned to Hunt, knowing Captain Semprun had a soft spot in her heart for the poor madman.

Her grin turned fierce.

Other cries were rising, now. The squadron was roused.

Her heart pounded within her chest, sending pulses of energy through her entire body.

She had never felt more alive.

There was no sense of fear. If she succeeded, she would have exacted vengeance and justice for her captain. If she failed, she would join him in hell, and they would laugh together at the injustice of fate.

But she didn't believe she would fail.

Suddenly, she believed with all her crashing heart that this would succeed.

A sharp bang sounded from off to port, and a cloud of gray smoke, glowing in the moonlight, rolled out over the water, obscuring the bastard's ship.

A distant splash behind her announced the fall of *Chasseur's* ranging shot; long.

Two more cannons roared aboard the brigantine, their shots falling closer and closer to her ship as she closed the distance.

She snarled. If only she could have somehow secured cannons for the *Amelie Carre*, she could have responded.

If she could have found anything to arm her with, she would respond to his attacks with more than ill will and a steady glare.

But if she responded with anything less than her apparent full broadside, it might raise enough suspicion to turn any wavering souls aboard the other ships against her.

They had to believe they were moments from destruction, or they would have time to consider the incongruity of it all.

Who did Greene believe was attacking? Were there enemies of his family she was unaware of? Could he think the Spanish had decided to take action against his attempts to bring the forced trade to Tortuga?

One thing was certain, she knew; there was no way he could suspect it was her.

She wanted him to know. She wanted him to understand that it was Maguire's first mate who was coming for him in the end.

That had been the one flaw in her plan; the one desire left unattended by all of this.

But she had decided, in the end, that it would be better to make sure of the enemy than to indulge in such petty revenge.

Still, her anonymity robbed the night of just a touch of savor.

A voice from ahead rose above all the others, shrieking orders through a speaking tube.

Greene, ordering the other ships to open fire.

Shanae swept the spyglass back over the other ships. There was frantic movement on all but *Jaguar*, but she couldn't make out its purpose. Were they about to fire on her? Were they about to fire on *Chasseur*? Without them, the rest would matter little.

The deck beneath her lurched as a horrendous crash shook the cog. *Chasseur* had found her range.

The other ships were not firing.

She looked up at the looming wall of the *Arbiter*. Was Boothe not up there? Could she count on no one?

Then, even as she watched the enormous ship swell before her, a flash snapped out from the forward-most gun. Smoke vomited down toward them all.

She fought the impulse to try to follow the shot with the spyglass and instead kept it trained on the *Arbiter*.

A shout of triumph from Vallance told her everything she needed to know. *Arbiter* had, indeed, fired upon *Chasseur*.

Boothe, at least, had succeeded.

Why the single shot, though? He was supposed to open up with six cannons at once.

Another roar, this time from *Syren*, and the water around *Chasseur's* stern boiled.

A light, sharp crack marked one of *Chainbreaker's* six-pounders.

A splintering crash aboard the beleaguered brigantine.

She bared her teeth in a primal, predatory smile that contained no glimmer of humor.

She muttered directions to the sailing master, ready now to bring the *Amelie Carre* around to block *Chasseur's* path to the open sea.

Overhead, she heard the fluttering canvas of her sails as they lost their wind. But they wouldn't need it now. They had enough headway to carry them into the brigantine's channel.

There was no way Greene could escape.

And then the world was shattered by a wave of sound so loud it was felt rather than heard.

Her head whipped around of its own accord toward *Arbiter*.

A stormfront of white powder smoke rolled across the water, obscuring the huge ship from view.

She reached for the wheel housing to steady herself.

Off her forward port quarter, *Chasseur* seemed to leap out of the water, shivering to pieces as it flew.

Her mainmast rose at an unnatural angle, foremast toppling like a rotten tree.

A ball of flame rose up out of the smoke and splinters, lighting the entire waterfront as if the sun had decided to rise early, and due south.

The waters of the harbor rocked with the impact, the air was filled with splintering, crashing, tearing wood, screaming men, roaring flames, and the heavy detonations of secondary explosions.

Shanae lurched to the railing, spyglass rolling on the deck behind her, forgotten.

This was not supposed to happen.

How would they find Greene in that hell?

Her throat burned, and she realized she was screaming.

Whether she was screaming at Boothe, Greene, or the other captains, she didn't know. She could have been screaming at fate, or the night, or Hunt's god for all she could decide.

A rending crash split the night off in the distance. Through the thinning smoke the *Arbiter* resolved. Something was very wrong with the galleon.

The lines of the ship's hull were not true. They did not draw an even line from stern castle to forecastle.

Each element was dipping drunkenly toward the water, away from the other.

Boothe had fired the entire broadside, and it had broken *Arbiter's* back.

She spat a curse into the water, knuckles white on the railing.

They had known the old ship couldn't survive its own broadside.

Boothe had known.

He must have gone mad.

Closer to hand, the *Chasseur* was settling into the water. The harbor all around was filling with burning bits of flotsam and screaming, crying crew.

The *Arbiter* was not on fire, but its doom was just as evident, its crew just as desperate to escape.

Boats were falling into the water all around as survivors tried to escape the two dying ships, and the other ships tried to send them assistance.

An eerie stillness settled over the harbor, broken now only by the distant cries of the dying and the desperate, the soft roaring hiss of fire meeting water, and the groaning of two ships settling into the sea's embrace.

Time seemed to stretch into a nightmare punctuated by the odd, disassociated sounds and the flickering, fitful light of the dying fires.

She screamed again.

"Captain!"

The voice barely penetrated her despair.

She turned to see Vallance pointing off to starboard.

She followed his finger, looking out over her own crew dropping the anchor to arrest the remaining headway.

In the distance she watched as the crew of the *Jaguar* lined the side of the frigate, pulling survivors from the harbor, surrounded by small boats.

A figure emerged from one of the boats, bedraggled and wounded, blood staining some white wrap around its head.

Red light flashed off blonde hair flying away from the bandage.

The red light of the flames.

Or was it red despite the flames?

She looked around desperately and found her spyglass up against the forward rail of the quarterdeck.

She lurched to the starboard rail, extending the spyglass with an alarming snap, and struggled to steady it in her shaking hands.

Crewmen aboard the *Jaguar* hoisted the figure in the bandage over the railing and onto the main deck.

As it fell, she saw the hair again.

Strawberry blonde.

The man turned to look out over the devastated harbor.

She screamed again, seeing things unfold even before they occurred.

"No!" She ran to the other railing and called down to the *Syren*, the closest ship of the squadron.

"*Jaguar*! Fire on the *Jaguar*!"

She waved. She pointed. She screamed again.

No one heard her.

She watched as the *Jaguar's* anchor rose out of the fire-dappled water. Overhead, her lines swarmed with crew as her sails dropped, pulled tight, and the frigate began to slip toward the mouth of the harbor.

She turned toward Vallance, but there was nothing the helmsman could do.

She could demand the crew weigh anchor, but the *Amelie Carre's* position meant she would never be able to come about in time. They would have to rig a spring to turn her in place or use the boats to muscle her around.

None of the other ships seemed to have noticed the frigate moving toward the open sea.

Greene was on board Fowler's ship and had somehow convinced the coward to carry him to safety.

She pounded the railing.

She wanted to break something. Or kill someone.

She glared across the water at the wreckage of the *Ultimo Arbiter*, still settling against the bottom, surrounded by bobbing crew and the boats of their would-be rescuers.

Damn the man!

What had Boothe been thinking?

Behind her, the sails of the *Jaguar* disappeared into the night.

Chapter 32
1675 - Windward Passage, In Route to Jamaica

Aidan watched Shanae as she paced the freshly painted quarterdeck, not daring to interrupt whatever dark thoughts churned within her mind.

Before them, *Chainbreaker* and *Laughing Jacques* ranged ahead, scanning the southern horizon for any sign of the *Jaguar*.

Behind them, *Syren* and their own *Bonnie Kate* followed, ready to sweep in whatever direction necessary to trap the more ungainly frigate against the prevailing wind.

If it hadn't been for the altered cog, the squadron could have made much better speed, and he wondered, not for the first time, why Shanae had demanded they stay in company with the ship as they made their way south.

His first surprise, after the sudden destruction of the *Chasseur* and the *Arbiter*, of course, had been the eagerness of the captains to join their cause.

It had been clear that Captains Semprun and Hamidi had never fully trusted Greene, nor his claim that Captain Maguire had left the island for Jamaica after the altercation in the jungle outside of Cayona.

Even they had not assumed the captain's death, however, and they had taken that news hard. Captain Houdin had been ready to support Shanae's case, of course. He had been there throughout the entire ordeal. But there had been no need.

Greene had installed his own creatures aboard each of the squadron's ships, as he had aboard the *Arbiter*. But they had been easily dealt with once Shanae's messengers had reached the captains. Aboard the *Kate*, Sylvestre had had the command, but had refused promotion to captain, maintaining that the crew believed Captain Maguire would return eventually.

The man's black and white striped mane had looked sad and bedraggled as he had bowed before Shanae, begging for her forgiveness.

It had been one of the few moments she had shown any emotion at all, however, for which Aidan was glad.

She had smiled a sad half-smile and raised the older man by the elbow, refusing his deference. Then she had asked him to command the ship for one last journey, as she needed to remain aboard the *Amelie Carre* for a little while longer.

That had been when she informed them of her next plan.

It had been in Captain Maguire's cabin, surrounded by his things, the room left untouched by Sylvestre and the other *Kates* despite the captain's disappearance.

Shanae was certain Greene would be making for Jamaica. There was nowhere else for him to go. It wasn't as if Fowler would agree to go home to England, where nothing could await him but the rope.

And Greene had no way of knowing that his old home was not the safe harbor it once had been.

Shanae and Hunt had been busy, with the solicitors the captain's hidden fortune had secured.

Greene might dock in Port Royal, and his family no doubt, maintained influence over the governor there, and the apparatus of the civil authorities, but they lacked the full power and prestige of their fortunes thanks to Captain Maguire's financial maneuverings.

Greene might make it to Port Royal, but his family would be unable to provide him with the kind of support he would need to replace the *Chasseur* or threaten the squadron again.

That was, if Greene was making for Jamaica.

Shanae was certain, but no one else was.

That also might explain the last changes to the *Amelie Carre*. A new name, the *Avontuur*, had been painted across the ship's broad stern. A Dutch name, that should be just the fig leaf they would need to sell the obviously altered, French-made ship to the factors in Port Royal.

The cog would fetch them a pretty penny, the Brethren calling Jamaica home would know the true story of the *Amelie Carre*, and the squadron's stock would rise accordingly.

He knew he was unable to follow Shanae's calculations, trying to secure a place for them all in Port Royal. But an undamaged cog dressed to look like a galleon should provide enough gold to buy almost anything, as far as he was concerned.

There would be no usual distribution of shares, perhaps, but that was a small price to pay for securing themselves a new home in this bustling, protected harbor.

It wouldn't feel like home for a long while, but if it was where Captain Maguire had wanted them, that was good enough for Aidan Allen.

He cast a glance back over their wake, to where the *Bonnie Kate* rolled under light sail. The brigantines would never be quite so fast with the wind clipping their bows as the sloops were, but they still struggled not to overtake the big, ungainly cog, even as the sloops struggled not to pull away.

He turned forward again to look at the sloops, and his eyes fixed on the *Laughing Jacques*, seemingly of their own accord.

Somewhere belowdecks aboard the *Jacques*, Boothe was hiding.

The fact that Boothe had survived his own folly was the height of irony, something Aidan had learned from his captain.

Many of the men and women aboard the *Arbiter* had died when the decks collapsed beneath the combined weight of the galleon's guns after her keel had snapped.

It must have been hellish aboard that gundeck and below, as the world shattered around them, water crashing in, timbers crashing down.

And somehow, Boothe had managed to swim away without a scratch.

Aidan knew that was less than a blessing, as far as the *Arbiter's* former first mate was concerned.

Shanae had said nothing to him, but there wasn't a soul in the squadron who doubted how she felt about the man who had single-handedly thrown victory to the sharks for his own petty sense of vengeance.

Shanae had refused to acknowledge Boothe, and the others had followed her lead. Soon enough the man had skulked belowdecks and hadn't been seen again.

In fact, Aidan wondered, for a moment, if he *was* still aboard the *Laughing Jacques*.

But then, he had to be, really. There wasn't anywhere else for him to go. It wasn't as if he would have been satisfied with the life of a woodcutter. And there would be no safe harbor in Tortuga for any of them anymore, once the French heard what had happened to the commodore and the squadron that had provided the island with the bulk of its protection from Spanish predation.

No. Boothe was somewhere aboard the *Jacques*, skulking in the shadows. Why, Aidan was certain he didn't know. And that was the least of his concerns.

What were they going to do when they arrived in Jamaica? If they found the *Jaguar* at anchor within the harbor, were they going to brace the frigate right there before everyone? Was it going to be a full-on engagement within the confines of the harbor? Beneath the great guns of the English forts?

He doubted they had enough gold left to bribe those forts into silence.

Or did Shanae mean to board the ship by herself and drag Greene out by the hair?

At this point, given her mad-dog attitude, he wouldn't have wagered on any one course of events.

She was capable of anything.

He settled back against the railing with a sigh. They would know soon enough, even at the pathetic speeds the newly christened *Avontuur* could manage.

Something told him Shanae Bure was going to pursue Greene to the ends of the Earth, and he knew that he would follow her that far and beyond.

And as he glanced again at the ships of the squadron, in company all around, he realized that he wasn't the only one.

*****

It was an intriguing experience, sailing through the small islands and mangrove stands that sheltered the entrance to the Port Royal harbor. Generally, most of the sailors Aidan knew would avoid mangrove stands, knowing full-well the treacherous shallows they might mark. But the channels into Port Royal had been established for years, and as long as the *Avontuur* maintained her course, they would be fine.

Ahead, behind the last stands of low trees, the buildings of Port Royal rose out of the water like some ancient myth. And between him and the structures was a forest of masts marking the harbor.

Laughing Jacques had already entered, making toward the northern quay, while *Chainbreaker* had raised her canvas and was keeping station to the left of the entrance. Behind him, he watched as *Bonnie Kate* followed, *Syren* joining the sloop on guard.

They weren't about to let Greene escape again.

Shanae had kept *Syren* and *Chainbreaker* out on purpose, of course, knowing that the crews of those two ships were going to have the hardest time finding acceptance in the English town. But between the prestige the *Avontuur*-ne-*Amelie Carre* as a prize offered, and the status they would gain by bringing down the Greenes, Shanae believed even the freed slaves and women of those two ships would be able to call Port Royal home.

The last of the mangroves fell away, revealing the bustling harbor of England's primary port in the region. The deeper sections were crowded with cargo ships of every description, flying flags from almost every nation of Europe. Along the quays and docks were many smaller ships, including most of the buccaneers the English governor had enticed to the island over the years to bolster his own naval defense.

Aidan was no one's fool. He knew the Brethren who had made Jamaica their new home had offered something in return. He could only imagine the uneasy truce that had to exist between the buccaneers and the small British Navy squadron housed between the two big forts off to starboard, their biggest ship, *Venator*, riding heavy at anchor in the middle of the formation, ready for a fight.

Port Royal was young, but it already rivaled Tortuga in its heyday.

Shanae came up onto the quarterdeck adjusting her pistols and sword belt. She hadn't changed her clothes, but something about her bearing seemed to remind him of the captain just before he'd head off to a meeting of the captains in council.

Whoever she was going to meet, she meant business.

"Bring her as close into the docks as you can, Aidan. And make her secure. The factors will want to board her for an inspection before they hand over the kind of coin we're asking for." She gave him a grim smile. "Be nice."

She shielded her eyes from the burning sun and looked up into the rigging. The men from the *Chaucer's Pride* had done the best they could to shift the old girl's sail plan as much as possible. Between the new construction and the newly positioned spars and rigging, her resemblance to the late, lamented *Amelie Carre* should not be unduly noticeable.

The hasty repairs they had managed on the damage *Chasseur* had inflicted before Boothe destroyed her should not be evident to a cursory inspection.

Then her words registered.

"Wait a minute. *I'm* to bring her in? *I'm* to be nice to the factors?" A chill of panic set into his throat. "Where will *you* be?"

She glared out over the port bow and nodded. He looked, shading his own eyes, and then gave a sharp exhalation.

Jaguar.

She had been right all along.

Aidan shook his head. He had never doubted her, he realized.

In the world he had inhabited for the last few days, he knew they would find *Jaguar* here.

The ship was situated as far from the mouth of the port as they could have managed, just offshore of the northern docks, where the *Pride* and most of the other Brethren vessels would be.

Her gun ports were closed, sails furled, anchor chain set and still.

Her deep brown paint glowed in the sun, highlights from her cream detailing glinting in the water around her.

He wanted to sink her where she rode at anchor.

"Are you going over there?" He turned back to Shanae. "Not alone you're not." He looked around for someone he could order to fetch his weapons, but she put a hand on his shoulder.

"Aidan, he's not over there." He tilted her head toward the town. "He'll be running for his father's house, near the governor's manse." She gave his shoulder a hard pat, then turned toward the ladder down to the main deck.

"Keep the squadron together. When you've dealt with the factors and the gold's been shifted to the captain's accounts, return to the *Kate*." She glanced toward the wheel, where Derrick Vallance was doing his best to appear oblivious. "Any of the *Prides* who want can go with you. See the others paid off from the factor's account and send them back to their ship."

Aidan felt a sour tug in his stomach.

Send them back to the *Chaucer's Pride*.

It wasn't like Captain Kay was going to be needing it anymore.

He nodded. "There's still no reason you have to go alone. I can come with you." He waved a vague hand toward Vallance. "He can deal with the factors. He's more than proven his worth—"

She shook her head and then turned, grabbing him by both shoulders and leaning her head into his.

The strangeness in his stomach turned. He felt warm.

"I need you here, Aidan. Don't worry; everything will be fine ashore."

He shook his head as he watched her descend.

It wasn't that he thought he would be any great asset if things went wrong.

He had seen Shanae fight often enough; he knew she could take care of herself.

Hell, if things went south on them, it was far more likely that *she* would be rescuing *him* than the other way around.

But he felt like he needed to be there with her all the same.

And the feeling in his gut was still there, too. What was that all about?

She was in the waist of the big ship now, passing along orders, watching as they lowered a boat, and then, with one last wave, her face grave, her smile almost sad, she was over the side and gone.

He stood there for a moment, locked in indecision. Then he moved toward the starboard rail, shooting Vallance a dark, warning look as he passed the helmsman, and leaned over the rail.

Far below, the *Avontuur's* newly painted boat was pulling for the distant shore with all the speed it could manage.

It was going faster than he would have expected.

Then he focused on the enormous shoulders of the man doing the rowing, and he cursed.

Why would she bring Fabien Astier and not him?

Certainly, the hulking brute of a Frenchmen would be more intimidating than Aidan's own, more normal size. But if things got hot, could he be trusted?

Aidan spat over the side into the bright blue waters of the bay.

He'd had enough. When the factors came, he would deal with them, and then he would go home.

It had been far too long since he had been aboard the *Bonnie Kate*. He had spoken with several of the *Kates* before they left Tortuga, including Sylvestre, Ruiz, and even Isabella. He knew he'd be welcomed with open arms.

Well, maybe not by Isabella. She had seemed rather cold at their last meeting.

But still, the others had been happy enough to see him again.

Then all they would need would be to have Shanae back, and then maybe things could go back to the way they were.

He slumped against the railing.

Without the captain, of course.

His eyes tightened and he turned to look again at *Jaguar*, floating placidly in the sunlight.

No matter how much he tried to pretend, or avoid the realities of the situation, he couldn't.

This entire affair was far from over.

Chapter 33
1675 ~ Port Royal, Jamaica

Watching her boat pull for shore, Boothe cursed his position.

None of the squadron captains had offered him a berth for the return to Jamaica. Each of them knew what he had done, what he had cost them, and were angry with him in their own right.

On top of that, none of them seemed eager to cross Shanae; and she had made no secret about how she felt about him now.

In the end, he had been forced to beg for space belowdecks aboard the *Laughing Jacques*. Houdin was the most easily approached of the captains, and even the little fat man, usually so easy-going and polite, had made the request difficult to make.

And he had made it plain that, although relenting, it was not something he was eager to do.

And so Boothe had crossed the Windward Passage in the cramped little sloop, bearing up as best he could beneath the glares and muttered curses of the crew.

Those he had once deemed the lowliest members of the squadron now felt, with some justification, that they were far above him.

He had taken cold meals alone in the funk and the dark of the cargo deck, or huddled alone on the main deck, when the smells and his own despair had driven up into the sunlight.

It had been the most miserable journey of his life, but he was determined to remain with the squadron and to make right what he had turned askew.

But now the woman he had wronged, no, the captain he had betrayed, was moving away as fast as that French bastard bodyguard of hers could row. She was heading into town, he could see, rather than the northern docks where he might have expected her to go, or the factors' establishments along the southern mouth to the smaller deep harbor.

He turned from the railing to find Captain Houdin standing behind him, watching the boat close with the quay.

"I need a boat." The words were out of Boothe's mouth before he had thought them.

Had he thought, he would have couched the request in prettier terms, but he would have asked, nonetheless.

He needed to follow Shanae Bure.

"I don't much give a drowned rat's ass what you need, Boothe." The man's wide grin made the words all the harder to follow. "You begged for a scrap of deck, and you got it. The rest is up to you, no?"

Boothe shook his head, gesturing toward the disappearing boat. "Captain, I have to follow her. You want to be rid of me? Lend me a boat, just long enough to get to shore, and you'll have seen the last of me aboard your ship. You won't have to deal with me again, I promise."

Houdin gave him a look through narrow green eyes. "You could swim across, and I'd be just as shut of you." He looked down at the water. "Fairly certain there aren't any sharks hereabouts. And the barracuda generally stay along the less-peopled coastlines."

Boothe stared at him.

And then the smile was back, although it still had an edge. "Albin!"

He started at the shout, looking around to see the young blond with the spotty beard emerge from the forward hatch.

"Ready a boat for Mr. Boothe, if you would be so kind, Albin."

The *Jacques's* scrappy young boatswain gave him a flat look, then nodded to his captain. "Yes, sir." And he was off, shouting orders to men twice his age who jumped to follow them.

The lad reminded Boothe a little of himself at that age, although he had been in the Navy then, and lived a very different life.

But when he thought about it, was it really that different?

He turned to thank Houdin, but the man was gone, standing by his sailing master at the tiller, discussing something that must have been quite weighty, judging from their faces.

"Boat's ready, Mr. Boothe." The tone belayed the respectful words, reminding him once again of his fall from grace.

The boy wasn't so much like him.

Boothe moved to the railing and climbed over, dropping the short distance down into the jollyboat. The Boatswain dropped gracefully in after him, followed by two surly-faced sailors.

They settled down to the oars while the boy perched at the bow, leaving the low stern for him; the noisome cargo.

As Albin started the two sailors with a sharply barked rhythm, he gave Boothe a steely glare and a snarling little grin.

Well, maybe he was a bit, after all.

*****

He tried to thank the young boatswain as he climbed up the old, dried out ladder on the quay, but the boy already had his two men pushing the boat around. None of them were paying him any heed at all.

He thought he caught one of the sailors taking a sideways glance at him, but the man looked away too quickly for him to be sure.

Boothe brushed off his knees, looking around the big cobbled forum. As unimportant as the men and women of the *Laughing Jacques* had made clear to him he was, the citizens of Port Royal clearly thought even less of him.

No one gave him so much as a glance as he stood there, trying to decide which way to go.

She might have gone to the factors to make the arrangements for her bastardized cog before continuing her pursuit of Greene.

Because she was pursuing Greene, He had no doubt.

The Greenes lived on the same wide boulevard as the governor, on the far side of the little island of Port Royal town. It shouldn't be too difficult to find them, even given the sudden downturn in their fortunes.

But that wouldn't have been where Shanae would go first, would it.

It wasn't a question. He knew where she was going to go.

She'd need to check the lay of the land before launching her next attack. She would need to collect information.

And there was only one place the girl would know to go, hoping to gather intelligence on the Greenes and the events occurring in Jamaica.

With one quick glance toward the business offices to the south, he turned north, moving into the maze of narrow streets much sooner than he needed to in order to avoid the dusky little hulk of a sloop that rocked at her moorings there, almost as if the *Chaucer's Pride* were mocking him for his part in the fratricide of the ship's captain and masters.

He didn't know what it said about him, that a ship could make him so uncomfortable and dredge up such strange pangs of conscience, but he didn't need to run into anyone he recognized from his attempts to press a crew for the ill-fated *Amelie Carre*, anyway.

As always, the confined tunnels of the city's poorer quarters immediately made him ill at ease. He was a man used to standing on the broad deck, with miles of clear sight lines between him and any horizon.

When he was sailing, that was. Even when he was in harbor, the decks of his ship were broad and clear.

The decks of the ship that had been his home for nearly two decades.

The ship he himself had destroyed.

If he made it through all this alive, there would be a lot he would have to answer for, beginning with himself.

None too soon he came upon the filthy little alley that housed One-Eyed Jack's. It was the only place she could hope to find a friendly face outside of Maguire's solicitors' offices.

He moved to the door. At this time of day, the place might not be empty, but it lacked the kind of crowd he would need to try to hide from her.

He waited, but the door didn't move. No one left or went in.

The filthy little windows were too high up, and too encrusted with salt and dirt, and the interior was too dark, for him to see anything going on within.

But if he went in, she was going to see him.

Still, if she wasn't in there... If she had, indeed, gone to her see her solicitors instead of stopping by this den of inequity first, he would lose any chance of following her if he waited here too long.

He moved to rest his back against the wall beside the door, doing his absolute best to appear casual, and then slid a bit closer to the door. When he felt his shoulder bump up against the door frame, he eased himself around until he was leaning on his shoulder.

What the hell was he doing? Had the last few days really unmanned him so thoroughly?

He would step into the squalid little pub with the bright light of day shining behind him, and he would demand to know what was happening.

She would know his worth. She would realize that there was no reason not to include him in her plans. There was no reason she wouldn't depend upon him to watch her back while she made her final move on Greene.

He reached out for the worn leather door handle.

No reason except that he had just so spectacularly ruined her last, well-conceived plan for justice.

In fact, by the time he was done, the wreckage of her scheme had been scattered, burning, across Cayona Harbor.

Why *would* she listen to him now?

Why *should* she listen to him now?

He rested back against the wall, cursing softly under his breath.

Whether he was cursing her, or himself, he didn't know.

He stood there with his back against the warm, moist wall, and struck it with the back of his head, slowly, several times.

When the door crashed open, he jumped. His hands came up to catch the splintered wood before it smashed into his face, and while he was dealing with that, the staccato echo of well-heeled boots marching off up the alleyway rattled off the surrounding walls.

Boothe eased the door closed, peering around the edge as it cleared his vision.

He was just able to see Shanae storm around the corner and out of sight.

Her back was rigid, her gait quick, and her footsteps continued to ring with authority even after he lost sight of her.

Rage had fairly radiated off her as she stalked away.

He stood there, unable to move.

He should follow her. That's what he had come ashore to do, wasn't it? He had intended to demand she let him help her.

Much as he had demanded Captain Houdin give him a boat.

Except that had only worked because the man wanted to get rid of him.

Maybe it was time Myles Boothe came to grips with the fact that no one owed him anything, moving forward.

He took a step to follow, but his foundering courage failed him.

If she was mad enough to kill him, he would have run after her and demanded a reckoning.

But she wasn't mad enough to kill him. Her opinion of him had fallen to utter and complete contempt.

Boothe knew he would have been able to withstand her hate. But her disdain was too much.

With a gust of breath, he turned on his heel and pulled the door to One-Eyed Jack's open.

Inside, it took a moment for his eyes to adjust. As always, in the daytime, the air was hot and thick inside. What relief the old stone might have offered disappeared past him through the open door.

The grimy windows offered little light, and the low lamps cast only a vague yellow glow over the scene.

Before him the short bar gleamed, cleaned and ready for the night's revels. The brown-haired bar girl, Liz, looked at him curiously, but he could tell nothing from her expression. There was certainly nothing here that he could see that might have set Shanae's anger ablaze.

The few tables in the front section were empty, and he had to peer deeper into the funk before he saw a couple of the tables in the wider common room had occupants. He thought he recognized the set of one man's shoulders, and things started to fall into place as he moved through the narrow door into that section of the establishment.

Captain Lachlan Porter's gray eyes watched his approach without emotion. The man's full white mane of hair was like a halo in the soft light, but his face was anything but angelic.

"I'm not certain I have anything to share with you, Myles Boothe of Tortuga."

Boothe decided to let that pass. "What was she after?"

There was no need to elaborate on who he meant.

That great fall of hair swung slowly back and forth. "Who are you, to order me around so? Mistress Bure's business is her own, and I'm not certain you have any claim to her, or it. And I certainly owe you nothing."

Boothe took a deep breath, trying to calm his own rising anger. "I'm trying to help her, Porter. I'm trying to make things right between us."

The man's answering sneer was almost enough to force Boothe's knife from its sheath. "From what I've heard, she's had enough of your help, Boothe. Might be high time you move on. The merchantmen are always looking for seasoned hands." A twinkle gleamed in his eyes. "Or you could always see if the Navy needs powder monkeys."

Another deep breath. He couldn't let this man bait him into a fight now. He needed to know what Shanae was doing so he could help her.

There would be no place for him among the Brethren anywhere, and certainly not in the squadron, if he couldn't address what happened in Cayona Harbor.

"Please." He settled into a chair opposite the old man. "I'm only trying to help."

He cast all his anger and frustration aside. There was only one thing that was going to convince this old sea dog to help, and that was genuine remorse.

And he had plenty of that to spare.

Porter looked down at the table, shifting his tankard a few inches to one side, and then an inch to the other.

"There's been a lot of talk among the merchant families of Port Royal lately."

Boothe forced himself to nod, assuming Porter wasn't just passing along idle gossip and had a point he was heading toward.

"Forced trade is a big deal here, and less of a black mark against the ship serving as catspaw as might be the case in Tortuga." He took a sip, and his eyes darkened. "Certainly, less of a black mark than Maguire considered it."

Boothe leaned forward. This seemed to be veering in a more relevant direction.

"The merchant families of Port Royal are deeply involved in the forced trade. Many see it as their patriotic duty, to strike at Spain anywhere they can." Another sip. "Or at least, that's what they say at parties."

Boothe nodded again, trying to control his impatience. While the old man was muttering over his small beer, Shanae was haring off to God alone knew where, into God alone knew what kind of danger.

"When Miss Bure began to put Maguire's plans into effect, the other families realized what the Greenes had been up to on Tortuga. With command of an entire squadron of buccaneers, they would dominate the forced trade." He shrugged. "The families didn't receive it well. Coming at a time when many of the Greene family assets were being locked down by the creditors, it was yet another blow to their status here."

Boothe was growing more and more impatient with each passing moment but forced himself to stillness.

Porter leaned forward over interlaced fingers, his eyes intent. His voice took on a heavy note. "Our governor, the Honorable Sir Thomas Lynch, has had disturbing news from England. Peace with Spain. A possible end to the forced trade." He smiled, but it was a ghastly expression. "No one yields power willingly, Mr. Boothe. The Assembly of Jamaica, and the Greenes in particular, will fight with every fiber of their being, with the king's blessing or no."

He began to realize what a viper's nest the squadron had sailed into. Not for the first time, he found himself cursing the machinations of the Old World, that so complicated their lives here. "Where did she go?"

For the first time since he sat down, Boothe thought he saw genuine emotion in Porter's gray eyes, and it sent a chill down his back.

"I honestly don't know, Boothe. But if she's trying to track down Greene's son, she's got to be headed toward their manse. Master Greene spends a good portion of every day, now, at the Governor's, demanding protection from what he calls 'foreign interference' with his business." A bit of the old grin returned. "I can only assume he means you lot. But honestly, I can't even begin to guess where she ran off to. She left after I told her about Greene and the governor."

Boothe shoved away from the table, rising and turning in one motion.

Maguire's big plans for the Greene's finances were all well and good, but Shanae was not so bloodless a creature as to care overmuch for such things.

She was pursuing a man, not a ledger book.

She was hunting Sidney Greene.

And Greene was hurt, and scared, and would be running for home.

Captain Porter shouted something else to him as he was leaving, but he couldn't hear as the rickety door to One-Eyed Jack's clattered shut behind him.

Chapter 34
1675 - Port Royal, Jamaica

The King's House, home of the Court of Chancery and the Assembly of Jamaica, was located at the end of High Street, the thoroughfare that housed both the governor's manse and most of the tall brick homes of the major merchant families.

Although the courtroom was often empty, the council chambers at the back of the House were often used for meetings of the Assembly, both formal and informal.

Shanae had learned much of the workings of King's House while pursuing Captain Maguire's financial vengeance on the Greenes.

Given what Captain Porter had told her about the shifting fortunes of the town, she knew there was a better than even chance she would find the Assembly of Jamaica convened in council for much of any given day.

She was going to destroy the Greenes that day, and see their fortunes spilled into the mud for what their son had wrought. And Sidney Greene, in particular, was going to pay an ugly price.

But first, she needed to see to it that the other families would step aside. Much like one buccaneer crew would not stand idly by to see another abused by outsiders, she knew the families of Port Royal, whether they liked the Greenes or not, would be loath to see them victimized by those they saw as their inferiors.

The final major flaw Captain Maguire had seen in Port Royal was the importance of the forced trade and the role it pushed upon the buccaneers. Rather than the fiercely independent adventurers of their own idle minds, they became nothing but tame guard dogs, attacking those they were pointed at, making heaps of wealth for their masters while holding back mere trinkets for themselves.

With the wealth the captain had secured for them, and the position among the merchant families they might purchase with the downfall of the Greenes, the squadron might well be free of the onerous elements of the forced trade, as well.

If the others could be convinced to let them.

She pushed through the bright white doors of the King's House and into the echoing interior without pause. The red-coated soldiers outside looked at each other as they noted her outlandish buccaneer's garb and the many weapons she carried in plain sight.

One opened his mouth, taking a hand from the shaft of his halberd to protest, but she was already inside.

"Young … young lady?" The soldier followed her, obviously hesitant. Her skin clearly marked her as at least part African, which had to be an uncomfortable reality for him. By her clothing she was a buccaneer, and a rather successful one. Her kind, no matter how you defined her kind, were not often seen on the High Street, let alone entering King's House.

She ignored him, moving through the building toward the conference room.

The soldier followed, clearly not knowing exactly what he should be doing. She had learned, after years among the squadron, that the best defense against an officious gatekeeper was a confident attitude and speed.

They never seemed to be able to think clearly, if you acted like you belonged, moved quickly, and didn't hesitate.

She came to the ornate door and pushed it open without knocking. The faces that rose to stare at her would have been comical under different circumstances.

"Miss Bure, this is highly irregular." Denis Flynn, the de facto leader of the Assembly, stood at the head of the table. She had dealt with him on several occasions while finalizing the purchase of the Greene family debts and calling in some of the less usual markers.

"Mr. Flynn, I have a request to present to the Assembly."

They were nothing like the formal council, where all twelve members would meet and decide the weighty matters of the island. These unofficial meetings only took place at times of great opportunity or stress. But she knew at once she had chosen the right tack, seeing them sit taller in their fancy chairs.

Such men always liked to be treated importantly.

Flynn's eyes narrowed. "I thought your accounts were in order from our last meeting. The Greene holdings are in a shambles. Governor Lynch is exhausted with the man's entreaties. Your revenge is complete. It is only a matter of time before they are forced to return to England."

"Revenge is not my business, Mr. Flynn." She stepped into the room, nodding her thanks to the confused sentry as if he had been her official escort through the building, dismissed now that she had reached her destination.

She was alarmed at how comfortable she felt in this environment, after only a few short weeks of working with Hunt and Captain Porter with Captain Maguire's finances.

She took an empty seat at the long table. "I come to you, gentlemen, to demand redress for grievances long suffered by my people, and long overdue for resolution."

The councilors exchanged uncomfortable glances, clearly not knowing what she meant.

There were many grievances imposed upon many peoples throughout the current system. By her birth and by her trade she could be counted among most of them. They couldn't possibly know to which ones she was referring now.

"Sidney Greene has brought about the destruction of several ships under my charge. He has proven himself to be a menace and a disruptive influence among the captains and crews of the buccaneers."

They seemed nonplussed at this. They saw themselves as the masters in the forced trade triangle, to be sure. Was it any concern of theirs if the dogs were squabbling amongst themselves?

She had to put this into terms they might understand.

"While attempting to secure an entire fleet for the services of the Greenes alone, Sidney Greene has disrupted that fleet. You have undoubtedly heard of the ships just entering the harbor?" She paused for effect, looking each of them in the eye. "And those now anchored just outside the harbor?"

Flynn grimaced. Having risen to the high seat upon the fall of Greene's fortunes, he was the most likely to be brought any news from the waterfront that might impact their deliberations.

"A formidable force, indeed. Two sloops, two brigantines, and a frigate, I understand? In company with a … strange hybrid, said to look like a cog mated with some fanciful variation of a Spanish galleon?"

Well, she couldn't expect her carpenters' hasty work to stand up to focused scrutiny in the harsh light of day. She shrugged.

"The *Avontuur*. I believe Dutch ships are still being accepted as prizes, in the current climate?"

Flynn exchanged a quick glance with the merchant sitting to his left, a younger man with short-cropped blond hair and hazel eyes. She could read their thoughts as if they were written plainly on a page.

The *Avontuur* was a large ship and would be a fine addition to the merchant fleets of any of these men.

The blond nodded and rose, bowing slightly to her as he moved past and out the door.

The others looked to each other uncomfortably, realizing only now that they had lost an opportunity.

And Flynn, of course, knew he had been given one.

She smiled at him, and he smiled back, briefly.

She would also be damned if she was going to disabuse the man of his mistaken assumption that the *Jaguar* was with her other ships.

"Still, Miss Bure," Flynn settled back in his chair. "You were saying something about your squadron, I believe?"

Her eyes tightened, and she made no effort to hide it. "Sidney Greene is responsible for many deaths among my people. He had brought about the destruction of at least two ships and threatens to disrupt the delicate balance in the region." She looked then at the others. "A balance that, I believe, has served you all well."

They looked uncomfortable at that, but none had the audacity to deny it.

"Miss Bure, we were in the middle of a rather delicate discussion. If you might move on to your point, we would certainly appreciate it."

She stood, towering over the men in the room, and locked eyes with each of them in turn, keeping Flynn for last.

When she was staring into his brown eyes, she smiled her most predatory smile.

"The Brethren demand redress, Mr. Flynn. I mean to take action against Sidney Greene, and anyone who comes between me and my quarry will rue that error."

He looked uneasily at the others, but none of them would meet his gaze. Captain Maguire had told her there were times when only one voice mattered, when only a captain's word carried weight, and the masters and mates would gladly cede those times to the man or woman with the biggest cabin.

She recognized that she had just placed Dennis Flynn into the Assembly's equivalent of that moment.

He returned her gaze for a instant, then looked away.

"Do what you must do. I trust you will try to keep the destruction to a reasonable level? The Assembly of Jamaica will not hamper your efforts, and I will see to it that Governor Lynch understands the delicate nature of the situation."

She nodded. "That was all I wanted to hear, Mr. Flynn. Thank you, and as always, it was a pleasure doing business with a man who understands the realities of the situation."

She left, smiling at the babble of rising consternation in her wake as the door closed behind her.

Dennis Flynn had just gained himself a hale new cargo ship. And Shanae Bure had just opened the path to Sidney Greene's destruction.

At the door she smiled and tipped her hat to the sentries, saving a mischievous wink for the tall dark-haired guard who had followed her into the House.

She could see the relief plain on his face, that she was leaving, apparently without killing anyone.

Not yet, anyway.

The Greene's manse was on the opposite side of the street from the Governor's residence and the King's House. The back of the grounds were on the water of Cagway Bay, the body of water that surrounded Port Royal.

It was brick, like most of the newer structures in the town, if anything could be considered newer in a settlement less than two decades old.

Port Royal had flourished under the aegis of the forced trade, and it was families like the Greenes who had benefited the most.

She stood across the cobbled street, leaning against a building and surveying the low wall with the tall manse behind.

Sidney Greene was in that building, somewhere. There were burly men standing by the gate, clearly guards despite their lack of uniforms. Maybe they were buccaneers, fallen on hard times. Or maybe they were mercenaries, or soldiers who had mustered out here in the colonies with no other trade to their names.

No matter the path that had led them to be standing between her and her prey, she would not feel the slightest compunction if she had to cut them down to get to him.

She took one last deep breath, then pushed herself off the building with her shoulder blades, standing steadily for a moment, and then stepped into the street.

Or she would have, if a strong arm had not seized her by the shoulder and spun her around.

"Where the hell have you been?"

Boothe's face was contorted in something that might have been anger, might have been fear, and might have been concern.

It better have been fear or concern, she thought, eyes hardening. The man had no right to bear her the slightest grudge ever again.

And he certainly had no right to demand anything of her.

She shrugged his arm off and could see in his eyes as he backed away that he realized how close she had come to drawing a weapon.

"What I do and where I go is no concern of yours, Boothe. Let's ignore each other moving forward, shall we? I won't kill you, and you won't let your shadow darken my path."

He jerked his chin in the direction of the Greene manse. "You going to storm the castle singlehandedly, are you?"

She looked over her shoulder to where the two guards by the gate were now watching them, their attention clearly caught by Boothe's histrionics.

She cursed, glaring down into the gutter, then back at the man who had ruined all her carefully laid plans. She stepped up close to him, hoping the guards might see this as a romantic entanglement rather than a disagreement over how to assault their position and kill the man they were hired to protect.

She tangled her fingers into the front of his shirt and pulled him close. "Step away, Boothe." Her voice was a blade-thin whisper through teeth clenched in a sick semblance of a smile. "Now. This is all that you have left me. Do you understand that? Will you deny me this as well?"

A sudden suspicion rose in her mind. Had Boothe been protecting Sidney Greene all along?

But before the heat could rise past her breastbone, she realized that couldn't be.

Boothe had tried to kill Greene with his ill-considered broadside. It was only God's perverse sense of humor that had allowed the would-be pirate king to survive the slaughter and make it to the *Jaguar*. And it was only Captain Fowler's cowardice that had let him escape.

She released the front of Boothe's shirt with a shove that sent him stumbling backwards.

But when she turned back toward the manse, she stopped.

There were more men standing around the gate.

Several of them were wearing the red-coated uniforms of Royal Marines.

She threw an animal glare at Boothe, but he was watching as well and missed her expression entirely.

She heard the clatter of hooves from beyond the wall and watched in growing horror as a party of five horsemen emerged; four more marines, with a man in salt-stained finery in the middle. They circled once in the middle of the street, and she saw him, in the center of the formation, as clear as day.

Looking down from his perch atop the roan horse, he saw her as well, and his eyes widened in terror before narrowing in blind, burning hatred.

Sidney Greene rode off down the street with the four marines in tight formation around him.

The man did not look back at her as he pounded down the cobbled High Street, and none of the others seemed to have noticed the exchange.

Boothe came up beside her, his own hatred plain on his face.

"The bastard. The puling, lubber bastard." He muttered the words under his breath as they watched the party disappear around a corner, heading south.

A huge figure poked his head around that corner a moment later, looking to her for further guidance, and she cursed.

She had set Fabien Astier to watch the approach toward the waterfront in case Greene dodged in that direction. But she couldn't have expected even a man of his prodigious size and ability to stop four armed marines on horseback, charging toward—

She stopped.

Boothe noticed the sudden change in her demeanor and turned to her.

"What? What is it?"

She began to run, following the vanished horsemen, but only coincidentally.

She was making for the main harbor and the waterfront.

Where her ships were waiting, watching for ships that might be approaching Port Royal.

They would even be keeping a weather eye on *Jaguar*, making sure Fowler couldn't escape their eventual vengeance for his part in Greene's escape.

But closer than the main harbor and her ships was the Naval Harbor.

The harbor where the marines might be expected to bring someone they were escorting.

Someone who might just have been able to secure some assistance from the new governor, eager to protect the forced trade that filled the town's coffers and kept it safe from foreign ships of war.

Her gut twisted as she ran past a surprised Astier, ignoring the pounding of Boothe's footsteps as he struggled to keep up.

Greene was heading toward the Naval Harbor with a marine escort.

The governor was helping him.

But helping him escape, or attack?

The only good thing she could think of was that the big guns on the forts surrounding Port Royal had not yet pounded her ships to kindling.

She could only hope that meant Lynch's assistance was not extending to open combat before the crowded waterfront.

But what was Greene doing, heading to the Naval Harbor?

She ran faster, feeling him escape with each jarring impact of her boots on the cobbles, the footsteps of the two men following her a hopeless counterpoint to her rising rage.

She was going to be too late.

Again.

Chapter 35
1675 ~ Portland Bight, Off Jamaica

Aidan took a moment to mop the sweat from his face. He had been running his crews ragged as the chaos of the *Bonnie Kate's* preparations to leave Port Royal with all haste surged around them.

Shanae had emerged from the surrounding buildings on the waterfront screaming in rage. The lookout aloft, who had been spending far more time with his spyglass trained on the *Jaguar* and the approach to the harbor than the town, had taken a moment to realize what he was seeing, but when he had, he'd called down to the quarterdeck, and Sylvestre had sent Perry pulling for all his crew was worth for the quay to fetch their captain.

Captain whether she accepted it or not.

Whether she wanted it or not.

But the true madness had only started when Shanae and Astier had scrambled up the side, the woman rushing through the crowds for the quarterdeck, shouting orders.

He couldn't remember the *Kate* ever having been so well-manned, with so many of the *Prides* still lingering after their return. Not many of those pallid ghosts had gone back to their own ship.

The crew of the *Laughing Jacques*, seeing the mad scramble aboard the *Kate*, had pushed off from their position on the decks, run past *Jaguar* with dark looks, and come up alongside the *Kate* before she could be brought about.

Shanae had shouted back and forth with Houdin for a moment, stabbing at the distant *Jaguar* with a finger all the while, and the *Jacques* had reluctantly furled her half-dropped sails, her sailors watching with disappointment while the *Kate* began to slide toward the mouth of the harbor.

Ahead of them he could see *Chainbreaker* and *Syren* making their own preparations, and beyond them he thought he could see a big ship flying the red and white ensign of the British Navy.

That struck him as odd. He hadn't noticed the ship slip out of the Naval Harbor in the chaos of his own work. It had to be the frigate, *Venator*. But why would she be leaving in the late afternoon?

He had far more pressing concerns, however, having been ordered with a bark from Shanae to have his guns ready, with full battle charges prepared, and more laid on within the magazine, ready to be ferried up at a moment's notice.

She had been bellowing orders from the moment her feet hit the deck. Her words had sent men and women scrambling up into the rigging, disappearing down into the hold, and scouring the ship for whatever they would need to prepare for battle.

Aidan had kept his questions to himself, then, recognizing her mood as an unforgiving, single-mindedly focused one.

Boothe had scrambled up after her Astier and been immediately ignored by the entire crew. No one wanted such a judas aboard, and the fact that he had weaseled his way onto the longboat was bad enough.

As they moved toward the mouth of the harbor, cutting between *Chainbreaker* and *Syren*, Shanae seemed to take note of the lost *Arbiter's* first mate for the first time.

"Get in a boat." She had snapped, surprising all around her.

Boothe had looked at her with eyes that managed to combine a heart wrenching plea and a growing anger together. Before he could respond, however, Shanae had drawn a long knife.

"You're not welcome on my ship. You can take a boat, or you can take a swim."

Perry had found the crew necessary to unlimber the smaller of the ship's boats and put it over the side even as they began to pick up speed.

"Go to the *Chainbreaker*." She was obviously talking to Boothe, although she refused to look at him, focused instead on the two other ships of the squadron that would be joining them on whatever she was planning. "Tell Hamidi what transpired ashore. Tell him where we think Greene is, and tell him to prepare his ship for battle."

Boothe's anger seemed to ebb at that, and with a nod, he moved down to the main deck, and then over the side.

He had reached *Chainbreaker* with little trouble, his pale face a stark contrast to the dark crew, and the faster, more maneuverable ship managed to sprint out ahead of them despite having to wait.

As the squadron eased out toward the wider bay, Shanae had the ship prepared for a full-scale battle, and they still didn't even know who they were going to be fighting.

In the lull, wiping the sweat from his forehead, he thought again about the *Venator's* odd departure, and his stomach turned to liquid.

Were they hunting a navy frigate?

And if they were, why in the name of all the saints was the *Venator* fleeing? She was easily a match for the *Kate* in open water.

Hell, even with the entire squadron, minus their own frigate, of course, they wouldn't have been a match for the *Venator*.

So, what were they doing?

He walked up and down the main deck of the ship one last time, casting his gaze over both the port and starboard crews, forcing the idle Prides out of the way.

All twelve of the nine-pounders were set, cartridges ready, double-shotted as Captain Maguire always favored for an opening salvo.

Whoever they were going to be fighting would know they'd been kissed after that first broadside.

Or his crews would be cursing for hours, clearing the guns if they didn't end up fighting.

Once he had assured himself that the guns were ready, he went up onto the quarterdeck, ostensibly to check on the two three-pound stern chasers.

Shanae had ordered every gun loaded, and he wasn't about to disappoint.

The crews running the two smaller guns were standing by their weapons, confused but eager to be into a fight.

It felt like a very long time since the men and women of the *Kate* were able to strike back at someone, and he knew from talking to them that those who had been left behind when Captain Maguire had taken up his position in the villa on the hill felt that even more keenly.

While he, Perry, Hunt, and a few others had been fighting across Tortuga, then Jamaica, then making the harrowing journey up the Windward Passage on a ship more than half under-construction, the rest of the *Kate*s had been sitting tight, living under the constant watchful eyes of Greene's minions.

Under the old commodore they had often felt his disdain for the weight of metal they carried, or for their lack of discipline when he was planning some grand feat. But they had never doubted the old man's faith in their fighting prowess or their commitment to the Brethren.

Greene's people had managed to convey such a deep sense of contempt and dislike for each and every one of them, many had started to doubt themselves.

Morale within the squadron had never been lower and had taken an even more drastic hit when they were told about the captain's murder in the jungle.

But now they were at sea again at last; unleashed upon some enemy, their teeth bared, ready to kill.

Even if Shanae had not yet told them who that enemy was.

She was standing beside the old Spaniard, Ruiz, by the wheel. Her eyes were scanning the horizon, back and forth without a moment's pause between courses. She wasn't looking through her spyglass, but there was no less sense of searching for all that.

"Guns are manned, loaded, and ready, Captain." He gave her a jaunty salute and a smile, but it faltered as she failed to respond.

And he thought he saw her flinch at the title.

"Shanae," he moved toward her, standing opposite Ruiz and scanning the horizon himself. "Who are we looking for?"

Chainbreaker was before them, off their port bow, ranging ahead in case their quarry had made a move for the open sea. *Syren* was just off their port stern, giving her the best chance to close with an enemy appearing from any quarter. Otherwise, there was no sign of another ship as far as the eye could see.

Off to starboard, almost lost in the distance, was the brown smudge of the Jamaican coastline sliding by, right on the horizon. Scattered across the sea between them and the land were the darker shadows of small islands, mangrove stands, and rocks, the nearest two or three cannon shots away; so no real danger even if someone had managed to lay an ambush there.

Shanae sighed, her face stone, and turned to him. "He's on the *Venator*, Aidan. Greene. He's on that frigate." She gestured with her head out over the bow. "He's getting away. Again. And if we've lost him this time, I don't know how we'll pick up his trail."

That made very little sense. "Why would he be on a navy frigate? What's the government got to gain, letting him use their most powerful ship?"

She smiled, but it had a poisoned tinge to its color. "It's not even close to the most powerful ship they have, once Morgan and this new governor return from England."

He shrugged. Captain Henry Morgan was a legend, and the man had lead several armadas of buccaneer ships across the local seas. But once they were sated, they would go their separate ways with no more loyalty to Morgan than to any other Brethren captain.

What *they* had was special: a squadron of buccaneering vessels that had served together long enough to almost match the British Navy for its cohesion and training.

At least, that's what they'd always told themselves.

He wasn't too eager to put that idea to the test against an actual, trained navy frigate crew.

"Forgetting Morgan for now, why would Governor Lynch just give his frigate to a little guttersnipe like Greene?"

She shook her head, this time snapping her spyglass open and rising it to her eye. "I don't know, Aidan. To appease the man's father? To get him out of Port Royal once and for all?" She cocked her head to one side in thought, lowering the glass. "Maybe he's bait for a trap?"

"I thought you had pulled the Greene's teeth? Would they still have enough influence for something like this?"

She frowned, going back to the spyglass. "Who knows what kind of influence he might still have back in England? And as I said, I don't know." She lowered the glass once more and turned to face him. "All I know is what I saw. He was escorted out of his family's compound by marines, charging headlong through the town for the naval harbor, and then, without warning, the *Venator* raised anchor and charged out of the harbor as if she was late for a battle."

"So, you believe he's on that ship, and it is trying to evade us, for reasons we can't begin to understand?"

She shrugged, slipping the spyglass into a pouch at her belt.

And then something else she had said earlier bobbed alarmingly to the surface.

"Bait?"

She waved that away, moving to the railing. "We need to make better time." She looked up, checking the wind, then turned to Ruiz. "Can we come a point or two more off the wind? I don't think they're moving out into the open. I think they're going to stick closer to shore."

"Why?" Aidan asked before realizing he wasn't going to get an answer.

Ruiz was glancing toward the distant smudge of Jamaica. "Treacherous waters in there, senorita."

Aidan rolled his eyes at the old man's Spanish affectations, but it didn't seem to bother Shanae any.

"I trust you to steer us true, Martin." She moved to the starboard railing and gripped it in tight fists. "He's in there, somewhere. I can feel him."

The crew aloft scrambled to shift the sails under Ruiz's shouted instructions, as the Spaniard nudged the *Kate* to starboard. Someone with a flag got *Chainbreaker's* attention, and Captain Hamidi brought his ship smoothly over, the more-nimble sloop far better able to take advantage of the wind and coming in fast toward land.

Another crewman with a flag roused Captain Semprun, and *Syren* turned as well, losing more of her speed than the *Kate* had, as her top women made their adjustments.

There was a tension that hummed across the crowded decks of the *Bonnie Kate* that he couldn't remember feeling in a very long time. The ship wasn't just out of harbor, hunting prey; she was unleashed, hunting a quarry that had proven its duplicity and demanded their complete, lethal attention.

There was not a man or woman aboard who would not have sacrificed themselves if it meant they might reach on Greene and bring him down.

The dawning horror of the Captain's death, suspected by so many and yet denied by almost all, had solidified into pure hatred and wrath among the *Kates* in particular. The other members of the squadron had seen the error of their ways, and of their captains, and were eager to cleanse their souls of those mistakes with Greene's blood and the blood of anyone who tried to help him.

That hatred and focus now thrummed around the *Bonnie Kate* like the heady charge just before a lightning strike. And when that bolt finally landed, he hoped it was going to ground somewhere other than into his ship.

The small, distant islands began to grow faster than he would have liked. The mangrove stands marking shallow regions rose up before them, and Ruiz managed to thread his way through the narrow passages as if the *Kate* was nothing more than a Taino canoa.

The closer those islands got, however, his more frayed his nerves became.

They were approaching the first of the larger islands, coming up fast on their starboard quarter, when Shanae turned to him. "Why don't you go down with your crews, Aidan? Make sure the number two gun is properly laid and have the others ready to follow suit in case the *Venator* comes out."

He shook his head. "Isabella can lay the gun at least as well as I can. I should stay—"

Shanae cut him off with a sharp gesture of one hand. "Go."

He gave her one last look, but there was no give in her expression. It was almost as if she had forgotten him already.

He slowly descended the ladder to the main deck, wove through the crews to where Isabella Sanz stood with the number two gun crew, and gave her a sickly smile.

"She wants me to lay the gun, in case they're hiding up ahead."

Isabella rolled her dark eyes. "Of course, she does." She stepped aside with a grand gesture that would have been at home in any European court.

He sighted down the length of the long gun, keeping both eyes open and shifting his focus through the depth of field between the ship and the approaching island.

As he stared down the length of cold steel at the ever-shifting pattern of green and shadow, he felt like he could almost reach out and touch the fronds.

The far edge of the island was gliding up as the *Kate* rocked gently beneath him. As each new yard of sea was revealed behind the island, he expected to see the red and white trim of the *Venator* lurking in wait.

They would be facing west as well, presenting their full, impressive broadside. They would most likely boast a heavier broadside than the *Jaguar*, with the power of the British Navy behind them for outfit and resupply.

That meant more than ten twelve-pound balls would be flying toward his head almost before he could give his own crew the order to fire.

To fire a paltry six nine-pound balls back.

The discrepancy, when presented in such stark, immediate, and personal terms, was chilling.

He felt sweat drawing a gelid, distracting path down his back beneath his shirt.

He tried to control his breathing, keeping his head down and his eyes focused.

The enemy's shot would be poorly laid. They had no idea where the *Kate* might emerge. They could not know exactly when to fire. They might miss their first salvo entirely.

By then, *Chainbreaker* and *Syren* should have joined the fray. It would be three against one, and all the maneuverability advantage would belong to the squadron.

Except that the three of them were still no match for the single frigate. And maneuverability would mean next to nothing in the bight, surrounded by islands, mangroves, and sandbars.

He took a deep breath, trying to hide the developing shake from Isabella.

The island continued to slide past the gun port, revealing more and more of the sea beyond.

And then they were past. The bight behind was empty.

The *Venator* was not lying in wait for them there.

He didn't try to hide his gusted sigh of relief as he stood, straightening until his back popped, and looking over to his fellow master gunner with a grin.

"Well, that was refreshing."

*****

They sailed past two more islands the same way, and Aidan began to wonder if he was losing years off his life from the stress and strain of staring over the gun at his own impending doom.

Chainbreaker had taken the lead again and was taking some of that strain off him, but he still found himself having to suppress a shudder as they came up on each new island.

Another was looming, and he would have to crouch down again any moment. He took the time to glance around, surveying the gun crews, and looking back at the quarterdeck where Shanae was staring off the starboard bow, hands on hips, every inch the stern, unforgiving captain.

He sighed.

There was almost no sign of the woman who had been his friend for years. The woman who had knocked more than one man down for calling her 'Maguire's little girl'.

Isabella gasped.

That was odd. Was she watching him watching Shanae? She wasn't usually a jealous woman, and there had never been anything more than casual between them. If she *had* noticed him looking at their former first mate, her first response would usually be mockery.

He turned to ask her what she meant when *Chainbreaker* exploded.

Chapter 36
1675 - Portland Bight, Off Jamaica

Boothe coughed, feeling something wet on his lips. He knew it wasn't water.

The deck of the *Chainbreaker* pitched beneath him, splinters digging into the flesh of his palms.

His ears rang, his vision was a dark swirl of colors and light.

What had happened?

The sloop had been swinging around the next little island in the bight, the third or fourth such glorified sandbar they had explored. Someone aloft had cried out, he had looked over to see a looming shadow emerging from the lee of the island, and that was it.

The *Venator*. It had to have been the *Venator*.

He tried to rise, but the deck was lurching beneath him. Through the deafening buzzing in his ears began to emerge a hellish cacophony of screams and cries.

He coughed, his lungs convulsing with the effort of trying to push himself upright. The cough felt wrong, thick and fluid.

A pain flared in his chest and he collapsed with a gasp.

He wanted to cry out, to plead for assistance.

But even his battered, addled brain could figure that no such help was coming.

Chainbreaker must have received the frigate's full broadside just as they cleared the island.

Which meant this had been a trap all along.

Greene had lured them out into the bight, knowing Shanae could not let him go, and had come about, swinging in behind one of the countless little islands and waited for the inevitable.

It just so happened to be the sloop *he* was on that had caught up first.

A world-ending crash sounded from somewhere off to his right; sound that was felt deep in the chest, as if a wave of pummeling force had just swept over the foundering ship.

Venator, firing another broadside.

He couldn't lay here, waiting to drown or burn.

He reached up with one shaking hand to try to clear his eyes, rubbing at the sticky mess.

He forced his eyes to open with a sickening peeling sound as the sludge of ash, blood, and God knew what else that gummed them closed gave way.

The nightmare resolved itself into an all-too familiar scene of devastation and death all around him.

Except that for decades it had been he who had inflicted such hardship on others. This was the scene that had welcomed him upon boarding countless prizes after a hard-fought chase, when the prey had refused to surrender, had struggled against the inevitable against all sense or meaning.

But that had been a righteous fight, then. The prey had been given every opportunity to strike their colors peacefully to the might of the Brethren of the Coast. Those who resisted got only what the immutable laws of nature demanded.

Chainbreaker had never been given a chance to surrender, *or* to fight.

He pushed himself to his feet on unsteady legs, reaching out to support himself upon the gunwale rail only to pull his hand away from the burning, tangled, splintered mess.

He looked down, then, at his hand. It was covered in blood and the dusty remnants of the ship.

He looked up to see that the sloop's mast had been shattered by a direct hit just a few handspans over his head. The mast, spars, and sail had fallen forward, shrouding the front of the vessel in smoldering canvas and tangled rope.

Bloodied men and women stood, sat, or stumbled through the wreckage. The best of them were trying desperately to help their fellows, while the worst sat where they were, apparently unharmed, but weeping into their hands.

Boothe shook his head, trying to clear it of the last ringing, and turned to look aft, to where Hamidi had stood with his sailing master, Billy Deever.

Hamidi was there, one arm hanging loosely at his side while he shouted for fire parties to douse the spreading flames. The short, fat quartermaster, Sefu Barasa, was holding his captain up despite a spreading red stain on his own leg.

There was no sign of Deever.

Boothe made his slow, painful way to the starboard rail.

He needed to know what was happening to the rest of the squadron. Was *Venator* trying to slip away, having removed Shanae's fastest ship from the equation? Or was this truly Greene's final ploy?

He hoped there was no further danger to the ship he was on. Clearly *Chainbreaker* was no danger to anyone.

Although, if *Venator* meant to end the entire squadron, she might well put a ball or two into the wreck as she sailed by, just to be sure.

There was a thick bank of powder smoke drifting lazily to the north east, trailing streamers behind it like the tattered banners of some ancient army.

Beneath those banners the *Venator* moved around the island.

The wind was not going to be anyone's friend in this battle, he saw. To come around and skirt the big frigate on its seaward side, Shanae's two brigantines would be in the teeth of the wind. There was no way they could maintain any speed at all, then, and might even find themselves locked in irons as the wind pushed them off their desired course.

If turned toward distant Jamaica, they would have the wind with them, at least enough to maintain steerage way, but they would be cutting it precariously close to the frigate.

There was no way Shanae would want to do that.

The disparity between the two forces already told a harrowing tale. Two brigantines against a navy frigate was no battle any captain would willingly entertain. They would need sea room and a fair wind to give them even a gambler's chance.

And they had neither.

Either Greene or the *Venator's* captain had laid this trap well, and his gut gave a sick lurch as he realized what he was about to witness.

Port Royal did not make it a point of hanging buccaneers. They had in the past, and of course they could always turn back that way in the future. But under the current regime, with Morgan rising so high back in England and the Brethren so important to the governor's plans for the defense of Jamaica, even bloody-handed pirates were more often acquitted than punished.

That wasn't going to happen here, though.

If the governor intended to follow the normal course of recent events, he never would have sanctioned the Greenes to use the *Venator* like this. And if the spirit of the times argued against hanging, that could only mean there was no intention of taking prisoners.

They were far enough from Port Royal now that, if the three ships of the squadron disappeared, if the *Venator* returned to the naval harbor with no comment or criticism, who would say a word?

He gripped the buckled railing and forced himself to watch.

Venator must have struck *Chainbreaker* with her port broadside, then immediately come about into the more advantageous point of sail, unmasking her starboard broadside and unleashed it on her next hapless victim.

He searched the waters of the bight to his right, fearing he would see nothing but wreckage and bodies, but there were still two brigantines there, one the deep green of Ireland, gold trim glittering in the sunlight; the other a glorious blue with similar detailing.

The *Bonnie Kate* and the *Syren* were still sailing.

It looked as if *Kate* had lost the top quarter of her mainmast. Both her royal and topgallant were gone, and he couldn't see through the smoke what might be left of the mast or spars.

She was carving her way forward, coming nearly into the wind, unleashing her starboard broadside, then coming about to fire her port guns.

Behind her, *Syren* was sailing a similar pattern, although her guns were firing with slightly less regularity.

It was a brave display of sailing and gunnery.

And it wouldn't matter at all.

The nine-pound balls might do some damage to the *Venator's* flanks, or they might be able to damage her sails if they loaded bar or chain shot. If they could do enough damage, they might be able to slip around the frigate and make for open sea.

But getting the guns on those low hulls to elevate enough to threaten the sails and masts as they closed would be nearly impossible. From the sharp sounds of *Kate's* guns, they were loaded with solid ball or maybe cannisters of grape.

He narrowed his eyes.

Why would she be firing grape as they closed?

The countless little lead balls sleeting across the deck might well slaughter some of the *Venator's* crew, and she might hope to break the morale of a lesser ship. But the British Navy crewed their vessels with men of stronger stuff. And again, the angle of her shots was far from ideal.

A ragged volley from *Syren* was definitely solid shot. He thought he could actually see several balls strike the towering forepeak of the frigate as they closed.

He turned again to Hamidi. "We need to do something!" He gestured wildly behind him. "They're going to die!"

He coughed again, his back tightening into a painful knot. He spat a gob of thick blood into the swirling mire at his feet.

The giant, dark-skinned man, his wild mane matted to his head with blood, stumped toward him. "What would you have us do, Boothe? Do you think they would take notice of our little guns? Would you like to fire a swivel up into the air? Would that make you feel better?"

Hamidi's voice was a low growl. "We are in no condition to take further part in this fight, you cretin."

Behind him he could hear the devasting roar of another broadside from the *Venator*.

"We will be lucky if we do not sink in the next ten minutes." The captain towered over him, then, squat Barasa still supporting Hamidi, glaring from beneath his steadying arm. "We need to see to that, and then, perhaps, we might limp back to port, if the frigate lets us."

His dark eyes were haunted. The eyes of a man who was losing some-thing precious and could do nothing to stem the tide as it was all pulled away.

"If there was something we could do to help her, we would." The giant stumped to the railing and looked out as the final act of this bitter farce played out. "We followed her out here, as we would have followed Maguire."

He bowed his head, and his next words were almost lost in the con-tinued tumult around them. "I fear our faith was misplaced. Maguire was wrong."

Boothe shook his head, grabbing Hamidi's shoulder and trying to force the big man around. He might as well have been trying to turn a statue, and so he came around himself, to glare up into the man's dark, blood-streaked face.

"No! There must be a way!" He gestured again at the *Venator*, looking almost close enough to touch. "She's just one ship!"

Hamidi snarled at him. "You're no fool, Boothe, no matter how you've been acting recently. You know saying that frigate is 'just one ship' is true only in the same sense of two minnows telling themselves the approaching barra-cuda is 'just one fish'." He laughed with a booming, hopeless sound. "This was all over the minute we came around that—"

A great crashing sound split the air behind them, and they all whirled as best their injuries allowed, to stare over the water at the two brigantines still flashing through the mild surf toward their doom.

Syren was falling behind, her entire mainmast collapsing with a splin-tering crack. Her sails billowed out with minor reports of their own as they spilled their wind, and the ship slewed off course as the women of her crew scrambled into the rigging, trying to cut the stays and lines that threatened to bring the foremast down as well.

"Damn." Hamidi whispered the word.

Boothe watched as *Syren* fell farther and farther behind her sister, leaving only the *Bonnie Kate* to continue her death run straight at the big frigate.

"Strike, girl. Strike your colors!" Barasa was muttered the order under his breath, his voice shaking.

Hamidi looked away again, shaking his head. "She won't." He looked at Boothe, and he couldn't tell if the giant was glaring at him with anger, pity, or sorrow. "She wouldn't. And neither would any of us."

Boothe nodded silently, then turned to watch.

Venator was not as maneuverable as the *Bonnie Kate* and could not get a full broadside off again on that single, nimble target. Her forward-most guns were popping off with regularity, however; the discipline and training of the British Navy telling with each well-placed shot.

The *Bonnie Kate's* bow looked as if it had been chewed by some giant beast, chunks missing, and one of her forward guns askew on its carriage.

There was other damage as well, in addition to the forecastle and the mast. Sections of rail had been blown away; a large hole had been stove into the forward bulkhead supporting the quarterdeck.

Her crowded deck was dark with blood and bilge water.

He realized with some distant part of his mind that many of the bodies over there belonged to Prides he himself had lured into this mess. The Kate was carrying far more than her normal complement of crew; and many of those now were scattered across her deck.

The little ship looked like it had been through hell.

And *Venator* was only getting started.

The men and women aboard *Chainbreaker* stood or sat in silence, now, their own pain forgotten. Shanae was clearly going to cut it close to the frigate, keep her wind for as long as she could, and then perhaps come about when they passed.

If she could survive one point-blank broadside to come around behind the frigate, she might be able to rake her with her remaining cannons, her cannon balls punching holes right down the bigger ship's length. Even with her smaller guns, such a blow might cripple the *Venator*, allowing the *Kate* to escape.

Except that she wasn't firing solid shot. She wasn't firing the kind of heavy metal that could do that kind of damage.

She was still firing grape, whenever Aidan Allen or Isabella Sanz could line up a shot.

"What the hell is she doing?" He muttered the words out loud, not caring who might hear.

Hamidi looked down at him, heavy dark brows lowered, then back across the glittering sea to the final stages of the battle.

Then the man smiled. Each tooth was outlined in wet blood, peeking through the tangle of dark beard.

"Well, I'll be damned." Hamidi's voice was filled with awe and admiration.

Boothe didn't want to reveal his own ignorance, turning back to watch the *Kate's* charge.

She was crashing through the waves like some ancient warrior's trusted steed, surging toward the *Venator* like a knight from the stories storming toward a monstrous dragon.

She had been firing grape, not solid shot.

He tried to penetrate the drifting smoke. The *Kate's* decks looked to be full of men and women, as you might expect, but they were not scrambling to make repairs or work the guns.

They were standing, still as statues, watching the terrifying sight of the *Venator* growing larger before them by the moment.

She wasn't going to try to slide by for a desperate raking shot.

She wasn't trying to slip by or get away at all.

It was clear the captain of the *Venator* came to a similar conclusion at the same time, as the big ship began to veer to starboard, losing her wind and headway in an attempt to bring her broadside to bear on her small attacker.

The small ship whose course did not waiver, driving straight for the center of the *Venator's* exposed flank.

He winced as that broadside fired, enormous cannons spitting fire and death and clouds of stinging brimstone smoke out into the bright light of day.

But the *Kate* was too close.

The shattering cannon fire flew clear over her, punching holes in her remaining sails, splashing harmlessly into her wake.

The *Kate* didn't need her sails anymore, however.

They had gotten her to where she needed to be.

And the *Bonnie Kate* crashed up against the *Venator* with a horrific rending, tearing sound. Both ships shivered at the grinding impact.

Before she had even come to rest, the *Kate's* crew was scrambling up the side of the *Venator*.

A massive crew, for a ship her size.

He turned in a fury toward Hamidi. "We need to get over there!" He was shocked to realize he was tugging on the man's vest, but he didn't care. *"We need to get over there!"* He repeated, shouting up into that dark face.

Hamidi wasn't looking at him but at the tangle of the two ships fused together by their impact.

There were cries from over the water behind them, and Boothe looked over to see *Syren* limping forward as well. Dominique Bienvenida was a fantastic sailing master, but the work she was doing at that moment, squeezing out every last knot from the tattered rags still clinging to their foremast, was incredible.

Hamidi looked around. Amidst the shattered wreckage of his own ship were two boats, *Chainbreaker's* own black and silver jollyboat and the green and gold of *Bonnie Kate's*; the boat Boothe had arrived on.

The giant nodded. Looking around, he began to point to men and women standing ankle deep in water and blood.

"Cassius!" The master gunner shook himself, looked up at his captain, and nodded. "Browne, Azizi, Cooke, get these boats ready!"

The crew of the *Chainbreaker*, those still able to stand, scrambled to obey.

Others, realizing what the captain intended, began to produce a dizzying array of weaponry from lockers, racks and the wreckage scattered across the deck.

Boothe picked up a wicked-looking boarding axe and moved to the side, where the green and gold boat was being pushed through a gap in the gunwale and into the water.

Over on the *Venator*, like a cliff overlooking some foreign sea, battle raged.

"Let's go aid Captain Bure, shall we?" Hamidi's blood-rimmed grin was savage, his eyes focused on the distant fight.

Boothe tried to respond, but no words came.

Instead, he merely nodded, hefting the big axe, hoping there was still time.

Chapter 37
1675 – Portland Bight, Off Jamaica

Shanae spat blood onto the clean deck of the *Venator*. Her jaw still stung from a glancing blow with the butt of a gaff hook, but there were plenty who were suffering worse than her.

She had strained her shoulder on the climb and taken a splinter to the thigh during the approach, but nothing could dissuade her now that she was so close.

The deck was slick with blood from her grape, with bodies piled up near hatches and in the lee of the bulwark.

She had surely wreaked a horrible vengeance upon these men who were not her enemies.

And she didn't care.

She glared about her. The sailors and marines had established positions at the forecastle and the quarterdeck, but once her people had taken out the topmen and their long guns, the crew were caught flat-footed, never having expected she would close and board.

She grinned, and she could feel her nerves slipping toward madness.

She had allowed herself to be ordered from place to place like a pawn in someone else's game for far too long. She had seen what Greene was when they had first met, and she had done nothing to stop his schemes.

Now the Commodore was dead, Captain Maguire was dead, and countless others with them.

She had no way of knowing how many dead there were aboard *Chainbreaker*. When that opening broadside had erupted from the far side of the island, the telltale bank of white smoke following the rolling thunder of the guns only moments before the little sloop had shivered to pieces, she hadn't been able to process what was happening.

She cursed herself for not having had Hamidi stay farther out to sea. There was no need for him to hug the islands to keep an eye out for the *Venator*. He would have been just as useful out of harm's way.

Instead, the big giant might well be dead, and there was no doubt others were for certain.

She scanned the broad deck of the frigate, looking for another foe.

The battle still raged at the ladder to the forecastle and the two stairs up to the quarterdeck. The occasional rifle shot down into the main deck was a danger, but for the most part the battle had devolved into a bloody hand-to-hand that men a thousand years ago would have been more than familiar with.

Her own pistols had been emptied twice in those first minutes of the fight. She had three of them, and their first shots had each accounted for a red-coated marine threatening her crew as they established a foothold on the main deck. As her *Kates* and *Prides*, who were all-but *Kates* now, too, had pushed forward, forcing the crew of the *Venator* and their marines back, she had reloaded two of the pistols; the third having cracked its pan when she struck an eager navy crewman in the head.

She thought she still had one loaded pistol, but she couldn't be sure. She was saving it, just in case.

The deck beneath her heaved and she looked to see a single mast rock beyond the starboard bow.

When the banshees of the *Syren* came scrambling aboard, looking for a fight and some vengeance against the men who had savaged their ship, she smiled.

"Repent, sinners!" Hunt's voice rang across the deck from nearby, where he had taken charge of the buccaneers trying to take the forecastle. "Your lord demands a sacrifice!"

She had thought to demand they show mercy to the crew of the *Venator*. They were trying to make Port Royal their home, after all. If the local navy held a grudge against them, it would only make that all the harder.

But it was a lot to ask for, after everything they had all been through, especially the recent bloodshed of the day. For her people to show mercy when the bloody fate they had so feared spun about them and threatened their opponents instead would have taken superhuman restraint.

She had not noted any particular bent toward mercy on the part of the English, either, so she didn't feel too bad.

Besides, these men had harbored Sidney Greene from her. There was no way she was going to lose him again, and she was willing to pay any price to bring him to justice for everything he had done.

There was a horrible high-pitched shriek and she turned just in time to see Hunt, his thin arms shaking, bodily throw a *Venator* overboard.

There were probably no sharks around, and he would most likely make it safely to the nameless island nearby, but she couldn't have promised him a long and happy life after that, regardless of who won the battle. Would the victors remember to save those who had gone into the water?

She would stay long enough to make sure of her own people, she knew. But would Greene? Would the English captain?

A cry announced another sortie from the barricade forward, and a line of sailors and marines rushed over the piled casks and crates, wielding sabers, axes, and long arms with bayonets affixed.

She took a moment to watch the action before joining in.

Hunt was a demon, as was almost always the case when the fighting got hot and close. He was fighting with his heavy cudgel, the gnarled white wood stained with blood. She watched as he swayed outside of one sailor's swing, the cutlass blade hissing just past his face, and then he leaned in the opposite direction as a boarding axe came crashing down into the deck, burying itself in the wet wood.

She had never once seen Hunt practice with any weapon at all, and watching him fight could be maddening as it appeared he just stumbled through a battle with no thought to strategy or technique.

Sure enough, he straightened from his latest lean and brought his cudgel down on one of his assailants' heads with an ugly crack. Without waiting to see if that man would fall – he did – Hunt spun around, flailing blind, it seemed, and laid the knotted head of his weapon into the ear of another English attacker.

Beside him, Aidan was standing guard, watching for an opening for his blood-slick blade.

She turned without surprise to see the giant Frenchman, Fabien Astier, standing beside her, wielding an enormous bill hook that looked like it would be more at home guarding some European castle across the Atlantic.

The man's green eyes were steady, as they always were in battle, and she had to remind herself again that he had been a simple merchant sailor just a few months ago.

A few months.

She wanted to spit. So much had happened, so much had been lost, in just a few months.

A few months ago, Captain Maguire had been alive, and the squadron had been feared and respected across the Caribbean Sea.

As if to emphasize the impermanence of this world, the *Venator* lurched again.

She turned, dancing out of the way as a mast rolled across the deck, taking out one of her own crewmen at the ankles.

The man screamed as he fell, and others bent down to help him, dragging him toward the bulwark and the *Kate* below.

She looked up. It had been the *Syren's* foremast, collapsed at last from the impact with the big frigate.

She grinned fiercely when she saw fist Captain Semprun then the enormous amazon Renata Villa climbing over the bulwark.

Semprun flourished her blade over her head while Renata screamed like a wounded beast of prey, looking around for her first victim.

She saw the eyes behind the barricade go round with fear as Semprun came up on her left, Renata on her right.

"Is he up there?" Captain Semprun's eyes were wild, her color high.

Shanae was forced to shake her head. "I don't know. We haven't gotten off the main deck yet. They're holding from the quarterdeck back and the forecastle, and they've held at all the hatches so far.

She nodded toward one of her own, a blonde woman named Anna Greene who was nursing a cut along the side of her neck with the help of Armand Carpentier, the French topman. "Anna took that cut trying to get down to the gundeck. We haven't been able to break through yet."

Sasha Semprun nodded, her eyes still wild, focused on the barricade. "Well, soonest begun is soonest done, I suppose."

The three of them, with the pressure of three crews now behind them, charged the barricade.

The fighting was fierce as the defenders stabbed over the pile with long axes and gaff hooks, trying to force them back.

Renata hacked into the shafts of the enemy weapons with her thick cutlass, battering some down and away while others simply shattered under her fierce blows. Captain Semprun fended off several clumsy strikes before rolling her eyes at the Englishman's tenacity. In one smooth motion she drew a pistol, aimed along the shaft, and fired.

The click-crack! of the pistol was deafening in the tight press of bodies, the cloud of acrid smoke catching in the back of her throat.

But the man holding the hook toppled over backwards, the weapon flying up and away, and Shanae pressed her way into the gap, lashing out to either side, laying open one man's arm, another man's face, sending their weapons tumble to the deck.

She shouldered her way into the opening, not stopping for a fearsome roar rising behind her.

When she heard a wet slap overlaid with a grim crack, she knew who it was, forcing his way beyond the defenders and into the narrow space of the forecastle behind the barricade.

The fighting was a chaotic blur from that point on. Aside from the few remaining marines in their bright red finery, there was little to differentiate an English sailor who had spent more than a few months in the local waters from a buccaneer. There were no women among the *Venator's* crew, of course, so it was a safe bet any lady was fighting for her cause. Other than that, if she didn't recognize the combatant, they could have been almost anyone.

The battle for the forecastle was vicious. She didn't know what the English sailors thought would happen to them if they surrendered, but they were refusing to ask for quarter while the buccaneers, still stinging from the gauntlet of fire that had led them to this pitched battle, weren't in any mood to offer.

At one point she saw an enormous black-skinned man with a wild mane of black hair charge across her path, a hapless marine being pushed toward the bulwark with eyes wide in disbelief as his booted feet slid across the deck. The man hit the low wall and was launched into the air beyond, splintering the railing with his passage.

When had Captain Hamidi joined the fight? Had he rowed across from his shattered sloop?

Shanae drew one forearm across her eyes and forehead to wipe away the sweat. She was exhausted; her throat burned from the powder smoke and the sun, and she was feeling weak from exertion.

When she pulled her arm away, the marine was almost upon her.

She remembered that moment, so long ago, on Bonaire, charging into the filthy, empty hut. That moment as she watched the Dutchman rise from behind the bed that had concealed him, shaking off the blanket and pointing the long gun right at Captain Maguire's head.

The marine had a long gun, too, but it must have been emptied a lifetime ago.

This weapon, however, bore the long, wicked blade of a bayonet fit into the barrel.

And that bayonet was flying straight for her sternum.

She brought her sword fanning around, but it wasn't going to be fast enough.

She heard Captain Semprun scream. She saw, in a swirling confusion of sound and light, Renata's eyes go wide.

Shanae's sword whistled as it sailed through the air.

Too late.

Greene was going to escape again.

Something bowled her over from behind with an animal roar.

"Poseidon!" Hunt looked nothing like the mild-mannered ecclesiast he must once have been, and she would be forever grateful for it. "My lord! Blood for you, Poseidon!"

The cudgel came down on the barrel of the long gun. The marine was carried forward by his momentum, eyes wide with sudden fear, and the bayonet buried itself in the deck, stopping him short with a grunt of pain as the butt of the gun was driven into his body.

With all the grace of a dancer and not an ounce of wasted effort, the cudgel came up again and struck the marine full in the face, sending him tumbling backward with a vacant look on his bloodied expression.

She smiled her thanks to the priest and turned about, cutlass leveled before her, but there were no more foes to fight.

A small knot of sailors and marines was being gathered up around the bottom of the foremast, empty hands raised, eyes round and wide. A combination of *Syrens* and *Kates* was binding them with course twine while others dismantled the barricade or made their careful way down the forward hatch.

There was still some fighting at the stern, but the mass of buccaneers amidships seemed to have forced their way down onto the gundeck through the main cargo hatches, and so the women moving down the ship's ladder from the forecastle met no resistance.

She checked the bodies with the help of Renata and Captain Semprun.

There were dead friends among them, but no sign of Greene.

She snarled and whirled, moving through the men and women of the squadron, hopping down onto the main deck without a pause, and stocking toward the sounds of fighting coming from the companionway between the two flights of stairs leading up to the quarter deck at the stern castle.

Above, the quarter deck was raucous, buccaneers cheering her on as they forced the knot of English sailors and marines into a corner.

The companionway was narrow, and she had to force herself past the mob as she headed for the fighting. She didn't have to knock anyone aside. The merest tap on a shoulder or pressure on an arm was enough.

Time seemed to slow as she walked; as if she was in a dream.

The sounds of fighting faded before her as she walked, almost as if they were receding, like an ebbing tide.

Would it be one of those dreams where she walked down an ever-stretching hallway? Would she never reach the room at the end?

But the door remained fixed in space and time beyond her patient crew. Her eyes focused on the finely carved wood as she walked among them, each stepping aside with solemn looks and nods of respect.

There were no smiles here.

"He's in the captain's cabin, m'am." One man said.

Another woman nodded. "Green, miss. He's armed."

Shanae paused. "With what?"

Aidan was standing by the doorframe, his hair dark with sweat, eyes alight with the fire of combat. "A blade. Nothing more." He grinned.

Of course, it *would* be Aidan who smiled here.

"He had a pistol, but it broke." He held up a pistol whose hardware hung loose and broken from around the lock plate. "I backed out once I got it. Figured you'd want to have words with him yourself."

She grinned, despite her thought of only a moment before.

And she drew her own pistol.

The door was closed but opened with a nudge of her foot.

With slick cutlass in one hand and pistol in the other she pushed open the door, scanning the well-appointed captain's cabin as she sidled in.

He was in a corner, clutching at a bloody shoulder wound, eyes wide and white in a powder-stained face. The green fire of his eyes was out, extinguished, for the first time since she had met him, with an overwhelming tide of fear.

"Leave me alone, or the governor will hear of it." His voice wavered as he issued the threat in a thin voice. The small sword he held out before him shook. It was a fine weapon for gentlemen duelists, but no match for the heavy steel of a cutlass.

She smiled. "I don't think Governor Lynch is going to much care what you have to say, when he sees the condition of the toy he leant you."

She looked around the cabin. Greene had not been alone when he had been hounded into this last refuge. There were three still bodies in red coats and two sailors sprawled against the walls. The furniture looked to have been very nice at one point, before it had been shattered in the fighting.

"Do you know where the captain of this vessel is, Mr. Greene?" She moved sideways, keeping her eye on his blade. "We'll need his help, I think, to get us all back to Port Royal after this little misunderstanding."

"He went below, the coward." Greene spat. "And it's Captain Greene, Bure; not mister."

She almost laughed, then. The man was a lunatic. It was the only possible explanation for the delusions he clung to, even now.

"Captain of what, pray tell? I believe your ship was blown out from beneath you, the last time we met." She stopped moving, having come to the wall.

"Why did you do it, Greene?" She lowered her own sword.

She needed to hear it. She needed to hear him say it, in his own words, before she could end this.

"You're a fool." He spat, finding a reserve of courage somewhere deep in his being. "You're all fools. Times are changing, and the days of the Brethren are numbered." He seemed genuinely angry, and that gave her pause.

"I could have made something better out of you! I could have made something that would have mattered!"

"And all you had to do was kill...?"

"Yes!" He barked the answer, desperation and newfound courage shaking his voice in equal measure, she believed. "Yes! I killed Hart! The old man was even more fool than the rest of you! And I had Maguire killed as well! He wouldn't listen to reason!"

Then, as if cut off by a slammed door, the man's words ended. He stared at her for a long moment, then his breath returned in low, shallow gasps. "But you're smarter than either of them! You would have worked *with* me. You could *still* work with me! Together, we could reforge the squadron into a weapon that would win us the entire Caribbean! Once Morgan and the others are out of the way, working out of Tortuga—"

She raised her pistol, and her arm did not waiver in the slightest. "I think that's just about enough, now, Mr. Greene."

"Yes!" The snarled word snapped out from the doorway, and she cocked her head in that direction, straightening when she realized who it was.

Boothe stood there, shoulders heaving with the force of his breathing. The man looked as if he had walked through hell. Long gone were his carefully trimmed beard and mustache, now the hair on his cheeks and lips were nothing but a ratty dark brown scruff, all design and artifice overgrown like I once-refined garden. His finery was faded and worn, ripped and tattered from his recent ordeals.

But the greatest change these weeks had wrought were in his eyes. His black eyes were rimmed in red, their whites yellow, and they were wide, filled with hate and completely devoid of sense.

"Shoot him!" Boothe barked the words, stepping into the cabin without even looking at Greene. He was staring at her with those crazed eyes, and so when the Port Royal scion charged him, he was caught completely unawares.

Greene flew at Boothe with a desperate cry, taking him in the side and driving him against the forward bulkhead.

"No!" The man's own finery was filthy; he probably hadn't had time to change since *Chasseur* detonated beneath him.

"No!" He screamed again, struggling to get his gentleman's hands around Boothe's neck.

Boothe snarled, struggling back, slapping the other man's hands away and landing several heavy blows against his assailant's ribs, but failing to dislodge him.

Shanae watched for several moments, not entirely sure she cared if one of these men killed the other, then she waded in close, flipped her pistol to grip it by the barrel, and brought the butt of the grip down on the back of Greene's head.

The wet crack was dull in the confines of the cabin, and he dropped bonelessly to the floor, draped across a sputtering, struggling Boothe.

"God damnit it, girl, why did you take so long!" He pushed Greene off him and rose unsteadily to his feet.

"Now, kill him!"

With a weak groan, Greene began to stir.

"Kill him!" Boothe's shriek bounced off the low ceiling, ringing in her abused ears.

A very strong impulse to strike the man across the cheek with the pistol nearly overwhelmed her.

"Please, no." Greene raised one hand to his ear, and it came away bloody. "Please."

The man's voice was a whisper, like a ghost trying to communicate through the veil of death.

Eamon Maguire might sound the same, trying to reach out to her even now.

The pistol was righted again without a thought, the barrel pressed against the man's bloody forehead.

He looked up at her with pathetic eyes, one almost completely occluded in a cloud of invading red.

He was defeated. There would be no more threat from Sidney Greene. No one would listen to him, there was no more money to be found this side of the Atlantic Ocean for him. Even if he won back his freedom somehow, the man was finished in his own mind; the only place it really mattered.

She lowered the pistol.

No!" Boothe screamed. "No! Not after everything he's done! Not after everything he's cost us all!"

She looked at him, his face contorted with hatred, and sighed.

"Bind Greene. Have him tied to the mast until we get back to Port Royal."

Aidan shouldered his way past her, his grin still firmly fixed in place.

"Happily, ma'am." Two other *Kates* followed him, hoisting Green to his feet and pulling him gently from the room.

"You had no right to let him live." Boothe spat the words as he sagged against a heavy desk scattered with papers and splinters. "Your claim on his life was no stronger than half a dozen others here on this ship alone."

"I think she made the right choice."

Shanae turned to see Sasha Semprun standing in the doorway.

"I agree." The towering shadow of Thomas Hamidi moved up behind the dark-haired captain of the *Syren*. "Greene will be dealt with by his own. His life is worth more to us now than the satisfaction his death would ever bring."

"And Bastian will concur, I believe." Captain Semprun's eyes were sad, but she smiled at Shanae.

"The captains in council approve." Hamidi rumbled, nodding his head as he came into the cabin.

Aidan returned from escorting Greene onto the deck.

"He said the captain is belowdecks?" She looked at the *Kate's* master gunner. "Can we find him, preferably alive?"

With a jaunty salute, he left again.

"What are you planning on doing with your prize, Captain?" Semprun's smile was warmer, now.

The words made little sense to Shanae, however.

She stared out the door after Aidan, remembering Greene's slumped shoulders and empty eyes.

Was this victory?

There was still so much to be done.

Chapter 38
1675 ~ Port Royal, Jamaica

The back section of One-Eyed Jack's was cramped with the new table, but no one was going to complain.

Not considering who had bought it.

There were other pubs, taverns, and ale houses in Port Royal. There were over fifty at last count, actually. And many of them were nicer, better-appointed, and better smelling than One-Eyed Jack's.

But as Aidan stood at the bar, one elbow thrown over the dark wood, waiting for Liz MacDonald to fill two leather jacks with small beer, he reflected that there was nowhere else he'd rather be.

The big table was in high spirits; the squadron in a celebratory mood. But Shanae had insisted her mug contain nothing more than the watered-down drink, and Aidan had decided to follow suit.

He nodded his thanks to Liz when she pushed the cups across the bar and smiled when she waved away his attempt to pay.

One of the strangest rules of apparent civilization: when you were flush with coin, it was much harder to spend it.

Not that he was complaining.

At the big table he squeezed past several people to get to Shanae, sitting in the middle with her back to the corner.

He put one cup down before her and settled back into his chair, just off her right shoulder.

"There's still been no sign of *Jaguar*." Captain Houdin's smile was weak. He had not been his usual, jovial self for days. Aidan believed the man felt guilty he had missed the battle of Portland Bight. Never mind that he had been ordered to stay behind and keep an eye on the *Jaguar*.

Fowler had stayed put all that day, but in the confusion of their return, with the severely damaged ships of the squadron escorting the battered English frigate back into port, he had slipped away.

Houdin had left later that day to try to find him. He had been searching ever since, but to no avail. This time he had been gone for over a week.

"No one on Tortuga has seen him, either." He swallowed, shooting a sideways glance at Shanae. "But there was other news."

Aidan hid his own smile behind a raised cup. Ever since their return, the other captains, masters, and mates had been treating Shanae differently.

He liked it.

"Well, if you're not going to tell us, I'm not sure why you're sitting at the table, Captain Houdin." Shanae's tone was cold, lacking the gentle mockery he might have expected.

"It's the French. They've sent a new governor."

"That's one option off the table, then." Captain Hamidi muttered, settling his massive bulk deeper into the large seat that had been found especially for him.

Captain Semprun shook her head. "We weren't going back to Tortuga anyway, Thomas. Let's not pretend that we might. That's one port that will be closed to us for quite a while."

"Not that we would want to return." Renata Villa looked uncomfortable; her impressive stature folded into a small wooden chair. "Have you forgotten how we left Cayona Harbor?"

There was a roll of soft laughter around the table, and Aidan smiled with a nod, although he didn't join in.

"So, what does it mean to us, then, that the French have reclaimed the island? They are not so effectual that this should alter our plans in any way." Sefu Barasa, the midnight-skinned quartermaster from the barely floating *Chainbreaker*, had very little patience for politics, of either the local variety or the European.

Captain Semprun looked at Sefu, then at the other captains. "It means we, in particular, will not be welcome in Tortuga for a while, at least. It also means that it is not likely that Fowler will attempt to put in there. There's no argument he can make to a new governor that would distance himself sufficiently from the mess we left behind."

Cesar Japon, Houdin's dapper little quartermaster, barked a laugh. "And even if he could, so what?" He rested one arm on the back of his chair. "I'm still not certain why we even care where Fowler has gotten off to."

"It's not so much that we care where he is, as that we care where he is going." Shanae took a sip of her beer and nodded thanks to him. "The squadron has a claim on *Jaguar* that no gathering of the Brethren would deny."

"And since you cost us the last frigate...?" Japon all but leered at Shanae over the long table. It was all Aidan could do not to throw his beer into the man's face.

"If you think the *Venator* was ever ours to lose, you're a bigger fool than I imagined." Hamidi's rumble cut off the rising rush of responses to the little Spaniard's shot.

"The return of the *Venator*, and the polite fiction of its capture by Greene and our happily running into them in the Bight are the foundation of our official welcome in Port Royal, Cesar." Captain Semprun was speaking slowly, as if to a child.

"And the beating we dealt her is the foundation of our welcome by the rest of the Brethren that call the island their home." Hamidi smiled from his throne.

But Japon was not so sanguine. "That damned ship would have fetched us—"

"Where?" Like a rifle shot from a fighting top, old Captain Lachlan's question brought all activity around the table to a halt.

"What?" Japon turned to glare at the white-haired old man.

"Where do you think you could sell off a prize like that?"

The Spaniard faltered, then rallied gamely enough. "I could sail it right into Porta Bello." The misplaced pride in the man's tone was not winning him any friends that Aidan could see. "Any number of Spanish ports—"

"Would be closed to you. Have you not been paying attention? Peace has broken out between the English and the Spaniards. Tortuga is in a shambles. Who would you sell an English frigate to, then? The Dutch?"

Japon settled back in his seat with a sour look and belted the last rum from his tankard.

Shanae leaned forward. "We don't much care about the *Jaguar*, do we? She was always too big for most of our work."

Aidan snorted. "Hell, she kept in harbor almost as much as the *Arbiter*."

That got another round of laughs from almost everyone around the big table but the bitter Spaniard.

"No, a welcome port here was more than worth the trade for the *Venator*." Shanae continued, but stopped when Renata Villa put her heavy cup down with a loud thud.

"I think you are missing a major point, Shanae." It was Hamidi, not her own captain Semprun, who reached across and patted the dark-skinned giantess's arm. "There is a reality here no number of legendary feats is going to change."

"This is a fine new table you've acquired for this latrine trench, Shanae. But it will take more than a table to make this a home for some of us." The *Syren's* quartermaster's dark complexion somehow managed to look even darker as her anger swelled.

Aidan looked back toward the bar, wondering how the locals might be taking this assault on their establishment.

Liz the barmaid and Jamie, the owner, were leaning in towards each other, muttering away, both committed, it seemed, to avoiding any acknowledgment of the new table dominating the common room.

"This is all well and good for most of you. But slavery is still very much in force here on Jamaica. The English look no more eager to release our people than the Spaniards." The tribal tattoos sparkled on Renata's shaven head.

"They hunt the Maroons here like animals." Sefu Barasa's anger was no less hot for the fact that he had never worn a chain.

"But you're free!" Captain Houdin's forced smile was not reassuring. "You are in no danger here! Free Africans walk the streets here every day!"

"How many?" Hamidi turned his dark gaze upon the much smaller Frenchman. "Enough that we will not feel like animals in a zoo? And what should we feel as we walk past our fellows, still in chains?"

"But you're free!" Houdin repeated, confused.

"Freedom for me and not for thee is not a creed I care to live by." Hamidi folded enormous arms over his huge chest and stared down at Captain Houdin.

"None of us wish to live that way, Thomas." Shanae leaned forward over her beer. "The—"

"The situation is complicated?" His laughter rumbled through the close room, but there was no humor in it. "That is easy for you to say, Shanae. Your skin—"

"Can pass, Thomas?" Her face was flat, now, eyes dark. Aidan felt a sympathetic jolt in his own gut. "Be very careful. You are drifting dangerously close to making an identical case as Bastian." She smiled a tight, feral grin. "The same case you just shut down so well."

Hamidi shook his head. "No, I will not be silenced so easily. You can make a claim to belonging here. A claim—"

"A claim just as strong as the one I can make to belonging with you and *Chainbreaker's* crew." She settled back in her seat. "And just as strong as those claims are the arguments of close-minded men that I don't belong here at all."

"You have been welcomed—" Captain Lachlan looked disturbed by the course of the conversation, but his words died at a gesture from Shanae.

"I can belong everywhere, or nowhere, depending on each person's point of view." She looked around the table, then, and met each of the captains, mates, and masters in the eye. "I can live at the whim of every bigoted fool traipsing down the center of every street in the world." She turned her head slowly to look, steely-eyed, at Captain Hamidi, Barasa, and Renata Villa. "I refuse them that power."

Renata looked discomfited, but Captain Hamidi's anger was still obvious. "And so you would walk down the streets of Port Royal, knowing that at any moment you might turn a corner and meet a man or woman of your own blood, wearing chains, and you would have to walk on by?"

Shanae shook her head, her own anger rising now. "Captain Maguire always—"

"Captain Maguire was an excellent captain, and a good man, but he always ignored this last hurdle to his own dreams and ambitions." Hamidi seemed to quiet a little, but there was still fire in his eyes. "Would you have us make our home in a land where our people are treated as property?"

"The situation here in Jamaica truly is complicated, Captain Hamidi." Lachlan had both his hands up in a calming gesture. "I understand your concerns, but—"

"Unless you were hiding in a bush somewhere nearby the day I won my own freedom with blood and fire, I would guard the next words to drop from my tongue, old man." Hamidi's anger surged back. "I will not stand idly by as my people suffer under the lash and the yoke." He turned to Shanae. "And none of my crew will, either."

Their glares locked, burning over the table. Beside Captain Hamidi, Renata sat rigid, adding her own black-eyed gaze to the conflict.

"This is not going to be solved today." Shanae spoke at last, her face as still tight, her eyes wary. "But it occurs to me that change is more easily achieved from within, over time, than from without, through force and steel. Our people might yet be freed on Jamaica, and we would be in a stronger position to help them from Port Royal than anywhere else we might drop our anchors, hundreds of leagues away."

"The Maroons, in the mountains, would be an interesting people to visit, in that regard." Lachlan offered up the comment in an off-handed manner, but the way he looked sidelong at Thomas Hamidi, Aidan could tell there was more there than he could hear.

The captain of the *Chainbreaker* stared at the old Port Royal captain for a long moment, then back to Shanae, then to Renata.

He put a hand on her shoulder and muttered something in her ear, easing back into his own chair.

Renata shook her head violently. "No." She stood. "This place will *never* be my home." She stood, her chair clattering back onto the hard floor behind her, and stalked through the confined common room, out the front room, and slammed the thin door behind her.

"Tortuga was never our home, either." Thomas bowed his head. "I fear there will be no place for us on this side of the Atlantic."

Sefu patted his captain on the man's broad back. "I keep telling you, Captain: my people along the Barbary Coast would welcome you, and all our crew, with open arms."

Teeth flashing in a humorless smile, Hamidi shrugged. "Maybe we'll have to go that far, one day." He looked up at Shanae, then, and shrugged. "Until then, we will stay." He held up a hand. "As many of my people who wish. I will not force any of them to stay on with me if they cannot stomach the smells of the plantations from the mainland."

Shanae nodded her thanks, then looked around the table. "We do not have to stay in Port Royal, but it is now an option. And I cannot think of anywhere else that might welcome us, battered and bruised as we are."

"When Morgan returns—" Mathias Sylvestre had been one of Captain Maguire's closest confidants, and therefore knew better than any of them what the pirate, Henry Morgan's return to the New World would mean to them.

"We'll have to deal with that when it happens." Shanae waved the concern away. "He's been gone for years. By the time he comes back, between stealing the *Amelie Carre* and selling it to the brokers as the *Avontuur*, our return of the 'pirated' *Venator*, and Captain Maguire's financial ruining of the Greenes, we will be well-enough established, we should be able to weather even Henry Morgan's ire."

"And we know Greene is gone?" Boothe's voice was ragged. He had not yet recovered from the incident in the *Venator's* captain's cabin. He had caused no more trouble, had had no more angry outbursts. But neither had the spark returned to his eyes, either.

He had spent the bulk of his time aboard the *Chaucer's Pride*, with the remnants of the sloop's crew. Aidan thought they had been going over the ship, looking to bring it up to fighting trim. But Boothe had made no claims on the squadron's coffers, despite the fact that it had proven plenty deep enough to see *Chainbreaker* nearly rebuilt from the keel up, and *Syren* and *Bonnie Kate* extensively repaired.

Aidan had no idea how much gold might be left in the counting houses of Port Royal under their names, but however much it was, Boothe had asked for none of it.

"He is." Lachlan nodded. "The governor sent him back with *Venator*."

The others smiled at that. It had turned out that the big frigate had suffered enough damage and loss of crew in the battle that she needed to return home to England for repairs and refit.

"His family went with him, hoping to intercede with the maritime courts as soon as they arrived."

"Surely he won't escape again? They take piracy very seriously, back in England, I hear." Shanae didn't appear concerned, despite the words.

Lachlan nodded with a smile. "This entire series of events was very unfortunate for Governor Lynch. With Morgan returning to the Caribbean from England with his successor, he needed to be able to prove he had regained control of the situation here. After your return of the *Venator*, he had little choice but to seek his scapegoat elsewhere." The old man shrugged. "Greene may not be paying for his actual crimes, but the crimes he is accused of bear a mortal burden. I don't think we'll be seeing him back this way again."

"Even if he came, there's not much for him to return *to*." Hunt was sitting at a side table, but with one elbow hooked over the back of his chair so he could better follow the captains' conversation. "They might have accounts back in England, and they might have friends, but Captain Maguire made sure they had nothing here that could grant them any power or protection at all."

Lachlan smiled and tipped his head in the madman's direction. "Thus clearing the way for whatever the future may now hold."

The captains exchanged glances, finally all looking at Shanae.

Aidan wanted to think that she was sitting at the head of the table through happenstance, but he was starting to wonder if anything happened to Shanae Bure by accident.

"So, for the time being, Port Royal will be our home?"

The others nodded, but they did not take their eyes away from the woman who had grown up among them.

It was said Sasha Semprun had been with the captain when he found Shanae, all those years ago. Most of the others had been with the squadron back then or joined soon after. They had all been a part of the girl's upbringing.

And each of these captains, with their closest advisors, mates, and masters, were now looking at her, waiting for her to speak.

In a world so divided, with the ripples from Europe's wars ready to capsize the most well-founded ship without notice, these hardened buccaneers were looking to a young girl, a half-breed escaped slave, for guidance.

Aidan looked down at the table again. The table Shanae had purchased almost as soon as they had received the governor's grudging reward for the *Venator's* return. The table that had made One-Eyed Jack's feel a little bit, just a little bit, like home.

She was sitting there beside him, either ignoring the looks the others gave her or completely misreading the moment.

But she was sitting at that table.

And that seemed to argue that she understood more than she was letting on.

And for some reason, he found that more reassuring than all the rest of it combined.

Chapter 39
1675 – The Windward Passage

There was nothing like the harnessed power of the wind, straining against the canvas overhead, pushing a well-founded ship toward her destiny.

The decks were silent save for the muttered conversations of the crew, the creaking of cordage and lines overhead, and the undignified squawk of a gull disturbed from his perch in the tops.

Off to starboard, the rebuilt *Chainbreaker* surged through the waves, carving a white furrow through the sea. Off to port, a newly stepped mast performing as if it had been in place for a decade, *Syren* loped along, her figurehead gazing defiantly northward. *Laughing Jacques*, on *Chainbreaker's* starboard quarter, completed the loose formation as they cut through the passage, headed toward their old home.

The squadron that had spent so many years operating out of Tortuga was smaller, now, but it was far more dangerous for all that. The dross had been burned away in the furnace of battle and betrayal, and the metal left behind had been forged into a lean, deadly weapon to turn against whomever they wished.

The gray shadow of a sleek sloop haunted the squadron's wake. It was considered by many of the Brethren to be ill luck to change the name of a ship, but Boothe had had no trouble from his new crew. None of them seemed overly enamored of the *Chaucer's Pride*, anyway.

She would never have admitted it to anyone, but Shanae thought Boothe had stumbled upon the perfect name when he christened the *Pride's Fall*. Her new paint, a gray that matched her old faded black almost perfectly, was more than a little eerie.

Shanae stretched, pacing back and forth in front of Martin Ruiz's wheel. She turned and smiled at the old Spaniard.

He was the only crewman who had been with Captain Maguire all those years ago still serving aboard the *Bonnie Kate* the day she had been found.

Well, the only crewman aside from her, she supposed.

She didn't know why she had made them chase her so far out to sea for this.

She had known what they were asking, without wasting the breath, in One-Eyed Jack's, sitting at that ridiculous table she had purchased.

She couldn't have said why she bought the table if pressed at the point of a pistol. It might have been hubris, of course. She was willing enough to see that much weakness in her soul.

Or perhaps it had been nothing more than a desire to celebrate, in some concrete fashion, the utter defeat of her enemies.

She smiled, her hair floating forward under the fitful gust of a northerly wind. Greene was gone, probably halfway across the Atlantic and headed toward an admiralty court thirsty to hang as many pirates as they could manufacture.

Captain Maguire was avenged, and she was free to pursue whatever the future might hold.

She felt her smile slip. She saw again the faces of the captains staring at her, waiting for her to speak.

She knew what they had wanted.

Of course, she had.

But did *she* want it?

From what she had seen, Solomon Hart had never been made happy by his self-aggrandizing tile of Commodore.

Hart might have brought them all together once and created for them an environment in which the strengths and weaknesses of a group of people might be combined to stave off the general malaise that had claimed so many of the Brethren of the Coast.

Whereas most crews had either moved to Port Royal and become pawns in the forced trade or given up their beloved ships altogether and moved inland to become woodsmen, the squadron of Tortuga had managed to stay together. If they hadn't prospered, they had at least *survived*.

She wondered what their time in Port Royal was going to be like. She had already been approached by Dennis Flynn's factor, with offers to enter into an alliance against a small Spanish consortium.

The language of King's House and the Assembly of Jamaica might flow like poetry and honey, but it was as blood soaked as any pirate's boarding cry.

The merchant families of Port Royal meant to harness the squadron into the forced trade just as they had every buccaneer crew that had put into that God-forsaken hell hole in the past ten years.

Which had made sending his envoy back to him in tears very satisfying.

It had also convinced her that spending too long in Port Royal would be bad for their souls as well as their instincts, and she had suggested they all head north, shake down their ships after the extensive repairs and refits they had undergone, and perhaps glide past Tortuga for old time's sake.

No one was going to begrudge them a fat French merchantman, if they should happen upon one.

She had suggested the outing, but she had not ordered it.

She had refused to take up the mantle they had silently offered her, and she was bound and determined to keep it that way.

Who was she, that she might lead an entire squadron of her Brethren in these hard times?

Could she keep Thomas Hamidi and his crew content, under the knowledge of how Jamaica produced all that sugar they shipped back east?

Could she keep the women of the *Syren* safe in Port Royal.

She laughed out loud at that thought. As if any of the women on Captain Semprun's ship needed anyone else's protection.

But honestly, why would any of them follow *her*?

She saw Aidan in the waist of the ship, walking among the guns, checking each one with Isabella beside him, laughing at some off-hand joke.

She felt something stir in her chest when she saw them together, but she couldn't have said what it was. And as captain, now, it wasn't something she was going to investigate.

"Ahem." Someone cleared their throat just over her shoulder and it took every ounce of her self-control not to leap off the deck.

She spun, fully intending to tear whoever it was down where they stood, but her eyes softened just a bit when she saw Hunt standing there, hat in hand, empty smile back in place.

"Yes, Hunt?"

"Ma'am." He dipped his head in a shy bow. She was still getting used to that. She had never agreed to take the position of captain on the *Bonnie Kate*, but there she was, undeniably standing on the quarterdeck as if she owned the ship.

Hunt tilted his head off to the left and she looked that way, her brow furrowing as she saw the flags waving aboard the *Syren*.

"It's time, Ma'am. You've run far enough."

*****

The three of them stood on the main deck of the *Bonnie Kate*, the sails overhead throwing ghostly half-shadows over them, offering little relief from the tropical sun.

Hamidi was covered in sweat, his great mane hanging limp. Sasha Semprun looked as composed as ever, dressed in practical garb that left no doubt to her efficacy as a fighter, while doing nothing to hide her gender. Captain Houdin's smile was there, but still wounded, as it had been since *Jaguar's* escape.

"You wouldn't see us ashore before we left, Shanae." They were letting Sasha do the talking, which probably made as much sense as anything else. "We decided to let you lead us north a ways, that we might have a chance to talk once again."

Shanae looked out over the rails, over the stretch of rolling sea. Other than the other four ships, there was nothing to see for miles and miles in any direction.

Boothe had not joined the other captains when he had been informed of this impromptu meeting, but he had dipped his ensign in acknowledgment.

If anyone felt even less accustomed to their new role than Shanae, it had to be Boothe. She wasn't even entirely sure he felt that he was a member of their little family anymore, although he had left Port Royal with them, with or without an invitation.

Shanae looked back at Sasha, squinting from the hot sun, and nodded for her to continue.

"You have been coy, Shanae. Which, I suppose, it what I should have expected, from a woman raised by Eamon Maguire."

That hit a little harder than she was expecting, but she thought she hid it well, masking her moment of discomfort by turning to look first at Thomas, then at Bastian.

"We have each spoken to our crews. Every man and woman among us has had a say, as is our way." The words sounded formal, and carried with them a strange note of steel, like chains, that Shanae found frightening in a way she could not have explained.

"And, having spoken with our crews, we have then taken council together." Thomas Hamidi seemed to be standing even taller than his usual towering stature.

"And, happily we found ourselves and our crews all in agreement!" Bastian Houdin's self-confidence might have taken a blow the day of the battle, but his humor showed through the clouds, for just a moment. "Even Boothe showed up. Although I'm not sure who invited him." His smile slipped, and he looked to the others. They shrugged, not as concerned, clearly, as the smaller Frenchman.

"Solomon Hart built the squadron. He brought each of us, or our ships, into the fold, creating a community the likes of which had not been attempted before, and which has not been successful since." Sasha's mouth twisted as if the praise for the old man tasted bad in her mouth.

"He created something special, but he was never elected to lead us." Thomas's face was stern. "He assumed the title and role of Commodore on his own."

"And we let him, because what he had created was new. None of us really understood what it might entail." Sasha looked more puzzled and less poisoned, now.

In fact, all of them looked as if they were waking from a strange dream.

Maybe they wouldn't do it. Maybe this was it, and the strange dream was about to end for good and all.

She wasn't sure how she felt about that. She was fairly certain Captain Maguire had never intended for this to last, formally, much past the shift to Jamaica.

But Captain Maguire was gone, and there was a comfort in the familiar she was not ready to give up after having already lost so much.

She merely nodded, encouraging them to continue without saying a word.

Maybe they weren't here for the reason she thought they were after all.

"Hart was never elected to lead the squadron." Thomas repeated.

Sasha smiled a strange, sad smile. "You have been."

The words took a moment to register. In her mind she had already reconciled herself with a world in which this cup had passed her by.

But here it was.

She looked at the three captains standing around her, but she looked the longest at Sasha Semprun. Sasha had been with Captain Maguire since his arrival in these waters. She had sailed with him for years, and he had been instrumental in helping her to acquire *Syren*.

Often, Shanae had suspected there might have been something even more between them, once.

Sasha Semprun was a superlative captain. *Syren* was always where she was supposed to be, with spot-on timing and every gun ready to fire. The women of her crew were the best trained, most loyal buccaneers in the squadron.

If anyone were to take up this mantle, it should be her.

But Sasha shook her head before Shanae could draw breath to speak.

"We have all had a hand in training and teaching you, Shanae. And you learned at the knee of the best of us for most of your life."

"The men and women of the squadron know this, and they know you." Bastian's smile was now unalloyed. "We all want you at the helm."

"You are the only person my crew trusts implicitly." Thomas put one enormous hand on her shoulder. "You live bestride so many worlds, Shanae Bure. It could only be you." He smiled gently at her, but she thought there might just be a hint of pity in that smile as well? "It was always going to be you."

She felt as if the air had disappeared from the main deck. She looked down, gathering her thoughts, and saw Aidan out of the corner of her eye.

He smiled and nodded, once, with conviction.

She looked back to the captains.

This could be a disaster. What if she destroyed the squadron?

One bad decision and everything could be gone in a moment.

What if *Venator* had landed a single solid blow on the *Kate* as she closed?

What if she had been killed on the *Amelie Carre*?

Or at Kralendijk?

Or in half a hundred other engagements in her admittedly brief life?

And if they were all counting on her when she succumbed?

The squadron could die because of her.

But she hadn't died. *Venator* had not landed that fatal blow. She had wielded the squadron like a dueling master with a blade. She was honest enough with herself to admit that.

She had taken the *Marie Lajoie* and the *Courageaux*. She had taken the *Amelie Carre* and defeated both the *Chasseur* and the *Venator*.

She had freed the squadron from Greene and set them on this path where their destiny was theirs to decide.

She walked away from the captains without a word, taking a winding, indirect route around the main mast, up the ladder onto the quarterdeck, and next to the wheel, where Martin gave her a small, tight smile through his salt and pepper goatee.

She turned to find the captains had followed and were watching her expectantly.

Thomas and Bastian looked concerned, but Sasha was smiling through a veil of unshed tears.

"I accept."

She forced the words out before her damned self-doubt could choke them into silence.

A great cheer rose from the entire ship.

Evidentially, the crew had been listening into the conversation after all.

As the cheer reached the other ships, first *Syren*, then the two sloops erupted in raucous roars of celebration as well.

She couldn't keep the smile from her face, then.

Thomas was the first to put out a hand, and they clasped wrists. Bastian was next but drew her in for a quick hug as well. Sasha made no pretext of gripping hands, and instead hauled her in for a long, tight embrace.

"So." Thomas stood once again, fists on belt, and surveyed the squadron around them.

There was suspicious sheen in his eyes.

"Were to first, Commodore?"

The others looked at her, and she saw the tightening of Martin's eyes at the title.

"I believe we should continue on to Tortuga, Thomas." She smiled, walking to the forward rail and leaning over the bulwark.

"But first, let's be clear."

She looked out over the *Bonnie Kate's* bow at the wide-open sea ahead.

"You can call me Captain."

Types of Ships

Brig – a two-masted, square-rigged ship, often carrying ten to twenty guns

Brigantine – a two-masted ship with a more complex rigging plan that was swifter and more maneuverable than a sloop, generally used for piracy, escort, and cargo, carrying between ten and twenty guns

Fluyt – a Dutch sailing ship used almost exclusively for cargo, might carry between four and sixteen guns

Frigate – a fully rigged naval ship built for speed and maneuverability used for scouting, escort, or patrols; characterized by one armed deck and one armed or unarmed deck, carrying between 24 and 56 guns

Galleon – a large multi-decked, heavily armed cargo carrier used by many European states from the 16th through the 18th centuries, usually with three or more masts and carrying as many as 74 guns

Long Boat – often carried on larger ships to ferry people and goods to land, these boats were generally 23 to 34 feet long and carried between six to ten oars; most could be rigged with a single sail for slightly longer distances and swift boarding actions; long boats might carry a small gun or a mounted swivel gun

Ship of the Line – a large military vessel intended to be used in the line of battle, often having more than one gun deck carrying anywhere between 60 to 110 guns

Sloop – a smaller, single-masted sailing ship designed for speed, with a single gun deck of up to 18 guns